The Hobsons of Rainbow Creek

★ A TEA PARTY NOVEL ★

Also by Steven Michael Hubele

Almost Full Circle: A Tribute to Dad

The Hobsons of Rainbow Creek

★ A TEA PARTY NOVEL ★

Steven Michael Hubele

The Hobsons of Rainbow Creek

This is a work of fiction. All of the characters, organizations, and events portrayed in
this novel are either products of the author's imagination or are used fictitiously.

Published by: Steven Michael Hubele

ISBN-10: 098858770X
ISBN-13: 978-0-9885877-0-0

Printed in the United States of America

Dedication and Acknowledgments

To my daughters, Amanda and Allison Hubele, whom I teach but also learn from frequently. My daughters inspired me to keep going and to pursue my dream of writing this book. If I had listened to the naysayer who said it was too difficult to write a novel with a main character interested in politics, I may have put a halt to this project, and that would have been a big mistake. Instead, I felt driven by the hope of fulfilling the challenge of entertaining readers and at the same time encouraging them to take a stance.

I remain especially grateful to the St. Louis Publishers Association for significantly broadening the availability of *The Hobsons of Rainbow Creek*, helping to expand its presence from word-of-mouth sales to the online market and bricks-and-mortar bookstores. The advice and assistance I have received have been invaluable and exceptional.

Thank you to everyone who has encouraged me along the way, and to you, the reader, for joining Arthur Hobson on his journey.

— Steven Michael Hubele

Contents

Prologue xi

1 The Early Years 1

2 The Neighborhood 19

3 Paying Attention to Politics 43

4 Overlooking Policy at Northridge High 69

5 Few People Benefiting from Fair-Weather Change 83

6 Faded Memories of the Sandlots 115

7 Agreeing to Speak 121

8 Friendship 127

9 Adjusting to the Real World 167

10 Planning for a Bigger Platform 185

11 Recognizing the Whispers of Support 241

12 Johnny's Notes Listening to Ms. Staley 285

13 Arthur's Health Care Letter to the President 291

Epilogue 299

About The Author 309

Sometimes clouds fall to the ground.
However, there are no trees in the sky.
Beyond all the endless blue, open space,
Maybe an angel will teach us to fly.

Part of what we know
Gets swept under the rug or thrown back in our face,
Never to resurface again.
Without documentation, there is no time to experience another embrace.

The same walls that keep us safe,
Can crumble and fall oh so fast.
Keep it real and live a worthy life
Before the memories are cast.

—Steven Michael Hubele

Put it before them briefly, so they will read it,
clearly so they will appreciate it,
picturesquely so they will remember it, and above all,
accurately so they will be guided by its light.

—Joseph Pulitzer

Prologue

This is the story of the residents of Rainbow Creek and their middle-class lives as told by Arthur Hobson. Arthur has spent nearly sixty years living in Rainbow Creek studying his neighbors and researching his apprehensions. He believes there is a connection between researching, reading, writing, listening, and living better. A writer and speaker interested in politics, he is also a husband, father, teacher, coach, drug counselor, sales representative, and politician, and yet he does not feel like any of these things. He feels much bigger than any one stereotype of a person. He is sure he knows about a bigger picture of the things that inspire and make people happy, and it was not a fulfillment brought about by fame and fortune.

The more he lives, the more he works, the more he researches, the more he thinks, the more Arthur prepares himself to write and speak to the public. Arthur is tired of the many masterful politicians who promised to be good listeners and do thorough research to learn the truth about issues in order to work toward change and fairness for all people and yet did none of those things. He does not think politics should be about twisting words to give fancy speeches to expedite policies that benefit people who have not earned anything.

Arthur Hobson has always been a curious person, a lifelong student interested in discovering ways in which each individual could play a small part in making life better for others. He has desperately tried to learn from his mistakes and those of others. He has studied the big picture of the world to try to understand where the smaller pieces fit. For Arthur, painting a verbal picture to tell a story is the easy part of writing and speaking; the exploration of how events affect life and reflecting on true feelings to make an emotional impact is often the most difficult. With all the time and effort he has invested in researching both sides of issues, he feels the facts are the most important parts of his work.

Like an old male elephant that wanders off into isolation living a solitary life, Arthur, like the author of any book, sometimes must stay in a room alone to think and get his thoughts down on paper. He also needs time to get out and experience life by listening and looking at the stars, imagining he can fly higher than any bird so that he can get a better look at things. He works at the community center, joins the Tea Party movement, tries to help his younger brother, and stays close to his daughters, Sandra and Susie. He studies history because he needs to know the past. Without the truth about the past, there cannot be a better future. He studies and speaks about addiction, racism, legislation, stereotypes, politics, and historical events so others can learn and shape their own opinions over time to help improve society. Becoming an ally takes work, but if you truly believe in what you are doing, anything is possible.

"Every Christian can work to become an antiracist, influencing others of their own race," Arthur says. "Everyone can learn more about other religions, and just because someone has a different religion, that does not make them a bad person. Working with diverse peoples is a great way to learn about other cultures and become more comfortable with your own. There are so many racist comments heard every day by people of all color, and that should just stop. Do the people making the racist remarks even know the people they are directing their comments toward? Can they prove that all races fit a stereotype? The answer to both questions is no."

Through the study of history, Arthur hopes to learn why politicians make mistakes and tries to learn how to do things better, because history is not supposed to teach us how to go backward; it teaches us to go forward. To Arthur it seems politicians ignore life's lessons, building campsites at the bottom of a hill under a tree, rather than in the open field at the top of the hill, so that every time a little rain falls, their campsites wash out. While the history of the middle class has its share of heartbreak, Arthur finds everyday heroes and dreamers in his neighborhood that share some of his visions for America too. The lives of the residents of Rainbow Creek reveal their pursuit to fill basic needs, discovering the things they love, recognizing things they are good at, and permitting each other to dream for more. They are concerned about authorities deciding when to take over parts of their journeys, because they are sure the Constitution sought to prevent much of the interference they see now. It takes courage, Arthur professes, to live ordinary lives. Ordinary people do not live like celebrities, but many of them are stars. He hopes that legislators will one day take notice.

So many people ask themselves the same questions: Who loves me? Where should I work? Where is my next paycheck coming from? Do I drive a decent car? Do I have a great view from my condominium or a safe home in a good neighborhood? Arthur wonders about much bigger questions: How was the universe created, and why am I here? Am I making a difference in this world? What are my politics and passions? What do I believe in? Is there room for religion in politics? Is there room for politics in religion? Which politicians should I vote for and what specific laws and regulations do people need in order to make our world a better place to live? How will it all play out? Is there an end game, an ultimate purpose? Children need adults to guide them, but where do adults go for guidance? Our lives, he realizes, are unique works of art. "Nobody can answer all these questions perfectly," says Arthur, looking back from his journey through life, "but to know what we know today is a remarkable achievement. Most of us need a creator and wish we knew more about how our decisions on earth affect our relationship with God."

Arthur shares his thoughts with anyone he can. "We all have that fire burning inside, but sometimes it just goes away, because we never took the opportunity to use it. Sometimes, our spirit is broken, and there does not seem to be any hope for progress. Why do I not get any of the breaks? What is the truth? We could spend a lot of time on debates or discussions central to the development of this concept. However, if we work hard, overcome obstacles, and are honest with ourselves and other people, we will have more opportunities to feel good about our choices." To his daughters he says, "The only way you are going to accomplish anything in life is by working hard, though you may not get all of the rewards or keep everything you've earned." He tells fellow Tea Party Patriots, "Whether you are a writer, sales representative, mechanic, construction worker, teacher, businessperson, or engineer, there is no substitute for hard work. If we work hard, we win. If we do not, we will not. Nevertheless, try to have a little fun along the way." Sometimes, even to himself, Arthur's life feels like more of a burden than a benefit. Though some people roll their eyes at him when he talks too much, most respect him because he tries so hard to prove that he means well, mainly wanting everybody to feel successful. However, he knows it is important to maintain wit and perspective in spite of hardships or losses.

If you asked Arthur, he would tell you the Hobson family needed three lives to get everything done: one to learn, a second to do, and a third to teach or write about it. It took so much effort just to understand life as he was living it. Yet, after more than forty years exerting himself as a researcher, writer, speaker, and teacher, working as an employee at the local community center and as a Tea Party advocate, and adjusting to changing family configurations, Arthur sees life is about more than his personal struggles. He sees how government policies affect people, and he wants the middle class to have a more resonating voice.

For too long Arthur Hobson and some of his best friends were noticing more government forces working against them than ever before. They were tired of all the drug busts and shootings on the news, all the corruption, all the new regulations, the mounting national debt, and the increasing number of bad influences in the lives of hardworking good people in America. No one was doing anything to fix the real problems of society. Too many people were still on welfare, still out of work or dying from drug overdoses. Arthur and his friends wanted people to start paying attention to the real issues. Arthur was ready to act.

The Early Years

Early on in his life, Arthur had not yet contemplated all the things that made his blood boil and what problems were serious enough to make him react. Driven to find his passion, he read and studied all he could about human brains and discovered that everything we do or say comes from our brain planning some kind of muscle movement to accomplish a task. Sensory neurons and muscular neurons connect our muscles to our brains. Our brains plan for movement now or at another time to accomplish a short-term or long-range goal. These plans tell us on an individual basis when to move, where to work, what to say, and how to write. At an army level, every conflict, every arms escalation, every war on the planet is about the energy needed to carry out the plans. In short, everything we do comes from planning.

Knowing that, Arthur conceived a plan of his own. He was ready to change lives, and if he could somehow help American citizens understand how the middle class evolved, he was sure they would begin to understand the discontent so many Americans were beginning to show. With this goal in mind, Arthur studied history and paid attention to time hoping to achieve some historical perspective about all the crap happening around him and his family in Rainbow Creek. He would waste no more time.

Time is every moment there has ever been or ever will be. It is a system of measuring duration, during which something exists, happens, or prevails. Prevailing conditions take place during a period of history, an age, or an era. Sometimes we use time to record the pace or speed. Sometimes time is bad, such as when one has to serve a prison term or when government makes bad policies in a race against time. Sometimes it is good, such as when one is on time, from time to time, or ahead of time, before it is too late. Time after time, we repeatedly make time to work, play, and travel. Time clocks, timekeepers, timepieces, timers, timeshares, time sheets, timetables, time zones, and timeouts help us keep track of time. Sometimes out of necessity, we pay installments on time. Sometimes we waste our time, but if we use it wisely, its existence is time-honored. It is not honorable for our government to abandon our principles only to suit the times or to gain favor.

While only Arthur's imagination could ponder much about what was lost in prehistoric times, he was proud to be included with the part of society that researched and documented printed words helping shape the future. The story of civilization is a short narration when compared to the story of the earth from its beginnings in time as an unwieldy whirl of gases, dust, and water vapor. Looking into the future, Arthur had hopes of a sophisticated life for more people because of an endless expanse of opportunities around the globe. As a writer, however, he could only write about what he read or learned about history, or what he knew, did, or saw in his own lifetime. He would reach back as far as he could to discover the true origins of the middle class.

On March 18, 1968, Robert F. Kennedy made remarks at the University of Kansas, and teenaged Arthur, tagging along with his father, Atwood, now fifty-seven years old, listened to the speech. They were visiting the campus for his older brother Kevin's commencement ceremony. It was a historic day that Arthur had not forgotten.

If we believe that we, as Americans, are bound together by a common concern for each other, then an urgent national priority is upon us. We must begin to end the disgrace of this other America. This is one of the great tasks of leadership for us, as individuals and citizens this year. Even if we act to erase material property, there is another greater task. We must confront the poverty of satisfaction, purpose, and dignity that afflicts us all. For too long, we seemed to have surrendered personal excellence and too many community values in the mere accumulation of material things. Our gross national product, now, is over $800 billion a year, but the gross national product, if we judge the United States of America by that, that gross national product counts air pollution and cigarette advertising, and ambulances to clear our highway of carnage. It counts special locks for our doors and jails for people who break laws. It counts the destruction of redwood and the loss of our natural wonder in chaotic sprawl. It counts Whitman's rifle and Speck's knife, and the television programs, which glorify violence in order to sell toys to our children. Yet the gross national product does not allow for the health of our children, the quality of their education, or the joy of their play. It does not include the beauty of our poetry or the *strength of our marriages, the intelligence of our public debate or the integrity of our public officials. It measures neither our wit nor our courage, neither our wisdom nor our learning, neither our compassion nor our devotion to our country. It measures everything, in short, except that which makes life worthwhile. It can tell us everything about America except why we are proud that we are Americans. Some men see things as they are and say why. I dream things that never were and say why not.*

Less than three months after the speech, Sirhan B. Sirhan assassinated Robert F. Kennedy. Two years after that speech, travel on Route 66 started to disappear as a more modern interstate replaced it and big cities grew modern too. Several decades after that speech, Kennedy's son became a resolute defender and an advocate for the environment, committed to making a positive difference in the quality of water we drink and air we breathe for present and future generations. He writes almost extensively on environmental issues and he prosecuted big businesses and big governments alike for polluting the environment. Today Kennedy's ideas about preserving the environment and recycling raw materials are more relevant than ever before.

After listening to the Kennedy speech with his father, Arthur felt inspired much as his father did when leaving for Pearl Harbor just two decades earlier. He turned his attention to listening to politicians and military generals speaking about strategy. A litany of underground forces still destabilized Vietnam, and though his little brother Johnny no longer lived at home, he was back in the States, home safe from the war and finished serving the military. Because of his growing love for his country, Arthur wanted to do something worthwhile to help the cause. His father and his little brother put their lives on the line in conflicts far away from home, and he wanted to make a difference too. Countries halfway around the world were now neighbors due to the explosion of television. Arthur, learning truths from his father, worried that because more countries were doing more trade, they were using different negotiating policies for some of the same resources to the world. He already understood that the air of smug entitlements by many Americans would eventually lead to problems, but he wondered if politicians understood how to plan for the future.

The decade before Vietnam was defined by the new technology of the era: television. At first people considered televisions luxury items; only twenty-five Rainbow Creek households owned one in the early days of the fifties. Arthur's didn't, but he sure remembered being fascinated by his neighbor's. No one quite understood how it worked, a process of transmitting images by converting light rays into electrical signals, a receiver reconverting the signals so that the images reproduced on the screen, but they loved this new broadcasting thing. By the sixties, residents considered televisions a necessity and TVs sat in almost every household in the US.

But before televisions really took hold, a different kind of revolution--an industrial revolution--was in force. Following the end of World War II, US manufacturing facilities were all intact and businesses started expanding to make room for the return of our soldiers who needed work. Soldiers from both sides destroyed infrastructure and manufacturing facilities in Europe and Japan, almost everything during the war. After the war, the Japanese, Germans, French, and Italians bought brand items from the States because we were the only country making things. The US economy boomed for two decades until Europe and Japan had time to rebuild their manufacturing base and infrastructure.

World War II also brought about the explosion of the automobile industry, further promoting the popularity of Route 66, and gas service stations developed near highways all across the country. Travelers saw long stretches of Midwest American corn, which grew as high as a Clydesdale's mane. Gas stations became premier service shops with service bays offering new tires and quick fixes for travelers in need. In a time before big-box stores and shopping malls, Main Street in Rainbow Creek consisted of a drugstore, shoe store, florist, the Five and Dime, a bank, a bar, a bakery, a music store, and a confectionary. One of the advantages of living in a small town is the residents don't have to wait in long lines at the grocery store, license bureau, auto repair shop, gas station, post office, and numerous other places to buy supplies and search for various forms of entertainment. Each store had its function in middle-class culture, and as America grew up, Sears, JC Penney, and Stix, Baer and Fuller came to town and all three companies advertised on the radio and in the newspapers. Most families in Rainbow Creek and just about every other town in America for that matter purchased an automobile. Fast-food restaurants were popping up everywhere. Many adults thought America was growing too fast. Waste and pollution became daily topics of discussion on the news and at the Hobson dinner table when Arthur was a boy.

It was a new time for many Americans, and many people consider this the blooming, if not the birth, of the middle class, but as Arthur looked back fifty years hence, he thought they were wrong. He thought the middle class had its roots somewhere before he was born.

In 1955, Arthur's parents, Margaret and Atwood, had three sons between the ages of nine and twelve, Kevin the oldest, Arthur the middle son, and Johnny the youngest. They lived a hardworking life in Rainbow Creek, one full of adventures, fun, and tough times.

The three boys loved riding their bikes to the confectionary, called simply "the Confectionary" by all the kids in the neighborhood, and collecting baseball cards, especially Stan Musial cards, but also other St. Louis Cardinals players who were doing well, and hoping the team might win more World Series trophies.

One summer afternoon, nine-year-old Johnny rode his bicycle alone to the Confectionary to buy two packs of baseball cards. Each pack of cards included a three-inch-by-two-inch stick of bubblegum covered in a thin dusting of vaporized powdered sugar. The lower level of the Confectionary, mostly built into the ground, had a walkout back entrance, but the sliding door was always locked. However, a patio with two bike racks was available for young customers who wanted to park their bicycles and walk around to the front entrance. Johnny, as he always did when his brothers chaperoned his bicycle trips to buy baseball cards, parked his bike in one of the racks, walked up the hill on the side of the building, and entered through the front entrance of the store. On most other errands to the Confectionary, Johnny and his brothers bought items for their mother—a half-gallon of milk, a loaf of bread, a stick of butter. Margaret usually only requested one or two items from each of her sons, because that was all any of them could fit into the small wire baskets fastened behind the seats of their bicycles. On this trip to the store, Johnny was requested to bring back just one item, a can of string beans, for the family dinner that night.

After paying for his two packs of baseball cards and the one can of string beans for his mother, he thanked Mrs. Keithly, the store owner, and walked out onto the sidewalk. He anxiously opened his two packs of baseball cards and let out a yell of, "Oh, yeah," when he saw a card with a picture of Stan Musial posing in his famous stance in the batter's box. Excited, Johnny ran down the hill on the side of the store to retrieve his bicycle, so he could get home and brag to his brothers about his good luck. As he turned the corner at the bottom of the hill, glimpsing the bicycle rack on the patio, he saw a very large fifth-grader cutting the chain securing Johnny's green three-speed Schwinn bicycle to the rack. Johnny was used to older brothers and seeing big farm boys around Rainbow Creek, but he had never seen such a big kid with such a young face. He thought the boy must have been two hundred and fifty pounds. The huge size mismatch did not keep Johnny from fighting back.

Johnny: "Hey, get away from my bike."

Big kid: "Shut up, squirt, I'm taking your bike. You can get another one when you are big enough to reach the pedals."

Johnny: "I can reach the pedals, and I have two older brothers who will kick your butt if you don't leave me alone."

Big kid: "Maybe I will just kick your butt right now."

The fifth-grader pushed Johnny to the ground. Johnny jumped up and pushed back. The bully pushed Johnny harder, knocking him to the ground again. Johnny jumped up again and punched the big kid in the arm. This time the boy did not hold back, punching Johnny in the face with a combination, causing his nose to bleed and blackening one of his eyes. In just a matter of a few seconds, Johnny was battered and bludgeoned, left only to watch as the thief quickly pedaled away with his bicycle. He was only nine years old, but the altercation suddenly convinced Johnny the world was not fair. Stan Musial played fair, treated other human beings right, and worked hard to improve his techniques. This big kid just stole his bicycle without doing any honest work in exchange for the right to own it. A few seconds to cut a chain, a couple of pushes and punches and the bigger kid takes the little kid's bicycle.

Feeling worse about the loss of his bicycle than his hurt face, Johnny told his family about what happened at the Confectionary. For several months after the treacherous child-hood mugging, the trio of Kevin, Arthur, and Johnny traveled together, to run motherly errands or buy baseball cards, to go to school or the ball park. Secretly Arthur hoped he and his two brothers would cross paths with the thief so they could "make amends," but they never did. However, near the end of the summer that year, they did find Johnny's bicycle, destroyed and mangled into a hundred pieces in a wooded area near the Confectionary. Many people are good at making others mad, but this bully took the hurt to a higher level. Watching from the kitchen window, Arthur saw Johnny sitting dejectedly under the large oak tree in the backyard at the Hobson House. He had a feeling this would not be the last of Johnny's troubles in the world.

Unlike Arthur, oldest son Kevin was more interested in analyzing things that existed in front of his eyes. He loved tearing things apart, finding out how mechanical things worked and if he could figure out some kind of solution to make a thing work better, hoping he could sell his inventions someday. Kevin found it especially hard to accept criticism from someone striking down his ideas after he stayed up countless nights long after three o'clock, perfecting a design or building a scale model, whether the project was for school or just for fun. He could not leave one of his own ideas any more than he could have stayed around longer to help care for a sick relative. If he was going to be a high achiever, he had to expect big things for himself.

Arthur, on the other hand, looked at the world by analyzing the big picture. After reading *Uncle Tom's Cabin* on the sly, he fell in love with politics. He was sixteen years old and obsessed with fighting against inequalities. Everything around him began to feel like it was about the elite versus the common person, the bully versus the weakling, the rich versus the poor, and the intellectual versus the uneducated. He committed himself to becoming a writer so he himself could become an agent to honest social change. He wanted his own voice. Negative news stories were overshadowing the historical impact of every comment he heard. He wanted to read literature and hear speeches that did more than just popularize an idea or a stereotype. He thought both should help inspire people to do better.

When Arthur read *Uncle Tom*, it moved him. He saw Tom as a noble, long-suffering Christian slave. But by the time Arthur was reading it, more than a hundred years after it was first published, "Uncle Tom" had become an epithet for African Americans who were accused of selling out to whites. This made no sense to Arthur, as throughout the book, far from allowing himself to be exploited, Tom stands up for his religious beliefs and is grudgingly admired even by his enemies. It tormented Arthur to know history didn't remember men like Uncle Tom as noble heroes and praiseworthy men, instead as men who had sold out to whites. Knowing cruel slave owner Simon Legree ordered Tom whipped to death out of frustration to break his slave's unshakeable belief in God, it just seemed incredibly wrong that anyone would purposely tarnish his name. Legree was the evil man who abandoned his sickly mother for a life at sea, and he ignored her letter to see her one last time at her deathbed. He raped women slaves who despised him. Yet many people made out Uncle Tom to be the bad person.

There was one thing in particular that Arthur took away from *Uncle Tom's Cabin*; it opened his eyes to what he found the most dreadful part of slavery: the outrages of feelings and affections that came with the separating of families. A few years later Arthur would reflect on this and see a certain connection in his own life, if to a lesser degree, when Kevin went away to college and Johnny went away to fight in the Vietnam War. All these "take it or leave it" deals in which he had no say or choice surrounded Arthur Hobson's life.

Compared to his brothers, Johnny was more of a free bird, often less engaging than the older boys. He expressed himself through music and only enjoyed the limelight if he had a guitar in his hands. Girls were always calling the house to talk to Johnny, and though most of the time he stretched the phone chord as far as it would go so no one else could hear, he seldom talked for more than a few minutes. He preferred using his free time to practice his guitar, privately trying to manufacture his dream into a reality, but scared that all the negativity in the world might suck him into a giant hole. He was right to worry. Soon after graduating from high school, Johnny was drafted and off fighting the war in Vietnam.

One thing Arthur heard often about himself as he grew up was how much he looked like his father, Atwood. In a lot of ways he acted like him too. Arthur thought his family history might lead him closer to the truth about the beginnings of the middle class and so he began to research it. What he found was a whole lot of pain and heartache, joy and achievements.

Atwood Hobson was born in turbulent times. The grandson of immigrants and son of a homesteading father, he was no stranger to hard labor, yet he always worked to stay educated. Not so many years before he was born, the collapse of intrusive governments and civil uprisings caused by wars, famine, and political differences made much of the world unsafe territory for anyone without power who tried to speak up. Immigrants like Atwood's parents, Ulysses and Juliet, arrived in America from many European countries in search of freedom in the land of milk and honey. After a while, they all became just Americans. They united to fight against oppressive tyrants and communism and they rarely went back to their homelands. When men did go back, they did not return to live or visit; they went back to fight for their democratic beliefs as soldiers in World War I.

Atwood was a young teen during the Great War, but by the time the Depression hit, he was well aware of what was going on around him. Loss of confidence, a depressed economy, poverty, work stoppages, plant closings, bank closings, and fear of communism all combined to wreak havoc on America, a state soon worsened by propaganda spread by the Hitler regime and a collision course with Japan. The Japanese were loading up their cargo ships with scrap metals and other materials discarded from American factories and shipped back to Japan by way of ports on the California coast. Why no one paid attention to this before the onset of World War II seemed unimaginable to twenty-seven-year-old Atwood. He had started dating a girl named Margaret Garfield, who was about to turn nineteen, and thoughts of the future were on his mind. Though she was young, Margaret was the most intelligent girl he had ever met. She complimented Atwood's weaknesses and always seemed able to add insight to a conversation. Sitting on the porch at the Hobson House on a warm fall night, Atwood begged an answer from Margaret.

Atwood: "Who is profiting from all the recycled steel and copper leaving American ports for Japan?"

Margaret: "I don't think the Japanese are using all this metal to build cars; I think they are using it to build airplanes, to make better ammunitions and stock military arsenal. At least that is what I gather from listening to my father talk about the high price of steel and copper."

Atwood: "I have been thinking about enlisting in the navy. My friend Frank gave me the name and address of a naval recruiter here in Rainbow Creek."

Margaret: "Only honorable men think it is important to help protect our country. If you are serious about enlisting, I will wait for you until you return home. Even though our country is enjoying peacetime, I will worry about you. I don't want anything to happen to you."

This was all Atwood needed to hear. One month later, he was working detail on a submarine in Pearl Harbor. He and Margaret exchanged letters regularly during the first two years of his rapid rise to the rank of chief petty officer. Then on December 7, 1941, the Japanese attacked the island of Oahu. The attack killed or injured more than thirty-five hundred Americans and sank or badly damaged eighteen battleships of the Pacific fleet. The *Arizona* battleship sank, with constant oil bubbles surfacing as a reminder of that horrible day. In addition, the Japanese wiped out a fleet of three hundred and fifty airplanes. Living in Rainbow Creek and every other town or big city in America during the war years that followed was just plain hell for all except the very fortunate.

There was some speculation about the possibility of what might happen if a nuclear chain reaction was unleashed in a way that would allow a bomb to build energy without any control. Robert Oppenheimer was the head of "science" for the Manhattan Project along with a dozen other scientists, who all played crucial roles in getting the weapon designed and built. The first demonstration of "the gadget" (the code name for the first atomic bomb) was at Trinity site in Alamogordo, New Mexico, and it proved that the weapon would detonate and that the chain would build as predicted. After three years of war, the US used the atomic bomb to retaliate against Japan and attempt to end the war. The first bomb, code-named "Little Boy," was dropped on the city of Hiroshima, Japan, on August 6, 1945, at 8:16:02 a.m. and exploded above the courtyard of Shima Hospital, with a force equivalent to over twelve thousand tons of TNT. The second bomb, code-named "Fat Man," exploded over Nagasaki, Japan, at 11:02 a.m. on August 9, 1945. It exploded with a force of twenty-two thousand tons of TNT. Within five years of both bombings, more than 410,000 people, six civilians to every soldier, died as a direct result or from bomb-related causes.

Up until this point, Nazis were an army of ideology triumphing over reason, depriving humanity of religious and political differences and murdering more than six million Jews. The Germans gassed men and women, buried children alive in sandpits, and threw babies to their deaths from hospital windows. American soldiers, including Atwood Hobson, regrouped to put an end to the war. When the soldiers came home, many of them married their sweethearts and went to work helping reshape the economy with a new industrial revolution. When Atwood returned to Rainbow Creek, he learned that both his parents had died while he was away. He took comfort in Margaret and married her as soon as he could.

Margaret: "Work here in America was really hard when you were gone, but now that the war is over, life will be fairer. I spent most of my daylight hours at the factory shooting rivets into fabricated metal parts and airplane wings."

Atwood: "Like most people in this country, we will just have to start rebuilding our lives. I am not sure what I can promise you, but whatever happens next, I know you are the person I want to share it with."

Margaret: "You are very sweet, Atwood." Margaret gave him a long kiss on the lips.

Atwood: "At least most of the time now, we will be rewarded for our work. We have an opportunity to make life better for our children and grandchildren."

Margaret: "If God blesses us with children, how many would you like to have?"

Atwood: "Well, it would be nice to have a little help around our property. Whenever I was lying in a trench, with bombs exploding all around me, I would think of children's names to help me get through the stress of fighting. Sometimes I dreamed about you and me, and children playing on a big swing hanging from the big oak tree in the backyard. I decided I liked the names Kevin, Arthur, and Johnny for a boy, and Aubrey, Sarah, and Annie for a girl. Every soldier had his own special mind game to play in order to avoid thinking about the possibility of never coming home. That one was mine."

When the GI Bill provided returning World War II soldiers with money for college and down payments on home mortgages, the popular image of the middle class took off. In Rainbow Creek, construction crews built thirty-five rural houses on large lots of a small leveraged dairy farm, and a few local returning GIs realized the American Dream. Similar projects in every state made it possible for returning service members to afford homes in these new suburbs. Atwood and Margaret, however, refused the government assistance and moved onto his parents' land and into the Hobson House to care for the property that had gone unattended while Atwood was off fighting the war. There were so many things for Atwood and Margaret to be thankful for: the backyard barbecues, a car in the driveway, and their loving relationship among them. The hottest craze of the times, owning a black-and-white television, was just a couple of years away.

Ulysses A. Hobson was the grandfather of Arthur Hobson and his two brothers, Kevin and Johnny. Even after living such a long accomplished life, Ulysses never could have imagined the fantastic events that would surface in the lives of his three grandsons. He never could have imagined the high rate of divorce, the extent of heroin addiction, or the difficulties of raising children in modern society. Fulfilling basic needs and permitting his family to love him were the only two things important to Ulysses early on in his life. Arthur wondered if his generation might hold the answer to when the middle class came to be.

Of all the presidents Ulysses admired in his lifetime, his favorite was Theodore Roosevelt. Roosevelt was a Harvard University graduate, hardened by the death of his mother on the same night as the death of his wife during childbirth, yet he somehow managed to tread along after a prolonged grieving period. He also knew what it was like to lose a fortune, as he lost more than half of the cattle on his Dakota Territory ranch during one of the hardest winters on record.

A young Ulysses followed the actions of President Roosevelt by deciphering telegrams at his Revenue Office and listening to early accounts of easterners traveling west. The president was able to overcome mainly because he had a loving daughter named Alice to take care of. He learned to heal his soul by spending time in the outdoors as a real working cowboy before moving to New York to pursue a career in politics. Ulysses felt that Roosevelt had real grit and he stood up for what he believed in when challenged, bringing meaning to his life and circumspection to others. He knew that allowing lawlessness breeds more lawlessness and eventually anarchy. Roosevelt thought the main job of government was to protect its citizens, not interfere in their personal lives or business affairs, and Ulysses agreed.

In 1901, Ulysses married Juliet Mathews and the newlyweds started building a new life and a house on an estate they happily referred to as the Hobson House Property in Rainbow Creek, Missouri. They could not have known then that their descendants would live in the house for generations. During a time when farmers and rural families wanted and needed children to help with chores and rugged living conditions, Juliet lost two early pregnancies to miscarriages. To help with the grieving, the couple put all of their effort into improving their home and their property. To Juliet, who was ten years younger than her husband, her home was the culmination of expression from her heart. She orchestrated a dimension of time and memory and a personalized dimension of emotion, collecting artifacts, sewing her own linens, and framing self-made paintings to hang on the walls. The transitions of her furnishings and the resolution of the architecture all built by the hands of Ulysses, as in soothing music, had strong effects on the moods of each of them and who they were as people. Juliet's focus on her home helped her overcome her losses and made her feel comfortable and safe. She wanted her home to feel like a journey of small discoveries for her husband or any future children or visitors. No matter what, she refused to accept the dead ends in life or feelings of being unappreciated. She was sure that if a wife managed a home correctly, climbing the stairs of the front porch could feel like preparing to walk into paradise.

One day, with exterior of the Hobson House nearly complete, Juliet walked up the stairs of the front porch to find Ulysses resting in his favorite chair.

Juliet: "I love you, Ulysses."

Ulysses: "You also."

Juliet: "You also? Thanks, Mr. Romance."

Ulysses: "Someday I will write you a love song. Any great singer starts slow at the beginning, tells a touching story in the middle, and finishes hitting the big notes at the ending."

Juliet: "OK, that makes up for it."

Ulysses: "You mean for not helping you more with the chores, feeding the chickens and our horses?"

Juliet: "No, I am being sarcastic--for that 'you also' comment earlier, you knucklehead!"

Ulysses: "Oh yeah, I guess that comment didn't sound right. I hope you don't make me shave a heart on my chest and walk around town with my shirt off."

Juliet: "You wouldn't. If you do that, I will braid my hair, put beads on the strands, and move to Oklahoma to join an Indian tribe."

Ulysses: "Um, please don't do that. You know I love you and need you here."

Juliet: "Finally, you said you love me. You were starting to sound like a politician or a general who drives people into the weeds instead of amongst the beautiful blooms and majestic trees."

Nine months later, Atwood Hobson was born. Ulysses and Juliet were delighted to have a healthy son.

Juliet and Ulysses were hard workers, but they knew they were lucky too. Others were much taken for granted. One day Juliet learned of an old childhood friend, Gloria Gates, who had moved to New York to work in the garment trade several years before and died, her life stolen away in a fire. Of all the groups of courageous Americans of their generation, the least recognized were the female garment workers who organized a strike against unfair bosses who paid them just two dollars a day for working long hours, seven days a week, in deplorable sweatshop conditions. Citizens learned more about their cause after a hundred and forty-five of the women died in a horrific fire on the ninth floor of a garment building one year after a strike against the company. The tragedy, known as the Triangle Shirtwaist Factory fire, shined a light on American values of fairness, honesty, and safety in the workplace. Some historians say this event triggered the beginning of the true spirit of thought, which later led to government regulating businesses. Up to this point in American history, politicians did little to enact regulations to protect against practices of dishonest businessmen. If bosses tried to take advantage of workers' values, there were little or no regulations stop their deceptive practices and little chance of punishing bosses, who seldom worried their wrongdoings would come back to haunt them. If the free market was to work for everybody, workers needed to be part of the team establishing important guides for fair pay and safety in the workplace. As long as early American workers were One Nation under God, they believed they were part of the greatest nation in the world. Maybe without even realizing, when workers were angry, they were shaping the beginnings of strong union platforms.

Ulysses always had a fascination with the quests of the bourgeoisie because people's dreams always seem interrupted by misadventures with wicked social satire. In the Western world, between the late eighteenth century and to this point in his life, a range of groups across history formed a social class characterized by middle or merchant classes that derived some social and economic power from employment, education, and wealth. They differed from the distinguished social classes whose power came from being born into an aristocratic family of titled landowners granted special privileges by the monarch. The bourgeoisie emerged from traders and manufacturers taking risks, financed under the control of old money. In Ulysses' mind, the city dwellers of the bourgeoisie owned the means of production, not the big money of big corporations or big government. The wealthy classes of early capitalist societies emerged from the middle class and a caste of poor serfs and immigrants who brought their own lifestyles and values. Many people throughout history were limited from progressing to the bourgeois because of measures beyond their control, but some just elected to settle without reaching for more out of life. Ulysses believed that when the bourgeoisie gain power, a potential loss of wealth and control emerges, so that rich businesspersons and politicians understandably see this as threatening to their power.

Studying the word *bourgeoisie*, Ulysses discovered this French term evolved from the Old French word *burgeis*, meaning an inhabitant of a town. *Burgeis* derives from the German word *burger*, meaning a market town or village that sells commodities such as leather or beef cattle. Visitors from Hamburg, Germany, introduced ground beef patties, called hamburgers, at the 1904 World's Fair in St. Louis. Ulysses loved when a new word perfectly explained something, but the sales pitches of the German prognosticators telling fairgoers that the hamburger would drastically reshape the economy in every town in America were a bit of a stretch for Juliet and him. No doubt, states witnessed gradual increases in numbers of middle-class people buying ground beef at the market close to their home in cities and towns across America, but many other industries were changing and evolving in places like Rainbow Creek. Farmers, once working to feed their families, opened grocery stores to make money and feed others. Customers of grocery stores, who once only cooked to feed their families, opened restaurants to make money and cook for others. Industrial manufacturers started producing utensils, plates, napkins, equipment, and cleaning supplies for restaurateurs, and so on and so forth. The middle class was branching out and getting stronger.

That was Ulysses' story. But before Ulysses came Edward and Mary.

Ever since he was a very young boy, Arthur had heard stories about his great-grandfather, Edward A. Hobson, who lived through the potato famine that caused so many families to migrate to America for a chance of a better life. Edward Hobson was a merchant, banker, politician, tax collector, railroad executive, and officer in the United States Army during the American Civil War. Most known for his determined pursuit of helping turn back the

Confederates at Morgan's Raid, and though captured late during the war, he was able to negotiate his release before Confederate General Robert E. Lee surrendered to General Ulysses S. Grant on April 9, 1865. The Confederates claimed to be fighting for their country's freedom, while at the same time denying freedom to generations of black slaves. Lee's surrender effectively ended the war and signaled the start of abolishing slavery, the root cause of the war. On March 8, 1863, a baby named Ulysses A. Hobson was born to Edward and his wife, Mary. Edward did not see his son until the war ended and he was able to return home.

Mary: "Work here in America is still as hard as it was in the old country. Now that the war is over, maybe life will be fairer. All is destroyed, even the rails, fencing of all kinds, trees, bushes and shrubs. Nothing is left that would hide a chicken. I never expect to witness another such sight. It is my hope that future generations will reflect upon this war on American soil, even though this battle amongst American citizens is melancholy to think upon because of the massive losses. Some of our neighbors were for the Union and others for the Confederacy, and family members even fought against one another. Everyone feared one another. Under such conditions, all work and undertakings came to a stop."

Edward: "At least most of the time now, we will be rewarded for our work. We have an opportunity to make life better for our children and grandchildren. I no longer have to worry about bushwhackers knocking on the front door and confiscating your labors or hurting you or our baby in the middle of the night while I'm away fighting."

Mary: "One night we were visited about three o'clock in the morning by the bush-whackers. I was awake with baby Ulysses when they burst into the house. They took our guns and then they went upstairs, took some wool blankets, and searched the dresser drawers. They even took my hairbrush, but thank the heavens; they didn't hurt me or Ulysses."

Edward: "We were in awful battles and our company was cut to pieces. I saw Captain Gibbs fall and started toward him when another bullet struck and killed him. I am afraid many of the boys who did come home, came home with serious injuries. I guess I am one of the lucky ones who just tires talking about it all."

Mary: "I promise we will not eat boiled crow for dinner, but until things get situated, we might have to eat a little humble pie at the start. Do you think some deer meat might make it to the kitchen table this winter?"

Edward: "War taught me to prepare long before the eleventh hour in order to earn my stripes. But even with all the preparation, no soldier could ever prepare for all the killing he had to endure amongst his own people. Yes, I will shoot a deer. Killing a deer will feel nothing like the emptiness felt killing another man."

Soon after the end of the war, Edward started engaging in business in Rainbow Creek. He joined the Republican Party and a few years later, made an unsuccessful run for clerk of the State Court of Appeals. By 1880, he was a delegate to the Republican National Convention and a strong supporter of Ulysses S. Grant's candidacy. After winning the presidential election, Grant rewarded Edward for his help by appointing him the Collector of Revenue in the district surrounding Rainbow Creek.

Arthur knew he was getting closer. He was beginning to get a sense of the origins of the middle class, yet he still felt it must run further into the past. He would keep looking. What was life like when Edward and Mary arrived, he wanted to know. What about the generations before Edward? His studies told him immigrants from countries like Ireland, Poland, Italy, and others, trying to free themselves from the struggles of their own upbringing, made the journey to America in search of their dreams. Some of the most impoverished people in Europe immigrated to America. Before that it was the Puritans and the British, the French and the Spanish, looking to establish colonies and bring fame to their homeland.

For the first fifty years of European settlements in America, a relationship between the government and schools did not exist. Frontier America was arguably the freest society that has ever existed. Parents had complete control of their own laws and their children's schooling. There was no government, no agencies, no legislation, and no certification or regulatory requirements. Life was simpler concerning these aspects of life on the range, and parents could choose whatever they wanted for themselves and their children. Nevertheless, there were always the "reformers" who thought they knew better than everyone else and thought they had the right to impose their views on others. When leaders formed governments and made policies, sometimes they made rules for their own welfare, not for the wants of the people. But generally, most of the British North American colonies that eventually helped form the United States were settled by men and women, who in the face of persecution refused to compromise their religious convictions and fled Europe. The New England colonies were conceived and established as "plantations of religion." Some settlers arrived for secular motives—to catch fish or farm the land—but the great majority of people left Europe to worship God in the way they believed to be correct. They believed that their success would prove that God's plan for Christian churches, Catholic and Protestant, could be successfully realized in the American wilderness. Colonies were planned as commercial ventures, but were led by entrepreneurs who considered themselves Christians working diligently to promote the prosperity of the church.

As Arthur saw it, the founding of the United States was simple. In the early 1770s, the king of England ruled the American colonies for monetary gains only. Even though the Americans were all the way across to the other side of the Atlantic Ocean from England, Americans still felt forced to obey the king's laws and send tax payments to the king. The colonists were angry because they were paying taxes without having a voice in representing their values and concerns. They resented paying taxes to a government that did nothing to represent them or help them. That anger led to the Boston Tea Party in 1773, when colonists threw forty-five tons of tea from Britain into the Boston Harbor so they would not have to pay the tax on it. A "Committee of Five," as it was called, included five of America's most famous historic figures, Benjamin Franklin, Thomas Jefferson, John Adams, Robert Livingston, and Roger Sherman. The members of the group asked Thomas Jefferson to write the first draft of a statement requesting independence from England. Once all the members agreed on any changes, they announced their freedom, the Declaration of Independence was completed, and the document was sent to an unhappy king. The Boston Tea Party demonstration and the Declaration of Independence led to the Revolutionary War and the war led to a colonial government free from rule by England, and a new nation was born.

Looking back ever further, Arthur read about the ancient Greeks, who used slaves for the benefit of their families. They were not black men, but white men held captive in war. There could be no talk of racism, simply oppression. Aristotle, one of the great Greek philosophers, declared slaves inferior beings that were justly subdued, deprived of their liberty and a chance at a good life. He learned from this story that maybe we should not put so much faith in our leaders and other great thinkers. They are human beings just like the rest of us and we should think more for ourselves.

Arthur also studied about the Egyptians and how they started infrastructure programs and employed people by building pyramids, and how the Romans broke loaves of bread, baked fish, and built chariots to get around and transport goods. Medieval kings ruled by making laws for all the people, some good ideas and some not so good, sometimes ending in wars of conquest. Wars were fought because one group wanted to take something from another group or because leaders wanted to occupy an idle workforce. He read about the Mayans, who were master farmers. They accomplished amazing feats, building pyramids too. They kept track of time with calendars, charts, and records of weather patterns by using symbols to express complex ideas. They engineered reservoirs, canals, dams, and levees. Then around 800 AD their entire civilization suddenly disappeared. The Mayans vanished from the earth. Some scientists think severe drought caused their demise; some think it is possible that the Mayans' water system became rampant with waterborne diseases; yet others figure they all died during a civil war.

Arthur also studied the Middle Ages and he learned that during this period, most people fit into one of three categories, the church, the noble, or the serf. The serfs were the peasants. However, there was another group of people called the freemen, some of whom belonged to the noble and some to the serf. The freemen included merchants, artisans, accountants, stewards, musicians, and some generally skilled riff-raff, and all these people were probably the closest members of what might gain consideration as a middle class. The clergy were separate and were formally supposed to be classless, though class to a larger degree, because of the varying settings of each church and the richness of the donations from different congregations, especially in England and Scotland, sometimes influenced them.

What all of Arthur's research finally confirmed for him is that the middle class began well before Christopher Columbus and his crew arrived in the Americas. Long ago, middle-class stature started to develop and meant having a domicile and enough dried meat and vegetables stored to make it through the upcoming winter season.

Now Arthur had his answer. The middle class had a long and honorable history that started with the beginning of civilization. Understanding this history, Arthur knew, would lead to understanding and living a better future for all. If he was going to get this great country heading in the right direction, he needed to help young people learn this important lesson. But how?

Rewrite the history books, thought Arthur.

★ 2 ★

The Neighborhood

P resent Rainbow Creek residents will never have a chance to repay the original inhabitants of the land for the work they did clearing trees and shaping trails as they founded their town. The Sauk, Creek, and Fox Indian tribes created the trails to travel back and forth on what now is Broadway and Main Street in the downtown square of Rainbow Creek. Every Indian chief's headdress was full of feathers as beautiful as the rainbow and as bright as the flowers and butterflies along the streams in Rainbow Creek. The chief earned each of the brightly colored feathers by making intelligent decisions and earning respect from fellow tribesmen. For many years after the US government stole the land and redistributed the Indians' wealth, all the birds in Rainbow Creek seemed to fly with feathers of darker colors.

Rainbow Creek, situated within a ribbon of wilderness, separated the land haunted by the ghosts of family farmers to the west and the railroad tracks at the outreaches of town to the east. A three-mile-long creek zigzagged through the middle of town. The creek gave residents a sense of direction when trying to find a business address or just about anything else, seldom leaving anyone lost or needing help from a map. Arcs containing all the colors of the spectrum formed regularly in the sky because of the refraction of the sun's rays off the large pebbles and the red clay base of the creek every time rain or mist fell. This is how Rainbow Creek earned its name.

During Arthur's early childhood days, his father, Atwood, tried to teach him "white collar" was a near synonym for making it to the middle class, but only if by work done in an honest way. "Blue collar" was the synonym for struggling in the working class, sometimes for not working enough hours, sometimes for not making a better wage. Thus, to consider belonging to the middle class, a man needed a job done in clean conditions that did not involve excessive heavy manual work. Atwood perceived a working-class job as one done in dirty conditions, usually requiring gloves or some type of protective clothing. Though Arthur never bought the argument, he realized his father just wanted him to have a better life than he had. As Arthur aged, this class distinction faded away with the rapid technological changes since the 1980s. Almost all jobs in modern society now require working with some type of computer, mobile device, machine, or equipment with microchips inside of them.

Today the most common measurements of class are those used by marketing researchers in the advertising industry to classify people in large cities and small towns that read or watch particular media, and advertisers are mainly interested in consumption habits. Atwood taught his sons a different way. If he let his mind settle for all gains, all progress, and all new ideas, then life would have no taste, and a fat and content human being settles for mediocrity. Sloth, laziness, thinking the government should bail out everyone from his or her problems and being unwilling to work are all reasons people fail. It certainly is not a bad thing if a person wants to work hard for things that are more than what one needs. The three Hobson boys weren't raised to spend their entire life taking for themselves, thinking only about the immediacy of living, without ever contemplating or following up on ideas to make this country better than they found it.

A strong middle class always leads the recovery of a strong economy. The middle class links arms across our great nation to figure out ways to create new industries and bring new jobs to stimulate growth in the economy. They find new ways to offer products and services that make our country better, and along the way, they earn honest money from honest work. The middle class is good at creating clusters of successful businesses like franchises in one city and then expanding in another. There was once a time in places like Rainbow Creek when a person could walk into a store or office, fill out a job application, and walk out with a job. However, with the struggling economy and so many people out of work, that is not a safe hiring practice anymore. Many of the town's baby boomers thought they would never lose their jobs. It is very unlikely now that a high school dropout could march through the front door of a business or factory and receive a lifetime job. Few jobs in Rainbow Creek paid new workers enough money now to give them a chance to climb the ladder, realizing dreams of buying a house, two cars, a motorcycle, a time-share, a bass fishing boat, and a new computer system along the way.

Rainbow Creek, a slow-growing place along the road in the Midwest, was trying during the 1950s to build its reputation as a successful, prosperous community with elements of small-town charm and other amenities. Restrictive air-quality standards were certainly not a problem in this community back in the fifties. The downtown section was full of nineteenth-century brick buildings, home to shops and restaurants and most of them locally owned, like the fittingly eccentric sweet food shop called Mom and Popcorn. The sweets shop sold homemade candy, imported licorice, and popular baked goods made in-house by Mom, the owner. Local taxes collected by the shops and restaurants supported the public school system, the parks, and roads, and helped ensure the public amenities did not decline or decay. Nevertheless, even though Rainbow Creek had many attractions, the biggest reason families gave for deciding to live there was the town's charm and potential.

Teachers and parents in Rainbow Creek were not the kind of adults who told children they did great when they scored a 40 percent on a test, struck out four times in a baseball game, or failed to perform one of their designated chores around the house. They believed positive reinforcement for everything a child does at an elementary age gives that child a false sense of reality, and as an adult, such children become wise guys because they learned as a child to think everything they say or do is the best way. They thought it better for parents and teachers to give helpful suggestions and even an occasional negative comment to push children to do better and ramp down reason for excuses for bad grades, because well-thought-out teaching approaches never hurt anybody before all this politically correct stuff. Besides, when children become adults, they often must learn to push in areas where they are uncomfortable, and though this makes them nervous, they feel alive and proud after accomplishments.

Whenever Kevin, Arthur, or Johnny hung out with Frank Lambert from down the street, Carol Lambert was the acting mother for the Hobson boys. *Dr. Spock's Baby and Child Care* book sat on the coffee table at the Lambert house. Carol insisted her son Frank say "please" and "thank you" and if he didn't use these words correctly, she would inform him about the wrongness of acting rude. She knew what other mothers would come to know later. Class is an aura of confidence, gained from preparation and having manners. Class has nothing to do with money. Class is accepting a challenge without running scared and using self-discipline to prove you can meet the demands of life. She never pulled away or retreated into her own little world when other kids were at her house. "You kids don't know how good you have it," she would say if one of them complained too much.

If teachers and parents coordinated efforts to use the right approaches, then they believed their town would not have children who grew up to be adults that have a sense of entitlement without earning the right. They would not have drivers on the highway who think they own the road; they would not have adults suing McDonald's because their children are getting fat; they would not have adults who must have more possessions than their neighbors, and their children just might end up gaining a little more common sense. Parents who decide to raise their families in Rainbow Creek are usually the types who like to live up to their ears in work, taking care of the yard, cleaning house, scrubbing bathrooms, recycling their trash, doing laundry, helping their kids with homework, shopping for groceries, cooking meals, taking care of cars, and holding down productive full-time jobs. Though they have little time to waste on themselves, they do not mind making sacrifices for their children. They prefer this to spending their lives idle and staring at the clock on the wall or the television. To a trained outside observer, it appears that moms and dads in Rainbow Creek are as strict as they need to be in raising their children, though they all have somewhat different parenting styles. For the teenage girls in the neighborhood, it was obvious that parents tried to teach them not to just sail along adjusting for boys, wanting them to have patience finding their own identity, prepared for a future of more boys than they ever dreamed of or wanted chasing them. During the fifties, most mothers lived life as was expected, taking care of their husband, kids, and house, because a woman who worried about a career or a better education was considered something less than a true woman, though they secretly dreamed of more for their daughters.

Arthur Hobson had a lot of help from his parents and teachers during his boyhood years, making it through the good times and the bad times, growing as a human being living in the Midwest. From his parents, Arthur learned his storytelling skills. The biggest gift his parents gave to him and his brothers was to tell bedtime stories of the olden days. Atwood fathered with discipline, a learned skill from his duties in the navy, but he was always fair and he had a kind and gentle side too. His stories usually involved talk about street politics, exciting stuff like undercover work by spies, submarines blowing up enemy ships, or play-by-play game enactments of past champions with gestures and sound effects. Atwood listened when a kid told him a story. He made a child feel his stories were important. He had street smarts and taught his boys to pay attention too.

Atwood knew way ahead of time that the world would go global. Watching more children playing and the growth in his own small town, he was paying attention to a world population growing at an even faster pace, especially in China. With all those people, he knew China would someday compete with the United States for reign as the world's economic superpower and that their immense militarism would have to be respected.

Margaret was a member of the National Endowment for the Arts, the most important group a typical middle-class American woman needed to join, she thought. The average middle-class Midwestern woman read ten books in a year, though exceptionally avid women readers in Rainbow Creek read as many as fifty books or more on an annual basis. Margaret read two books per month. She probably would have enjoyed reading more, except that she cared deeply about raising her three sons and the family home sat on the outskirts of a suburb. Women in town read more than men read, and read more in all book categories except history, biography, and sports. It was ironic to Margaret knowing that men wrote almost all of what later unpretentious women readers considered the literary classics. She also had a propensity to work crossword puzzles like nobody else on earth. She hoped her love for words and the English language rubbed off on her children, as she tried to teach each of her three boys to overcome obstacles with their minds and spirits. She tried to give her sons some perspective about growing up and the dangers in the world. For her, no topic was too big for a child. She never left them out of the conversation because of their age.

When Margaret was a little girl, Franklin D. Roosevelt was campaigning for the presidency on the promise of the New Deal. Seventy-five years ago, Roosevelt came up with a creative solution in which he asked American workers to contribute to a social savings account that the government would manage on their behalf and would be there for their retirement. Social Security has been the most successful social program in the history of our country, supported by both Republicans and Democrats by a 77–6 vote on passage of the bill. But today, the government estimates that more Americans now receive income benefits from government than they pay into it. When our ancestors wrote our tax policies, everyone paid payroll taxes, but today only 47 percent of American households pay federal income taxes, and Social Security is primarily financed by a percent payroll tax, split equally between employer and employee. Social Security pays monthly benefits to about 53 million Americans today. However, with the recession and high unemployment, less money has come in than anticipated and lately the system has been drawing on the reserves. The Congressional Budget Office estimates that the reserve fund and payroll taxes will cover full payment of benefits for another thirty years.

Other parts of the New Deal were supposed to bring about change and expand government in order to provide more jobs, chiefly on public-works projects. Later, after a swearing-in to the presidency, Roosevelt proposed that farmers set their crops on fire in order to decrease supply and drive up prices. For farm families like Margaret's parents, the Garfields, this kind of leadership could not stand for long. At the same time, Margaret was beginning to develop her own political philosophy about individualism and freedom and the effects of too much government interference. She hated that so many facets of the New Deal seemed to kill the entrepreneurial spirit of the men in her family and town. She saw many of the changes as impractical, because too many self-reliant, independent, courageous, and prosperous men in her community were all of the sudden penalized from every direction.

Atwood's father, Ulysses, was also paying attention to Roosevelt's new government model. After the federal government under FDR decided to separate the banking industry from the investment industry with the passing of the Glass-Seagull Act, Ulysses watched to try to understand the eventual outcome. Brokerage firms had to make a decision. The players could declare their firm a bank or they could deal in investments as a brokerage firm. Firms could not do both. At the time, firms like J. P. Morgan and Company decided to remain a bank. The investment partners at J. P. Morgan walked out and formed Morgan Stanley, so that they could remain in the capital formation and investment business. Ulysses was too worried about keeping food on the table to worry about what new rules the government was making to establish boundaries between banks and brokerage firms. Besides, his family and fellow citizens were living through the Depression. But he did take notice when one operation was given special privileges.

The government allowed just one company by law to remain in both functions. The company was Brown Brothers Harriman. Roosevelt specifically decided to do a favor for his friend and supporter, Averill Harriman, who controlled the president's family bank. Coincidentally, President George W. Bush's grandfather was also a prominent banker at Brown Brothers. He ran the show; his name was Prescott Bush. For the next several decades, it became apparent to Ulysses Hobson that the general decision separating the banking and investment functions was the better idea he endorsed. But he hated federal policies that arrange a special deal for one company here and another special policy for another company somewhere else. Ulysses never knew the name for these kinds of negotiations, but it was the biggest launching of lobbying by a special-interest group up to that point in time.

The mentality necessary to run a bank was radically different from the managerial expertise necessary to run a successful brokerage firm. To Ulysses' way of thinking, brokerage firms were supposed to help investors earn dividends by investing in legitimate and solvent companies, while banks were supposed to help individuals and families with day-to-day personal transactions and loans for immediate essentials. Despite this, several decades into the future, financial advisor Sandy Wyle would manage to convince President Bill Clinton to get the Glass-Seagull Act repealed so that he could fulfill his personal vision of running large banks and investment firms at the same time. They did not care that the management teams of both firms had conflicts of interest, as long as the two friends could make lots of money. A huge advantage was gained because they now could hedge their bets in the direction of the known regulatory changes before they happened, making lots of money. Atwood, riding an Amtrak train home from a business trip in Chicago, after meeting with a potential client, met Sandy Wyle. Wyle was on his way to meet with regional Federal Reserve executives in St. Louis. Atwood never met President Clinton, but after spending just twenty minutes talking to Sandy Wyle on the return trip on the train, he had nicknames for both men, "Slick Wyle and Slick Willie."

No wonder the small banks in Rainbow Creek and other small towns could not stay apace of larger banking competitors. No wonder so many investors lost money investing in small bank stocks. No wonder 80 percent of the wealthiest people in America are financial executives of large firms. They could not get there without special relationship deals with the government. Though Atwood did not live long enough to see the latest financial messes, he was not so naïve to think these shifts in wealth could possibly happen so fast without some kind of corrupt involvement. Sandy Wyle did not wait for industries to prosper or new companies to start doing business. He had the rules changed in his favor. Displaying his arrogance, he positioned a plaque in his office with his picture and a statement that read, "I shattered the Glass-Seagull Act." Middle-class investors lost a lot of their hard-earned money because of special arrangements that stacked the deck in favor of large banks, investment firms, and their presidents. It soon became apparent to Atwood that for the last half-century bad behavior hadn't been regulated by the politicians and executives making the rules, and the country was the worse for it.

Three decades before any talks of repealing banking regulations began, Atwood had already begun teaching his middle son about money, politics, and other important life lessons. One afternoon in the summer of 1965, Atwood and Arthur were drinking lemonade while sitting on the wooden picnic bench stretched across the backyard patio at the Hobson House, having just finished cutting the grass and trimming all the hedges on the property. Open to the fresh smells of the manicured yard and partners to degrees of lessening formality of the free undulations of the woods in the background, Atwood and Arthur saw a black waterbug scurrying across the patio and carrying another dead waterbug on its back. Atwood wondered what killed the waterbug. "Was it something that kills other living things?" Arthur asked his father. "Do you think the two water bugs were related to one another? Do you think the one waterbug took advantage of the other waterbug, causing it to die?" Atwood replied, "I don't know, but relative to their tiny size, water bugs are very strong creatures. It is amazing how fast they move carrying double their own body weight, almost as fast as when making a solo getaway." Arthur remembered many things his father told him; Atwood taught his son to pay attention. "An aristocrat might hire someone to take care of his bug problem or any other problem, but a man of the bourgeoisie will watch for a brief time and solve the problem himself, saving himself some money," he told his son.

Most of the men of Atwood Hobson's generation worked in difficult environments but they stayed dedicated to earn a paycheck and feed their families. They did what their bosses told them to do, because bosses did not allow workers a lot of flexibility, and other opportunities did not always present themselves, especially during the war years. Middle-class workers climbed telephone poles for utility companies and worked in dangerous weather conditions. Men worked in hot factories manufacturing products to make life easier for their families at home. They built roads and bridges over difficult terrain. They built high-rise commercial buildings and underground tunnels, which made getting to work easier for others. They worked to achieve the American Dream.

Margaret Hobson loved spending time at Vintage Book Store, tucked away in an unassuming part of town between a secondhand clothing store and a flower shop. Well-dusted shelves in the store ran to the top of lofty ceilings, and she seldom saw anything to clutter the floor except for conveniently placed stepladders to help customers reach the higher books. The owners of Vintage, Shane and Nancy Braswell, discriminating buyers, looked for interesting and unusual books. Any book chosen had spines that were tight and covers intact except in the case of a rare book where a little battering around the edges was acceptable. The booksellers at Vintage filled needs for any reader with general-interest books, self-help guides, obscure works on design, Hemingway novels, reedy volumes of poetry, beat detective thrillers, and volumes of the experiences of individuals during the Civil War and World War II. Margaret knew to ask the owners about rare books, which occasionally arrived at the store and were kept behind the cash register for only the best customers. Margaret thought of Vintage as the type of place where people who cared and paid attention gathered to honor writers and thinkers who had made things better for future generations.

Margaret believed a home that had one or two walls considered book-filled with hardcover books of top quality neatly stacked side-by-side on shelves of mahogany or oak cases distinguishes itself from other residences where family members didn't read. "When people don't read, they usually think with a narrow mind, exposed only to a limited number of viewpoints and often their lives are messy because of it," she often told her three sons. "For a person who reads, it becomes more important to be aware and to always remember. Reading can soften a lot of ills and whip a soul back into shape." For her it was all about capturing her sons' passion and enthusiasm for subjects at an early age. Who did the work up to this point and left it here for you? What happens next? What is at the other end? She wanted her boys to plan their own adventures and offer some value to society. She wanted her sons to plan for what they would see in the future.

"From all life experiences, then reading and studying and researching even more, the freedom of opinion in book or press is the foundation for the sound and natural development of any people. Every time you open a book, you open a world of possibilities. When you cannot comprehend what is inside a book, most of your possibilities will vanish," she adamantly revealed to her sons. "Most professional or skilled jobs parallel with middle-class men and women with good reading skills," she continued. Of all her sons, Arthur was the one who best grasped this concept from her. "Books are not dead," Arthur remembers his mom telling him and his brothers, over and over, when they were young boys. "It is cool to read; to be successful, to be good at something, people need good reading skills. People can't ignore this fact." It was a lesson Arthur would never forget.

Margaret's medical history listed only one condition before her first child was born. She later told her doctor that raising three boys caused all the maladies she suffered in old age. Maybe she was correct in trying to reverse the trend of how young people nowadays seem to blame their parents for all of their problems. Toward the end of Margaret's life, her shoulders began to break down. She had spent so many years gardening, doing laundry, cleaning house, and bent over working, that she finally wore all the cartilage down between her bones. It got to where she could barely raise her right arm to brush her hair. Not much later, her heart began to trouble her. Yet, even when the doctors told her they would have to pry her chest open to reconstruct four bypasses, insert an artificial aortic valve, and implant a pacemaker, Margaret's strengths never wavered from the person she was, a valorous giant.

When Margaret died of complications from the major heart surgery, there was friction in the family amongst the three sons, grown men by now. Kevin and Johnny believed Arthur was their mother's favorite son, and this had always been a sore spot. Johnny particularly did not handle the news well. While Kevin and his new bride, Shirley, flew into Rainbow Creek as soon as they heard the bad news, Johnny never showed up for the funeral services. This wasn't so much of a surprise to Arthur. Whenever Arthur was able to connect on the telephone with his youngest brother, Johnny started the conversation with, "You never …" or "You always …," setting up an instant negative tone in the discussion. Such blanket statements halted comfortable communication and made Arthur feel unfairly attacked, though most of the time he was able to control his emotions. He avoided falling into the trap of firing back with directives such as, "Please act like …" or "Please don't do that …," which would only lead to more unhealthy resentment with no room for any of the brothers to maneuver.

After a long day at work, three months after his mother's death, Arthur retrieved a rambling, nearly incoherent message from Johnny on his answering machine.

"Oh, Arthur, there is something I want to say to you. I have been working jobs here and there, but I do not make as much money as you, so I cannot help you with mom's funeral expenses. There is one other thing I want to say to you too. Maybe now that you are not spending so much time with Mom, almost as if you two were boyfriend and girlfriend—I mean she was your mother, not your girlfriend. She is … I mean you were her son, not her boyfriend. Maybe now you can find a real woman to spend the rest of your life with, and yeah, you can say whatever you want. You think I am crazy, but I am the only one in the family who speaks the truth. I do not hide behind … Uh, uh; I am not a fake person. I am down to earth and I just do not have the money everybody else does. I do not pretend everything in my own little world is perfect. And like I told Mom when she was sick, I don't pretend like everything amongst family members is perfect."

The message clicked off; Johnny had hung up. Arthur sensed a crisis was about to erupt.

Arthur found it difficult to understand the resistance he was feeling from his two brothers and why each of them seemed to push away from any family cohesiveness.

Johnny was acting too secretive and Kevin only worried about himself and his career, showing little concern for family responsibilities. Arthur's marriage to Jane had its share of troubles and he had two daughters to take care of, but certainly, Johnny's forgetfulness did not fog his mind so much that he forgot his brother was still married to Jane, Arthur thought. Because Johnny had not lived in Rainbow Creek for many years and he did not speak to Arthur on a regular basis, he never could have anticipated that Arthur and Jane were having problems in their marriage. Though the comparisons Johnny made of mother and son to boyfriend and girlfriend sickened Arthur, he took the insults as a sign that a fiasco of money and career problems overpowered Johnny, not jealousy or hatred of his brother. Johnny had talent, but his partying blinded him from the notion that he always seemed to take the easy way of doing things, never challenging himself to take his music success to the next level. Then when things did not work out, because he did not make the extra effort, he blamed others for his own mistakes. If he had a comment to make or an issue to address with anyone who called him, he would state his mind and then unfairly hang up the phone. He thought he gained an advantage, but all his roguish behavior did was to make every conflict worse and obligate more time and effort in the future to straighten things out. He allowed himself to forget about all the messages he left offending people and he went about his business, unencumbered by any sense of responsibility to do more than complain, all the while playing the victim of a situation getting worse, one that he perpetuated himself. No matter what others attempted to tell him, he did not try to find ways to set his foolish behaviors aside and boldly do something to make meaningful change in his life. It was time for Johnny to act courageously instead of acting like a moron, but he was not listening.

Johnny was treating others the same way losers treat people and he was learning how to invert reality. He told others he did not like people, but the truth was he did not like himself. If anyone approached him, he blurted out accusations and walked away without giving anyone else a chance to respond. He quit communicating with the outside world, no longer answering his home phone, ignoring e-mails, and turning off his cell phone. He was blind to the problems, sicknesses, surgeries, and eventual death of his mother as well as all the other minor struggles, even though Arthur tried to call Johnny to give updates of his family members and friends. At least his parents were not still alive to experience all the madness. Johnny was fighting in Vietnam when Atwood died, unable to experience closure then either.

The Rainbow Creek community as a whole reached a point of numbering a more diverse cross section of people than the representation of trees and shrubs growing around town.

Brown Bark Hickory, White Pine, Black Walnut, Ivory Silk Lilac, Flowering Dogwood, Japanese Willow, Yellow Crabapple, Bur Oak, Honey Locust, Sugar Maple, Pink Magnolia, Forsythia, Pyracantha, Mock Orange, Viburnum, Wahoo, and Burning Bush flourished in the growing neighborhood. But similar to the way disease was spread by insects, killing off the Red Buckeye and Lacebark Elm trees, many people were hurting from a struggling economy, high unemployment, and damages to their homes from so many storms with high winds, local weather forecasters attributing it to global warming.

With the financial stability of the whole world seeming to plummet and everyone feeling the pinch of tough economic times, Jane and Arthur exhausted all attempts to try and weather the troubles in their marriage, without running to an attorney's office. Neither person wanted to deepen their own financial situation by paying expensive consultant fees or selling houses in a market when home values were at unsurpassed lows and financing questionable.

The news not picked up initially in the neighborhood, Arthur and Jane did separate, and she and their two daughters moved away three years after moving into the subdivision. Arthur worried that since he was a father used to seeing or talking to his two daughters almost every day since the moment they were born, adjusting to seeing his girls only occasionally would be difficult. He thought how such arrangements were difficult even in movies. Not long after his marriage to Jane, Arthur set aside the political dreams he had nurtured since his teen years, out of a sense of obligation to his wife and children, believing he needed to have a more stable job if they were going to live in a good neighborhood. Now that he was about to be single again, he determined to get back into the realm of politics. His job as an inside sales representative had never excited him, so when he was offered a job at the local community center, he accepted. He quit his sales job and accepted a director's position that would afford him an opportunity to build his platform for the possibility of a future career in politics.

His old neighbors had difficulty understanding some of the negative rumors being circulated about the generous, red-faced, tall, balding, former industrial sales represen-tative, the man they remembered riding his bike around the subdivision with his two daughters on Hill View Avenue in the rain. It seemed strange that Arthur, who was one of the nicest people in the neighborhood and whose own roots were in Rainbow Creek, should be in trouble now with his marriage and his position in the community. Yet, it seemed things had not been right in the Hobson family for some time.

Arthur and Jane, young professional pioneers of Rainbow Creek, were the first couple to lay down money on a plot to build a house on Hill View, before any homeowners fell on hard times a decade later. They bought the smallest ranch home offered with a brick front, and then engaged themselves for several years planting greenery, building a deck, and renovating the basement for more living space. Though three generations of his family had grown up at the Hobson House, Arthur was happy to relinquish the property to Jane, because in his mind, this newfound interest in following the Tea Party movement would probably require more traveling. Besides, the house on Hill Avenue was all he needed as his home base.

The house on Hill Avenue was part of a larger estate, a newer development consisting of seventy-five homes in a multi-bathroom style with attached two-car garages. Though the development wasn't known to the wealthy in the rest of the state or anywhere else for that matter, the mortgage industry had lent money to retirees and middle-income families at very low interest rates. The construction of the development and the paving of the extra-wide streets that connected all the houses temporarily enhanced the economy for a couple of years in Rainbow Creek.

One rejuvenation plan that came from the mayor's office that was right for the citizens of Rainbow Creek was the renovation of a structurally sound vacant building used in a creative way commercially. A large vacant commercial building was converted into a community center in a central location of the Rainbow Creek municipality, complete with a gymnasium and large banquet rooms, started hosting events for all ages. The community center created opportunities for citizens to use the fitness rooms, hold dance classes, run basketball camps, play volleyball games, organize business meetings, furnish services to people at a grass-roots level, and even serve luncheons to senior citizens. As the community center started filling daily schedules and adding special events, Kay Applebaum hired Arthur, and he became increasingly involved in his work there as a community organizer.

The affluent, high-society members of Rainbow Creek all seemed to live on large estates just within the boundaries of the far reaches of town. Most people of the Rainbow Creek bourgeoisie, including neighbors who lived in Arthur's newer subdivision development and those who lived in the old downtown section of town, tried to entertain themselves because they did not always have the money to travel, stay in fancy hotels, eat at five-star restaurants, or hobnob with celebrities. They told jokes, wrote songs, read books, participated in games, played cards, and hung out with friends. They watched a lot of cable television, very different from the few choices of black-and-white television of yesteryear. Residents liked sophisticated humor that did not rely on clear innuendo. To them comedy did not require gutter-talk to get a cheap laugh, and thoughtful humor appealed more to Rainbow Creek patrons than raunchy comedy. They believed it was much better than the kind of humor that just needs a couple of four-letter words and a missing punch line to get a belly laugh, which is much of what they were seeing on television today.

The real question for Rainbow Creek residents was who ultimately would get to make decisions about their lives? This is the basic question about politics. Are decisions made by individuals or do they cede the right to make those decisions to some government official who knows so much better about their life than they do? What doctor do they see, where do they live, where do they want their children to go to school, what insurance do they buy, what charities do they support, where do they shop, who do they marry, what hospital do they go to, and how do they save for retirement? Politics is really about who decides the answer to many of the important questions in a person's life, the individual or someone else. Are people educated enough to decide for themselves and smart enough to want to know what's in the fine print, or do they let someone else run their lives?

Jane was quiet and unassuming and did not belong to any groups. She did not go to college and did not particularly like cultural events or professional sports. She knew things like not to plant annuals before May 1 because there is a good chance there will be a freeze before then in Rainbow Creek. Like her husband, she worked a full-time office job and dropped her kids off at daycare every weekday morning. From her first day in the middle-class neighborhood of Rainbow Creek, Jane was unhappy. She did not like having to work so hard to have more. She did not like when teenagers descended in the woods behind their house to party and drink cheap beer in the wee hours of the morning, becoming louder as they became drunker. This kind of nonsense was not what she and Arthur bargained for when signing the contract to purchase a nice home in Rainbow Creek. When she could not take it anymore, she would jump out of bed, open up a window and holler, "Hey, you guys all need to go home. Some people have to work in the morning!" The teenagers certainly were not afraid of Jane, but by this time, nearly partied out, they usually went home. Tall, hair dyed, young, always tired, and driving a red Ford Explorer, she carried all the hours of her week in that vehicle. On Saturday errand runs, the usual stash behind the driver's seat might include a box of diapers, baby wipes, other baby supplies, two car seats, bags of groceries, a gallon of latex paint, 10 pounds of dog food, and a bottle of wine. She was already living the life many of the other mothers would experience after settling in to their new homes in the neighborhood.

It wasn't all bad. She loved her kids. They often provided amusing stories for her to tell at the office. One day when Jane was still new to the neighborhood and running late for work, her daughter Sandra already off to school on the bus, Susie strapped in the backseat, and with Jane maneuvering in the morning rush hour traffic, an amusing conversation took place in the car one morning.

"My skirt looks and feels a bit tight," complained Jane.

"We can go shopping this weekend to buy you some new outfits for work," said five-year-old Susie, consoling her mom from the backseat. "You always buy me clothes that are one size bigger so I have room to grow into them. How old are you mom?" After Jane told her daughter her age, Susie replied, "Wow, Mom, you've celebrated a lot of birthdays and you ate a lot of birthday cake. This is probably why your skirt feels a little tight."

In earlier years, when you could still drive an SUV without guilt and there was little traffic, the collective task in Rainbow Creek was to relearn certain life skills that your own parents had fled to the suburbs to unlearn: How to encourage dogs to poop in somebody else's yard, how to determine which neighbors to befriend, how to determine the needs of the local public school, how to juggle trash pickups and grass mowing days to lessen the noise all seemed important issues. How to determine what items are worth saving for the recycle bins, and how to decide on what kind of locks and alarms to protect your home, all seemed less important.

The neighborhood buzzed with concerns. Was it true you could still get full service at certain gas stations? Was it possible to find an auto repair shop or dealer who sold great tires and great prices? Was it possible to find a place to recycle old paint and pesticides? What bells and whistles were worth the added expense on your next appliance purchase? Was it true that most TV dinners contained dangerous amounts of salt? Was it safe to use coffee filters twice, or could a pot of coffee be reheated the next day? Why was the red Ford Explorer making those weird noises? What charities should a person donate to and how much? Where should a person bank or shop for groceries? Citizens made most of the decisions in their own neighborhoods, with government playing a lesser role, because at that time the local newspaper and radio were the only connections to the rest of the world. Television was still in its infancy, and personal computers were unheard of.

For Arthur, it all boiled down to deciding when an issue was important enough to pick a battle. There were more relevant issues of the day, like was it possible to raise happy and healthy kids by sending them to daycare while parents worked full-time, who to vote for in local, state, and national elections, and how to respond when a neighbor calls a person from another race *nigger, chink, kraut, mick, kyke, wop, dago, camel jockey* or *sand nigger*. Every individual has to decide which issues need more attention and which matters are worth fighting for in life.

At the Hobson House during the mid-1950s, in the hours Atwood and Margaret viewed television, network executives and the government tightly controlled programming. Around-the-clock broadcasting was unheard of back then. In 1956, for example, television broadcast on weekdays between 9 a.m. and 11 p.m. There was also a period between 6 p.m. and 7 p.m. when there was no programming broadcast. During this time, parents tricked their children into doing homework and thinking that the evening's television had finished so they would go to bed without complaint. Lawrence Welk, Jackie Gleason, and Jack Benny entertained adults at night. *You Bet Your Life* and *I've Got a Secret* were hit shows of the times.

In the early years of rural television, there was only one channel, the BBC, broadcast in Rainbow Creek. One of the most popular of the early programs was a game show called *What's My Line*. A panel of four would ask questions of a member of the public to determine what his or her occupation was. Families gathered around the set to watch the show. Soon more channels followed and in most of the programming during the early years, the emphasis was on history and Westerns, not so much about current affairs. Black-and-white televisions were the norm at first. Among the first television shows, about 100 sagas were Westerns. In these shows, cowboys told stories of survival and heartache, setting the standards of right and wrong, teaching kids like the Hobson boys about heroes overcoming the villains. *Bonanza* and *Wagon Train* were two of the most popular Westerns for many boys. Soon after the Westerns were the arrival of the serious dramas and the two doctor shows, *Ben Casey* and *Dr. Kildaire*, very popular with young girls like Jane. *Ed Sullivan* was the mainstream variety show that brought the Beatles, the Monkees, and the Rolling Stones to teenaged Johnny. A myriad of secret agent shows, such as *The Man from U.N.C.L.E.*, *The Avengers, Mission Impossible, I Spy*, and *The Mod Squad*, and a trio of popular family shows, *Ozzie and Harriet, Lucy and Ricky*, and *Leave It to Beaver* kept middle-class Americans entertained.

All across the country young men like Arthur had a crush on Elizabeth Montgomery, the actress who played Samantha in *Bewitched*, a sitcom about a beautiful witch that aired in the late sixties. With an affection that stayed with him as a grown man, Arthur was sad when he learned she died of cancer in 1995. The beautiful actress was appealing to males, not just because she was pretty, but because she was a tomboy who did not like to shop. Montgomery had strong political views at a time when it was not so easy to go against the grain, and Arthur respected that. She was an outspoken champion of women's rights and gay rights throughout her life, sharply contrasting with her conservative father, who was once a media advisor to President Dwight Eisenhower. As a favor to her former *Bewitched* co-star, Dick Sargent, she helped grand marshal the Los Angeles Gay Pride Parade. Several years later, she opened the public's eyes with a documentary she helped make about the Iran-Contra Affair, the shadow government of assassins, arms dealers, drug smugglers, former CIA operatives, and top US military personnel running foreign policy unaccountable to the public, following their own rules and ultimately suspending the Constitution. The documentary film, *Cover-Up*, revealed the hostage deal with Iran that included a delay to release American hostages until after the 1980 presidential election.

The Iran hostage crisis was a diplomatic turning point between Iran and the United States where 66 Americans were held hostage for 444 days, after a group of Islamist students and militants took over the American Embassy in Tehran in support of the Iranian Revolution. President Carter called the hostages "victims of terrorism and anarchy," adding that the "United States will not yield to blackmail."

The Shah of Iran railed against the American government, denouncing it as the "Great Satan" and "Enemy of Islam." But when the Shah was diagnosed with lymphoma, he requested to be treated by US doctors. His request was granted, but that was the straw that enraged a mob of Iranians to storm the American Embassy and take hostages. Though eight American servicemen died in a failed attempt to rescue the hostages, they were later released into custody, just minutes after President Reagan was sworn into office. Iran wanted to wait to see if Republicans gained power with a transfer from Carter to Reagan before completing any deals. Some political analysts believe the crisis was a major reason for President Jimmy Carter's defeat in his run for a second term. In Iran, the crisis strengthened the political power of those who opposed any normalization of relations with the West. It marked the beginning of sanctions and weakened economic ties between Iran and the United States.

Five years later, Reagan administration officials secretly facilitated an illegal sale of arms to Iran in hopes of securing the release of another group of seven American hostages, further funding the Hezbollah Contras through un-appropriated strategies of Congress. Several investigations ensued over the next few years, and in the end, fourteen administration officials were indicted, including then Secretary of Defense Caspar Weinberger, John Poindexter, and Lieutenant Colonel Oliver North of the National Security Council.

On December 24, 1992, nearing the end of his term in office after being defeated by Bill Clinton the previous month, President Bush pardoned six administration officials, namely Elliot Abrams, Duane Clarridge, Alan Fiers, Clair George, Robert McFarlane, and Caspar Weinberger. In Poindexter's hometown of Odon, Indiana, a street was renamed John Poindexter Street. Bill Breeden, a former minister, stole the street's sign in protest of the Iran-Contra Affair. He claimed that he was holding it for a ransom of $30 million, in reference to the amount of money given to Iran to transfer to the Contras. He was later arrested and confined to prison, making him, as satirically noted by Howard Zinn, "the only person to be imprisoned as a result of the Iran-Contra Scandal."

On a more pleasant fall evening in 1995, with their daughters Sandra and Susie spending the night at a friend's house, Jane and Arthur invited Victor and Karen Anderson, their neighbors from across the street, for dinner. Jane served baked chicken, mashed potatoes, dressing, candied yams, string beans, and cranberry sauce. Although he thought it wasn't really necessary to put on airs, Arthur ran to the grocery store to buy a gallon of premade iced tea, a bottle of wine, and a loaf of freshly baked French bread just minutes before the guests arrived, to appease Jane. At the dinner table, the conversation flowed freely.

Victor: "So, what has everyone been watching on television lately?"

Karen: "I like these old reruns of the *Gong Show*. However, I think the show's producers tested the limits of television broadcasting when they decided to show two young women licking popsicles in a provocatively seductive manner. Network executives fell asleep and failed to notice the skit until the program aired."

Jane: "Do you guys remember the popular rerun of the night a sketch received really long laughs involving Johnny Carson and Ed Ames on the *Tonight Show*? Ed Ames was showing Johnny Carson how to throw a tomahawk. Someone drew the outline of a human figure on a large plywood cutout. Ames threw the tomahawk. It landed right below the cutout figure's crotch. The look on Johnny's face was priceless. The way he waited to speak and his reserved timing of waiting to laugh was hilarious to anyone watching the show."

Arthur: "As a young boy, I loved watching the Bob Hope Specials. I will remember him for his clean humor; no one did it better. Grateful veterans will always remember his trips to war zones putting himself and his traveling staff in harm's way. I even enjoyed watching the golf tournament he put together for the foundation he started, The Desert Classic Charities, but I heard rumblings that more money was dished out, 500 percent more money, to the purse for professional golfers than to charitable causes."

For all inquiries, the Hobsons of Rainbow Creek were good resources because Arthur was a businessman who stayed abreast of the political scene and Jane tried her best to be a working mom and a mother to her two girls, though she wished she could stay home all of the time to raise her daughters. Though Arthur had thinning hair, he did not worry about erectile dysfunction, getting older, or having one foot in the grave yet. He sometimes bragged but Jane was famously averse to speaking well of herself or ill of anybody else. Her two daughters, on the other hand, were a favorite topic for bragging. This character trait appeared a little odd because she looked at her daughters and saw her own reflection, a reflection of years of experience, laughter, well-earned lines of worry, and a hope of a lifelong friendship. In the reflection were memories of trips to the emergency room in the middle of the night, secrets told in strict confidence, and questions asked when only an honest answer would do, all remembered like photos in a yearbook album.

Jane worried a lot and always had a to-do list for her husband. She always wanted help with the children, partly because of her lack of confidence and partly because she worried whether she was raising her children properly. Watching her retrace her steps so many times made any onlookers feel like they were watching a movie, and when she rewound the scenes to take another look trying to catch more of the small details, they felt trapped in a maze with nothing to drink or eat. The continual series of worrying missteps are not particularly lethal each on their own, but taken all together serve to bring down a movie with great potential. She thought her children were extremely ill and needed to see a doctor every time they came home from daycare with a cough, headache, or runny nose. Her addiction to the girly sitcoms and reality shows on television seemed related to her never having the desire or the time to read books anymore. There were people with whom her lack of confidence didn't sit well—who detected she enjoyed surrounding herself with some level of misery in an attempt to keep others away from her space and with fewer demands of her. Nevertheless, most people found her genuine and it was hard to resist a woman whom your own children loved so much and remembered all the holidays and always brought a dish when visiting family or friends.

Jane had grown up on the other side of the railroad tracks, just a mile away from the northeastern suburbs of Rainbow Creek, and earned average grades in school. After completing her sophomore year in high school, she transferred from the only private Catholic high school in town to the only public high school. One strange thing about Jane, given her strong ties to her parents and siblings while growing up, was that she knew very little about her family roots. Years passed without anyone from her side of the family, not even her parents, coming to visit Arthur and Jane at their home in Rainbow Creek. If you asked anything directly about her parents, she became defensive, saying, "My parents are old and retired; they just want to be left alone," and the conversation would end.

Arthur often struggled to understand his wife, the woman he thought he was supposed to understand more than any other person on earth. Sometimes Jane was overly negative with him and overly protective of her personal space, possibly behaviors she learned from her parents. At other times, though, she was a worrier, she seemed genuinely interested in conversations with other people, and she rarely thought ill of what others did. Jane basically saw the world as a good place and if someone made a mistake, she thought there had to be a reason for it.

Karen Anderson was the only other mother on Hill View Avenue who had been living in the new neighborhood as long as Jane had. She'd come to Rainbow Creek having been a physical education teacher and volleyball coach to wealthy kids at a rural private school. After several years of working there, she was fired from a district in the western part of the state because she cursed at a girl for bad behavior. No longer considered consonant with good judgment in any school setting, private or public, even a seldom-cursing teacher could not stay on the district payroll by the early 1990s. Karen became one of those distracted, break-taking part-time recreational supervisors at the county-run YMCA. Karen's husband, Victor, was already retired and drew a monthly pension and a Social Security check; without that income, it was hard to see how the Andersons could afford a house in Rainbow Creek. Victor played a round of golf twice a week and watched lots of baseball and football games on TV. Arthur had known Victor all his life; Victor's childhood house was only a half-mile from the Hobson House property. When the Andersons bought the house on Hill View, across the street from the Hobsons, they were neighbors again.

Growing up, Arthur told the story many times about how his good-spirited friends, Gary and Larry Bordeaux, built a turtle pit in the their backyard during their early childhood days. Gary painted a "G" on the shell of his box turtle and Larry painted an "L" on the shell of his turtle. When the two boys became teenagers, after years of caring for and playing with their turtles, both decided to release their box turtles into the wild at a state park several miles away from their home outside Rainbow Creek. The next summer, Larry's turtle, with the "L" painted on its shell, managed to find its way to the Andersons' backyard. The boys knew dogs could find their way home after getting lost miles away, but for a turtle to do this was very unusual. "Gary and Larry are mere mortals, but this curious story about turtles may well live forever," Arthur told his high school friends. For many years, it wasn't unusual to see a box turtle crossing a street or coming out of a wooded area in Rainbow Creek, until the massive flood waters hit the area creeks, streams, waterways, and rivers of the Midwest in 1982. Now it seems as if box turtles have becomes an endangered species in the area.

Some jobs were lost forever in Rainbow Creek as well. Milkmen no longer brought dairy products to the front porches of houses. Appliance repair technicians no longer made service calls to chip away ice buildup from the freezer or fix an element on a stove. No longer did diaper trucks deliver cloth diapers to mothers with small children, due to the shift in more convenient throwaway brands. Telephone service technicians no longer made house calls to repair rotary phones and they seldom wired old-fashioned landlines. The hardware store no longer hired the one man responsible for sharpening scissors, hand clippers, and handsaws. Scissors are now mostly cheap enough to throw away and replace when they wear out. Gas-powered chainsaws and weed whackers replaced handsaws and clippers.

By the late nineties, Karen was the only woman in the neighborhood who refused to convert to all the modern ways of the technological world. She still cursed a lot, refused to buy a cell phone, hated computers, bleached her hair, wore tie-dyed shirts, and came home late on Tuesday nights. "That's my volleyball tournament night," she explained whenever anyone tried to make plans with Karen on Tuesday evening, as if everybody should aspire to play pro-style volleyball. One night she quietly let herself into the Hobsons' house with the key they had given her and lifted her sleeping daughter, Samantha, from the sofa where Jane had tucked her under a comforter. Jane had volunteered to look after Samantha on the evenings Karen was out, and Karen had taken advantage of her for a ton of free babysitting. It could not have escaped Jane's attention that Karen never repaid this hospitality and ignored Jane's daughters. Karen always talked to Arthur out at the mailbox or at neighborhood functions while dressed in her flimsy outfits and tight pants, praising Arthur's knowledge about politics and sports and always laughing at his stupid jokes; but for many years the worst that Jane would say of Karen was that some women have a tough life and if Karen was sometimes mean to her it was probably because she was tired. Jane didn't see Karen as the control freak she was, always pretending to live someone else's dream without wanting to take the initiative to pursue living her own dreams, giving advice to other mothers when she never really earned the right or raised the correct issues.

Karen and some others around the neighborhood thought Jane and Arthur were an odd match. Arthur was an independent thinker, who leaned toward the policies of the Republicans and thought everybody else should have to work for their good fortunes and learn to muster the courage to take some risks. He tired of liberals always telling citizens the only way for positive change to work is for more government to oversee more programs from the top down. His view was that the country as a whole had drifted away from the pleas of most of our former presidents. "Government socialism is becoming revered and capitalism reviled by too many Americans due to the pervasiveness of liberal propaganda and the lack of a historical viewpoint," he bemoaned.

Jane, on the other hand, was no great risk taker and certainly not a feminist. She liked relaxing on the couch watching her television programs with the aroma of something baking or cooking in the kitchen. She seemed disinterested in politics or sports. If you mentioned ideas from a political candidate's speech or statistics from a box score, you could see by her face she was not interested. Instead, she became aggravated and would yeah-yeah any further comments about the two subjects. It was obvious that the only thing that mattered to her were her two daughters--not her friends, not her fellow employees, not politics, not sports, not even her husband. The biggest dreams Jane ever voiced to Arthur were what to eat for dinner and what to plant in the garden. Because Jane did not talk much and did not express her feelings to Arthur, he felt like the invisible man at home much of the time.

There was one thing they agreed on: Jane and Arthur were both engrossed in the lives of their two daughters. Sandra was a blessing to her parents—an avid reader, star pitcher on the softball field, loyal daughter capable with all the latest technology, and protector of her little sister. Beautiful, opinionated, a leader in her circle of friends, Susie was also sanctification to her parents—a great student, a good basketball player, honest, soft-spoken, pretty, well liked by her friends. Jane loved bragging about her daughters. Unfortunately it seemed she liked even better to spout off about her and Arthur's marriage difficulties with relatives, coworkers, neighbors, or anyone else who would listen. Most of her stories took the form of complaints, as if she enjoyed living in an environment full of drama and heartache with little connection to the big picture of the world.

"He is a narcissist," she told other wives in the neighborhood during one long winter filled with an unusually large number of arguments. Both Jane and Arthur were asserting stands to get their way, and the closest neighbors overheard them.

Arthur was aware of the long-term toxicity he and his wife were creating with their arguments. He could feel it pouring into their marriage like chemical waste dispersed over a period of many years that cause a stench. When he thought of it he was reminded of the millions of tons of waste by-products that clutter our nation, electric companies dumping tons of coal ash into wet ponds across the country, as half of our country's electricity is powered by coal. In Kingston, Tennessee, a major ash spill was one of the worst toxic waste accidents ever in America and it happened the same year Arthur and Jane started contemplating a separation. The spill rumbled over hundreds of homes and killed several people, polluted the water supply, and left the town deserted. The electric companies preached that the coal ash was safe as dirt, but in reality, it was full of arsenic and cadmium. The Environmental Protection Agency, an entity that spends billions of dollars for much lesser causes, did little to check what this county's electric company did with its hazardous waste. In the past, electric companies sold coal ash to golf courses to use for building mounds, filling holes, and covering rocky earth. The Heartland Electric Company sold millions of tons of it for use on one golf course, in which large amounts of toxic metals were absorbed into the water supply in one section of town. Many other electric companies around the country relied on this form of recycling and called it beneficial use. The coal ash was also used as an additive in cement mix, in the manufacture of bowling balls, in carpeting, and in kitchen counters. It was getting to the point where you just couldn't trust any of the utility or energy companies, because they all seemed to lie and take shortcuts to chase a fast dollar, no matter who they might hurt. Feeding the coal-fired generators at electric plants by strip-mining the ancestral hills across America denudes every last frontier of native habitat and is one of the biggest concerns of global warming. Even if electric companies improved their environmental practices by one-hundred-fold, some concerned environmentalists say more work would be needed. Drive within a mile of any of our major rivers and you will discover another problem: the smell. This was disheartening to Arthur. The Hudson, Ohio, Missouri, and Mississippi Rivers aren't just muddy; they are full of chemical waste products. The water was not clean because the rivers pick up all kinds of debris and chemicals dumped along their banks and it had a way of seeping into the supply tables. For Arthur, the whole process was eerily similar to all the detritus that got stirred up when he and Jane argued, and once things had been said and done, they could never be erased from the memory banks.

"Is he having an affair? Is he abusing you?" Karen asked Jane one early Saturday afternoon, when both ladies went out to their crosswise mailboxes at the same time.

"No," Jane said. "I just wish it would all stop."

"What's the problem, then? The whole country was brought to a standstill over a cigar, a stained dress, the definition of the word *is*, and a lying president," Karen stated condescendingly.

"He's questioning everything I do. We argue about the difference between adults and children, about what to eat for dinner, about how to vote in the next election, about how to discipline the children, about how to spend our money, until finally it's me lying in bed just wishing it all would stop."

"He is a complicated man who isn't happy focusing on one thing," said Karen, hoping Jane wouldn't internalize this comment as a criticism toward her.

"He thinks he can fix the world," said Jane, rolling her eyes toward the sky. "Family life can get complicated, that's for sure," said Karen. "I think most mothers struggle with raising their children. If you shelter children too much when they are young, they rebel when they're older. If you give children too much leeway when they are young, they think they know everything when they are older. It is a fine line raising kids."

"I really do not need to be preached to about how to raise my children," said Jane. She was beginning to feel like she was being talked down to.

"Just like the government shouldn't keep raising spending by trillions of dollars, putting pressure on everybody, parents put too much pressure on their children, expecting them to succeed in areas where they themselves failed," said Karen, still forcing her opinions on Jane.

"Well, I just figure that most of the time the truth has a certain ring to it and people find their own ways to work things out," said Jane.

"It is a mistake to look at just one thing when addressing any complex problem, like the economy, for instance. To fix the economy, politicians must find solutions for housing, jobs, education, and health care. They must address all of these issues in an integrated way or they are kidding themselves and the public. It's the same thing here: you can have the nicest home in the neighborhood, but if all the family members living inside the house aren't happy, then the adults have to look beyond the material things and do a better job understanding and communicating what is important to each individual. Am I starting to sound like Arthur?" confessed Karen.

"Maybe you have talked to him more times than I realize," replied Jane, as both ladies turned and started walking back inside.

The more Jane complained about her home life, the more involved Arthur became in his life outside of the home. He spent more and more time playing golf on Friday afternoons, working as a time clock official and scorekeeper at pickup basketball games on early Saturday mornings, and working long hours running public services at the community center on Saturday nights. He met local campaign organizers at the community center during the week and met with local councilmen and women on weekends. He became involved in all of the affairs of the neighborhood watch association, put signs in his yard for his favorite Republican candidates at all levels of politics, went to school board meetings, and read any books about politics he could get his hands on.

The older generation of Rainbow Creek believed the education of children steadily climbed downward for the last three decades because of the irresistible forces of video games over the print culture. The grand dames talked freely about a clear distinction often made between pre-video game kids and post-video game kids and their grasp of basic geography, science, and history. To them it was still a story of bad news for the community to see a decline in book, newspaper, and magazine reading by young people. The good news was that reading novels in Rainbow Creek was continuing to increase and it affected citizens at all other ages and education levels. Nearly 85 percent of adults in town read novels for pleasure on a regular basis because they knew reading created citizens that are more informed. In their community, it was almost impossible for politicians to blame public ignorance as the main reason for local problems, and if they did, they then became labeled as a "know-it-all aristocrat" and were run out of town. Arthur did not think any politician who used patronizing rhetoric would have a chance to stay in office if he did not understand the problems of the middle class. The middle class was just as likely to live in urban centers as in the suburbs. In fact, *Time* magazine once described the middle class as people who "sing the national anthem at sporting events and mean it." Arthur did not like it when senators or mayors assured voters that they were just plain folks. He thought it came across as phony. He did not like it when billionaire senators and millionaire mayors without military experience professed that they would make sure dead soldiers had not died in vain, because they will see to it that the government of the folks, by the folks, for the folks will continue its extraordinary work. Then Americans watch these same politicians force underhanded deals and listen to more slick rhetoric that follows. Locally, Arthur was tired of people paying for things they did not need, did not want, and did not vote for. He wanted jobs for unemployed people, affordable health care, and improved schools because it was long overdue. Life with Jane was coming to an end, but his life in politics was just getting started.

★ 3 ★

Paying Attention to Politics

People of modern society living in all areas of the United States have, for the most part, become more aware of their surroundings in recent years, largely due to the ramifications of the two planes that flew into the Twin Towers on September 11, 2001, the one plane that flew into the Pentagon, and a fourth plane that was stopped from completing its mission. Because brave passengers on the fourth plane sacrificed their lives by causing it to crash into a field in Pennsylvania, Arthur was inspired to do more with his life and help shape the direction of his country in a small way. These terrible events brought citizens together in a way not seen since World War II, and the Hobson family was part of the national following that professed, "We Americans shall never forget those who died at Shankesville, Pennsylvania, the Pentagon, the World Trade Center, or other places where heroes were just trying to help."

By January 2009, Arthur was heavily involved in the Tea Party, attending events as far away as New York and Pennsylvania. Protestors in New York were angry about an 18 percent tax on non-diet soft drinks imposed by former governor David Paterson. Arthur stood on the riverbank and watched participants dressed in Native American costumes dump soft drinks into the Susquehanna River with an endorsement from Texas Congressman Ron Paul. As soon as the Tea Party started winding down in New York, Arthur joined patriotic citizens loading onto a chartered Greyhound bus and heading for an event scheduled the next afternoon in Philadelphia.

Speakers in Pennsylvania were warned about using foul language because, as Arthur was told, nearly eight hundred people at other settings in the state were arrested or summoned to court that year for cursing, many times threatening violence. Some of the violators were ex-military. Police arrested one woman for disorderly conduct stemming from swearing at a principal from her daughter's school after the principal asked the protest group to move farther away from the school. Arthur figured the school principal must have been a Democrat, because from what he heard, the school was barely visible from the corner where the group gathered nearly a quarter mile away. In another case, a federal appeals court overturned the convictions of two men who used profanity in addressing a Park Ranger. The court ruled that though their behavior was very disrespectful, it was not criminal.

After spending the night in a Philadelphia Holiday Inn and getting some much-needed rest, Arthur awoke at 7:15 a.m. to shave, shower, eat breakfast, and prepare for the day's events. He was excited about giving his first speech at a Saturday afternoon Tea Party gathering in a big city away from home.

"The free exchange of ideas, even when voiced crudely, is central to American democracy. However, expressing yourself without using curse words will validate that you are making a more thoughtful argument for sure," Arthur told a fast-gathering crowd of three to four hundred people in Philadelphia. "For now, protesting nonviolently at rallies and criticizing government officials are still some of the most important freedoms we have in the United States."

An angry heckler stood in front of the makeshift stage near the podium where Arthur was talking into the microphone. After he had said just two sentences, the man taunted Arthur by shouting, "Hey, buddy, I can tell from your accent that you aren't from around here. What do you know about what the people of Philadelphia want these days?" Right then the guy affirmed what Arthur's friends had told him about Philly fans. They love when hometown boys are doing well; otherwise, they hate you no matter where you are from.

Arthur: "I live in the Midwest, in a small town called Rainbow Creek, about an hour south of St. Louis by car, and about an hour south of Chicago by jet. Believe it or not, people in the Midwest do more than ring cowbells all day long. Midwesterners are real people and sometimes when we open a barn door, we find some inspiration and come up with new ideas that will help others living on both coasts."

Heckler: "Well, there aren't any barn doors in downtown Philadelphia."

Arthur: "Would it have made more sense if I had said a bedroom door, the door of a sports car, or a refrigerator door to explain myself? You must care about the direction in which our country is headed or you wouldn't have taken the time to attend this rally. If you let me speak now, maybe you and I can talk later about issues important to you."

Heckler: "Whatever, man."

Arthur had learned a long time ago that it is more important to be yourself than to adjust to everyone else. Other people tell you to stay positive, he thought, because they have a selfish desire of demanding that others keep their life easy. He tired of people who were only interested in immediate entitlements that were free and easy. Not surprisingly, the heckler never showed to speak with Arthur after he finished his speech.

Arthur was determined more than ever to speak or write about the truth, to talk to the people, to research the topics and travel to the destinations of interest, where events take place. He joined Tea Party leaders and organizers who were willing to do this in unusually short amounts of time because information was flowing fast and freely through computers and mobile phones. He was beginning to reshape his personal timeline, and it struck him how exciting it was to have this new experience, this new journey of opportunities. He wasn't collecting buttons, mugs, hats, and T-shirts; he was collecting ideas. Everything he was learning, he wanted to bring back to Rainbow Creek.

Arthur liked reminding people that the computer age is only about as old as a college student, and even though middle-class Americans make the world's best computers now, government and private industry must continue to invest in the best tech security in the world. "The world that seems so familiar today, a world with mass transit, interstates, cookie-cutter subdivisions, state-of-the-art sports stadiums, skyscrapers, laptops, mobile phones, grocery superstores, malls, fast-food chains, synthetic oils, synthetic fabrics, and many other modern conveniences, is just a wink of time when compared to the entire history of human evolution. Progress has been moving fast," he announced at the Philadelphia Tea Party rally.

Smart politicians, numbering very few in the beginning, started courting the grassroots conservative coalition's eager-to-work followers and they tried to tap into their influential social and fund-raising networks.

"The rise of the Tea Party Express is a classic example of the self-correcting forces initiated by courageous Americans when absolutely necessary. We must honor our Civil War soldiers, the colonists of the Boston Tea Party, the American soldiers and citizens of the two world wars, our Korean War and Vietnam veterans. We must also remember those people who fought for what they believed in, the striking female garment workers of 1911, the civil rights marchers, the seventy thousand responders and the guardian angels at ground zero in New York. Our modern-day Tea Party is fighting to keep America intact too," Arthur told small audiences of listeners in Philadelphia. Some in the crowd were barely old enough to vote, but they were aware enough to think it important to attend the rally. They often wore T-shirts silk-screened with the letters T-E-A and the message "Taxed Enough Already."

Out West, conservative author Michelle Malkin encouraged bloggers to stage a rally in Denver on February 17, 2009, the same day President Obama planned to sign the stimulus bill into law. In Denver, walking around and talking to people, Arthur noticed a large number of straw hats with the words "Don't Tread on Me" embroidered on the bill and small American flags wrapped around the top. Three weeks later, he joined other representatives and Tea Party Patriot cofounder Jenny Beth Martin as they went to Upper Senate Park on Capitol Hill in the pouring rain to protest the impending health insurance vote. They went again to Washington in early November to stage one of the largest rallies in Tea Party history during the final congressional debates about the Patient Protection and Affordable Care Act. Tea Party Patriots carried multitudes of signs. One sign read, "Do you want a politician and a lawyer when you get sick, or do you want a doctor?" Another sign read, "Free stuff is never free."

Members of the Hobson family and so many people across America were waking up for the first time in decades, tweeting one another about politics, healthcare, and their personal beliefs on their mobile phones and on the Internet. In truth, America was founded as a constitutional republic, not as a democracy where majority rules. The majority is sometimes wrong. By this time, rejection didn't scare Arthur. He was fighting the good fight and he was all in.

"Our founding fathers took great pains in avoiding the words *rule by majority* or the word *democracy* when scripting the official work we call the US Constitution," Arthur told citizens in Philadelphia, Washington, DC, and St. Louis, spreading the Tea Party message. "Let's hope more of our future members of Congress are statesmen and patriots, rather than politicians. The fall of any empire is always caused by greed accompanied by power, destroying the greatness of a country," he concluded. Arthur was sure most politicians were about shifting policies in their favor to make their own lives and the lives of their friends better. All this rhetoric about creating jobs was really just about rearranging the marketplace, by taxing or subsidizing operations of a politician's choice. Their policies should not be all about beating the other party; they should be about fixing the problems of the country. He wanted citizens to demand fairness and to understand the specific truths about the Constitution.

Arthur and a growing number of Tea Party organizers, including former Democratic President Jimmy Carter, suggested that the people of the United States seemed more divided with their politics than at any time since the Civil War. Complaints about political issues spread like wildfire over talk radio airwaves, twenty-four-hour cable television channels, town hall meetings, and blogs. Arthur professed that many of our problems have become so large and so complex that our inexperienced leaders rarely agree on how to fix them because they do not understand all of the ramifications. The administration and Congress did not seem to be listening. All these politicians were telling citizens how to live and how to think without giving them a chance to speak their opinions. A whole country of citizens was becoming better at listening while the politicians were talking too much and not listening enough.

While on the Tea Party trail, Arthur uncovered a recurring conundrum in inner cities. Poor families living in older two-story homes set up their basements with an apartment address. When sons or daughters turned eighteen, they moved into the basement, applied for a welfare check and food stamps, and smoked all the pot they wanted in the privacy of their newly arranged digs. Tea Party members began citing this type of welfare abuse as to why the government should allow the middle class more influence.

Neighbors in Rainbow Creek worked hard at their jobs. When they came home from their jobs, they worked some more. They trimmed their hedges and planted flowers in the spring, painted their houses and washed their cars in the summer, raked leaves in the fall and shoveled snow in the winter, and mowed their yards for three seasons of the year. They cut firewood and threw a few logs in the fireplace when the weather turned cold. When they finished all their work, if they were lucky, there might be some time left to play a round of golf, take in a baseball game, or play with the kids. Through the journey in time, the Hobson family and their friends who speculated about their personal beliefs and their place in the universe, often examined concepts of class and social status, good and evil, and the existence of God. They learned from the Greatest Generation and they shared some of their memories in common and some evocative of Generation X and Generation Y, and some resonate on their own. They thought about challenging issues, relating their findings to others, and at decisive moments they even tried to inspire other people in some facet or another.

Arthur perceived the brief history of the early years of the United States as evolving from a wide-open landscape into a modern middle-class society where the Hobson family and many other middle-class Americans are now, at the start of the second decade in the twenty-first century. He was concerned about authorities deciding when to take over parts of people's journeys, because he was sure the Constitution sought to prevent much of the interference. Too often, the middle class felt forced to deal with more of the big mistakes and corruption evolving in the government and in people's daily lives. Whenever given a chance, Arthur offered his unique perspective on politics and governing practices affecting the middle class. He went to great lengths to support the absolute necessity to protect the middle-class structure of society, making it a big part of his life's work. He led a charge for a more far-reaching assessment devoted to stopping illegal drugs and showing how this culture is destroying families. He wanted his in-depth study of drugs and alcohol presented to the people who need help the most, those with a family member addicted to drugs. His thoughts about professional sports and entertainment surrounded the question, why do Americans watch certain television programs and support outrageous salaries to so many professional athletes?

Many people consider themselves highly intelligent individuals, but Arthur found it odd that so many of them fail to make good decisions about the most important issue, their own health. They spend too much time stressing about making fast money, smoking, drinking, and chasing their romantic dreams and an out-of-control social life. He was sure rackets devised by our government and dishonest businesspersons took much of people's money. His daughter Susie helped convince him that more citizens needed to demand more from the government about the importance of keeping our air and water safe. Arthur Hobson was becoming obsessed with challenging people to think about what concerns they support and to refine their political beliefs and make changes in their own lives to make the world a better place. Americans were celebrating the one-hundredth anniversary of the birth of Mark Twain and the two-hundredth anniversary of the birth of Charles Dickens, two great inspirations to do better. It seemed to Arthur that every hundred years, in England before and now in America, one great thinker is produced who writes about the important social issues of the times. Though only faintly resembling the stature of Twain or Dickens, Arthur enjoyed a passion for writing and giving speeches, and he wanted others paying attention to social reform even more now, because change was happening faster than people were taking time to notice.

Arthur loved to uncover earthy stories recounting important issues concerning middle-class life in America today, especially when they expedited change that affected others for decades. Arthur took close, hard looks at government policies and programs, some that did not seem to work and some tolerated for way too long. Though he placed a few humorous stories meticulously within the pages of his speeches, what was not so funny was that millions of Americans refused to recognize the hypocrisy of and the brutal-izing results of bad practices by government on businesses and individuals in middle-class society. Fixing widespread off-course American culture would be difficult, but he was sure a challenge from the people was long overdue. Through the eyes of Arthur, his family, friends, and neighbors were starting to understand his powerful attempt to address serious issues embedded deep within the culture of the community. Some were following Arthur's lead and taking more control of their own lives, trying to put a stop to all forms of assault and corruption by dishonest adults who were supposed to care about the next generation and making the world a better place.

Arthur watched as Barack Obama, on occasion, used tactics from the lecture style of Dr. Martin Luther King Jr. When the audience was responding positively to points of his agenda, Obama ramped up his voice, drawing out diction and slowing dialect and brogue the way King had done. King was a minister from the South where he refined his speaking skills at uplifting revival worship services. King came by the speaking pattern naturally, but Obama arrived at this pretentious imitation after regular mentoring lessons from Jesse Jackson on Saturday afternoons, preparing for the campaign trail. He was doing everything he could to avoid losing another election, like the one lost for the seat from Chicago's black South Side for House of Representative against Bobby Rush, a former Black Panther.

According to Arthur, the basic needs of all human beings are to eat, pray, learn, protect, get medical care, and make arrangements for anyone who dies. For these reasons, he believed there would always be a need for farmers, religious leaders, teachers, consultants, research scientists, law enforcement officers, corrections officers, soldiers, doctors, nurses, construction workers, and morticians. Ways to do things will change, but these jobs will never disappear. Technology and science will keep giving us methods for doing these jobs differently, more efficiently, and better, helping people earn free time to enjoy backyard barbecues, listen to rock music, smell great aromas rising up from the oven, eat homemade pies, watch movies, enjoy recreational sports, and sit around talking about nothing.

If President Obama wants to appear genuine, good counsel would tell him to just be himself and stick to the facts. Our society has enough lack of humility and if the president quits speaking about discourse and starts solving the real problems of our country, he will earn more respect. He makes an impression, but it will be up to Father Time to judge his legacy. If senators start speaking to each other instead of past each other, some goodwill might improve his legacy.

Very few young voters are aware of a speech Obama gave in Egypt more than a decade ago, in which he said, "As a student of history, I also know civilization's debt to Islam. It was Islam that carried the light of learning through so many centuries, paving the way for Europe's Renaissance."

Arthur was a serious history buff and he hated when others put their own spin on retelling the past. He hated it even more when a storyteller became upset when someone with more experience or knowledge about a topic challenged their faulty retelling of history. He hated when in the storyteller's eyes, he or his adversaries are always the victim, always the victim of some injustice, even when he knows the truth. Arthur wanted our leaders to stop all the lies. He wanted political transparency.

The future president's speech was way off base and loaded with deception. During the Islamic invasion of the Byzantine Empire in Turkey toward the end of the eleventh century, Muslim warlords forcibly took over Christian churches and turned them into mosques. Remains of Christian saints were dug up and given to dogs. To stave off one of those digs, Christians moved the bones of Saint Nicholas, the generous fourth-century bishop of Myra, to Bari, Italy. The focus put on the move introduced the bishop's gift-giving traditions to Western Europe honored by Christians all over the world today. The Renaissance was a revival of interest in art, architecture, paintings, sculpture, and philosophy by people who had to try to rebuild their lives after fleeing the Islamic invasion of the Byzantine Empire.

In the following two hundred years, nine crusades between Muslims and Christians took place between the Black Sea and India. A Muslim warlord named Tamerlane led massacres that killed an estimated 17 million people. He eventually captured Moscow and buried two thousand prisoners alive in cement. Seven centuries later, Muslims and Christians are still fighting over causes in the Middle East.

Arthur understood that one group does not have a monopoly on evil. He just wanted our political leaders to be more even-handed in their descriptions when explaining historical events and present situations that affect millions of Americans.

At first Americans were told, by the Bush administration, that the war in Iraq was being fought over "weapons of mass destruction." After this argument proved to be false, most Americans believed the fighting between mainly Christians and Muslims was really about keeping open the lanes of oil flow to the West.

President George W. Bush and Vice President Dick Cheney thought the Iraqi people would instantaneously rebuild their own country after the mission they called Shock and Awe and the overthrow of the kingdom of Saddam Hussein. Shortly after that mission, Bush told his country the combat was over and we had won. However, the problems in Iraq ran much deeper than American leaders had anticipated or understood. The Iraqi people were so battered and bludgeoned from all sides for so many years that their trust of any form of government leadership was lost and paid for in blood. Though the US military toppled Hussein early on in the conflict, the fighting continued for several years before troops started coming home from Iraq and the level of violence declined dramatically. Two million items of equipment and seven thousand tons of ammunitions were finally dispersed and shipped home ten years after the war started, ending a massive war effort by the military. The war has left crumbled buildings and huge amounts of debris and garbage lining the streets of Iraq. Rats' nests of wires and generators supply some power, but there is little running water and there are only a few electric poles or power lines.

On regular occasions, Arthur talked to his friend Frank Lambert about politics and military strategy. One afternoon, Frank called Arthur to talk.

Frank: "Hi, Arthur. I just wanted to call and tell you about what a customer friend told me after coming home after serving three tours in Iraq."

Arthur: "Go ahead. What branch of the military was your friend in?"

Frank: "My friend is an Air Force fighter pilot. He told me about what it looks like flying over Iraq. Looking down from the window of his airplane, he saw a vast, bleached-white desert. In the distance, he saw blue-gray mountains, and just below his airplane, he saw a river that looked like a ribbon of green cutting through the white desert sand. It was the Euphrates River and it is not far away from the Tigris. When he made his descent in the airplane, he noticed large white and tan mounds of rubble on either side of the Euphrates. These mounds are the remains of ancient settlements begun more than seven thousand years ago—ancient walls, temples, and brick houses lying in crumpled piles. When he landed the airplane in Baghdad or Basra, he saw more mounds of debris. However, this time the rubble marked the remains of modern buildings leveled in the last ten years of war."

Arthur: "Seven thousand years after the building of ancient settlements, there are still too many conflicts and too much rubble. It is just unbelievable how long conflicts have been fought in that region of the world."

Arthur tried to join the army when he was eighteen, but a medical condition concerning his colon kept him from military service. Despite occasional uncomfortable symptoms of abdominal pain, bloating, and diarrhea, he controlled his irritable colon by managing his diet and lifestyle. His condition and disappointment at not gaining acceptance into the military did not deter his curiosity for foreign policy and for trying to understand the decisions of top brass. Without any war experience of his own, he sometimes relied on his brother Johnny or his friend Frank for their opinions. Johnny and Frank both fought in the Vietnam War. Johnny had been out of touch for a while, though, so Arthur mostly discussed war issues with Frank these days. Not too long ago Arthur found out Johnny was staying in Atlanta when his daughter Sandra received a birthday card from him. The envelope had an Atlanta postmark but did not have a return address.

Arthur: "Even with our combat troops sent home from Iraq, the war is not over. There will be more suicide bombings and even a civil war is possible, but don't you think American soldiers have borne the brunt of this problem long enough?"

Frank: "Yes, violence and war have been part of life for people trying to survive in this part of the world for thousands of years. We did overthrow Saddam Hussein, but we can't want the solutions for peace more than the Iraqi citizens want it for themselves."

Arthur: "More soldiers have died in the wars in Iraq and Afghanistan than in the 9/11 attacks, and ten times as many injured, while Americans keep going deeper in debt from an already trillion-dollar unfunded war. Do you think soon it will be decided it is time for all our boys to come home from Afghanistan too?"

Frank: "I don't know, but I hope our president doesn't just base his decision on politics by withdrawing troops immediately in Afghanistan because of his desire for reelection. According to military leaders, withdrawing troops in September is riskier than waiting to do it in December, because the cold weather will lessen the number of enemy fighters willing to brave the harsh elements. Afghanistan is a big sinkhole that has gobbled up large dynasties in ancient civilization, forcing Russia to withdraw after massive losses in recent history. It is a very difficult place to fight a war—full of underground tunnels, harsh desert sands, extreme weather, and a stony mountain terrain. Despite these hard circumstances, our all-volunteer military is still asked to complete the burdensome tasks we place upon them. Withdrawal of troops must be done in a slow and methodical manner."

Arthur: "From what I see on the news, the terrain looks terrible over there."

Frank: "Any exit strategy must involve a plan that enables our soldiers to hand off the mission to the Afghan military, so that they can leave cautiously. Getting truck convoys to safely navigate dirt roads in mountains and strategically bring home heavy equipment is difficult when snipers are blowing up tankers. NATO forces, truck drivers, and contractors trying to rebuild infrastructure are under a constant barrage of militia tactics against the cause."

Arthur: "General Patraeus was given a very difficult task in Afghanistan. He is trying to do more training of the Afghan people in hopes of building their own army, large enough and capable enough to defeat the terrorists. What kind of Afghanistan do we want? A contained Afghanistan? Is this acceptable enough? Or do we want to try to eliminate al-Qaeda, which may be an impossible task. Do we threaten to withdraw aid or make further sanctions against countries that are unwilling to help us in the fight?"

Frank: "The elderly are the most respected people in the Afghan communities. There are about fifty elders in most small-town hierarchies. They are usually hardened people who are somewhat knowledgeable about local politics, but because they are illiterate, it is difficult for them to bargain for positive change. They do not want their civilians bombed and they want to be involved in the decision making when setting policy. Sometimes they befriend those who can help them survive harsh conditions, not necessarily those they agree with on politics."

Arthur: "Winning in Afghanistan is supposed to be about empowering the people to run their own country, like teaching farmers to grow their own crops, not growing poppy plants and not just giving them free food. So are you saying these people are willing to die for their faith and their tribe affiliation, but not necessarily for their country?"

Frank: "Many times it's not about the politics; it's about people trying to survive. The Afghan people are always in survival mode because 90 percent of the adults are illiterate. Adults who can't read a short grocery list, much less a book, face far-reaching consequences. These high levels of illiteracy affect virtually every social problem they have as a nation. The enormous scope of illiteracy in Afghanistan is seriously affecting their global competitiveness and is costing taxpayers in America billions of dollars, because so much time and money has to be spent to teach basic methods of nation building. Illiteracy puts much added pressure on Afghan citizens because when people can't read, they can't carry their weight in the workforce."

Arthur: "In America, when some of our characters give up on carrying their own weight, they apply for aid and disability. While some Americans truly suffer from injuries and health problems, this does not explain the 38 percent jump in disability applications by out-of-work people last year. The rest of us are supposed to be satisfied with lower pay, bad mortgage deals, lousy stock-market investment returns, and subsidized government healthcare, all paid for by borrowing from China. I do not think Afghanistan is the only country now in a waiting game. Americans need a little awareness too."

According to Arthur, the current state of community affairs in hometowns across America is in a waiting game too. The retired seniors of the middle class are tired of strangers ripping them off, and they are putting a hold on spending any money in their dwindling savings accounts in hopes of influencing better government policy geared toward them. They want thoughtful and well-developed policy that puts people to work and revs up the economic engine that drives our great country. They are tired of both sides, Democrats and Republicans, taking shots against each other and want them to clean up their own houses first. The political system seems dysfunctional when our politicians repeat bumper-sticker sayings without any details about how to make better policies. It is hard to see any effects of change when costs have put off spending for seniors and young people years into the future. Politicians are more concerned with their parties than with what they are supposed to be doing, representing the people who sent them to Washington or elected them as their local voice for their town, district, state, and country.

One of Barack Obama's favorite phrases, "We will move forward," was a line he often used in his campaign speeches directed at young people. However, a speaking blunder made during the campaign has stuck in the craw of older voters, which made it difficult for them to move forward with his policies. The slip-up happened during a speech in Oregon when he mentioned that he visited all fifty-seven states. Anyone who is a resident of Hawaii or Alaska often hears the term the "lower 48" referring to the other forty-eight states. Any true American knows there are fifty states all together. How is it possible that a man running for the highest position in the land could say something so off base? A true resident of Hawaii, a true American, would never have difficulty remembering how many states there are, never, no matter how tired he was. The May 9, 2008, blunder in Oregon by the freshman senator at the time followed the obligatory "delighted to see you" opening of his speech.

Citizens in Rainbow Creek and other communities were at a crossroads on deciding how much government is good for America. This question spurred intense arguments during the presidential debates of 2008 and continues to do so today.

John McCain did make Senator Obama squirm during the campaign. *Joe the Plumber* became the moniker for the person McCain talked about as an example of a middle-class worker who worked hard to earn his money and did not want any rule changes that would shift more of his discretionary spending. McCain called Obama "Senator Government," but Obama voiced no response to the remarks, instead using a tin-ear strategy to take focus off his spread-the-wealth policies and his spend-spend-spend plans.

Arthur noticed that often when politicians talk, they seem trapped within their own baseless narratives, reluctant to listen to, much less credit, anything that contradicts what they chose long ago to believe. Politicians lie, especially when they want to win an election, but some do it with ease and flare while working the campaign trail. "Electing politicians is a little like buying bananas," Arthur often said. "Buy your bananas a little green, so the uneaten ones in the bunch do not go bad after the first day you bring them home." Surely, Arthur figured, President Obama must think about some of those promises he made while on the campaign trail. Surely President Obama must ponder why it is that European countries expect the United States and the UK to shoulder the burden of the wars in the Middle East alone. This is a joint problem in which our friends should help, even if some of our allies are not completely happy with America at this point. Did he give any more thought to ousting lobbyists in Washington like he promised during the campaign? No. Did he keep earmarks out of all new bills and legislation? No; in fact, after the election a special deal to the state of Nebraska offered an exchange for getting a senator's vote to help sway healthcare legislation, mostly a partisan outcome. All these special healthcare provisions for states that give tax breaks to corporations like Gator-aid, indoor tanning salons, and other businesses violate the principle that all federal legislation needs to benefit the general welfare. Executive orders are not supposed to ramrod legislation; their intention is for use in national emergencies such as moving troops during terrorist attacks or aid for natural disasters. Regarding the healthcare policy debate, when asked whether the proposals made sense and whether government had the right to assert this power according to the Constitution, Nancy Pelosi said, "The Constitution was the last refuge of the scoundrel who lacked serious policy arguments." To stay clear of the ridiculous comments, President Obama avoided the situation and never once mentioned Pelosi's gaffe to the public. He was more interested in and most comfortable talking to young people, especially when he had plenty of time to prepare a commencement speech like the one he gave to all college students in May of the following year.

"You are graduating today in part because those who came before you had the courage to look past their differences, face down their common difficulties, and perfect their union. Young soldiers pushed forward at Lexington, Gettysburg, Normandy and at Kandahar. It was graduates like you, who looked across a continent and built the railroads, highways, schools, and universities, that have fueled the most prosperous economy in the world. It was a thirty-three-year-old Thomas Jefferson who wrote the Declaration of Independence; a thirty-three-year-old Elizabeth Cady Stanton who organized the Seneca Falls Convention, the first national women's rights convention; a twenty-six-year-old Martin Luther King Jr. who began his journey to the mountaintop; and a twenty-year-old Bill Gates who started one of the most transformative companies on Earth. All of these Americans faced long odds. All of them faced doubt. Many grew up in tough times."

One month after President Obama's speech, Arthur professed at a Rainbow Creek subdivision association meeting, in front of two dozen of his neighbors, messages he agreed with and relayed for the Tea Party:

"It is time for all middle-class citizens to say, 'This is our America too.' We have to protect the sovereignty of the nation and all the working middle-class citizens that are the day-to-day operations of our country. Our leaders must ease restrictions and lower taxes on businesses so employers can hire the unemployed and poor. A redistribution of wealth is taking money away from the middle-class people who earned it, to finance more government programs, and allowing the wealthy to have more power. It is no accident seven out of ten of the wealthiest suburbs in the country are in Washington, DC. We have to keep building on what we have earned; we do not want our livelihoods torn apart and our money redistributed. Taxpayers can't continue to bear the costs of companies' risks, the same companies which have earned millions of dollars for taking those risks."

Neighbors voiced their concerns about taxes, health insurance, and the economy in general. People in Rainbow Creek were paying attention to politics more than they ever had in the past. As a young man, President Obama studied and lived in Indonesia, before furthering his education at Harvard. For a different perspective when he was in college, Arthur studied politics of nations in Europe, countries more successful and freer than Indonesia. It is easier for Europeans to accept social welfare policies when it appears the money pays to support programs for local citizens, not like in America where much of the money is spent to manage vast numbers of refugees and unskilled immigrants that cross the border into America illegally. Citizens start to wonder if they are working for their own families anymore. It is the same feeling they get when the politicians spend enormous amounts of money to buy visibility and spread propaganda at election times. Politicians believe that if they tell lies long enough, people will begin to believe them. Just as the tactics of dishonest salespeople will catch up with their business later, the tactics of dishonest politicians will haunt their party down the road.

In the decades since Arthur was a young boy, European markets opened up, and their tax rates decreased; public monopolies were dismantled, and more competition sprung, but problems still existed as people tried to adjust to a new world economy. People accepted many new European trends and they did not want to go back to the old way of doing things. People simply increasingly managed without too much government interference in their lives. Incomes and consumer prices are slowly stabilizing, bringing more people into the middle class. Social Democrats have failed to see this and have not changed their thinking to appeal to this new world society. "If there is a lesson to be learned from Europe," Arthur says, "it is that policies hell-bent on increasing government expenditures are simply not an option anymore and politicians should listen more to the ideas of the middle class."

After the Rainbow Creek subdivision meeting ended, Jane and Arthur invited Karen and Victor over for dinner. Though in the back of her mind, Jane thought this might be the last dinner she shared with her friends from across the street, she wanted to tell Victor and Karen in person that she and Arthur were broken up at this point. She wanted the Anderson's to know she was trying to stay amiable with Arthur, keeping in mind the best interests of their two daughters. Arthur and Victor were happy talking about politics, though both men were guilty of straying away from local issues by overly discussing global problems, boring some people at other functions.

Although Arthur loved Jane's beef stew, he would have been happy to eat anything when talking politics with others at dinner. The beef stew, made from a family recipe, was not a favorite of all their guests, but Karen and Victor appeared to love it. Victor, who often kidded Jane about her cooking, chewed on a big chunk of buttered French bread and a large spoonful of stew, moaning in delight as if it were the most delicious food he ever ate. He had Arthur, Karen, and Jane in fits of laughter. Whether he genuinely loved the beef stew or pretended for Jane's sake, no one was exactly sure, but it was probably more the latter.

Arthur said, "The problem with searching for the truth about government is that it is very difficult for anybody to relate to a trillion anything, especially now that the US debt is approaching $15 trillion from all the economic activity in every area and aspect of American life."

Victor added, "I just read in the newspaper that, in 2000, 12 percent of the average Missouri worker's median household income went to cover premium costs for health insurance through their employer. By 2010, the same household will be paying about 20 percent of its income for health insurance."

Karen said, "The more of a family's income that's spent on health insurance costs, the less there is to pay for food, housing, utilities, transportation. Forget about any fancy vacations for Victor and me. Families find themselves scrambling to cover the rising cost of living in the present, with less hope for the future."

Arthur said, "I figure almost one-third of a worker's paycheck goes for federal taxes, state taxes, local taxes, Medicare taxes, and Social Security taxes. Employees work the first four months of a year before they realize any discretionary spending at all."

Victor opined, "Soon the politicians will be telling us about a new tax on the toilet paper we use. Why are we always hearing about these ridiculous stories where our congressmen choose to occupy their time with matters such as school lunches, gay marriages, what color to paint their offices, and talk about their dreams of help from the sugar plum fairy? We are living in unprecedented times and they should be focused on the real threats to our country, such as the economy, jobs, cyber security, and the dangers at our Mexican borders."

Arthur added, "I think it would be a crazy idea for any politician to make drastic changes to our financial and healthcare systems before focusing on jobs, when so many people are struggling to make ends meet. First and foremost, people have to get back to work."

Arthur paid much more attention to politics than the average person. He ate and breathed it like an Olympic athlete who is obsessed with his event or a master chef who is preoccupied with a dish. When he heard about a "stimulus plan," but no details were ever explained about how the money would create jobs, Arthur was suspect of the plan. The same president who proclaimed during his inauguration "on this day we have chosen hope over fear" soon warned Americans that the US economy would be forever destroyed if the stimulus bill was voted down. The warning was so over-the-top that former president Bill Clinton warned our new president against declaring such grim pronouncements in the future. When President Obama met with congressional leaders to sign his stimulus bill on the first Friday after his inauguration, he listened to concerns of overspending by Republicans, but crashed any hopes of real dialogue by crassly telling them, "I won." The stimulus bill included zero Republican recommendations and failed to get a single Republican vote.

Philanthropist billionaire Warren Buffett talked about the perils of our country and the seriousness of the financial crisis. He said, "Lending should be about people with intelligence and character, not flash and property." Buffett made his comments on a segment that was played repeatedly on CNBC's stock channel in the months following the financial crisis. Collateralized debt obligations, as Buffett warned, so many times are a form of derivatives that spread risk and uncertainty about the underlying assets more widely, rather than reduce risk through diversification. Credit rating agencies failed to account for large risks in case of a housing value collapse or a financial recession when rating derivatives.

Early Tea Party organizers kept a close ear to the messages from Sara Palin.

"It is not just the tactic of using Republicans for bipartisan photo-ops, and then cutting them off from helping make any of the financial or healthcare decisions, that irks Obama's opponents. There are issues such as the swift reversal of Bush policies on abortion and embryonic-stem-cell research, which are dear to the Republican base. In addition, in another tricky fabrication, Obama's top advisor and chief of staff, Rohm Emanuel, orchestrated a public relations stunt trying to frame talk-radio host Rush Limbaugh as the real leader and head of the Republican Party. Emanuel is the same person who said, 'You never want to waste a good crisis.'"

The Tea Party followers remembered when President Obama promised that he was going to rebuild this economy stronger than before. Nevertheless, the president's futile stimulus handouts did not help matters. Twenty-three million people in the US still did not have jobs. The Republicans wondered why anyone could think the best way to improve the economy was another welfare program and only policies that help small businesses and increase jobs will help the economy. Many private sector healthcare workers worried that their jobs would disappear with government-run healthcare.

President Barack Obama, when he visited town meetings and talked to the press, talked about small businesses fighting for and creating jobs and the old theme of "Made in America." The new president missed the point. Small businesses in Rainbow Creek do not fight for jobs; they fight to make a profit. Small businesses everywhere try to increase their number of customers, find ways to keep expenses down, and work hard to try to provide the best possible product or service. Jobs follow profits. Running a small business requires negotiating a thicket of regulations, fees, worker's compensation, identification permits, and certificates of insurance, self-employment taxes, and paying for health insurance, one of the biggest expenses. The prize for business success is the privilege of paying higher taxes, but they should be fair; otherwise, if these companies get big enough, they may leave the country in search of lower taxes.

President Obama was the largest recipient in political history of millions of dollars from the financial and securities lobbyists, but he was still blaming the Republicans for the bad economy. Arthur was trying to figure out if the president was listening to other politicians in a way that drew them to want more conversation with him, or were they speaking to him, rarely able to figure out what he really thought. Members of the Obama administration repeatedly talked about a GDP growing at a 2.5 percent rate, but always failed to mention the real issue of the dollar losing half its purchasing power in a decade. Arthur's study of history taught him that the best way to gage the intellect and experience of a leader was to look at the experienced men he has around him. When things are going bad, PR people always try to repackage their politician as a more tolerant and mature individual, as their ideological views remain the same. Arthur was curious to see how the president related to Congress, the Supreme Court, oil company executives, healthcare officials, mortgage bankers and taxpayers. Would he take the time to discover real insight or would he rail against arguments no one is making to distract us from his real agenda? Arthur found it fascinating to watch how these things played out.

John Paulson and other consumer advocates raised awareness and blew the doors off the magnitude of the problems in the mortgage industry. He and other bankers knew the mortgage loans they were putting together and selling were junk, loans to people they knew could never pay them back. They knew because their own analysts told them so. Unscrupulous, lazy ratings agencies were at the heart of the mortgage crisis. Hundreds of thousands of mortgage loans failed to meet basic underwriting standards of years passed. It became so bad that Wall Street insiders were creating products to bet against their own customers and the institution of banks in small towns and big cities all across the United States. Stockbrokers and bankers pushed policies that benefited them personally, with little or no regard for the customer. Even regional mortgage banks in Rainbow Creek that knowingly sold citizens homes they could not afford, later took the homes back during the foreclosure process.

In the past, banks wanted the government to relax regulations because they could not do what they needed to do to make money. Then when the rules were relaxed, the bank executives went crazy picking the pockets of customers, and a financial crisis spread like the plague. Bank executives became so lazy and so corrupt that they could not even sign their own names to mortgages and business loan documents. They farmed out the paperwork to boiler-room companies that hired young people with little work experience to sign phony signatures on as many as four thousand documents per day. Many of the doctored documents hurt people whose houses and businesses were foreclosed on. If you think only a few bad apples working for small local banks used this method, you are wrong. This illegal documentation practice was used at all major banks in all fifty states during the financial crisis and after it, as banks tried to recover money from bad loans. Therefore people found out those banks need some regulations, but the right kind of regulations with well thought out provisions by politicians who work for homeowners and businesses. Too many businesses are still struggling and too many Americans lost jobs and homes.

Sandra and Susie were a little worried about their father because they hadn't heard from him in several days. They discovered their worrying unnecessary once they read the messages he left on their Facebook pages in case they were looking for him. Arthur was on a mission trying to find out what the Tea Party was saying about the economy. The Tea Party Express, now the nation's largest political action committee, was making three stops this week in St. Louis, Kansas City, and Springfield, Missouri. Arthur attended all three rallies, adding nearly eight hundred miles to the odometer of his car in just four days.

Local organizer Scott Boston kicked off the Missouri leg of the tour, speaking to several hundred liberty-minded individuals converged at the top of the steps underneath the Arch on the St. Louis Riverfront, to protest our elected officials in Washington, DC. Boston told the audience, "The issue is the fact that our elected officials are not listening to their constituents." Someone in the crowd hollered, "People don't want taxation without representation." Arthur heard another person holler, "People want jobs." Signs in the crowd read, "We've Had Enough" and "Our Last Stand." Arthur noticed about a dozen people throwing tea bags into the Mississippi River.

The wordiest sign Arthur scoped out was the one a middle-aged bearded man in the crowd at the rally in Kansas City was holding. It read, "We are tired of our politicians giving pork to people who haven't earned anything."

The rain hit Springfield about the time the Tea Party organizers began setting up the stage and the canvas-tent-top booths, used by organizers to sell promotional items and raise money for travel expenses. The rain slowed the event, but three hundred people turned out anyway, to wave their small American flags and listen to a wide range of speakers, including gun-friendly Bob Dixon, Missouri sovereignty leader Jim Guest, and an abide-by-the-Constitution rock-singing grandfather.

The Tea Party now stood for six simple principles: no more bailouts, reduce the size and intrusiveness of government, stop raising our taxes, repeal Obama healthcare, cease out-of-control spending, and bring back American prosperity. These principles are etched in large letters on the sides of the Tea Party Express touring buses. Not just the members of the Tea Party, but 80 percent of the American citizenry wanted Congress to pass a balanced budget. But it just didn't happen because neither party was willing to sacrifice while the other side prospers. For too many citizens, politics in America felt like owning a car with the biggest engine, but the steering wheel is missing.

Mortgage lenders in Rainbow Creek, Heartland, Fieldcrest, and just about every other town in America, lowered the necessary down payment to buy a house from 20 percent of its intrinsic value, a normal requirement for a home mortgage fifty years ago, to down payments of 5 percent, 3 percent, 1 percent, and even no down payment on some loans. Once considered great investments, home mortgages were now risky business. The federal government spent many years intervening by giving advice to lower the perception of risk, which actually helped cause the financial crisis. In ten short years, the government piled up more debt than in the two centuries following the signing of the Declaration of Independence.

Animal Farm and *1984* were required reading for Arthur, Jane, and their friends when they were in high school. The two books were still required reading when Sandra and Susie attended high school too. The books relate what happens to animals and people that free themselves, but once again become enslaved through violence and fraud. Arthur liked both works written by George Orwell, a man who paid attention to politics and satire, prophesying a world lay to waste by warring dictators, when leaders commit fraud and enforce failed policies. Orwell wasn't afraid to get his hands dirty, working as a porter and dishwasher at night, so he could talk to people and write during the day. He wrote about barnyard animals revolting against their vicious drunken masters, similar to how politicians arrive in office with grand plans, only to submit to a tyranny erected by their own administration. Because the stories are relevant across several generations, compari-sons can be made between the animals and characters in the stories with politicians and citizens today. Vultures prey on dead things near the fork in the road and other living things trying to hide during the day. Snails and frogs sleep during the day and come out at night because they can lose too much of their green from the sun. Pigs roll around in the mud and slop, never overcoming their dirty activities. Thoroughbreds do most of the work to win large sums of money for their owners, yet the horses never experience prosperity. Boars use their advanced sense of smell to hunt unsuspecting prey. Spiders work at night as predators to catch smaller bugs in well-hidden webs with no chance to escape. Each species of firefly has a special light signal it uses to attract other credulous fireflies of the same species. Moths work best at night when the air is chilly and damp and they use this time to pick up scents with their antennae. There are a thousand comparisons that a man could make between a cheating politician or immoral stockbroker and the nightly activities of insects, rodents, and aggressive barnyard animals. Charles Ponzi was one. Bernie Madoff was another.

Bernie L. Madoff, who is serving a 150-year sentence in federal prison, captained a multibillion-dollar Ponzi scheme that swindled money from thousands of wealthy investors. Living in the penal system, his past, present, and future are now all in one. His former clients received phony quarterly statements that showed consistently positive returns, even during turbulent market conditions—because the accounts were not real. People fail you, children disappoint you, moths put hole in your clothes, but rarely are there men who rob you of as much money as Madoff robbed his clients. When the SEC charged him and his investment firm, Bernard L. Madoff Investment Securities LLC, with securities fraud, Arthur started thinking about running for mayor and cleaning up some of the lesser frauds in Rainbow Creek.

The month after the stew dinner with Victor and Karen, Arthur was again speaking in front of his neighbors at a subdivision association meeting. "If a mechanic, a doctor or a job applicant had a track record of acting irresponsibly," he intoned, "lying, or cheating, patients and customers would not want to deal with that person. Yet in the case of presidents, voters often overlook the signs of past poor choices and poor character, and focus instead on their charismatic speaking abilities and pompous acting skills on TV. The strength of character of a candidate is his past accomplishments, not his influencing skills, which will determine whether he or she will be successful as president." He continued, "Presidential candidates are in two businesses, politics and government. In politics, they are brilliant when giving speeches and marketing themselves. President Obama used all the latest technological tools to market his messages and aligned himself with Mario Lopez and other hot celebrities on the campaign trail. Lopez appealed to many young voters after his success on *Dancing with the Stars* and as host of *Extra* and *America's Best Dance Crew* on MTV. In the business of government, presidential candidates and very few senators, for that matter, know anything about running a business, much less the entire government. Most of their activity focuses on whatever is in the headlines for the moment and whatever will get them more votes at their next election. Besides starting earlier than any other presidential campaign in history, candidate Obama took trips to Jordan, Israel, Afghanistan, Iraq, Germany, France, Britain, and over five thousand other campaign stops to help gain information to use in forming rhetoric for speeches used to gain votes. John McCain traveled to Canada and Mexico trying to build business relationships to help the economy. The presidential candidates campaigned for eighteen months."

The audience applauded. Arthur enjoyed speaking to people who listened to his message. He went on: "Older, experienced voters knew that no politician or other individual is as smart about an issue as he thinks he is. If elected to the presidency, an experienced politician knows mostly who he is. A younger politician elected to this position is still working through that process during his presidency. When debating an issue in politics, in the courts, or in academia, it is no longer good enough in today's world to just establish the best way to do something. The winning party has to defeat and humiliate its opponent. Even though we hear a great deal about discussing issues and talking things out by the parties involved, it is rare to see a fair and enlightening exchange of ideas and viewpoints. The job of the US president is the highest position of power on earth; it is not a behind-the-scenes job. Because of all the media and all of the technology, never has a president had to face so many problems under so much scrutiny as he does today."

By the end of his speech Arthur was exhausted, but he knew he had connected with more than one in the crowd. He took his seat. With so many issues facing average Americans, he knew he wasn't going to be able to sit around idly very long. If a community organizer, without military or corporate business experience, could rise to the position of President of the United States in less than a decade, certainly he could do a lot more to help his own community. He was working within the trenches of the Tea Party to hone in his personal beliefs about modern politics and deep-rooted American values.

Not long after that night, Arthur started working to support candidates who believed the challenge of any administration is to build an economy that is rich enough to support our children, the elderly, and the sick without completely damaging the source of the money, the middle class. He felt the biggest problem in meeting this challenge was to find ways to fix the unfortunate corruption and the piling on of the middle class by unscrupulous individuals. He believed if the current pace of corruption and legislation continued, in twenty years, the middle class would become the socialist class. Free people would work to pay for hundreds of government welfare programs with little or no money left for discretionary spending. To Arthur, freedom was already starting to feel like it was headed in the wrong direction. At neighborhood association meetings and when visiting with people at the community center he often asked, "When was the last time anything was micromanaged in Washington, DC, and the program was deemed a fleeting success? Washington needs to remember our country is called the United States of America, not the United States of Europe, not the United States of the Middle East, not the United States of China, not the United States of the World. It is time for more empowerment of people at the state level and less at the national level."

"'Only in the US of A. Yo momma's not in Europe, who's the beast in the Middle East, why talk finer about China, no hate in the state'—that's how teenagers rap to each other these days," one mother sang to Arthur during a big screening of the presidential debates at the Rainbow Creek community center, free to residents. Arthur wasn't the kind of person who rolled his eyes at the expense of others, but he did believe that humor can go a long way in building relationships, so he smiled at the woman after her attempt to rap the words.

Arthur always tried to stay on point and didn't want to get into shouting matches with any of the patrons he was trying to sway toward his way of thinking. Back when he was with Jane, she often told Arthur it was pointless to argue with other people because it only made them mad. Besides, grownups were supposed to act civilized when working out their differences. Whenever Jane attended a rally or a meeting, she would tell Arthur on the way there, "Arthur, don't get into any heated arguments." Arthur could not help it. He had to try to prove to everybody that he understood politics and he knew how to fix things, especially in his own town. Though other people were intelligent and well versed, Arthur lived and breathed politics twenty-four hours a day, and at first, he would not accept the ideas of people who did not agree with him. He thought others lied through their teeth and never took the time to understand the issues. Jane worried that Arthur might someday get in a fistfight, or worse, with an angry citizen mad at the government or an angry worker laid-off by his boss. Arthur did not think about bizarre things that did not end well because he was stubborn, and though he sometimes overreached, Jane knew not to undercut his authority or undo anything he accomplished at meetings.

Arthur hated that the government was allowing seven-figure lobbyists' donations from undisclosed individuals from unknown destinations to dictate our politics. Wild West days came to his mind, a time when there were no limits and no rules. Goldman-Sachs, nicknamed "Government Sachs" after the bailout, seems to be as powerful as Washington. Political will always ties to money. One of Arthur's favorite declarations was, "Just follow the money and you will find the cause." He thought Fannie Mae and Freddie Mac lobbied for a Democratic president because Democrats are more likely to sponsor social programs and bailouts. After Democrats took control of the Senate and House in 2009 and with nearly five million homes in the foreclosure process, he hated that Fannie

Mae and Freddie Mac received $259 billion, the single largest bailout in American history, because it was said, "They are too big to fail."

A few months after Jane moved out, the hard feelings between her and Arthur began to soften. She stopped by one Saturday to drop off clothes for Susie, and found Arthur alone in the kitchen, preparing his notes for an upcoming speech. Jane never was much for politics, but she reached out to Arthur to talk about what he was passionate about. She asked what he was working on.

Jane: "All this tangled talk about politics, who are we supposed to believe, national networks, Fair and Balanced Fox, CNBC, CNN, C-SPAN, local news stations, or the Internet?"

Arthur: "What we need to do is find out who is paying to sponsor the broadcasts to get a clearer understanding of the opinions on a specific topic. If we know that George Soros, Warren Buffett, the Republicans, the Democrats, Big Oil, General Electric, Goldman-Sachs, or some other lobbyist with thick wallets is sponsoring the broadcasts, then we know the news is slanted. Our leaders have become followers of polls and they help friends who are the biggest donors during campaigns. They are unwilling to risk their careers in politics by compromising to bring about the policies needed, and they only talk about issues in the abstract."

Jane: "I want to know who is responsible for the financial meltdown."

Arthur: "Every penny of taxpayers' spending and income is subject to audit by the government, so shouldn't the expenses and earnings racked up by our politicians be subject to audit? A green audit might be best, because then there would be an analysis of how people who riff about the environment are living their own lives. We would know which politicians give speeches telling the rest of us how to reduce our carbon footprint and then ride in limousines and hop on private jets to fly back to homes where they pay a thousand-dollar-per-month energy bill."

Jane: "So you think middle-class taxpayers pay for the corruption and wastes of the wealthy and the welfare programs for the poor?"

Arthur: "That's exactly right. Ethiopia is one of the poorest countries in the world because it is run by political thugs and drug lords. Its political leaders are nothing but thieves in expensive suits. Ethiopian thugs jail more journalists than any other nation, assuring the controlling party in power is able to repress its people. American politicians use sneakier ways to control a much more gigantic cash flow."

Jane: "I would hate to live in Ethiopia, with thugs controlling every facet of life."

Arthur: "Property and civil rights mean nothing in Ethiopia. The judicial wing of Ethiopia is a corrupt model of failure that takes whatever they want from the people. Ethiopia wasn't always as poor as it is today, but despite billions of dollars of foreign aid, the vast majority of the citizenry is hungry or starving to death."

Jane: "How do Congress and our military leaders decide which countries to go after when dictators are repressing their people? I would hope it has nothing to do with skin color."

Arthur: "More than anything, I think it comes down to which countries are more important to our trade agreements and whether they are rich in oil. Does a country make products or sell commodities that are important to us?"

Jane: "I guess if it really mattered, more often wars would be started over human rights violations and not oil."

Arthur: "You would think our black president would do more to stop two of the worst men in the world, the dictators of Eritrea and Sudan. Isaias Afewerki, dictator of Eritrea, deprives his citizens of all freedoms and religious beliefs, and he imprisons and tortures activists and journalists. He aids and empowers the terrorists in Somalia. Omar al-Bashir, dictator of Sudan, bombs civilians and has killed an estimated three hundred thousand people in Darfur since 2003. He has embezzled billions of dollars from his people. The International Criminal Court has charged him with genocide and crimes against humanity."

Jane: "For sure Americans are much better off than the poor people in Eritrea, Sudan, and Ethiopia. But there are a lot of decisions about issues in recent years that just don't seem fair to the average citizen in the US."

Arthur: "Our own government deprives the citizenry every time it expedites favors to fellow politicians, hands millions of dollars to handpicked solar companies, former coadjutors, and corporate lobbyists, or bails out friends of large corporations to promote its agenda."

Jane: "Instead of the IRS agents worrying about us penny-pinchers, they should be investigating the flow of money coming in and out of Washington."

Arthur: "Too often in life, the person who makes the most noise gets the rewards instead of the one who is most deserving or most qualified. According to public records, the largest discrepancy in family income exists in Washington, DC, where 8.5 percent (more than any state in the country) of the people are considered wealthy—making over $200,000 per year—and twice that number of people (more than any state in the country) are under the poverty line and making less than $25,000 per year. California and Illinois are two of the most hardnosed states to do business in, due to a difficult regulatory and tax climate. Texas and Virginia are doing the best job of wooing companies and are considered the favorable states to do business."

Jane: "To my point, sounds like the IRS should be doing more audits in Washington."

Arthur: "I agree. Businesses and individuals get audited by the IRS. Voters would like to see a detailed audit of the spending from the Democrats' trillion-dollar stimulus bill to find out where all the tax dollars went."

Jane and Arthur had never really talked like this before. It made Arthur happy. They left the kitchen and took up seats on the couch in the living room to continue their conversation.

Jane: "Americans are always surveyed whether they are satisfied that President Obama and the Democrats in Congress have the best interests and needs of the American people as their number one priority. I was called at least five times this year by workers of the Democratic Party asking about my approval rating of the president. Shouldn't some of the money and effort go toward real, concrete fixes, instead of all this money spent on reelection efforts?"

Arthur: "Why do we never read about audits of any government welfare programs or see any of their financial statements? Why is there never a newspaper headline that says, 'Government Welfare Program Ends Because Its Intended Goal Has Been Reached'? Have you ever heard of a government program that came in under budget and served as a model of efficiency and performance? If cutting out the middleman lowers the price of things, why do we pay the government to stand between us and the free market if a program isn't working?"

Jane: "When an employer asks an employee how company funds are being spent, you'll never hear a boss say, 'There's no need to see receipts, I'll just take your word for it.' It's sickening to know that politicians accept bribes when many couples are working two or three jobs to try to make ends meet."

Arthur: "Maybe we should start talking into one of those long horns fans bring to soccer matches, and hope that a caring government official in the crowd is listening. Just working one job is hard enough, but working two jobs can make life very stressful for some people. Most challenges we take upon ourselves in life that can have great rewards also have the possibilities of tremendous disappointments. The upsides and downsides vary depending upon a person's position in life. Some people work two jobs because one job may offer better pay, but the second job helps pay for health benefits. I know I have always worked long hours because I wanted to save a little for when the car breaks down or to help send the girls to college. Not many people these days are saving money, because they want to try their hand at investing whatever is left after paying the bills."

Jane: "I know you have always worked hard to support our family. Did you ever find yourself getting angry because I controlled the checkbook, paying the bills and deciding what to buy most of the time?"

Arthur: "Most of the time, I didn't spend a lot of money on things anyway. I still keep a hundred-dollar bill in my wallet in case of an emergency. I am more interested in this growing grass roots organizing by the Tea Party, protesting against those responsible for the bank failures and the mortgage crisis. I think the current and prior administrations, along with the Wall Street executives, can share the credit for these fiascos."

Jane: "How do you think Rainbow Creek or our state of Missouri fits into this mess?"

Arthur: "As of today, only nine states have a triple-A credit rating from all three of the major agencies in charge of this commission. I am happy to say that I read Missouri is one of the nine states, with Iowa, Utah, Georgia, North Carolina, Virginia, Maryland, Delaware, and Indiana also joining the list. All Americans have a responsibility of fairness when it comes to money, but some Americans have a better awareness of upholding their responsibilities. Just as the Freedom Riders forced changes to bring down the 'Whites Only—No Colored' signs and abolished the Jim Crow laws in the early sixties, the Tea Party is bringing more focus to the improper monetary policies and job creation bills in our nation. Paying attention to the pulse of the nation, Tea Partiers are tiring of listening to the loudest voices instead of the most intelligent ones. When our senators lay out a new plan and call it a jobs creation bill, but all it does is subsidize unemployment compensation and public-employee jobs, there is no chance for progress or profits. The bill feels like Peter is robbing Paul, taking from the rich and giving to the poor, to no effect, no increase in jobs, just another policy that penalizes success and subsidizes failure."

When Jane spoke next, Arthur was surprised by what he heard. It was rare for Jane to be so honest and forthright with her feelings.

Jane: "The politics of our country is similar to our marriage. You focused so much of your attention on problems at work and seldom had any time to spend with me. When we did have a little time to spend together, we couldn't agree on how to spend it."

Arthur: "In general, baseball and local politics are the ties that bind people around here. We never had that."

Jane: "I just don't have as much interest in sports or politics as you do."

Arthur: "I know you don't."

Arthur was quiet. It had been nice talking with Jane like this, but ultimately nothing had changed. They had no common ground. It was clear their marriage really was over.

"I know you don't," he repeated.

Arthur was reading up on the Tea Party again. They wanted to know why the House Oversight Committee had no control over the welfare system in the US. Does the committee know about all of the problems within the system, or does it just not care? The Tea Party thought the HOC should be centralizing and organizing to prevent the misuse and abuse of over eighty welfare programs run by six different agencies, because there still was no main central computer. Some abusers were getting checks from multiple agencies and no one knows how much they are taking in or how many programs they belong to, programs paid for mostly by middle-class taxpayers. Arthur learned at the latest Tea Party gathering that if one added up all the publicly released figures from all eighty programs, you would find one in five Americans belongs to at least one welfare program and approximately $350 billion is paid out each year, this money representing about 20 percent of the entire federal budget. The problem is not quite as bad in Rainbow Creek, but still one in seven residents knows where to go to get a doctor's affidavit and an application from a welfare agency in order to supply enough paperwork to snowball the process for claiming disability payments from the government. Arthur was starting to wonder if politicians think all the people who go to work every day always feel good and never deal with any anxiety or pain. They must, because they keep passing legislation that allows additional welfare programs so people receive disability payments for carpel tunnel, back pain, sore joints, neck pain, headaches, stiffness, and any ailment they can convince a doctor that the symptoms keep them from having the ability to go to work. Everybody goes through struggles and most people with non-life-threatening health issues cope the best ways they can. Just as an illegal immigrant is a dishonest undocumented worker, Arthur thought, a welfare thief is a dishonest documented worker.

Researching history, following the Tea Party and giving speeches himself, Arthur was defining his own beliefs about what makes a great leader. He was sure great leaders lead by example. He was tired of hearing the current administration talk about mistreatment of poor people, when there are so many welfare cheats. He was tired of hearing about how badly terrorists are treated, when an overwhelming number of soldiers have done such courageous work. When a serious problem arises, great leaders stay involved to find a fix. They don't go on vacation and request that others find a solution. Arthur now realized that brilliant speakers don't always turn out to be great communicators and negotiators, no matter how well a speech is delivered, especially if their values fail to connect with the people. All the leadership discussions from the Tea Party made him think about his daughters charging debts close to the credit limits on their first credit cards. When this happens, a father doesn't ask the bank to raise the limits; he is supposed to advise his adult children to exercise more responsible spending. His hope for the future, when he looked at his girls, was that they would continue to grow as trustworthy individuals and work hard towards earning the things that make them happy in life.

★ 4 ★

Overlooking Policy
at Northridge High

When exactly Sandra became such a conscientious student, no one knew for sure, but it started early. She always received As on her report card, was always on the honor roll, and was a member of the National Honor Society. Fathers of pretty and talented daughters always worry that some boy could talk them into having sex too early and damage all of their dreams for the future. Fathers do not want to hear their daughters' names passed around as the promiscuous girls at school. Arthur did not want either of his daughters to turn up pregnant before they were wise to the ways of the world and in a position to financially afford raising a child. He did not want either of his daughters to grow up to be women who never look in the mirror to understand their own faults, always blaming others for what is wrong surrounding their personal lives.

According to Jane, the lesson she learned from listening to the constant battles between her two daughters and Arthur was that children were compelled to obey their parents because parents paid the bills. Jane recognized this in stark contrast to other parents who handed out tens and twenties to their children whenever they asked; creating a sense of entitlement that seemed to envelop children. Arthur and Jane both wanted their girls to earn things and learn ambition. Moms who hired Sandra to babysit in the neighborhood knew her to be conscientious and they noticed how she transferred some of her own discipline to their children. The younger children in the neighborhood loved when she came to their house to babysit because they knew they would learn something and have fun at the same time. Sandra was the only girl in the neighborhood who went door-to-door asking the elderly homeowners if she could shovel the driveway after a winter snowstorm. Sandra was average weight and only five-foot-three, but she was strong. The boys around Rainbow Creek did not seem to mind the competition and a couple of them took time to flirt with her when crossing an icy street. By the time Sandra was fifteen, she was already waiting tables and cooking in the kitchen at the Heavenly Gate Retirement Home located ten minutes from her house.

The job at Heavenly Gate paid a good enough wage for Sandra to pay for lunches at school and have a little spending money for clothes and entertainment. Now a junior at Northridge High, she refused to wear overly revealing clothes and excessive jewelry, even though many of the other girls pushed the limits by wearing Goth outfits or hippie clothes from the sixties. A popular tenth-grade boy, named Roger, started writing love letters filled with misspelled words to Sandra. If Sandra wasn't so enamored by Roger's good looks, she might have realized the boy's writing skills showed he needed to pay more attention in class. The two of them were part of a small group of students passing hundreds of pieces of paper with scribbled writing before the teachers wised up and tried to put an end to the illicit learning practices.

Many times, young teachers bring a level of energy and enthusiasm that is contagious to the students as well as the more tenured teachers. Sandra's favorite teacher was Mrs. Olson. Mrs. Olson, an English teacher, always had fun and interesting assignments for her students. One day she asked the class to count the number of *f*s in the following sentence:

Finished files are the result of years of scientific study combined with the experience of years.

"How many did you count?" she asked. "Did you count three? If you did, look again. The correct answer is six. The brain processes the word *of* as if it were a *v*." The class got a kick out of that. Mrs. Olson believed unique and simple assignments like this one, used each day over the course of the school year, kept the sometimes overwhelming project of educating and motivating students fun and interesting, while still sticking to the plan of the curriculum.

Mrs. Olson spoke to the parents of her students at a special assembly she scheduled the evening of the first day of the school year. She told them, "We all owe our children and everyone else's children a better education. They are the future of the country. Thirty years ago, mothers started to go back to work, and no longer were they waiting at home for their children when they get off the school bus. With their busy schedules, mothers barely have enough time to make dinner, much less time to make sure their children do homework. We must remember that raising responsible children is more important than raising children with lots of material possessions. The catch, though, is that children are responsible only if someone is there to make sure they are responsible, so fathers and older siblings need to jump in and help. When parents abdicate their role as the primary source of values, morals, self-esteem, fairness, proper diet, and exercise, we fail our children and we fail in giving support to our schools."

"We need to change the mind-set of expecting teachers to be parents to our children," she continued," and allow them to teach. They should not spend their days disciplining children and worrying about losing their jobs because not enough students scored high enough on standardized tests. Children are not on this earth to rule the lives of their teachers and parents. Instead of a sense of entitlement, children need structure and they need discipline and common sense. They really do not need to always dress in the latest labeled fashions and designer accessories, and they need to do their own laundry.

We must remember that if we do not teach our children how to act when they are alone, they will succumb to loneliness and other more serious troubles. As individuals, all children need to take a break from the world and all the media. Such things as doing chores around the house, preparing a family grocery list, helping make dinner, or reading a good book can accomplish this. No matter how many people own cell phones, to text at the dinner table in front of family and friends is considered rude. Life is about balance and moderation. Children need at least one person, besides the teacher, who is committed to their education, and they need to know that somebody cares. Students need to realize that they forfeit their chance for life at its fullest when they do not give their best effort at school. When students give a minimum effort to learning, they get a minimum of opportunities in return. Even with parents' help and teachers' best efforts, in the end, the students' effort determines how much and how well they learn. With a determined effort, students attain the knowledge and skills to control their own destiny. By learning to study with self-discipline, students become lifelong learners able to apply their talents with high expectations and able to turn challenges into opportunities."

Along with responsibility, discipline and education about finances were also impor-tant to Arthur. Early on he taught his daughters about money. He wanted his girls to be smart about their finances rather than being the kind of people who grow up swindled by politicians and motivational speakers who will not counsel you to think until you give your credit card number to their outfit. "Buried in the fine print," he explained to Susie and Sandra, "you'll see the credit card slip advises that it will begin charging a forty-nine-dollar monthly fee for their newsletter and investment counseling services unless you send a cancellation notice in writing to Tampa, Florida, by midnight Saturday. Don't be fooled by the shiny packaging." Arthur wanted smart, alert girls who wouldn't be taken advantage of. He also wanted girls who wouldn't try to take advantage of the system. Still, they were bound to make mistakes.

Attempting to be an entrepreneur herself, Sandra started selling packaged deals for a spring break trip to Cancun, valued at about seven hundred dollars per person, to students who were juniors and seniors at her high school, before the teachers wised up and forbade her to run a business on school property. Afterward, Jane made sure to tell the mothers of classmates that they could come to her house to sign up for the travel plans.

"It's not an unfair request from the teachers," Arthur told Sandra. "You were bene-fiting from scheduled time already allotted for learning. I didn't notice you complaining about the rules when they were working in your favor."

"Most of the time I was presenting the information to friends during my lunch period. I used my own money to purchase all the marketing and sales brochures and was hoping to make enough commissions to pay for my own expenses on the trip. I made a deal with Mrs. Ginger Miller, the agent at Shining Star Travel Company, so that if I signed up twenty students, my airfare and hotel and food expenses would be covered by the agency. Juniors and seniors at my high school were eligible for the spring break trip to Cancun. The arrangement was simple. I just had to get contact information and sign up people. Mrs. Miller took care of the money and details."

"You were exploiting your friends and the teachers were trying to put a stop to it. Don't you understand that?"

"Why didn't you warn me?"

"I thought I did."

"You just warned me that others might not be able to afford the trip in this tough economy and I could lose my investment."

"Well, at least you didn't lose any money, but you can't sell vacation plans on school time when you are supposed to be learning and listening to the teacher. I didn't think you would discuss the details of the Cancun trip with your friends during class. I guess I was too trusting in thinking you would do this work after school hours."

"I'm getting too old to try and live on babysitting money. It's not like I am shirking all of my other responsibilities. Everyone thinks I was scheming to take advantage of my classmates, when in reality I was helping everyone. The more students I signed up, the bigger discounts the travel agency was willing to give all of us."

"Just make sure you respect your teachers. Each teacher has a room full of kids to worry about every day. You have to understand that your mistake was trying to do some of your business on the teacher's time."

"My teachers are so boring and everything they are teaching I learned last year. I had an opportunity to make enough money to pay for my entire trip. Becoming an adult sure is confusing."

"Sandra, making money is important, but you have to play by the rules. Some of the students have not turned eighteen yet and you need written permission from their parents before they can go on the trip. The school administration has rules and they have to be fair to everybody."

"Right—everybody but me gets treated fairly."

Though Sandra was still visibly upset, Arthur thought this was the end of the discussion. As long as his daughter stopped doing business during school hours, and Mrs. Miller took care of the money and permission slips from parents, everything would be fine. Surely this matter wouldn't become any more complicated for a father and daughter seriously doing their best to understand each other's perspectives.

The next day at school, an unfamiliar girl accused Sandra of stealing her boyfriend because she had invited him on the senior trip. The girl slapped Sandra in the face. Sandra pushed back and a catfight ensued in the hallway near the entrance to the school library. Other students started congregating near the two combatants and within a few moments of pulling hair and a couple of minor scratches to both girls, the vice principal broke up the fight. The vice principal spoke with the school secretary concerning the incident, and the secretary called Arthur to attend a disciplinary meeting at the school. Arthur was worried that this fight could affect his daughter's permanent scholastic record.

"I called you here to discuss Sandra's three-day suspension from school," said Vice Principal Thompson.

"Mr. Thompson, I know Sandra was selling senior trip packages on school property, but now that the issue has been addressed by me and Mrs. Hobson, isn't it a little extreme for her to miss her schoolwork? She has never been in trouble at school before," Arthur argued.

"Your daughter isn't being suspended for selling senior trip packages at school; she is being suspended for her involvement in a fight with another girl in the hallway. Another girl accused Sandra of trying to steal her boyfriend," Mr. Thompson explained.

"Who hit first?" asked Arthur.

"Well, the other girl slapped Sandra first, but she pushed back and we have a 'no tolerance for fighting' policy at our school," said a stern Vice Principal Thompson.

"What is a girl supposed to do when an unfamiliar student is pounding on her face? I taught my daughters early on to defend themselves and voice their opinion if someone is bullying them," Arthur stated.

"Violence is a serious problem, Mr. Hobson, and we have to nip it in the bud. Let me show you something. Here is a note that a teacher intercepted a couple of weeks ago. This male student is experiencing emotional problems and threatening violence."

"What's up or down in your life. There is shit in mine. Do not even trip off these people in here anymore. People are going to get hurt. See if anyone says anything else to me afterwards. I am the center of the universe, the star, and everyone else is a useless speck of matter."

"We were able to set up counseling help for this family and therapy for this male student before things turned tragic. The boy is going to classes in an alternative setting run by some well-trained and experienced educators who have devoted their lives to working with troubled youths. Unfortunately, I also know of another account, which had a terrible ending. A boy in the Heartland School District killed his girlfriend after she dismissed their relationship. In a fit of rage, he hit her over the head with a baseball bat and then set her car on fire with her body in the backseat. After police interrogated the suspect, they found the boy had a history of heroin abuse. Drug paraphernalia was found stashed in various hiding places at the boy's home. You are an intelligent man, so I know you understand what administrators are up against." Vice Principal Thompson raised both hands toward the sky as if he could use all the help he could get.

"Yes, I certainly understand, but I just wish political leaders, educators, businesses, police, and the National Guard would do more to try to put an end to the violence surrounding the drug culture, because drug use robs these kids of their clairvoyance. The people surrounding the drug trade and people with drug addictions are committing many of the serious crimes in America. I certainly do not think we should be comparing this catfight between my daughter and this other girl to a murder or the violence surrounding the drug culture. I think drug use is behind most of the major problems in our schools." Arthur paused. "I will talk to my daughter," he added.

"Never should our children pay for the mistakes, bad decisions, and corruption of politicians. When public school districts are forced to lay off teachers and eliminate educational programs, students settle for less, instead of reaching for more. These decisions put more pressure on teachers to accomplish their objectives. With fewer teachers, the students learn less math and science and fewer skills that young people need to enter the job market. Anyway, this is another topic for another day."

"It might not appear that I am making sense complaining about people not doing anything about drugs and violence, while at the same time arguing my daughter shouldn't get in trouble for her involvement in a fight at school. I'm just saying I think it is wrong to tell a people not to defend their selves."

"There is a lot wrong with our schools, but most of the problems come from external influences," said the vice principal. "We must first solve the external problems schools face. The schools have not failed; we have failed the schools. There are many ways to save them. A diamond is merely a lump of coal that does well under pressure. While it is true that every man, woman, and child has a national duty to make an honest effort to contribute to society, an uneducated public will be the weakness that causes our society to fail. Parents have an obligation to teach their children to recognize the reality of the need for an educated society. It is good to think each student's life's journey will duplicate humanity, but it's even better to believe it will advance humanity. 'A mind is a terrible thing to waste' was declared by the United Negro College Fund. I think they had it right."

Instead of speaking about a separate rant about his political beliefs about education, Arthur wanted to make sure he left Mr. Thompson's office within the context of the reasons he was called to meet with him, the well-being of students, school violence, and selling vacation packages on school time. Torn between the seriousness of the subject of fighting in school and the desire to lighten the mood, he decided to take a risk against a man very capable of matching wits to make a convincing argument.

"Did you hear about the vandal who threw a rock through the driver's side window of a Jeep in the hotel parking lot during last year's Cancun trip?"

"No, what happened?"

"The vandal took the car for a joyride, but he returned the vehicle to the parking lot sometime before dawn. Besides the broken window, no other damage was done to the Jeep. However, paper wrappers from a Mexican fast-food restaurant were spread all over the front and back seats. After a detective from the Cancun police department investigated the case, he told the group staying at the hotel, 'Let this be a lesson to everybody. Never take anything that's *nachos* (not yours).'"

"You had me going for a minute. That's a good one. The work of school administrators isn't all doom and gloom. Most of us have a sense of humor. Humor is ageless and timeless. So where do we go from here," said Arthur.

"I'm sorry, Arthur, like I said, our school has a 'no tolerance' policy for fighting and both girls are suspended for three days. They are not allowed on school property during this time," said a confirming Vice Principal Thompson.

"I don't want you to think I'm one of those fathers who take care of all their child's problems. I will support your decision, but I need to know if this incident will appear on Sandra's permanent record. You know, she earns very good grades and up to this point she has had hopes for an academic scholarship," said Arthur.

"If Sandra is not involved in any other incidents by the end of senior year, this incident will be erased from her file. Talk to your daughter. I need to get back to work, so have a nice day, Arthur." Mr. Thompson stood up from his chair and handed Arthur his latest monthly newsletter, due to be mailed out later in the day. Arthur read the newsletter on the walk out to his car. It said:

Dear Parents/Guardians,

Not so long ago, our politicians used white Bibles and black Bibles to swear by oath in courtrooms, when making policies for white and black children in the South, before the civil rights movement and desegregation took hold. If we do not read, do not study, and do not get involved, we keep the same assumptions we have always thought, with no room to grow. To heck with the politicians; parents/guardians have to make the effort to change the environment of public schools at the local level. The formal school setting sometimes gets confusing and complicated, but parents/guardians have to take a leap of faith to do more to support the schools. People have to care as much about other children as they do about their own children. Our country does more for recycling our garbage than we do to help educate our children in some of our struggling public schools. People care more about pets than they do about the neighbors' children. Motivation, the foundation of every effort, exists behind every achievement. Educational methods are best when teacher and student have a heightened interest and a desire for truth and understanding of the subject matter. What makes the teaching process difficult for teachers is when you have students who read at a third-grade level and others in the same classroom who read at a tenth-grade level. That is what teachers are up against, not to mention the culture on the streets in general. Children from affluent neighborhoods hear about 35 million words by the time they enter high school. Children from poor neighborhoods hear about half as many words, and the gap is widening with all of the advances in technology.

What skills do we teach our children? Are we preparing and educating our children for the future? Should we at least teach students to achieve excellent standards in core academic subjects? How do we answer these aforementioned questions and still address all aspects of the costs to operate a school? In most schools, curriculum is determined by vague guidelines established by state and local authorities. The mere act of revising a curriculum each year, and then combining it with expectations, is bound to bring some improvement. The mere fact of paying close attention to curricula makes a mediocre school better. Physical education, art, music, creativity, and imagination are essential parts of the curriculum. The stimulation of the artistic part of the brain complements quite nicely the steady focus needed in math, science, and analytical thinking. Physical education became the norm in schools after the First World War raised concerns about the fitness of our soldiers. With so many overweight children today, physical education is just as important. Many teachers feel that foreign languages need inclusion in the curriculum at earlier ages, especially Spanish and Chinese, because it starts children on a bilingual path, which helps reinforce their English grammar and prepares them for our global economy.

Today we celebrate mediocrity and bad behavior by watching reality television shows. Cheaters, Desperate Housewives, Laguna Beach, Survivor, Fear Factor, and Big Brother are unscripted dramatic programming staged by untrained actors, people with bad behavior living in a situation where a prize is awarded at the end of an event and regularly watched by fans. It is permeating every fabric of our society. Vulgar language and disrespectful behavior seem to be everywhere you look: in schools, in stores, at the park, and in our neighborhoods. We can do better. Please keep talking to your children about the importance of their education. We need them to lead us into the future.

Thank you,

Paul Thompson

Vice Principal

Arthur left the vice principal's office unhappy but more sensitive to the violence issue, and upon walking down the hall, he heard the f-word at least three times and saw two boys roughhousing near the library. Though well versed in politics, he wasn't in any position to argue with the vice principal, and he hated the thought that some of the wealthier parents in the district used their influence by making large contributions to the school district to take care of problems or gain favor.

Vice Principal Thompson had said schools faced more problems today than fifty years ago. Was he right? It seemed the most common problems faced by teachers in the school districts of Rainbow Creek, Fieldcrest, and Heartland from 1940 through 1970 included talking out of turn, chewing gum, passing notes, making noise, reading comic books, running in the halls, breaking dress code, not turning in homework, and damaging school materials. Twenty-first-century teachers in many American school districts encounter more serious problems, such as absenteeism, drug abuse, alcohol abuse, pregnancy, vandalism, guns, violence, robbery, gangs, sexual diseases including AIDS, abortion, and even suicide and murder. Society's problems not only affect but also infect schools. Some classrooms are overwhelmed with sociological problems and a growing burden on the teachers to get everything right. Somewhere down the line, parents started expecting their teachers to be doctors, social workers, psychologists, and family counselors, a reality in school systems today. Vice Principal Thompson felt his school was way ahead of the curve if he made sure his school was void of drugs, alcohol, and violence. He was correct in believing this was a good start to saving the schools. The difference is while fifty years ago throwing punches settled fights; disputes are sometimes settled with guns today. A gun in the hands of an immature adolescent with a prefrontal cortex years away from being fully developed is a recipe for disaster, and Mr. Thompson was doing everything he knew how to avoid losing any more young people.

Thompson viewed schools by their very nature as expressions of opinion—which certain things to teach our children—and philosophers have been debating these issues since the time of Plato. The Quakers of England discussed ways to improve their schools in the seventeenth century and, at the same time, tried to keep individual religious beliefs separate and personal. John Dewey created not only a school but also an entire movement based on his vision of child development. When George W. Bush became president, he started the program "No Child Left Behind." Some people feel that President Bush created another level of unproductive wasteful spending, with too much money spent on bureaucracy and not enough spent on instruction in the classroom. Others criticized President Bush for spending so much money on the war and not enough on educational instruction. But without the protection of our democracy, our schools would not enjoy the freedoms of choice we have today.

Vice Principal Thompson and Arthur Hobson were the type of men who respected all those who worked overtime in the mine or factory, or who cleaned hotel rooms and scrubbed floors at night, all the while trying to save enough money because they know what an education can do for their children. They want their children to have a chance at a better future. They want their children to get a college education because they know that of the millions of Americans who have advanced graduate degrees, only 3 percent of them are unemployed.

People in the Rainbow Creek School District still argue the same issues of yesteryear, such things as money, taxes, class size, budget, curriculum, safety, teacher-student ratio, extracurricular activities, religion, dress code, lunch programs, safety concerns, and many other important issues. However, Vice Principal Thompson was trying to steer educators in his school away from clerical work because he was sure teaching had to be much more. He was tired of watching his teachers jump through hoops with their one-size-fits-all mandate by the government, worried only about upholding regulations and test scores and trying not to get sued. Just as every adult is different, every child is different, with different interests and passions, yet teachers instruct all their students the same way. Thompson wanted his teachers to allow for creativity during class time, so there was a balance with math and science the rest of the day. He wanted his teachers to do their best, because in many other countries he noticed a trend occurring. In many other countries, colleges only accept the most creative college students to study education. In these countries, admission to study education is harder than for medical or law school, because their cultures value their teachers as the country's most important assets.

Rainbow Creek School District was typical of most educational systems in small US towns, doing a little better than the average district. But US schools as a whole have dropped to twelfth in world rankings of education. Canada is first. South Korea is second. Russia is third. Japan is fourth. The children living in the city of Shanghai, China, scored at the top in reading, math, and science compared to students in the rest of the world. The Asian countries as a whole are increasingly making education a priority of family life. It is not beyond the realm of possibility that China could someday outproduce every country in every product. China used to make cheap plastic toys. "How many wake-up calls do we need?" was a question Vice Principal Thompson often asked when soliciting improvements in education. "Maybe the government should have taken the $800 billion that it handed to millionaires and used it to improve our educational system. As long as the government shrinks the middle class, the slide in education will continue. In far too many families, the long-term focus of a good education has become secondary to the immediate needs and gratifications of day-to-day living," he worried.

The School Board of Rainbow Creek was accountable for a budget that was honest and fair, showing how much money it needed and how the administration wanted to spend it. The Board of Education's responsibility was to focus on increasing performance, increasing quality faculty retention, growing the use of valuable computer technology, improving facilities, getting value for school district expenditures, developing advanced and special-needs programs, funding extracurricular activities, and increasing discipline of students (meaning better-prepared students, not punishing them). Their focus was to rid schools of drugs and violence, increase graduation rates, eliminate illiteracy, restore higher rankings in science and math, and promote the significance of college-level classes completed during high school years for college credit. The board was becoming more aggressive in marketing the district's visibility and name brand, standing a greater chance of increasing community involvement and interaction that would bring needed new energy and bright new creative ideas. By addressing these issues, standardized test scores were sure to go higher.

A study by the Brookings Institute in June 2006 revealed that middle-income neighborhoods, as a proportion of all the nation's neighborhoods, declined from 58 percent in 1970 to 41 percent in 2000. The safety of the neighborhood, the quality of the school system, and the number of people working good jobs are the links to building a strong middle class and overachieving school districts. If Vice Principal Thompson witnessed something working in his school district, he tried to make it the rule and not the exception. One school in Rainbow Creek was lousy fifty years ago and it was still lousy today. The school board was tired of this school doing things the same way when its policies did not work and its members were in the beginning stages of trying to innovate. According to Arthur, the reasons for failed schools usually involved some form of corruption or a lack of support from parents and guardians.

The astute people in town believed in investing in the future and in supporting their values with their pocketbooks. From buying electric cars to iPhones and iPads, vacation destinations to fair-priced ocean cruises, magazines to books, and healthy foods to practical fashions, people make decisions every day about what to spend their money on. An economy that improves the quality of a school system, the safety of the neighborhood, and the number of people working leads to a strong middle class. Because Americans had a lot at stake with the economy and democracy, Arthur tried to spread more optimism by seeking advice from people who saw themselves as contributors instead of victims, people who could turn ideas and hobbies into small businesses, instead of spending all their discretionary money on alcohol and drugs or at overpriced professional sporting events and concerts. He wanted to learn more about how honest millionaires make their money by working to create better ideas and why failed companies scheme to rob the public. Millionaires talk about new ideas and long-term plans, so he believed the middle class should think more long term, and not so much about instant gratification. If more people would just try to create a clear vision of the life they want, they would be closer to attaining it. By taking calculated risks, eliminating unnecessary expenses where forces are taking advantage of you, certainly anyone can learn to take advantage of good opportunities, anyone can improve his or her financial position, he thought.

From Jane's experience, taking sides with Arthur or Sandra about school issues would just exacerbate the situation, and it was clear to her she should stay out of any arguments and just let the events play themselves out. She was not too worried because Sandra was not the kind of student who was often in trouble at school.

Sandra was not the only girl acting up in class. A few of her classmates seemed blinded by the postures of their "bad boy" boyfriends, and they did not realize when they had latched on to a person who was genuinely bad news. Though these mischievous girls acted in more subtle ways, they were good at instigating bad behavior. Working in small groups one day, Sandra's classmate Bonnie Schreiber wrote in her science notebook a suggestive paragraph about the dragonfly nymph. It was a clear example of a girl's attention gone astray. Bonnie had intended for the boy sitting next to her to read her notes and flirt back, but she was too shortsighted to consider the boy might hand the paper in to the teacher. She wrote:

"The dragonfly nymph breathes by sucking water in and out of its tail near where the gills beat back and forth. The female dragonfly catches its prey by thrusting out their lower jaw, then encapsulating its head. The male dragonfly can pump itself up and down, propel back and forth, and it lasts a long time. The female dragonfly lays its eggs by submerging itself completely in a state of bliss."

Bonnie Schreiber was the third girl in a week to be suspended by Vice Principal Thompson.

In order to rally the school around a set of objectives, Mr. Thompson felt it necessary for teachers, parents, and students to feel a sense of community and to take stock of its current situation—the good things and the obstacles. He started a Parent Involvement Policy, adopting a plan in which each parent signs a pledge to donate fifteen hours of volunteer service to the school each year. He told parents in a letter:

"We have to quit making excuses for parents/guardians who don't find time for their children. Finding time for their children does not mean just buying things for them. Parents who refuse the pledge are sending the message that they do not care about making the schools better. Schools that have a strong contingency of parents/guardians involved in the program are making huge improvements in school districts nationwide. If parents/guardians follow through with their pledge to work fifteen hours of school community service per year, turning any school into a successful community is a reachable goal. Parents/guardians are successful if they teach their children by example how to be self-reliant. Parent/guardian committees focusing on safety, lunch

programs, cleanup, recycling, maintenance help, painting, data entry, organizing book orders, hall monitoring, field trips, fund-raising, concessions at sporting events, commencement, and many other activities help raise the standards to empower schools with a sense of community. Beautifying the school simply by filling walls with photographs and students' works greatly adds to the learning environment. Children growing up in families when parents don't stress the importance of education are more prone to relying on welfare programs, using drugs, not voting, and doing little to improve their situation on their own."

Just as Margaret Hobson made every effort to teach her boys the importance of reading, Vice Principal Thompson preached that improving academic achievement started at home. He insisted it was wrong information to hear that the government, the media, and the nation's teachers—with no mention of the role of parents and guardians—cause the plight of our children. Parents are the major fabric of the school; they influence students more than the administrators or the teachers. Parents can help raise the academic standards of their children by supporting teachers, expanding the use of computers and technology at home, staying involved with homework, and monitoring the progress of their children. Parents help by encouraging their children to find something that they excel in, whether it is a sport, art, music, writing, or some other activity; they learn and have fun at the same time. Hands-on activities help increase self-esteem in other aspects of the students' lives.

To show his commitment to an improved education system, Mr. Thompson kept a framed copy of a published report on the wall behind his desk in his office. "If an unfriendly power had attempted to impose on America the mediocre educational performance that exists today, we might well have viewed it as an act of war. As it stands, we have allowed this to happen to ourselves. We have dismantled essential support systems, which helped make gains possible. We have, in effect, been committing an act of unthinking unilateral educational disarmament." These statements, published by the US Department of Education's National Commission appeared in a report called "Excellence in Education, a Nation at Risk: The Imperative for Educational Reform," back in 1983. It was a call to action that Arthur was already answering.

5

Few People Benefiting from Fair-Weather Change

As Sandra neared graduation from Northridge High, Arthur was reminded how fast time passes. He reflected back to the day when his father, Atwood, told his doctor he was experiencing a lot more headaches than he ever used to. After extensive tests and x-rays, Atwood found out he had an inoperable brain tumor and was given just a few weeks to live. Johnny was fighting in Vietnam that year, and it was a very difficult time for Arthur, watching his father die and worrying about his brother. "He's been worn out," Arthur said sadly, "by a lifetime of hard work." Nevertheless, Atwood was determined to remain independent and enjoy his family during the last stage of his life, and for a few more weeks, he kept driving his old Buick Skylark to the diner for coffee in the morning and the golf course clubhouse for cards in the afternoon. At the news of the tumor, Arthur and Jane worked hard to pay medical bills and make arrangements with Atwood's bank. Then, just a couple of weeks after they tied up the ends to most of the financial issues, Atwood died, and Arthur called the funeral home to make plans to bury his father. The rushed pace of everything gave Arthur little time to mourn the death of his father, as he kept most of his memories to himself and delved into his work.

A few months later, when the will was read, the family learned that Atwood had left his house on the hill, ten miles outside Rainbow Creek, exclusively to Arthur. When Johnny and Kevin heard the news, they wanted to rent out the house and use the income to help pay for expenses for their mother to live at a nursing home. Jane insisted that Arthur honor his father's wishes that he care for his mother and keep the home in the family. By not selling, but keeping the property as an investment, Atwood believed its value would continue to rise through the years. While Margaret lived in the house in the years following Atwood's death, her wish to let Arthur make any important decisions about the property halted any more discussions about what the boys should do about caring for their mother.

Interrupted from reflecting on the past, Arthur sprang up from his chair to answer a knock at the front door. It was Jane delivering another box of Susie's stuff, two pairs of shoes and a scarf handed down from Sandra. Jane stayed long enough to catch the updates about the Muslim community center and mosque controversy on TV. She watched with particular interest, partly because she knew it must be uncomfortable for the president to comment on whether or not to allow Muslims to build a community center two blocks from ground zero and partly because she worried about how new conflicts might affect the safety of her two daughters and the next generation. Even though Muslims have the same right to practice their religion as everyone else in this country, there was controversy because of the sacred location where they intended to build the center. Because Obama's middle name is Hussein, some Americans always accused the president of siding with or appeasing the Muslims, no matter what he said to the people or the press. Since ignorance breeds contempt, the president decided not to wear religion on his sleeve. Religious profiling is as detestable as racial profiling in his eyes. "Religious freedom is an important right in this country. If it is a right, then it is a right. Otherwise, what good is a right? It's as if you have freedom of speech, but are told to shut up, and not getting a chance to voice your opinion," said the president. "A general contempt for a whole group of people is ridiculous. By examining one case, you can sometimes shed a little light on another. Many people don't know that American citizens, who are also Muslims and work at the Pentagon, already share chapel services with other faiths at a rebuilt section of prayer space where the plane hit the building on 9/11."

Jane: "That doesn't surprise me that Muslims work at the Pentagon."

Arthur: "Me neither. But it does bother me that the Muslim organization wants to build the mosque near ground zero, and it bothers me even more when they apply for grant assistance from the federal government to do it. How bold is that? This type of move adds fuel to the fire. Where is the separation of church and state as written by our forefathers in our Constitution?"

The news report went on to note that opponents of the Islamic center were saying that as long as Christians cannot build a church in Mecca, Muslims cannot build an Islamic center or mosque near ground zero in Lower Manhattan, New York. The Tea Party organized more meetings when they found out that the US State Department provided funds to Cypress to refurbish mosques and supply their people with new computers while American taxpayers were struggling to make ends meet. They told members of Congress that spending hundreds of millions of dollars trying to buy relationships in Cypress showed weakness, while Muslims were laughing all the way to the bank. The Tea Party felt this type of foreign policy was an insult to conservatives who work hard for their money and it did little to mend relationships between Christians and Muslims in Lower Manhattan. "We are emotional people first, not the reverse where we can just buy our way out of all our problems," said one unidentified speaker at a rally on the newscast. "We cannot assign value to things if we do not know the outcome of our policies. Governments are supposed to adjust politics to changes in the times for all people, not just to appease a certain religious sect. Two wrongs to make a right is the way of thinking which may be the match that ignites the fire in the hands of the terrorists," he concluded. Jane and Arthur sat on the couch entranced.

Johnny happened to be watching the news at that time as well. He noticed another twisting of the truth was happening again in the Middle East. Words did not matter and another generation was going to suffer because of the propaganda. The Taliban continued distorting the name of Islam. They contended that Americans were severely criticizing their religion. When Johnny's mind became clear to what was happening, he saw the Taliban as cowards because in many incidents they used children to fight their conflicts. Every time he heard about the Taliban fighters using a young boy to behead an accused traitor in a village of Pakistan or a group of men standing in a circle to stone to death a young woman lying on the ground, he had flashbacks to the travesties he experienced in Vietnam. Deluded Muslim suicide bombers in Iraq and Afghanistan are praised by Taliban leaders as martyrs for killing people who do not agree with the way they think, but Johnny was sure all they did was enrage more people worldwide.

Two decades since returning from the Vietnam War, Johnny now spent much of his life drinking too much, wasting his money on fast women, chain smoking, exploiting his family, and roaming from city to city when he wore out his welcome. He currently was living in Atlanta. Johnny never forgave the liberal press for describing the dead and wounded in the war he fought for as mostly conscripts of the poor and lower middle class. This angered him because he knew many of these soldiers as mostly enlisted men from all fifty states who were the most courageous people in our country, and why did it matter if they had money or not? Many of them gave up their lives fighting for our freedom. It angered him when America led the charge to remove dictators in Afghanistan and Iraq with little help from other peaceful allies, or how, after a horrific earthquake in Haiti and a devastating tsunami hit Japan, Americans took the lead there too, in supplying relief to the victims. He believed it was time for the US to send some of those European countries a bill to help pay for the costs of the war. He watched America spend most of the money attributed to the war, some say $2 billion per week, fighting the war in Afghanistan with little help from allies; he watched and hated China for spending about that same amount of money each week buying up minerals, metals, and resources all around the world.

With recent cuts to the Social Security Administration's operating budget, Rainbow Creek was hit with a potential shutdown of its service offices. Rainbow Creek, it seemed, was too rural to warrant its own office. One afternoon, Arthur drove to the Rainbow Creek service office, where Yolanda Zucchetto concluded every customer correspondence with a "thank you." Arthur explained to Yolanda that he was still receiving his deceased mother's checks. He had tried to stop them by calling the office, but he was on hold for nearly thirty-five minutes. "I don't blame your office for not dealing with phone customers faster, because you guys are being squeezed, just like everyone else," Arthur told Yolanda. "This is true. The politicians write laws to ensure more money goes into the pockets of their friends. Now they are cutting services to people who were promised benefits for working their entire lives paying into the system," said Yolanda. "I believe the free market and property rights regulate most things anyway, so I don't believe we need a lot of these new regulations, especially when politicians and bankers make the rules for themselves. Anyway, to end on a good note, thank you for closing out my mother's account," said Arthur. "You're welcome. I'll say an extra prayer for you and your family when I go to bed tonight," said Yolanda, making the sign of the cross before announcing, "I'll take whichever customer is next, please."

Arthur and Jane had always taken the girls to their grandmother's house for visits during the summer, often bringing along one of Sandra's friends from the ball team or one of Susie's friends from the neighborhood, their friends always describing the property as the house with the great big yard and woods with a creek behind it. As a consideration to Jane, Arthur decided to allow Jane and Sandra, nearing graduation, to live in the old house whenever the transfer agent finished a safety inspection. Jane and Sandra started going to the house during the evenings to organize papers, throw away trash, clean floors and carpets, paint walls, pull weeds, and plant flowers in the garden. Susie stayed home on Hill View with Arthur and he worked on his political notes for upcoming speeches. He knew becoming a good speechwriter was more about having lived enough than it was about using proper grammar and sentence structure. Arthur wrote in his notes:

Americans just want the truth. If our president or any of our politicians are worried about the repercussions of telling the truth, then what is the purpose of the truth? The greatest reverence we can pay to truth is to use it. A demagogue makes false claims to gain power, adjusting his politics to fit the group he is talking to. It is true that President Obama received a backlash of mistrust from citizens due to the reputations of past presidents. However, some of the mistrust he earned himself because of his overzealous and false promises made on the campaign trail and because he was not forthcoming on other questions asked of him. This entire fast-to-act new legislation is thrown at the American people, but we do not know what is in the workings of these bills. Part A of the wording of a new bill presented by the media sounds good, but part B is kept hidden from the public and we just do not know what is in that section of the bill. The president and the media seem to underestimate the intelligence of the middle class, simplifying all issues instead of explaining the details. Sometimes it feels like the administration has free rein to go after anything, even though individuals and small businesses have worked and fought hard for years to attain a level of success. President Obama is a brilliant man, but sometimes it does not feel like he is connecting with the people. Does he really understand the sacrifices made by military families? Sometimes it does not feel like he is showing empathy for the people. He is so aggressive with his politics to change everything, too much and too fast. Some things are working and do not need interference by the government. The hope is that our elected presidents have enough experience, have lived long enough, have made enough important decisions, and have enough intelligence to do the right things. Does President Obama understand the extent of corruption in America or will his policies just add to the mess? Does he understand that though elderly people occasionally drive an entire mile with their blinkers on, they reuse coffee filters, double-dip tea bags, wear old clothes, lower their thermostats to save energy, compensate for their aging bodies, live simple lives, and try to save costs wherever they can? Does he really understand American history? Does he know how to succeed as president? Will he earn deep respect from the American people because of his character? When those who have power are genuine and transparent, their policies work. When their policies are artificial and manipulative, they fail. Persistence, honesty, kindness, courage, and patience are all part of character, sometimes learned from a father or mother. When a country is run without a budget in place for four years, debt, doubt and decline worsen the outlook of how some people judge a president's character. They don't like being told by authority that consumers are spending more money because they feel great, when they are spending more money because prices have gone higher. Combining this with a welfare mentality of underclasses who feel entitled to redistribute money from successful businesses, and you get a worsening jobs outlook. A president undoubtedly influences some of the beliefs and values of the public to his very identity.

Over the course of the summer several of the neighbors brought their sons and daughters for visits at the Hobson House while Jane and Sandra were working on it. Jane seemed happier and she was fitter than ever. Neighbors remarked how responsible and talented Sandra was, and how nicely she and Jane seemed to get along. Mother and daughter did get along. Their love for each other was especially evident when both women watched old reruns together at night. Sandra loved sharing her laughter watching old syndicated shows with immensely funny episodes, such as Carol Burnett desperately trying to find something to wear on a date, and then appearing before the audience on the stairs wearing a set of green and brown curtains, hanging rod and all. "That's a beautiful outfit," says Tim Conway. "Thanks, I saw it in a window and I had to have it," says Carol Burnett.

Sandra really was a fun and ambitious girl. She worked at the retirement community waiting tables and cooking in the kitchen during morning shift, and helped her mother rehab the house in the evening. In the early afternoon on weekdays, she sat in a lawn chair resting in front of the house, listening to the birds chirp and glancing intermittently at any cars or trucks that drove passed the mailbox. Her mother's new boyfriend, Stuart, had undertaken stripping the old asphalt shingles and gluing down architecturally esthetic slate pieces on the roof. He did some electrical wiring and repaired a porch light too. Jane and Sandra were happy for the help.

Something became apparent to Sandra that summer working on the Hobson House, something she had been only vaguely aware of until then. All this time she thought she was just helping her mother, but in truth she was shaping her opinions about more important things. She was doing just what her parents had taught her to do. Now realizing that her time was important, she thought about how she would invest in her community. She pondered a culture overwrought with drugs, wondering if she would ever partake in any underground experiences, or would she always try to rescue others. She had lived her entire life in a small town and had yet to travel far. She pulled out a Kleenex from her pocket and wiped the sweat off her brow. Mostly the way she was, was because of what her parents taught her, and she did not want to feel bad about that, but she was inspired to define who she was and what she wanted to do. Before the end of the summer, Sandra signed up for night classes for the fall semester at the community college in town. Living with her mother, she was able to save a good portion of the money she made at the retirement home.

Arthur had not seen Sandra for several weeks, so he decided to drive out to the old house to check on her. He and Jane were currently on the outs, but he didn't want that to stop him from seeing his daughter. When he arrived, Jane and Sandra were sitting in lawn chairs sipping lemonade.

"So, Jane, the house is really starting to look nice. Have you guys had any time to relax and do anything interesting in your free time?" Arthur asked, leaning against the front panel of his Buick.

Jane considered the questions briefly and then looked straight at Arthur. "No, not really," she said.

"Are you tired of working on the house?"

"No, not really."

"Are you feeling isolated or bored out here near the woods?"

"No, not really."

"Have you watched any good movies lately or gone to any Cardinals games this summer?"

"No."

Jane continued to stare at Arthur with a cold, we-have-nothing-between-us-anymore gaze. "I do plan to go to check what's on television a little later tonight," she finally offered. "What about you, Sandra? You and Mom seem to be getting along well. Have you been enjoying the summer?"

"Dad, Mom has a new boyfriend. His name is Stuart and they met at the grocery store and he will be stopping by tomorrow," said Sandra.

Drawing from past confrontations in his own life, Arthur hesitated, trying not to say too much or too little. When writing speeches, he explained himself with a sense of objectivity, but usually using generalities. In this circumstance, he did not want to get in an argument with Jane or upset his daughter, so he spoke softly and to the point. He hoped his wit and intelligence was enough to calm the situation.

"Love is a subject not understood by many of the brightest minds of society," said Arthur. "Let me know if you need anything, Sandra. I need to get going. I have other work to do at home."

"OK, I love you, Dad."

"I love you too."

Arthur returned to his Buick and drove home.

All the long talks, all the weekend trips to play in softball tournaments, and all the difficulties shared with Sandra in the past had a purpose. The talks were not about proving who was right, the tournaments were not about winning every game, and the difficulties were not about causing suffering. All these experiences were about building respect, overcoming obstacles, and teaching whom to trust. Arthur and Sandra had built a solid father-daughter relationship. The great thing about children is that their loyalties never change while their minds and bodies are constantly changing. But all of a sudden, Sandra seemed all grown up. There was actually quite a bit of change happening all around. The country's president, a black Democrat and a former community organizer, was living in the White House with his family and mother-in-law. It did not cross Sandra's mind to question when presidents began to invite their mothers-in-law to live in the White House on taxpayers' dollars. Jane had a new boyfriend, Stuart, a mustached young heavy equipment worker she had met in front of a mound of cantaloupes in the produce department of the local A&P, for whom she decided to lose more weight. Out went the tie-dyed shirts and the flowery print dresses; in came the high heels, more makeup, and puffy hair. Separated from Arthur, Jane seemed happier than at any time in her married life.

Soon Stuart began spending nights at the Hobson House, shuffling around in a St. Louis Cardinals baseball jersey with his brown leather Wolverine work boots, and before long, he was setting up the attached garage as his private work space with all his power tools, landscaping equipment, and riding lawnmower. A bumper sticker on the back of his truck read, "I'm a Democrat and I vote."

One day while Jane and Stuart were working on the house, Jane plugged in her old metal floor fan, the one with the frayed wire. As soon as she plugged it in, sparks shot out from the electric socket in the wall and she set her hair on fire.

"I almost fried myself plugging in the fan and my hair got singed in front," Jane cried.

"Fiery hair sure stinks up the house," said Stuart.

"You could ask me if I am OK before you start with the jokes," said Jane.

"You knew that old metal fan had a bad wire and you continued to plug it in the wall anyway. What were you thinking? Are you OK?" Stuart finally asked.

"Yes, I'm OK, but I am going to go get my hair washed and trimmed at the hair salon. I'll be back in a couple of hours," said Jane.

"While you're out, why don't you take your little ass over to the hardware store and buy a new fan. Considering that summer is almost over, fans are probably priced dirt cheap now," taunted Stuart, oblivious to her feelings.

"Can't you ask me nicely, instead of telling me sarcastically what to do? Good-bye. I'll be back in a couple of hours," said Jane.

Toward the end of the professional baseball season each year, baseball fans in Rainbow Creek always watched the final Cardinals-Cubs series with added interest, especially if they were in the pennant race. But this year the Democratic presidential hopefuls were debating truly important issues on television, and residents in Rainbow Creek and elsewhere had to decide if they wanted to watch the debates or the baseball game. Arthur had two televisions blasting side-by-side in the living room and his three childhood friends, Gary and Larry Bordeaux and Frank Lambert, were at his house to watch both events with him.

After Arthur tuned in the first television to the debates, one look at the stone-faced people in the audience forced Gary to get up off his chair and walk into the kitchen to look for some chips and dip. He just wanted to watch the ballgame, but the others outvoted him for a spell.

Arthur: "When more viewers decide to watch the game than the debates, it's no wonder voters are so confused about politics."

Frank: "I know why people are confused about politics. Take the tax code. The Gettysburg Address is only 272 words long. You can find over 500 words about American history or politics on the back of a cereal box. A King James Bible utilizes 783,137 words to describe the Old and New Testament, while nearly 4 million words makeup the federal tax code."

Arthur: "We have a lot of things backwards in our country."

Larry: "Did you guys see the recent news broadcast where the reporter announced that poor and needy families were going to be given free computers? Why are poor and needy people given free computers if they are hungry and having a hard time paying their utility bills? Common sense would be to give them food and clothing. People can't eat computers; besides, everybody else has to work and save money to afford a computer, a great tool to own but not a necessity."

Arthur: "If you ask me, these people should have to do some community service in exchange for the free computers. Too often, our government just gives away things without ever thinking about who is paying for it. I guess if the recipients used the computers to search employment websites to find a job, it might be worth it. However, in reality, I think the people will mostly use the computers to play video games. We will just have to wait and see if the computers change anything."

Frank: "Why is it when politicians want the rich and the poor to compromise, it always feels like the average citizen pays for everything? Why is it when changes are made, we are never told what is really happening? Changes always feel like someone in the government is trying to pull the wool over our eyes, in hopes of supporting a secret agenda that takes advantage of the people in the middle."

Arthur: "I don't like the idea of all these highly paid appointees doing work supposed to be done by our elected officials in Congress. Many of these appointees have no military experience and no corporate experience. Politicians need to start acting as if they are spending their own money. Government shouldn't be about increasing spending each year to make it appear like our needs are based on appropriations." Larry: "I agree with you, friend. Some older voters hated the whole mantra of change—any kind of change—from the very beginning. The whole idea of making something different or changing the way people are used to doing something is difficult from the start. Everybody knows that. It is no surprise that change is difficult for Americans unless a new policy offers some benefits for the middle class. The middle class has been paying for everything for fifty years and they are tired of it."

Arthur: "During the economic collapse of 2008–2009, congressional members' wealth increased an average of 16 percent. How is that possible and why was it allowed while banks failed, real estate collapsed, automakers filed for bankruptcy, and investors saw their money disappear? It is as if Congress thinks that no one needs to work for a living, members are entitled, and if you need something, someone else will work to give it to you. It is no wonder people are cynical and angry with politicians. Congress adds pork, funds earmarks, takes bribes, embezzles campaign contributions, and steals money from welfare programs. Politics is supposed to stand for the general welfare of the population, not the welfare of a partial sector of the population.

Gary: "The heads of Facebook and Google, the Yahoo's and the fuck U's, the crooks in Washington and the do-gooders out West don't like it when people curse their policies, but I really don't like the much bigger 'f' word they throw back in the face of the middle class: *fraud*."

Arthur: "It's true. In the absence of a truly fair leader of the middle class, the Tea Party protesters are tired of the paper trail of injustices from criminals paying off the politicians."

Frank: "Some of these politicians must think we are stupid."

Gary: "I remember a time when I had to make a big decision in my life. Life experiences give us chances to find out what kind of people we are. A couple of decades ago, I was a collection agent sent to a young mother's apartment to collect a final payment on an equity loan she made. The young mother could not make the last payment and my boss instructed me to haul away a refrigerator she used as collateral when the loan was established. When I arrived at the apartment, the young mother was standing in the empty apartment holding her nearly-naked baby in her arms. The refrigerator was the only household item gracing the entire apartment. I had a choice to make. Should I haul away the refrigerator to pay off the debt and enhance my own position in business, but put the lives of the mother and baby in more danger, or should I pay attention to the serious reality of the situation and waive the last payment? I decided to choose the latter option and referred the young mother to a friend of mine who worked at the local unemployment office, hoping he could help the young mother find a job and childcare assistance."

Arthur: "Gary, you followed your heart. What you did was commendable. Too many people today are willing to walk over their grandmother for a fast buck. This is America and we are supposed to pride ourselves on our democracy, because we believe in honest work by honest bankers and businesspersons and an honest government with honest politicians. Real growth and prosperity will come when we stop the corruption. Certainly do not throw more printed money at the problem, because all this does is put off the inevitable, a devalued dollar and a problem that has not gone away. Build on what we have; do not tear it apart and redistribute it. There is a lot at stake."

Larry: "When you think about it, change isn't such a prophetic word. Change is part of everyday life, and no matter how one tries to resist change, there really is little one can do to stop most of it. But a few generations ago, the founders of Rainbow Creek learned that people don't like being preached to about supposed changes that are really just lies." With that the men turned their attention to the ballgame and the bowls of pretzel sticks and potato chips that Gary had brought back from the kitchen.

Gary: "Did you guys know the last time the Cubs were in the World Series, it was 1908 and there were only 6,120 fans in the stands."

Larry: "My brother memorizes a lot of weird baseball things. Since he's a Cardinals fan, he likes to rub it in to the Cubs fans every year."

Frank: "He's a baseball fan."

Gary: "Did you guys hear about the strange ending in the Detroit-Cleveland game the other night? The umpire blew a call that robbed the Detroit pitcher of a perfect game. With two outs in the ninth inning, the batter smashed a ground ball to the first baseman. Replays showed that the pitcher, covering at first base, got the throw from the first baseman and touched the base one stride before the runner, but the umpire inexplicably called the runner safe. To the pitcher's credit, he never said a word to argue the umpire's call and just proceeded to retire the next hitter. I think the missed call will eventually bolster the performance as the greatest game ever pitched, because the pitcher really retired twenty-eight batters, not just twenty-seven."

Frank: "I hope it goes down in history that way. Then, because the umpires never changed the call, a bad situation is turned around into a great situation, and the legend will get better every time the story is told."

Arthur: "What's amazing to me is the way so many fans keep supporting team owners that meet the outrageous demands of agents and star players. This is the story that someone should tell. The best hitters in baseball are now paid one million dollars per homerun, which is hard for me to understand. I used to love the game of baseball as a kid, and my dad taught me to appreciate the civic benefits of citizens rooting and supporting their local franchise. That was back during a time when it was easy to cheer for the home team. Too many things have changed."

Frank: "I agree with you, Arthur. While athletes entertain us for a few hours, there is nothing productive about their work that warrants them making such outrageous salaries."

Arthur: "It's getting harder to root for triple-digit multimillion-dollar athletes, especially those who cheated by using steroids."

Frank: "Professional athletes don't provide needed critical services, manufacture tangible products, or save lives. Yet, not only do they make outrageous salaries to play games, they make huge dollars for endorsing products and services. Commercials using professional athletes are so trite and phony. Why should an athlete get to tell others how to live, what rules to play by, and what products to use just because he makes a lot of money?"

Arthur: "I agree with you, Frank. A person with a background in medicine, science, education, business administration, social services, or health services offers a more intelligent discourse on matters concerning politics, health, new products or services. To many fans, the greed in sports has ruined their enthusiasm for the game. No athlete is worth hundreds of millions of dollars."

Frank: "Remember when all we cared about was playing ball on the sandlots and working on our old used cars together. Those were the good old days."

Gary: "With all the faults in sports—points shaving, game fixing, spying on other teams, dog fighting, gun incidents, athletes fighting in the stands, selling drugs, accusations of rape and even murder—fans continue to support professional teams. Though the mistakes haven't been good for the image of the games, the money continues to flow into the sports industry. A guy does wonder sometimes how it will all play out. ...

"Hey, did I just hear one of the debaters say, 'We need to pass this bill so we can find out what is in it'? That is unbelievable. These politicians must really think we are morons."

Frank: "I think the politician who said it is a moron."

Arthur: "What do voters want, more government or more jobs? What do voters want, one big government controlling all sectors of our lives or more opportunities for members of their families?"

Frank: "The government is acting moronically and now they want to limit the size of sodas, the number of chips in a snack bag, and the weight of a hamburger patty. Come on, folks. When is the intrusion in our lives going to stop?"

Arthur: "Government intrusions always start small before growing to unbearable levels. In the beginning, the first US income tax in 1861 to finance the Civil War was proposed at 3 percent. If you're paying attention, you'll see the same 'start small' approaches while you watch the way the Transportation Security Administration and the Affordable Care Act programs keep becoming more expensive."

Frank: "It's spooky, but almost natural; to think our officials are scrutinizing our every move in a dimly lit room under the streets of Washington, DC?"

Arthur: "Men who have effectively fulfilled political office have been practical, paid attention to national consensus, made a connection with the people, and have told the truth. From Washington, to Lincoln, and most recently Reagan, presidents who were able to earn the trust of their citizens were the leaders who effectively ran our country."

Frank: "When a politician says, 'The true engine of growth will always be like a certain company,' and the company goes belly up, he loses trust. Maybe he should have said, 'Let me and my friends take your money for four years, then we'll disappear completely from your lives.' Distorting logic to mislead people is insidious to me."

Larry: "Have you guys ever noticed how people in power pick their fights. Take the animal rights issue, for example. The powers that be will go after all the little old ladies wearing their fur coats, but they are OK with big bad bikers wearing leather jackets and wealthy aristocrats driving expensive cars with leather seats."

All of the men in the room nodded in agreement. Frank shook his head. "It's a real shame," he said.

The debates ended, Gary was allowed his wish of watching the end of the ballgame without the distraction of politics. The Cardinals beat the Cubs 2–1 in a pitching duel. The win put the Cardinals one game out of first place, but for the true-to-form last-place Cubbies, there is always next year. Leaving to go home, Arthur's good friends shook his hand and thanked him for his hospitality and the lively conversation.

The Rainbow Creek citizens who followed politics were starting to hear more about the Tea Party, which was initiated by Trevor Leach. The chairman of the Young Americans for Liberty in New York organized a "tea party" to protest an obesity tax proposal and call for fiscal responsibility on the part of the government. Several of the protestors wore Native American headdresses similar to the band of eighteenth-century colonists who dumped tea into Boston Harbor to express outrage about British taxes.

Other political protests against the unlawful—in fact, unconstitutional—force of power from members of Congress in the form of bailouts of enterprises that had engaged in acts of criminal activity were forming in cities across the country. The indictments from angry Tea Baggers were not limited to the executives of the nation's largest banks and brokerages. The corruption intertwined through Fannie Mae and Freddie Mac to ties with members of Congress, from stockbrokers selling worthless pension fund securities to judges who protected money interests on Wall Street and the president's order to print more money because spending was far above revenues. The Tea Party was started to bring awareness about the corruption of American politics and the blatant theft of money from taxpayers. Tea Baggers wanted politicians to show responsibility and judges to enforce the laws against any person responsible for robbing and pillaging hardworking citizens. Though at the beginning, the grass-roots movement was composed of a loose affiliation of national and local groups determining their own platform of conservative complaints, great organizational leadership helped the Tea Party evolve into an obey-the-Constitution agenda. The sightless determination to force an unconstitutional stimulus package through a mostly Democratic Senate and then the House of Representatives was a financial death knell for millions of Americans who hated the bill. Thousands of these Americans protested in freezing conditions in Washington, DC, in hopes of making their voices heard. They made signs with red, white, and blue markers, held American flags high, set up table displays to hand out literature, and went about their business of spreading their important middle-class message to the early media circles.

With one and a half billion Internet users in the world and forecasters predicting an increase to five billion users within five years, Tea Baggers thought it was an opportunity to hasten their approach so that "We the People" felt part of the process again and others around the world might watch with a newfound respect for Americans. The need for a more practical and pragmatic approach to progress was a common theme shared by those who hoped for a more prosperous economy and a better educated population. Entrepreneurship built America in the past and Tea Baggers were asking businesses to start showing the entrepreneurial spirit again to help create jobs. They were asking government to stop legislating rules and regulations that were curbing the creation of new jobs. The government was now spending six times more money on building prisons than it was on education, even though it is common knowledge that a majority of crimes are committed by individuals high on drugs and alcohol. If the Tea Party had its way, this spending ratio would be reversed, because people who know better, do better. Too many major campaign donors ended up with the business contracts, political appointments, and tax breaks. The word for this kind of governance is "cronyism."

All of these ideas were filling Arthur's mind these days. He was so busy preparing speeches and overseeing a sunroom addition on his own house he didn't have time to worry or complain about what was going on at the Hobson House. When Jane finally called him, late in September, after several months with Sandra refurbishing the old Hobson House, she wanted to know how Susie was adjusting to the new arrangement.

"She is doing fine and stays busy with her studies and her job. She isn't home right now, but she wanted me to tell you she received an early acceptance to the University of Missouri."

"That's great! Tell her I am proud of her."

"How's the house coming along?"

"The loud noise has died down, and now Sandra and I are concentrating on the finishing touches on the inside. You know, sponge painting and decorative wall painting and those types of things. We enjoy the girly stuff, colors and patterns, and finding knick-knacks to brighten the ambience."

"Well, I'll tell Susie you called and I'm sorry you missed her, but I need to get back to work. The director at the community center asked me to prepare an after-school presentation on the dangers of cigarette smoking to a group of teenagers tomorrow."

"OK, good luck with that. I'll talk to you later and send my love to Susie."

By 3 p.m. the next day, Arthur was standing behind a podium in Meeting Room B at the community center watching as about two dozen teenagers filed in. Arthur waited until everyone was seated and then began his talk.

Good afternoon, everyone, my name is Mr. Hobson, hope you all are doing well. I won't beat around the bush. Smoking is a bad habit. By the start of 2007, an estimated 45.3 million people in the US still smoked cigarettes. For most smokers who could go back in time and change a few things, one of those things would be to never pick up their first cigarette. While it may be too late to reach the people who have been smoking for twenty-five years or more and who probably don't have the intention of quitting anytime soon, it's not too late for you.

Of all the states, Missouri spends the least amount of money on antismoking ads. At issue is a strong debate on whether smoking bans lower health costs. Many argue that a major part of our country's increased health costs are a consequence of extending peoples lives suffering from chronic diseases. Others argue that health insurance isn't for every bruise or scratch; it's for people insuring against catastrophic conditions. But isn't smoking one of the major reasons for the onset of these diseases?

The additives used in the manufacture of cigarettes are something every smoker should know about. The list of nearly six hundred ingredients had long been kept a secret until citizens groups and health officials began to apply pressure in the 1980s and 1990s. American Tobacco Company, Brown and Williamson, Liggett Group, Phillip Morris, and R. J. Reynolds Tobacco Company finally submitted the information to the Department of Human Services in the mid- to late 1990s. Because of all the pressure put on tobacco companies by health officials wanting transparency regarding everything about the making of cigarettes, a black market now exists for cigarettes similar to the underground sales of street drugs. Millions of dollars change hands from doing business this way in large metropolitan areas every month. Though tobacco companies deny wrongdoing, it isn't unusual for truckloads full of cigarette cartons to mysteriously disappear and later be sold at the backdoors of retail shops and taverns in the inner city.

When a cigarette is burning, more than four thousand chemical compounds are created from the different combinations of ingredients, many of them toxic and/or carcinogenic. Carbon monoxide, nitrogen oxide, cyanide, and ammonia are all present in cigarette smoke. Forty-three known carcinogens are in mainstream smoke and secondhand smoke. Cigarettes are delivery systems for toxic chemicals and carcinogens that cause a wide range of illnesses, including cancer, emphysema, and heart disease. What happens with heart disease? The walls of the coronary arteries become damaged by inflammation caused by toxins in cigarette smoke that latch on to white blood cells and LDL and form a plaque that obstructs blood flow and oxygen delivery, a condition known as angina. Plaque eventually builds to a blood clot, which blocks blood flow, causing the heart muscles to stop.

Arthur paused there. He felt like he had grabbed the attention of the teenagers and he knew he better, because teenagers can make an adult feel like a flea on the hindquarters of a dog, about to sit down on the ground and scratch the pest into oblivion. Before Arthur returned to his presentation, an overweight boy stood up and spoke. "Hi, my name is

Albert and I know, some people call me Fat Albert, but I don't like it when they do. Mr. Hobson, as you can see, I'm somewhat overweight and I started smoking in hopes it would help me cut down on eating snacks, so I don't gain more weight."

"There are much better ways of controlling weight than by smoking, Albert. Proper diet, exercise, finding hobbies, and other lifestyle changes are better ways to curb weight gain, and they don't put your life at risk. Thank you for the participation." Arthur continued.

Cadmium, a chemical found in batteries, is extremely poisonous and when it is inhaled through a cigarette it can cause kidney damage. Tar is an ingredient found in roads and tires as well as cigarettes. A two-pack-a-day smoker inhales one gram of tar a day, which amounts to a quart of thick, gooey tar inhaled in a year. Toluene, commonly found in glue, is also found in cigarettes. It is a toxic substance that produces euphoria, but also irritation of the airways and lungs. Cigarettes also contain naphthalene, a main ingredient in mothballs. This proven poison causes reproductive and brain cell breakdown. Arsenic, used to kill rats, kills people too when they smoke it. It causes irritated lungs, abnormal heartbeat, and a score of other symptoms. Acetone is an ingredient found in nail polish remover as well as cigarettes. It is a harsh chemical that irritates your lungs and leads to cancer. The toxin phenol, found in plastics as well as cigarettes, can cause kidney and liver damage and reduced blood pressure, resulting in severe sickness and possible death. Ammonia, often used as a fertilizer as well as in cleaning supplies, speeds the delivery of nicotine to smokers and changes the reading of tar when used in cigarettes, making it seem lower.

It is amazing the amount of poison that exists in one cigarette. Tobacco companies add flavor to hide the dreadful additives, increase addictiveness, and improve taste. Filters on cigarettes are just a marketing ploy to trick consumers to think they are smoking a safer cigarette.

But the list goes on. Butane, DDT, formaldehyde, methoprene, and polonium are also added to cigarettes. The main use for butane is in lighter fluid. DDT is a banned insecticide. The main use of formaldehyde, ironically, is to preserve dead tissues. The main use for methoprene is in insecticides. Polonium is a cancer-causing radioactive element. Methyl isocyanines, when accidentally released at a manufacturing plant, killed two thousand people in Bhopal, India, in 1984.

If the illnesses associated with smoking aren't enough of a deterrent, consider this. Companies are starting to think twice about hiring smokers, even for outside workers, because of the added health risks and time wasted on the job. By hiring a smoker, companies subsidize the two hours of work per week wasted from lighting up. More time will be spent sweeping up cigarette butts and emptying ashtrays. Companies that do hire smokers have designated smoking areas and only allow smoking during breaks and lunchtime. Recent trends of many municipalities show that their citizens support a ban on smoking inside commercial or public buildings.

In addition, smokers pay more than nonsmokers for life and health insurance policies for obvious reasons: smokers are a bad bet. Further consider the rapidly increasing costs of cigarettes. People pay upwards of nine dollars a pack for cigarettes in New York City. At a pack a day, that's sixty-three dollars a week or more than three thousand dollars a year on a habit that could kill you! No matter how you look it, it is time to quit smoking.

Thank you for coming to my presentation and good luck in the future concerning all of your choices. Stay safe and have a great evening.

The group of teenagers clapped at the conclusion of Arthur's talk and a few of them walked up to shake his hand and personally thank him for the new awareness of subject matter presented to them. Arthur was proud to have contributed at least a little something to a concern that was close to his heart.

The newly built sunroom at the back of Arthur's house on Hill View was like a plant nursery, with glass sides, a tightly woven nylon carpet covering the floor, and a tan plaid asphalt shingled roof to match the house. Arthur referred to it as the "reading room" because besides the collection of great-smelling indoor plants assembled throughout the fifteen-by-fifteen-foot room, he had stacked his favorite books on wedge-shaped book-cases in all four corners and moved his favorite leather lounging chair there. One shelf of the bookcase Arthur saved for displaying a dinosaur, a turtle, a cactus, an angel, and a dish all made out of clay by Susie while she was in kindergarten. Arthur cherished these items and wanted to keep them in full view because he thought each work of art was way beyond expectations for such a young girl.

The day after he gave his presentation on smoking to the teenagers at the community center, Susie had helped him plant geraniums with red and white flowers and shrubbery to form a barrier from the wind and sun next to the air-conditioning unit. There were no obstructed views, and before long, the neighbors were complimenting Arthur and Susie on the sunroom and landscaping design. Some of the neighborhood moms, who never said hello to Arthur before, heard about his smoking presentation and now waved when they drove by the house. In the old days, Arthur had always been great with kids, teaching them softball at the nearby ball field, shooting hoops with them in the driveway, showing them how to draw animal caricatures—but now most of the kids in the neighborhood were in high school or away at college. Arthur was finding more and more ways to fill his days, but whenever he had time, he enjoyed drinking a cup of coffee in the sunroom, peering out the windows at any birds in the trees or small animals running across the backyard, and catching up on his reading.

Arthur labored like a workaholic so he could pay his bills, offer support to others at the community center, help Sandra with car expenses so she could get back and forth from community college, and save money to help send Susie to college in just a year and a few months. He always had been a good father and taught his daughters many things to deal with the real world even though his marriage was failing and he often tried to do too much.

Arthur was a decent man, but one of his weaknesses was that he spread himself too thin. He was interested in everything and the diversity of the subject matter of the books he read supported this observation. Arthur had his father's physicality and facial features, thin ankles, thin hair, thin eyebrows, blue eyes, and a tongue that stuck out at the left corner of his mouth in moments of concentration. His father saddled him with the presumption of success, preferring that he would rather err on the side of high expectations than low ambitions, hoping that Arthur would give him something to cheer about someday. Arthur would not have had it any other way. He'd begun his career at a metal manufacturing plant as a sales representative reporting to the corporate office, but he'd tired of always feeling shunted from making decisions, always needing approval from higher-ups to get anything done. On Hill View, he was always telling his neighbors about manufacturing plants he visited and how manufacturers made certain popular products. After eleven years of meeting with buyers, design engineers, and production managers, Arthur walked away from the job as a sales representative for stock and custom-made metal parts. Nobody suspected Arthur of harboring any feelings of discontent; he just was more enthusiastic about politics, writing, the environment, and giving talks at the community center and any other place where people would come to listen.

Months passed without much fanfare for any members of the Hobson family living in Rainbow Creek, as they all seemed to be adjusting to their new living arrangements. Arthur was settled into his daily routine of writing, speaking to local businesspersons, and working long hours at the community center. Jane continued working on the Hobson House, but was now enjoying many of the improvements along with her boyfriend, Stuart. Sandra had little free time, but she was happiest when she stayed busy. Susie was excited about her upcoming plans to live on her own and attend the University of Missouri.

Knowing that Susie would soon be going off to college, Arthur tried to stay neutral on any discussions that might stir emotions between him and her during the summer months. After Susie left home to study, he wondered if she would ever return to Rainbow Creek to live, or would she accept work in a far-away place. Once she graduated from high school, Susie spent the summer waiting tables at the busy All Sports Grill, sharpening her people skills and gaining confidence in helping solve problems. Arthur, who did not ordinarily brag about his own two children, vouchsafed to strangers how proud he was of Susie's accomplishments so far. She stayed clear of drugs and alcohol, held a job over the summers, kept her grades high, and had been accepted to start her college career studying biological sciences at the University of Missouri. At the same time, Sandra was making plans to buy her own condominium and leave the Hobson House, where she had been living with her mother for nearly a year. Jane's feelings were hurt and the two women were arguing more and more. Sandra wanted her independence and Jane knew how much she would miss her daughters.

The year before, in 2008, Congress started the first-time homebuyers' tax credit to help boost the economy and support the banking and housing markets. The program was supposed to help first-time homebuyers like Sandra buy a house. Under the plan, the Treasury offered an eight-thousand-dollar tax credit to qualifying shoppers. But many first-time homebuyers, including Sandra, experienced delays in the processing of their tax returns and their claims for the tax credit. The Treasury Inspection General of Tax Administration stated in an audit released shortly after Sandra filed her tax return, "The IRS continues to lack sufficient controls to stop erroneous and fraudulent claims for the first-time homebuyer tax credit." According to the audit, almost two million taxpayers received nearly $13 billion in tax credits under the program, including an estimated 14,132 individuals who received fraudulent credits totaling nearly $28 million.

Reports on television and all over the Internet showed some homebuyers got the credit before the tax break even went into effect. Some working teenagers who did not purchase a home, fraudulently claimed the first-time homebuyer credit. Some parents claimed the credit under a child's name. Nearly three thousand erroneous claims totaled nearly $24 million in credits for taxpayers who purchased their homes before the effective date of the credit. Nearly fifteen hundred prisoners, some serving life sentences, took in more than $10 million in fraudulent claims for phantom home purchases, and a large number of duplicate claims were filed under different names for the same home. In one case, sixty-seven taxpayers used the same home purchase to claim the credit. It was uncovered that even some government workers filed fraudulent claims from inside job positions. The first-time homebuyers' tax credit did help more than two and half million people who filed legitimate claims. However, the Internal Revenue Service will have to spend millions of dollars taking steps to try to fix this mess and enforce more legal actions. Dishonest people and corruption, pushing America in the wrong direction and bruising its reputation, once again ruined a program that could have been great for this country.

By the time Sandra finally received her income tax check in July, Susie had settled on a place to live, a studio apartment she found listed on the Internet. The university had an arrangement with the leasing agents at a large complex that housed incoming freshmen, current undergrads, and graduate students. With scholarship money, help from her parents, and the money she had saved from working as a server, and if she lived modestly, she could pay her bills.

In Rainbow Creek thousands of hardworking middle-class families struggled to live even while bringing in two or three incomes. A generation ago, the typical Rainbow Creek family lived on one income. Now it seems even two or three incomes are not always enough to pay the rapidly rising costs of housing, food, transportation, health care, and college while trying to save for retirement. Many middle-class families, though their earnings are broadly defined, had little room to wiggle if something catastrophic happened in their lives.

Arthur was more relaxed these days but he loved staying involved in his daughters' lives, and even he had to admit all these new living arrangements kept him away from all the whining and bickering from the old days. "Sandra makes all her own decisions now that she is living on her own," Jane often said. Jane did not tell Arthur that Sandra was letting some young man named Tommy move in to her condominium. Arthur would have loved if Sandra had confided in him about the arrangement, asking questions about subleases, financial considerations, sharing expenses, and rules of the condominium association. Arthur would have felt that he and his daughter were on the same page and he would have worried less, but she never approached her dad about the new boyfriend moving into her condominium. Arthur always explained things to Sandra when she was a little girl, especially when she was asking lots of questions. Now he wondered if he had answered enough of her inquiries. He worried if she would pay for all the groceries or would this person pay his fair share of the food and other expenses. Arthur was concerned because he was considerate and he paid attention to details. Who would do the dishes, take out the trash, clean the bathroom, scrub the floors, vacuum the carpet, do the laundry, and pay the bills? Arthur knew that Sandra was generous, but was this Tommy person generous too, or was he the kind of person who mooched until he wore out his welcome and used up everything he could? Arthur had a bad feeling about this person and he had not even met him yet. He also knew that Sandra was a grown woman and she made her own choices now, but he still wished in some ways that both his daughters were little girls staying in his house, safe and responsible, instead of vulnerable to the perils of the world. Moreover, at some point in their young adult lives, Arthur figured his two daughters realized that their parents are human and they make the best decisions they can with the options available to them. He wanted his daughters to be honest about what they wanted and then go for it.

In the summer months prior to Susie's going away to college, Arthur tried to find books about the real causes of poverty, but his search revealed little. He wanted more done to address what he was certain was the real cause of poverty, the abuse of drugs and alcohol. He wanted more done to fight crime in our cities and punish cheating politicians. He wanted to know more about why brilliant leaders begin careers with great and noble ideas, but end them as social failures. Everyone has faults, but Arthur hated when politicians purposefully hid information, did not explain it, inadvertently said something else, or acted indifferent as to whether their words meant anything or not. The vagueness and sheer incompetence of so many elected officials, acting as if nothing can stop the government, made him sick.

As soon as the Tea Party raised questions about certain topics, the concrete melted into the abstract and neither members of the media nor officials of the government seemed able to think in terms of speech, which made sense. Therefore, the public stayed confused about bad policies and problems never fixed. Everything the politicians were doing as cloaked in secrecy, far away from every registered voter.

Reflecting again on his childhood for a moment, Arthur remembered what his father taught him about mudslinging. He said, "Mudslinging is not merely a disturber of the English language, it is a destroyer of hope for our children."

Arthur was grateful to Sandra and Susie, and he always welcomed them back to his house. He often told them this too. He was glad his girls behaved like grownups and were not the kind of women who threw hissy fits over every little thing or always acted as if they were the victim. He hoped Sandra would call him once a month to invite him over to her condo for a delicious home-prepared meal because all that experience in the kitchen at the retirement community made her a great cook. He hoped Susie would call to invite him to make the two-hour drive to Columbia to play a round of golf or take in a college football game. Her college apartment sat on top of a hill overlooking an eighteen-hole golf course. A shuttle bus took students back and forth from strategic drop-off points on campus. All those arguments and fights when the girls were little and none of them seemed to make any sense now. Arthur and Jane yelling about stupid stuff, trying to gain a little power over each other in front of the kids, and before either realizes it, both children are gone and the closets and drawers in their bedrooms are empty.

As a college student living away from home for the first time, Susie found ways to save money. She lowered the thermostat, shopped at discount grocers and dollar stores, and consolidated trips to run errands in an effort to save gas. She bought nearly new clothing at secondhand shops and she used her worn-out clothing, not good enough to donate, as rags so she saved money from not needing to buy paper towels. She reused bags, bows, boxes, jars, plastic containers, buttons, and other items, mostly because she treasured these kinds of things during the college experience. She paid her bills online, saving money on stamps and envelopes. To her, the popcorn popper was almost a necessity for late-night snacks. She signed up, at a charge of nine dollars a month, with Netflix for easy unlimited access to more than a hundred thousand new and classic movies through the mail; she and her friends, who came over for movie night, took turns paying the bill.

Because Susie's apartment was small, she occupied the space with creativity and only the things she needed most. She stacked large plastic containers full of pants and oversized sweatshirts high in her closet. Jackets and dresses hung on the only rail in the closet. Her portable seventeen-inch digital TV set sat on top of her DVD player, which sat on top of a black wooden particleboard nightstand that she assembled herself. The books on her shelves were about strange places, wilderness lands, self-help reads that turn a person from good to great, consumer buying guides, and expository science works concerning living organisms and bacteria. Everything about her adolescent years was beginning to feel faint and far away. The one thing there was not much in the way of was food in the refrigerator or snacks in the pantry. At first, Susie's only food supplies consisted of a package of instant Spanish rice, a six-pack of diet Coke, unpopped popcorn, and a one-pound box of saltine crackers, all the sort of stuff that satisfied her for fifteen minutes and then left her even hungrier. It occurred to her, after three weeks of eating fast food, she actually needed to shop at the grocery store so she could start cooking for herself.

Arthur was sad about Susie being away, but he now had more time to devote to research, writing, speaking, and politics in general. Further, he was beginning to formulate a plan to run for mayor. He even officially joined the St. Louis Chapter of the Tea Party.

One night, reading a particularly thought-provoking article, it occurred to Arthur that some presidents and senators believe that since the wealthy have prospered at the labor of others, their money does not really belong to them. He wondered if big corporate profits were a measure of how effectively the wealthy had ripped off the rest of society, especially if corporate headquarters were relocated overseas to avoid taxes. With that belief, whatever taxes levied against the rich would be automatically justifiable. However, in the real world, he decided not all corporations acted this way, and the middle class did seem to pay most of the taxes on things.

Arthur researched relationships between big business and all political parties in American history and tried to figure out why failed policies did not work. Almost every time, he concluded corruption got in the way. The Federalists, Whigs, Dixie rats, Independents, Libertarians, Democrats, Republicans, Green Party followers, Socialists, Communists, Reformers, Progressives, and the leaders of the Labor and Union Parties all were guilty of legislating corrupt monetary policies to gain favor with the most successful businesses of the time.

Arthur believed a president must support the common good of all the people, not just big business, and not just themselves. The three elements of the common good are respect for life, improving the well-being of citizens, and peace in the homeland. Presidents make decisions about how much control the government should have. The American public listens to see if a president keeps his promises and they get angry when they are lied to, tired of promises made just to gain votes. They do not like it when a politician explains only the favorable part of a new policy to push a bill through. When leaving out important details of an explanation, it feels like the president pulled the wool over peoples eyes. They want all the facts of the big picture presented and then they want to use their individual intelligent thoughts to vote on making a decision about an issue.

Barack Obama, after only five months of experience as the US senator from Illinois, declared his candidacy for president, the most powerful position in the world. Obama's favorite slogan was, "Are you fired up? Let's go change the world." Arthur believed a better slogan would have been, "Are you fired up? Let us go make the world a better place. Some things don't need changing." Nevertheless, this is America and American voters decide their issues and their candidates at the polls. As a reminder, when we elect our presidents, we elect human beings with all their foibles and weaknesses. On November 5, 2008, Barack Obama became the 44th president of the United States of America, on a widely used theme of "Change has come to America." Voters hoped this president would enhance their lives. Arthur's friend Frank hoped the president would just tell the truth. Frank decided to call Arthur at home that night.

Frank: "Hi, Arthur, how are you?"

Arthur: "I'm good, just watching programming about our new president."

Frank: "That's what I'm calling about. I remember when your mom used to try to teach us that truthful lips endure forever, but a lying tongue only endures for a moment. I hope the president was telling the truth when he promised to cut the deficit in half. Instead of making promises to voters, I wish the president would tell our mayor to quit wasting local dollars to benefit his union friends."

Arthur: "Unions once made promises to big businesses too. At the beginning, when unions were building this country, their representatives bargained for safe working conditions and decent wages. However, their ever-increasing demands put massive pressures on businesses. Eventually, bargaining agreements became so good that workers started taking early retirement. Their pension pay packages allowed thirty-year employees to draw nearly as much money retired as they made while working, collecting checks for the rest of their lives. These types of pensions became unsustainable, running big businesses into the ground. With massive pension expenses on the books, many American auto manufacturers and other Fortune 500 factories closed, some bulldozed into oblivion."

Frank: "Even with all the lost jobs and closed plants in Rainbow Creek and around the country, labor union officials still use union dues to try and sway elections. They even borrow money to do so."

Arthur: "The practice of a politician supporting unions starts looking like a quest to abolish the private sector and make every American worker a government worker."

Frank: "Never in the history of the US has big business had to deal with so many demands. Until politicians, unions, and the private sector work together, big business will continue to keep a freeze on hiring."

Arthur: "So many career politicians have never run a lemonade stand, much less a national economy. What do they know about creating jobs for Americans?"

Frank: "I tire of politicians who earn their riches in a rigged government-dominated market, a system called crony capitalism. Then they pass more laws to take care of their friends and fellow politicians so they can exercise more influence and more power."

Arthur: "All this does is give an excuse to healthy men and women in the prime of their lives, who are struggling to find a job, to apply for physical disability and other types of aid. When all the trends in safety and technology should have meant a decline in physical disability payments, the government has dished out a sevenfold increase in recent years to people claiming they are unable to work."

Frank: "To all these politicians who keep telling us that government spending will expand the overall economy, why can't they tell us the truth? Their policies will shrink the private sector."

Arthur: "The one sure thing in raising a teenager is that they're still seeking guidance and they need structure and safety, and if a parent is only being their friend and not telling their children the truth, a parent can't create that. It's too early to judge, but the promises for all this *change* has a confusing beginning. The best intentions are sometimes fraught with disappointment."

Frank estimated his profits to be twelve points lower than the year before running his leasing business. He attributed much of the decrease to the costs of meeting compliance issues mandated for the automobile industry. He saw how the burden of regulation was especially high on small businesses, the real job creators and means of recovery during recessions.

For a president professing during the campaign that he has the answers to save the economy, a $50 million inauguration seemed exorbitant to Arthur, triple what taxpayers spent at George W. Bush's first inauguration. Celebrating the election of a new president is nice, but common sense tells us that much of the money could have gone toward more productive uses. The excitement of the election results and the reception galas that followed had an exhaling influence on Mrs. Obama as she announced, "For the first time in my adult lifetime I'm really proud of my country, and not just because Barack has done well, but because I think people are hungry for change." This was an unfitting announcement coming from the wife of a former state senator and now the president of the United States. Did she forget about all the brave soldiers fighting in Iraq and Afghanistan and past wars or how the country came together after the terrorists' attacks on 9/11?

From the beginning it appeared that the new Democratic administration was full of young staffers who might miss the boat by not realizing that the inside fight in Congress is very different from the outside fight of gaining the support of the people. Young staffers sometimes make mistakes in a rush to put their own stamp on history. When a president loses several inside fights, he focuses more on the issues from the opposing party. The differences of opinion and the widely differing proposals perpetuate public confusion, which leads to even less support for the president. The people the president chose to surround him will determine the quality of advice he receives and the goals implemented. "Americans can live with a politician who makes small errors in judgment but not large errors from the heart," became a foremost argument in Arthur's speeches to help build his mayoral platform.

Just as Arthur was sitting down to rewrite one of his speeches about the tragedies occurring today in the black community, the phone rang.

Sandra: "Hi, Dad, I am just calling to see how you are doing. Are you doing OK?"

Arthur: "Yes, I'm doing fine. I always enjoy when either of my daughters calls me to chat."

Sandra: "I like the word 'chat.' It sounds so hip, like maybe you are ready to start 'texting' and 'blogging' your views in a chat room."

Arthur: "Hey, we used the word fifty years ago, before computer technology was even a glimmer of anyone's imagination."

Sandra: "I know that, Dad. But seriously, do you think you will keep trying to improve your computer skills?"

Arthur: "I am improving a little at a time. I e-mail, search the Internet, and have a Facebook page. If I was still a young person, I might think about going back to college to study cyberspace security. The US needs more graduates trained in mobile payments, intelligent electricity grids, cloud computing, and electronic health records. The Department of Defense, financial institutions, retail stores, hospitals, universities, businesses, and power utilities need protection from cyber crime. Firms that specialize in cyber security are pulling together threads to form a strategy that will stop the three levels of cyber corruption, exploitation, disruption, and destruction of communication systems."

Sandra: "It's true, opportunities are vastly increasing for those with skills in cyber security. I read where businesses and government have spent more money the last two years in the area of security than they have in the history of our country, and with limited success. Many more talented data security specialists are needed to keep up with the exponentially growing numbers of criminals on the other side of cyberspace."

Arthur: "Just use your imagination about the possibilities."

Sandra: "Hey, I just remembered something funny. Did you watch Wanda Sykes last night?"

Arthur: "No, I didn't. What was it about?"

Sandra: "Well, she talked about the black Barbie Doll and compared it to the white Barbie Doll. She said African Americans are complaining that Walmart is charging less for the black Barbie Doll. She said they should stop complaining and be happy to save a little money now, because they will spend lots more on clothes, weaves, and nail products for the dolls in the future. It was hilarious. I wish you had seen it."

Arthur: "She is a funny lady; I wish I had seen it too."

Sandra: "If Dr. Martin Luther King Jr. were still alive today, do you think he would still feel the same way about everything today? Would he feel blacks and whites have done enough to eliminate racism in our country?"

Arthur: "There are still white people who don't like black people and there are still black people who don't like white people. Dr. King said, 'We cannot walk alone … ' Everyone has to do their part to diffuse politically charged rhetoric and racism when it rears its head. We all need to pay more attention to bizarre and disruptive behavior and the red flags that get ignored until a tragedy occurs."

Sandra: "Why do you think racism still exists? It seems to be more of an issue with people your age, not so much with my generation."

Arthur: "Some people, especially political figures, might not want to abolish racism because talking about it is part of the agenda that made their careers. Complaining, playing the blame game, and using the race card are tactics lawyers sometimes overstate, overplayed by politicians and no longer genuine in today's diverse society. The influence of minorities is part of all major circles. President Obama is the leader of the free world, Oprah Winfrey practically oversees the business world running her own network and promoting her favorite things, and Lebron James, Kobe Bryant, Albert Pujols, Alex Rodriguez, Tiger Woods, and Venus and Serena Williams garner much of the attention in the sports world."

Sandra: "Would you say wealthy, middle class, or poorer neighborhoods have the worst racism?"

Arthur: "Middle-class and poorer families are struggling in many towns and cities in America right now. I think some people use racism as an excuse. If an individual fights hard enough to get an education and works hard enough to show an employer he or she is an asset to the company and can help the business make money, anyone can be successful. Most successful people can tell you about the times when they sacrificed or had to make difficult decisions. They can tell you stories about working two jobs to help pay the expenses of starting a new company. They can tell you about a period when they were working full time while going to college full time."

Sandra: "I guess things aren't always how they are portrayed."

Arthur: "You told me about the Wanda Sykes episode. I was watching a *South Park* episode not too long ago where they did a spoof of *Wheel of Fortune*. Three contestants had to try to guess the seven-letter word from a category called "People who annoy others." Toward the end of the round, two white contestants refused to guess the word even though the Vanna White look-a-like had already turned over all the letters except one. The puzzle read N _ G G E R S. When the one black contestant's father yelled 'NIGGERS' from the audience, the host of the game show said, to everyone else's amazement, 'No, that answer is wrong, and please, audience, do not call out any more guesses.' The final letter was an A and the black contestant guessed the word, N A G G E R S. I thought that was really clever."

After a few more minutes of catching up, Sandra said she was off to a hair appointment and they hung up. Arthur smiled and returned to his writing. He wanted politics to be about fairness and qualifications, not skin color. The civil rights movement of the 1960s changed the landscape and made it so that African Americans, Caucasians, and all nationalities can live next to each other, go to school with each other, and work together. While Reverend Sharpton and others were traveling around the country spreading anger, Arthur donated one hundred dollars to an advocacy group wanting to build a statue near the library in Rainbow Creek. In memory of the Dred and Harriet Scott Decision in 1857, the statue was to be a reminder of the end of slavery. To gain anything worthwhile takes time and it might be time to make a collaborative effort to change things again. Arthur felt that maybe we should no longer have exclusive public events such as Miss Black America, the Black Repertory Theater, and black newspapers. Maybe we should no longer have it both ways. Reverend Sharpton would not be happy with Miss White America, White Repertory Theater, white-only newspapers, or segregated events for white-only anything, but maybe it is time our leaders stop exploiting the idea of a racist society.

The Tea Party followers started asking questions like, "When are we going to get away from having two sets of rules for ethnic groups, allowing certain individuals to choose the set that best fits their situation at the time? One hundred and two years of the NAACP and political rallies under the guise of the national coalition on black, civic participation for African American political power seems like enough time for everyone to get the message. Shouldn't our political rallies include participation by American citizens of all income levels and of all races and religions?" The Tea Party was against any form of government that only looked out for one race or one sector of the population and they wanted real answers. Maximizing social harmony is a goal of any government, but Tea Baggers just wanted fairness, not more policies forcing them to surrender their strongly held religious beliefs, pay for everybody else's conflicts, and costing them more of their hard-earned money.

Liberal media folks put a spin on the beliefs of the followers of traditional conservatism, meaning the Tea Party. Liberal journalists wrote that the Tea Party cheered for executions at prisons, and because they opposed health care reform, they shouted, "Let them die" to the individuals who faced life-threatening illnesses without any medical coverage. Though there were isolated incidents of this type of conduct by outer fringe groups, liberal talk-show hosts told viewers that Tea Party followers were anti-government, anti-Muslim, anti-science, anti-fun, and anti-changes represented by a president with dark skin. Tea Party Patriots told citizens the extremist group organized in the woods with an entire network of ammunitions had nothing to do with their organization, but still liberal zealots compared Tea Party followers to civil rights protestors who threw bricks at windows and looted stores. Any occurrence anywhere of screaming, rock throwing, or fighting, the zealots blamed on the Tea Party. Tea Party rhetoric was the reason for fires ignited during droughts in the West. The truth of the matter is that the Tea Party just wanted a responsible government, and they wanted an end to the runaway spending and outrageous mounting national debt. Everything was changing and no politicians were listening to the people who were paying for all the changes. The people paying for all the changes wanted their country back.

Arthur, along with the rest of the middle class, was realizing through the massive growth of communications technology that there is a much larger connection of suspicious activity between rackets created by Wall Street, regulations by government, lobbies of big business, and the illegal drug market than once suspected. All of these forces were creating ways to take more of the working man's money. The owner of a Laundromat or a self-employed construction worker should not have to work eighty hours per week to make ends meet. Workers fed up with more regulations wanted to put an end to deceit and corruption. As people took a harder look at patterns of recent history, they noticed some of the same rackets kept occurring. The Tea Party was telling politicians they refused to put up with bad politics and bad behavior any longer. They were wise to the dishonest power grabs of the men and women in charge. They were lashing back by changing their spending patterns, living with less, and deciding which cheating politicians they wanted out of office. They were listening to think tanks and joining rallies. They knew that if you are taught to think for yourself, you don't need a president trying to sell every step of his agenda to change our minds and try to justify what he is doing when the will of the people doesn't agree with him. It is no wonder that Americans became suspicious when our government began printing money or President Obama flew overseas to ask Chinese leaders to devalue the yen. It is no wonder the Tea Party wanted accountability when military and homeland security take up half of the federal government's operating budget and the bureaucrats awarding the rebuilding contracts are the owners of the companies getting the work. The Tea Party did not feel the government was exhibiting transparency when taxpayers were forced to bail out big financial institutions and the executives who caused the fiasco kept their high-profile jobs, no one went to jail, and then later the executives gave themselves huge bonuses again.

What has happened to the middle class? What has happened to the American dream? The Tea Party wanted answers to these two questions because income had decreased for a decade, the value of the dollar was down, and it was much harder to save for children's college, harder to stay in a house, and harder to save for the future. They were convinced too many congressional representatives were lobbying for Wall Street and not for the American people. The United States ranked nineteenth out of twenty-two countries, near the bottom of countries with the worst corruption, according to a CNBC report that aired on October 26, 2010. At the top of the list, Denmark, New Zealand, and Singapore have the least corruption according to the report.

Smartphones sped up the Tea Party Express, once considered just a small grass-roots organization. It appeared to Democrats that some of the characters running under the Tea Party banner were just entertainment for many Americans. Tea Party candidate Sharon Angle, running for US Senator in Nevada, demanded that government stay away from health care, even as she and her husband receive health care through the federal Civil Service Retirement System. Meg Whitman, the Tea Party candidate running for governor of California, talked about the devastation caused by illegal aliens, causing lost jobs, even as she has had to confess to hiring an "illegal" as her own house cleaner for the past nine years. Delaware's Tea Party candidate, Christine O'Donnell, campaigning under the theme of a "saner government," once bragged about dabbling in witchcraft at a satanic altar.

Reverend Sharpton declared Martin Luther King Day "Our Day," meaning black America's day, when Tea Party members organized a political rally on the same day. Some say making political statements on such days as 9/11 and Martin Luther King Day is wrong. Some say doing it on these days bring more attention to a cause. What makes America great is that we rally around a cause without bombing buildings or killing masses of people that disagree with us. Change-the-world idealism that supports worthy causes for all of us will better suite Americans than rebellious protests of ideals against one race, religion, or some other identity.

American voters decide their issues and their candidates at the polls. The Tea Party wanted more from its candidates. Tea Partiers did not want more sound bites; they wanted better ideas with substance. They wanted to hear more about saving Social Security into the future and ways to get the unemployed working again. Smart politicians started listening to patriotic Tea Party speakers who truly wanted to hear intelligent ideas from authentic campaigners who didn't dodge controversial issues and weren't afraid to take a stand, instead of giving standard answers to questions without any convictions.

In comparison to most of the intact families in the neighborhood, the new Hobson arrangement was working as well as if not better than most of the others. One woman, Ann Kratchet, who lived at the south end of the Rainbow Creek neighborhood, liked to talk to Jane when they met on the street, but they were not friends. Ann talked whether anyone was listening or not. She was known to spread rumors about her husband's anxieties, Jane's mental health, and the overwhelming struggles of Sandra and Susie, along with any other neighborhood gossip she could dream up. She herself was unhappily married and seemed to be trying to bring everybody else down to her level of unhappiness. Now that Jane had moved into the Hobson House, she didn't run into Ann as often, but one day Jane stopped in to the Rainbow Creek grocery store and found herself standing next to Ann at the huge watermelon display.

Ann: "Jane, what have you been up to? I haven't seen you. It's not true you moved out, is it? That's really a shame. You know, I was watching the news the other day and they were talking about terrorists and I immediately thought of Arthur. Have you ever noticed how so many anti-American radicals wear American-branded clothing, listen to music made by American artists, watch movies with American actors and actresses, and travel to American hospitals for medical care? Did you and Arthur hear about that terrorist who was questioned by Congress? His name was Abdullah Ibn Abdull Aziz Bin Abdulrahman Bin Faisal Bin Turki Bin Abdullah Bin Muhammad al Saud or something like that. I can never keep those names straight."

Jane: "No, I must have missed that on the news."

Ann: "A man who carries such a name only wants to confuse and speak some form of a sophisticated dying aboriginal language of his own. Terrorists don't pay their taxes, but if they did, a tax accountant would have fun trying to keep this name straight on all the tax forms."

Jane: "I don't follow politics as much as my husband does, but I'll ask him about the long-named Middle Eastern man next time I see him."

Ann: "Why does your husband even get involved in all that political nonsense, anyway?"

Jane: "You'll have to ask him, Ann."

Jane mostly stayed away from the more populated and busier sections of Rainbow Creek, hibernating at the Hobson House during a long stretch of snow and one of the coldest winters in fifty years. She stayed away from get-togethers in the old subdivision where her baked cookies were once a big hit. She refused any invitations from old classmates or softball moms for a night out, but she did like to drink a glass of wine or two in the evening while watching her favorite TV shows and having what Arthur imagined was less than earth shattering, mundane, unsatisfying, and boring sex on the couch or in the bedroom with Stuart. Maybe he imagined it this way because he wanted to believe his way of doing things was more politically erect when describing his own sexual congress.

For all her homeliness and skills around the house, Jane had never really felt close to anyone before, including Arthur during her entire marriage to him. She was starting to feel much differently about her relationship with Stuart. He became the prince of Jane's life, as she was wide-open to his flirtations and his charm of appearing to love everything he said or did. She swayed to his view of liberal politics, believing in everything the Obama administration tried to push on the American people, and especially Stuart's spin on the reasons why the policies made sense. This was her way of making Stuart feel important. Joe Biden, Nancy Pelosi, Hillary Clinton, and the Carnahan family could easily influence the new couple's way of thinking, as if they belonged to a cult for welfare politics. Stuart was especially excited when the administration extended unemployment benefits, which helped him collect a weekly paycheck during the extremely bad weather when construction workers and landscapers were laid off.

During stretches of bad weather, when Stuart was unable to work construction outside, he stayed home and tried to charm Jane like a politician tries to charm the citizenry. "Carpeting is the toughest floor material to keep clean. But I will get rid of all the dust particles, mites, and allergens from down deep in the fibers of all of the carpeting in the rooms where the carpeting does not have to be replaced," Stuart told Jane one morning during a torrential downpour. "Before doing anything, it is a good idea to follow the manufacturer's recommendation when cleaning carpets, either by using a freshwater steam rinse or a dry extraction powder," he told her. "For the rooms that need new carpeting, I recommend rolls of a carpeting product called 'Bliss by Beaulieu. Factory workers make this carpeting by using a technology, which prevents bacteria from growing while absorbing odors, allowing the house to smell fresh. Coupled with the Ecstasy Pad makes this carpeting the kind you will want to roll around on." That afternoon Jane placed enough Bliss carpeting for all the rooms in the Hobson House, and of course, all the carpeting she ordered contained tints of her favorite color, green.

Too much rain, sleet, and snow played havoc on the minds of people living in small towns like Rainbow Creek. Bad weather upends their routines and brings chaos to their daily lives. It plays havoc on watersheds, utilities, businesses, schools, and household schedules too. Snow and ice hinder driving for everybody in town because the municipality does not have as much heavy-duty snow-plowing equipment as the big cities do. For his part, Arthur spent the cold weather months researching politics so that he could make informed decisions. Instead of beating his kids, suing his neighbors, or cussing at citizens when they disagreed with him about politics, he tried to find out all the facts by deeply submerging himself into his work. He was getting more involved with the St. Louis Chapter of the Tea Party and working more hours and leading more projects at the community center. He used this time to energize himself as he continued to plan his run for mayor. The more involved with the community he became, the more sure he was that this candidacy was the right decision.

6

Faded Memories
of the Sandlots

Young Arthur had luck and God on his side. Through the skilled hands of Dr. Robert Murray, the good Lord blessed him and saved his life. When Arthur was just fourteen years old, Dr. Murray removed a baseball-sized tumor and two feet of Arthur's large intestine—a brand-new and risky operation. For the first time in his life, Arthur witnessed greatness firsthand. Inspired by the doctor's patience, professionalism, focus, determination, intelligence, ability, and passion for his work, Arthur knew he wanted to apply some of these same traits to whatever career path he chose.

Arthur had high energy as a child, which accounted for his frame staying on the thin side, allowing him to run fast and develop better than average athletic skills. By the time he entered college, his bigger appetite and devotion to a daily weight-lifting routine added thirty pounds of muscle to his frame. His surgery had not slowed him down.

Arthur's first memory of playing sports with his friends was at the sandlot. In faded years past, so many young boys played baseball in their backyards and on sandlots across the country that today when they go to a major league ballpark, it feels like coming home.

A half-century back in time, sandlots existed all across America, but very few of them were as special to Arthur as Ronnie's Field, which was managed by a friend, teacher, and coach named Mel. In the early '60s, Ronnie's Field was the meeting place for a group of boys who had their own secret ball club. If you were a boy between the ages of ten and sixteen and lived on either side of Church Road in Rainbow Creek, you qualified to play. The wide-open field was a place where the boys played ball every day of the week during the summer and sometimes on the weekends.

Frank, Kevin, Arthur, Johnny, Gary, Larry, Victor, and a dozen other boys from the neighborhood usually showed up at the sandlot during the warmer days of summer to do what they loved to do—play ball. Some of the boys who were focused when they were on the field playing ball seemed a little lost off the field, but their lives felt bolstered by the integrity taught by Mel.

Before a game, the older boys took turns measuring the distances between bases, chalking the base lines, and staking the ends of the foul lines on the first and third base sides of the field. A long rope tied across from stake to stake provided a home run boundary. Using their dads' lawn mowers, the boys cut the grass extra short in the infield, but let the grass grow a little higher in the outfield.

Evergreen bushes, maple trees, and oak trees lined the chain-link fence that separated the field from Ronnie's Drive-in. The fence provided a respite area for taking a break in the shade. Between games, a couple of players would jog to a nearby gas station and buy a few pops to bring back for everyone to share. The boys used this time to restring broken webbing of a glove or tape cracked wooden bats back together. It all worked on the buddy system. If you needed a dime for a pop, someone gave you one, because all that mattered was that everyone got refreshed, so the boys could play another game.

At first, the pickup games drew a handful of kids from both sides of the neighborhood. Then a few weeks into the warmer weather of August, Frank and Arthur, two of the older and more respected boys in the neighborhood and born leaders, started a telephone chain and organized the meeting time each day. Soon the secret ball club grew to more than thirty boys from the neighborhood. Some rode their bikes from two miles away, with their baseball gloves hanging from the handlebars and baseball cards popping against the spokes.

Mel, a young, beloved schoolteacher, umpired, coached, monitored the games, and taught the boys good sportsmanship. He was left-handed, but he still managed to catch and umpire while overseeing the game and making sure the boys laughed from time to time. During the school year, Mel taught at a tough midtown institution in St. Louis, so he was certainly qualified to chaperone any group of young boys out in the suburbs. He did it for free and without fanfare. The boys loved Mel and they had fun playing ball while staying out of trouble. They played when they wanted and for as long as they wanted, and they played for the love of the game.

Sandlot ball is almost nonexistent today. Organized Little League baseball organizations have replaced the sandlot games of the past, with fancy uniforms, signed consent forms, expensive equipment, concession stands, restrooms with electricity and indoor plumbing, outfield walls with advertising, board supervision, and a limited number of scheduled places to play. The baseball season is now shorter as athletes shift from one activity to another. One thing is for sure: the kids today are not having any more fun than the boys from the sandlot era had.

Ronnie's Field was a very special place where there was no clock. Arthur and the other boys forgot about their worries and just played baseball. The former sandlot is now a parking lot for a bar and grill, a movie theater, and a shopping plaza. Today Ronnie's Field is gone, but the kids who played ball there still tell stories about their experiences on the sandlot.

Arthur had put in a long day, and after he said good-bye to the last of the stragglers at the community center, he locked the doors and gathered his things to make the twenty-minute drive home. When he walked in the front door, Susie, dressed in green sweatpants and a large white T-shirt, was sitting on an oversized floor pillow with part of her focus on homework and part of her focus on the harsh noise blaring from the TV. She was back from Mizzou for a few days to visit.

"Hi, Dad, how did your day go?" Susie asked.

"OK," shrugged Arthur. "The number of visitors today was small, but the people who were there had nice things to say. How did softball practice go?" Arthur asked.

Susie looked down at the floor. It was obvious something was bothering her. "Do you think I've been happy with my life playing sports lately?"

"I don't know. Sometimes it is difficult to gauge the mood of teenage girls."

"Dad, I used to love softball, but now I'm starting to hate it," Susie said, crying. "I hate all sports."

Arthur sighed. In an effort to console her, he put his things down on the kitchen table and came back to hug her, although he was still confused.

"I'm a very good left-handed pitcher," Susie said. "I run as fast as anybody on the team. I can throw a change-up and a curve ball. Not many girls can throw a true under-handed curve ball."

"I can tell you are really upset—tell me the whole story," Arthur said.

"Well, when I first tried out for the team, I truly thought I was as good as any of the pitchers in the tryouts. I had played a lot of the girls when I was on the traveling team and had beaten all of them. But there are two other pitchers on the team—one girl is a senior and another girl is the wrestling coach's daughter—and there are a lot of politics involved when the coach decides who takes the mound during practice and games. Since I have been the coach's choice to sit the bench for varsity games, and occasionally play outfield for junior varsity games, I never know which team I'm on and the changes feel like a big demotion."

"I understand why you feel the way you do," said Arthur.

"I'm having a hard time building any friendships with my teammates too. Last Saturday there was a miscommunication about the schedule and I didn't think our team had a game, so I made plans with a friend from class to attend a football game. When another girl from my team told Coach I was seen at the football game when I was supposed to be at our softball game, I was forced to apologize in front of the whole team the next day at practice."

"Sounds like things have become messy. You know I'm not the kind of father who makes big donations to a school to win favors for my daughters. You know I'm not the kind of father who runs to the coach to solve my children's problems. I remember how much fun you and I had when we took some of those road trips to small towns for summer softball tournaments when you were younger. They were like minivacations for both of us. It sounds to me like softball, which was such a love of yours as a little girl, has become more of an irritation to you now. Any decision about softball, ultimately, is yours."

Though good left-handed pitchers were a commodity, Susie wasn't happy. She wasn't being given a chance to pitch or play much for that matter. She thought about her options. The next morning she headed back to college, and as soon as she got on campus she walked into the coach's office, returned her clean uniform, and quit the team. That was the last time Susie played organized softball. Arthur thought about all those days he and his daughter played catch in the yard and all the evenings they practiced pitching under the street lamps. It was too bad she was giving up something she had worked so hard for. Though some parents may have tried to force their daughter to continue to play, Arthur wanted Susie's decision to feel right, and he wanted her to take ownership of it.

Now that Susie wasn't playing softball, she became more interested in her studies and becoming part of the millennial generation's newest workforce, an optimistic bunch of seventy-five million kids. This generation is technically literate like no other workers in our history. Technology has always been an important part of their lives. They understand computers, notebooks, cellular phones, the Internet, digital cameras, and text-messaging devices. Like most young people from her generation, Susie was very good at multitasking, having juggled sports, school, and social media interests as a young teen. She worked hard, but she expected structure anywhere she studied or worked, and she was hopeful of even helping rewrite some of the rules. She and many young people like her acknowledged and respected positions and titles, and wanted a working relationship with their boss. This desire doesn't always mesh with this generation's love of independence and hands-off style, but Susie figured smart bosses know how to find the strengths of each employee by personalizing their work. Susie and others her age have one thing in common: they are relatively new to the professional workplace. Therefore, they are definitely in need of some mentoring, no matter how smart and confident they are. Susie responded well to personal attention because she appreciated formal mentoring with set meetings and plenty of feedback. She liked lots of challenges as long as the structure was in place to break down goals into steps, and she was offered the resources and information she needed to meet the challenges of her work.

Susie always had many interests, but nothing as intense as her love for animals. Her love for animals started at a very young age when Arthur would take her along to hit golf balls at a driving range ten miles from home. The owner of the driving range, Jeff Dalton, loved animals too and he allowed his domesticated canines, felines, and other pets to roam freely in a large fenced yard off to the side of the driving range. Families were fascinated by the arrangement because while parents hit golf balls, their kids played with the animals under the supervision of a hired conservationist agent who taught the children about pets and wildlife. Susie's two favorite animals were a black Lab with only three legs named Three Putts and a gray potbellied pig named Mud Hazard. Three Putts lost a leg after a speeding driver clipped the dog's hind leg. Dalton had witnessed the dog trying to cross a two-lane county road on a rainy night, and after the accident he had taken him to the All Pets Veterinary Hospital, where the Lab's leg was amputated. The speeding driver never turned back to check on the animal. Dalton agreed to care for Mud Hazard when a resident brought the potbellied pig to him because the animal grew too large for the man to keep concealed at his apartment. Mud Hazard loved to lie on the ground on his side and let children scratch his belly with a hand broom supplied by the conservation agent. Susie had her own pets to love also. She always had a smile on her face when she returned home from the driving range and saw her yellow Lab, Lacy, waiting for her. Susie loved her dog and often took Lacy for walks around the neighborhood and down a trail to the park.

Susie, like a lot of people who heard the story, cried when she learned of the black Lab that had walked down the aisle at the funeral mass for his owner, a Navy Seal killed in a helicopter crash in Afghanistan. The Navy Seal was laid out in his casket draped with a US flag. As the dog approached the foot of the altar, it let out a sigh and lay down on the floor to be next to his master. What Susie did with the rest of her free time when she was in high school was as vague as it is for all teenagers once they get their driver's license. She had lots of friends, including a special boy in her life, but according to her it was nothing too serious. She sometimes referred to a great movie she had gone to see or a great new song she heard on the radio. She really liked Kelly Clarkson and Carrie Underwood, who both seemed to understand how teenage girls felt about things. Her collection of music wasn't large, but when either of these two American Idol winners released something new, Susie rushed out to get it.

One Saturday morning, listening to the softer side of Underwood on her CD player and sitting over a plate of bacon and eggs, Susie asked her father, "Dad, I know we live in a decent neighborhood, but why are Northridge High and the Rainbow School District always so poor and always asking for tax increases? Whenever I visit another school, it always seems to have better technology, better libraries, and better facilities. I thought our schools had a relationship with the community and helped keep everybody's home values intact."

"That is a very observant but difficult question. Although the school district does get some revenue from sales taxes and new construction, there is not much undeveloped land in our area. Our district is mostly a residential territory with less than the average number of homes per square acre mainly due to so many big backyards. Because of that, the reality is our schools lose a small part of their budget each year due to inflation. Because there aren't a growing number of developments or houses to be taxed, each person has to pay more or volunteer time to help make up for the increased costs," said Arthur.

"Does our school get much money from the government?" asked Susie.

"With the changes in national education policies, more than four-fifths of our district's money must come from local sources, greatly depending on our residents to provide the means to fund the education of the students. Some school districts in Missouri have large office complexes, industrial manufacturing facilities, big stadiums, and corporate businesses that generate significant amounts of revenue without adding costs for educating any more students. You didn't know that I knew so much about the costs of education, did you?"

"No, but I thought you may have some ideas," said Susie.

"I don't know what all the answers are at this point, but it is something that needs more attention. I do know that the administration at Northridge has been doing more with less for the last ten years. Cuts have been made in salaries, insurance, energy costs, and the number of routes for bus transportation," said Arthur. "Even if a school district were the best district in the state, there are limits to how far any school board can stretch a dollar."

7

Agreeing to Speak

Kay Applebaum, the director at the community center who was known for her advocacy of education, children, and Meals on Wheels for the elderly, called Arthur and asked for his help. Heaven for Kay was seeing the community center full of children learning life skills from qualified instructors and sharing time during lunch with senior citizens. Kay married a doctor at the Evangelical Church on the north side of Chicago and came to Rainbow Creek forty years ago, when her husband took a position in pediatrics at Christian Hospital. Back then the couple was inspired by President Kennedy's request, "Ask not what your country can do for you; ask what you can do for your country." Kay thought motherhood was a very noble occupation, but she wanted to inspire more children on a larger scale, and her biggest dream came true when she was selected from a group of fifty applicants to run the Rainbow Creek Community Center. Seeing people of all ages journeying through the automatic doors at the front lobby of the center made her happy.

"Arthur, I received a phone call from an administrator at the Salvation Children's Home. The home is bringing a group of middle-school children to the community center and the administrator asked if we had anyone who could talk to the kids for one hour about the dangers of drugs. An epidemic of heroin use is sweeping our country. You did such an excellent job presenting your information about the dangers of smoking a while back that your name came to mind right away when I took this call," explained Kay.

"When are the kids supposed to arrive?" Arthur asked.

"Two weeks from today, at 9 a.m.," Kay said enthusiastically.

"Well then, that gives me just two weeks to prepare my talk. I better start working on it," replied Arthur.

"You are the best, Arthur; thank you so much. The administrator will be delighted."

Salvation Children's Home was founded nearly 150 years ago by a minister of St. Paul's Evangelical Church who saw a need in his mostly German Protestant congregation. Many of the children placed in the home at the beginning were orphans found roaming the streets and sleeping in the doorways due to outbreaks of cholera, a fatal disease destroying many families. At the turn of the twentieth century, wealthy members of the congregation donated enough money to purchase a forty-nine-acre apple orchard and build a school and living quarters on a hill ten miles south of Rainbow Creek. Over the years the home began to take in children with emotional problems as well as pregnant teens with no other way to care for their babies. Today the home is called on to help with children who have been kicked out of school for fighting or drug use. Arthur was honored and touched when he was asked to help.

Most mornings Arthur left the house after breakfast to meet his coworkers at the community center to discuss plans for the day before people started arriving for events and activities. Today would be a little different. Today the teenagers from Salvation Children's Home were coming to listen to Arthur talk about the dangers of drugs. Two weeks of preparing seemed to go by fast, but he was ready. When the big yellow bus pulled up in the circle drive at the front entrance to the lobby at 9 a.m., Arthur was waiting on the sidewalk ready to greet the driver and all of the students as they filed by. There were kids of many races and creeds, Caucasians, African-Americans, immigrants from Mexico, immigrants from Bosnia and Haiti, Asian students, physically challenged students and kids with learning disabilities. Arthur found all their differences interesting and challenging. Most of the kids on this field trip were sixth- and seventh-graders. Arthur knew that many of these kids had already experienced serious problems associated with using drugs, binge drinking, sexual abuse, physical abuse, and mental abuse. Some of the parents of these children had exposed them to drugs and alcohol every day before they were sent to jail and their children were ordered by the court to live and go to school at Salvation.

As he was drafting his speech, Arthur talked to health care officials at Christian Hospital who have raised fears of a hidden epidemic of alcoholism among the middle class. Surprising to some, a recent study found they are the biggest drinkers. In fact, 43 percent of middle-class parents exceed the recommended daily limit of two alcoholic drinks once a week. Arthur also spoke with teachers and counselors from social services as well as campus security who worked in liaison with the county police department. The teachers and counselors did not divulge specific information about individual students, but they did discuss the general guidelines of why the children were there and their needs to overcome their anger going forward.

Arthur realized he wasn't there to take sides or sort out all the facts about each child's situation; he was there to educate them about drugs and alcohol. He had a lot of experience working with all kinds of people and he could spot an instigator or a liar in a minute. The one-hundred-seat conference room at the community center was used for all types of events. Today, half of the seats were filled and Arthur began his talk as he always did, knowing how to take control and grab the attention of his audience.

"Welcome! How is everyone?" he began. "Now, most of you think you are totally innocent victims, right?"

A chorus of "That's right" resonated from students in the back rows.

"None of you deserves any of the punishments others are trying to give you and none of you should have to go to classes to further your education if you don't want to, right?"

Another round of "That's right" resonated from students throughout the room.

"You are always right about everything, right? Mommy and Daddy drink and party with drugs and didn't graduate from high school, so that's how it is going to be for you. So what if you have trouble explaining yourself and nobody understands you. So what if the police are always in your neighborhood arresting people. That's because the police are prejudiced against people who have your skin color and there will never be opportunities for people like you. These are the truths and Jesus Christ taught his followers that facts don't lie."

This time the room remained quiet and the students were starting to realize that Arthur was being sarcastic.

"Alcohol and drug abuse is happening on every city block, every rural mile, and every neighborhood in America. It is the biggest reason for squandered time and one of the most hurtful reasons devastating the economy because of missed workdays and lowered production. Little attention is focused on the economic ramifications of alcohol and drug abuse because of the difficulties of detecting and stopping it," Arthur proclaimed, charged up to make his point. He continued:

Family members know the roller-coaster ride of living with someone addicted to alcohol or drugs. Those with dependency problems live their lives in slow-motion and with depleted ambition and energy. Their thinking and feeling are impaired, as is their ability to make rational choices or to follow up on important decisions. Mood swings happen for no apparent reason other than anxiety or paranoia.

The craziness that overtakes the lives of families when a child or a parent or both are abusing drugs and alcohol can feel like a contagious disease. The need to deny the problem of their own family member leads to an epidemic of blame down the road when problems occur, which they always do. Most people have boundaries and are realistic about life, but those addicted to drugs and alcohol can't be relied on when they make promises because they don't tell the truth. They sometimes even brag about being drunk, using endearing terms such as drinking spree, lit, exhilarated, party hearty, happy hour, inebriated, tipsy, pickled, soaked, soused, fuddled, muddled, *and* stupefied. *Because so many people never admit their addiction to alcohol or drugs, it is very important for family members to continually encourage and congratulate them when they do try to stop using.*

No good comes from using heroin, cocaine, methamphetamine, or any other form of street drug. Use of these drugs dumbs down America and destroys families. They are extremely dangerous and expensive. Youth are wasting their money on all these drugs and liquors without considering the amount of debt they will have to face in the future.

When someone is in recovery, all alcoholic beverages should be removed from the home and all medicines and prescriptions secured safely under lock and key. Liquor, drugs, and debt are the main things that cause smart people to go astray. Keeping mind-altering or addictive items out of the house will help lessen the temptation of the addict to use and help to promote a healthier lifestyle.

Since September 11, 2001, we have learned a great deal about the connection between terrorism and illegal drugs, including the fact that our enemies in Iraq and Afghanistan have derived considerable income from the drug trade. This trade not only spreads addiction but is an inherent enemy of lawful order and democracy throughout the world. Just as heroin and cocaine destroy lives, so too do heroin and cocaine trades destroys institutions of law and government. It is the people using drugs that destroy the institutions. Without a demand for drugs, there would be much less destruction of users or institutions. The world would be a much better place for everyone.

Between the years 2005 and 2010, Chicago had the highest heroin abuse rate in the country. Over 100,000 addicts checked into hospitals for treatment during that time. During this same period, 500 people died in the St. Louis metropolitan area alone, from heroin use. White middle-class young adults between eighteen and thirty years of age make up the largest group of users, but no ethnic or social class is immune. That means you are not immune. Don't let it happen to you.

Arthur had been talking for about thirty minutes, and although he felt he had held the attention of the students, it was time to take a break. Besides, his throat was a little dry and he needed a drink of water. He told the kids where the bathrooms and snack machines were and asked them to come back to their seats in ten minutes. Arthur understood that teenagers were curious about things and they want to be nurtured, but they didn't like being lectured to about what they should like or dislike, do or not do, so he took the ten minutes to readjust his itinerary. When the students returned to their seats, he decided to use the rest of the time as a question-and-answer discussion.

"Does anybody have any questions?"

"Mr. Arthur, you think you know so much, you don't know why I used heroin," said a feisty Latino girl named Sofia. "Well, I'm going to tell you why. I used heroin to escape from the pain of reality. My father was also a heavy drinker and a drug user, and when he did not like something my brother or I did, he would punish us by locking us in a storage room in the basement for three or four days. He only came back down the basement once in the evenings to slide a pack of cigarettes and a meal under the door. My brother and I were able to drink water from a faucet protruding from the foundation wall inside the storage room. One time, after my father let us out, I reported the abuse to the police, and a detective arrested my parents and my brother. Foster care split up my brother and me."

Arthur barely hesitated. "I'm glad you are out of that environment you were in," Arthur said, "and I'm sure your life is going to get much better. You have reminded me of a story that I think shows how the police don't always respond the right way. When I was young, I cleaned offices while working my way through college. Late one night, when I was picking up cigarette butts on the sidewalk, near the front entrance of a business, some woman called the police on me because she thought I looked suspicious and was trying to break into the building. The cops showed up and ordered me off the premises. They thought they were doing the right thing but they weren't. They are human too. Now, does anyone else have comments?" At first no one moved. "Would anyone like to tell how they came to be at Salvation?" Arthur prompted. Slowly, a teenage boy named Michael raised his hand. Arthur nodded and Michael began to speak.

"My mom and dad and I live in a big house overlooking the Mississippi River. My parents always buy the latest technology and once a month my dad invites coworkers and business clients over for dinner parties. Since the second grade, I saw all this drinking and socializing, and by the fifth grade I was sneaking around drinking from half-full, unattended glasses of booze. Everybody thought my dad was this successful businessman who was a great guy and liked to have fun hosting parties for his friends and associates. He would walk around the party clutching his drink and making sure all of his guests had a drink too. He was like a little boy who discovered riding a bike for the first time and he wanted everybody else to have one so they could share the experience with him. He didn't really care about the legal age for drinking. I started sneaking liquor out of the liquor cabinet when no one was home. The teachers started to smell liquor on my breath and noticing my inattentiveness in class. The principal at my middle school thought a couple of years at Salvation might keep me sober and help straighten out my behavior and this is the reason I'm here listening to you talk."

"Thank you, Michael, for sharing your story." Arthur looked around the room and saw more hands go up. Each child had a similar story of parents oblivious to how harmful their actions were to their children. After listening to a few more stories, Arthur concluded, "All parents freak out about stuff, try to control situations and do harebrained things, but exposing children to alcohol and drugs is very harmful to them. Recognizing you have a problem is half the battle. You have all expressed yourselves with such confidence and told your stories so eloquently this morning that I have faith you will figure things out.

"Thank you all for coming. I enjoyed our time together. Good luck to all of you and thanks again for attending my presentation."

As the children left the building, Arthur truly hoped for the best for those kids. They had a tough road, but with support he knew they could make something of their lives.

It was the holidays again and Arthur found himself in a new situation. In Christmases past, Arthur's mother would come over for dinner, and sometimes Kevin and Shirley would come too. Susie and Sandra, when they were younger, would put on little skits that they had prepared, while everyone laughed and took pictures, enjoying the festive occasion. This year was different. Jane and the kids were out of the house and his parents had passed away. He was alone.

The day after New Year's Arthur fell asleep after the ten o'clock news. His dreams reminded him that he shared enough of the blame for his divorce from Jane. During their courtship, Jane had been drawn by Arthur's sense of adventure, but during the marriage, she wasn't comfortable joining in when it came to the unknown. She was happier watching from afar and happiest lying alone under a warm blanket on the couch watching television and in front of the fireplace during the winter.

When Arthur first started working long hours at the community center, Jane had an excuse for being tired because she was always driving Sandra and Susie to painting class, dance lessons, Girl Scouts, student council, basketball, cheerleading, soccer, softball, and any other activity the girls were involved in. Jane didn't feel safe letting other mothers or teenage siblings of friends drive her two daughters to activities around town on roads they weren't used to driving on. By the time the three of them returned home at night, and after they finished making and eating a quick dinner at nine or ten o'clock, the girls still had to do homework and wash athletic uniforms and school clothes before they could go to bed.

On weekends when her daughters were little, Jane always made sure to plan girly things at home. They baked cookies and cakes in the kitchen, changed hair color in the bathroom sink, and ate chocolate ice cream and caramel popcorn while watching the latest Disney movie in the VCR. Jane used her energy to maintain closeness with her two daughters, a closeness she didn't have with Arthur.

8 ★

Friendship

Justin liked to visit the Rainbow Creek community center every evening around suppertime before the nightly programs started and the supervisors and workers were to
busy to approach for just small talk. He walked from his home, jumping a neighbor's fence
just three blocks away and strolling down the sidewalk the rest of the way until reaching
the parking lot of the center. When arriving at the center, Justin liked to sit in a chair near
the snack vending machine in the lobby and close to the front desk near Arthur's office.
His first words were usually to Arthur and he would sneak up and speak into his ear from
behind, and before any of the evening programs started, saying, "How are you doing
buddy, I'm glad you are my friend."

Arthur would look up and he always knew who was speaking, "Nice to see you
Justin, hope you are doing well."

"Yes, I'm fine, thank you very much. They need to make you the big boss in charge
of all of the community centers and parks and swimming pools in our county. You are the
most brilliant person here."

"Wow, thank you for the nice compliment."

"They need to pay you more and give you more responsibilities."

Justin deduced this opinion of Arthur after the first time he talked to him during the
grand-opening of the center.

"Funny you say that, but I have been getting more involved with giving talks about
drugs to teenagers and writing political speeches for Tea-Party rallies."

"You need to make sure you get paid good money for your research and opinions,
OK?"

"Well I will see what I can do about negotiating contracts for hire. That didn't sound right, I mean making sure I get paid a decent wage for my time, you know what I mean."

"Yes, because you are the best."

Arthur tried to pay a little extra attention to Justin because his mom wasn't home most of the time and his dad was in prison for a drug offense, and in spite of it all, Justin had ambition cutting grass, shoveling snow, and washing cars for neighbors and he showed interest in his school work. Arthur hated it when he saw older adults giving teenage workers, waitresses at restaurants or sales clerks at the mall, a hard time, always finding fault with something. He figured teenagers should be congratulated for holding a job and going to school, not degraded in front of everyone for not working fast enough because some supposedly more mature person thinks their time is more valuable than everybody else's. So many adults criticize teenagers at first glance in meeting instead of smiling and telling them how much they appreciate their help.

Arthur didn't know the names of all the people who visited the community center, but most of them knew his because he was genuinely interested in their lives, their struggles and their successes. Admittedly though, it was easy for others to remember who he was because his name appeared on all of the activity brochures he designed, in stacks on the front counter in the lobby. Under glass on the wall in the lobby were the rules for all visitors who entered the building, rules Arthur created to help keep a safe environment at the center. Pamphlets about dance groups, volleyball leagues, basketball schedules, yoga classes, political meetings and other social events, all designed by Arthur, filled the clear rectangular hard-plastic pockets nailed to the wall.

After a cool windy night full of sporadic rain showers and high elevation lighting strikes, and a particularly busy shift at the community center, Arthur was glad to be home and finally able to sit in his favorite leather lounge chair to relax. He turned on the TV and listened to a recording of this morning's show, "The president and his White House staff are unaware of the Tea Party and the president will hold a press conference today," reported Dan Hearns on a replay of *Good Morning America*. Chuck Todd, an American journalist, chief White House correspondent and political director of NBC News, dismissed the Tea Party by saying, "Their ideas really haven't caught on." Arthur couldn't believe what he was hearing. He knew Todd as a contributing editor to "*Meet the Press, NBC Nightly News,* and *Hardball with Chris Mathews*. He remembered him as a contributing editor to *Countdown with Keith Olbermann*, before Olbermann resigned, tired of bickering and hearing what politicians say when they are on their soapbox, then watching a polarizing shift in attitudes and unable to accomplish smart policies. With all his experience and all of his appearances on these shows, to underestimate or to refuse to acknowledge the Tea Party was a huge mistake according to Arthur. To not even acknowledge the Tea Party was a slap in their faces, as if views were being forced on them without giving them any time for their voices to be heard. The comments fueled the fire and Tea Partiers started dreaming about even loftier ideals for growing their movement.

So many people of the Tea Party felt like they were ignored. When people don't like a president's style, it doesn't mean that they disagree with everything the president is trying to do. But when people feel ignored by a president and a spin is put on their politics, they don't even want to listen to him talk anymore, because in their mind, there are no good things happening.

The Administration was so busy trying to get things done; they stopped paying attention to the people. President Obama took some responsibility for this failure, but Tea Partiers still wondered if he really gets their message. He seems to take the Utopian route when forming his agenda, categorizing his thoughts into good, bad and wishful policies, regardless of what others think. Sometimes it feels like the intelligence of the American people is being insulted. The President said he is disappointed that he didn't spend enough time trying to sway us on his policies. Maybe an increasing number of people just don't like his policies. He calls for other people to start practicing civility, but his careless use of words offends people. Calling members of the other party "enemies" when they don't agree with him polarizes political parties instead of bringing them together. The road back for our politicians is to focus on specific details and practical fixes of problems instead of more talk to garnish votes for the next election. Arthur thought politicians needed to earn trust and genuinely apologize when they make mistakes. The old metaphor for the middle class, "Don't cry or we will give you something to cry about," doesn't work anymore.

With the president's success winning the election by gaining the support of young voters, it is questionable whether they are still paying attention to many of the issues. When Arthur heard young people say the decisions of the government don't really affect them, he knew they were not paying attention. He is certain we wouldn't want our brave young soldiers to hear them say that either.

A wall of issues to worry about is always present for any president. A much trimmed down version of the healthcare package passed without real bi-partisan support. Global warming discussions mainly faded away mainly due to so much focus putting a stop to the BP oil leak on the Gulf Coast. Education reform meant mostly education cuts. The wars in Iraq and Afghanistan hit seven years since their start, though some combat forces left Iraq to help in Afghanistan, while support troops stayed in Iraq. Bank bailouts that were supposed to save the housing market and the economy have done little to help the double-digit unemployment rate.

Arthur knew much about history and totally respected the freedom riders who fought for change and civil rights issues in a non-violent manner, but he didn't like the way longtime rebel rouser Reverend Al Sharpton forced his beliefs upon others. From what he gathered from all the information sent out from various media sources, including *Good*

Morning America, CNN, 60 Minutes, Media Matters, New York Times, and *Washington Post,* President Obama was building a friendship with Reverend Sharpton.

Reverend Sharpton didn't pay nearly three million worth of state and federal taxes he owed until he was caught cheating the government. He never apologized for walking hand-in-hand to support a young girl who made a bogus claim saying four white police officers raped her back in the 60's.

Near the turn of the century, minority infrastructure contractors wanted more of a piece of the pie when it came to work on bridge projects in St. Louis. The complaints raging from the black community and the chief executive officer of Kwame Construction caught the attention of Reverend Al Sharpton. In meetings with protestors, Reverend Sharpton was persuaded to join in a plan to shut down the highway guaranteed to gain a national audience. The plan called for protestors to line up next to each other in cars, gradually slowing down in all lanes of eastbound traffic on the interstate winding through the downtown area of St. Louis. The cars came to a stop and were met by hordes of protestors on foot. All told, an estimated three hundred protestors took to the highway that morning. Almost half of them, including Reverend Sharpton, were arrested and charged with disorderly conduct. Luckily there were no traffic accidents or injuries reported because of the highway shutdown. It would have been a bad morning for an ambulance using the highway to try and transport a patient to a hospital.

A decade later, businesses and state officials have awarded more minority contracts. But past experience of firms working on large projects, quality, and meeting the standards of contracts still have more weight than awarding work based on skin color. Some of the protestors have acknowledged progress was made and there are better ways to address inequities than resorting to some of the old methods used.

It might seem only a fantasy, but Arthur thought, "Wouldn't it be nice if terrorists, instead of blowing up infrastructure all over the world, used that energy to build infrastructure all over the world. Regions in the United States, the Middle-East and China sure need new roads and bridges. Think of all the people who would benefit. Think of all the international companies who benefit when they ship steel, commodities and other products needed at the work sites in these regions. Then lastly, the regions benefit as they receive goods and services faster and easier because of their new roads and bridges. New communities rise out of the ashes and next to the roads as they did during the U. S. Industrial Revolution after World War II."

Arthur was upset when he heard that President Obama appointed Reverend Sharpton to a post as one of his top-advisors on education. Sharpton, who made his career traveling around the country playing the race card, is one of our nation's most controversial people. All of us can learn from philosophies of a half century ago, but philosophies are different today. It is true Arthur once made the comment, "Why isn't Reverend Sharpton doing more to see that African-American males go to college and graduate?" Any moron knows influencing more African-American males to attend college is more important than re-shaping educational policies in another attempt at a fast fix only benefits lobbyists or Washington. Arthur didn't like the continuing premise to keep giving everything away for free to people who don't seek out the tools they need to further their own careers and succeed in the business world. But empowering an old-fashioned black Democratic leader who made a living "enslaving" the African American citizenry by selling ways to dependency on welfare programs and continuing to teach them that they are victims, didn't sit well with Arthur.

Whether he was wrong or right, Arthur became perplexed when politics veered away from fairness and qualifications and towards skin color. Though he was cognizant of the existence of a segment of people in the population who still lived as bigots, he refused to give them additional power by talking about their racist beliefs. African-Americans, Caucasians and all nationalities live next to each other, go to school with each other and work together. Slavery was abolished over one-hundred-and-forty-years ago and thanks to the courage of Dred and Harriet Scott, the 15th Amendment of the Constitution, the last of three landmark amendments that abolished slavery in the U. S., guaranteed citizenship and the right to vote to citizens regardless of "race, color or previous condition of servitude." When President Ulysses S. Grant signed the measure, four million former slaves and free African Americans at once were declared eligible voters. It took nearly another hundred years for 'Civil Rights' to change the landscape again. Nobody will ever know for sure how long President Grant or Martin Luther King thought it would take for the world to be free from tribunals in other lands who bind their people to lesser rights as citizens.

Like everything Arthur wrote preparing for a speaking engagement, at first, half of his notes seemed genius and half clumsy and bad to him. But because he had such a high level of perseverance, by staying the course and tapping the keys on his computer late into the night, his works always seemed to come together. No matter what the topic, once his speech was ready, he always sent invitations to the appropriate audiences, hoping they all would attend to listen to him talk. From the miscellaneous account, he was usually in position to pay his friend Justin a fair wage to help fold brochures, stuff invitations and stick stamps and address labels on envelopes. The invitations went out to hundreds, sometimes thousands of residents in Rainbow Creek and surrounding municipalities. The weather turned warmer and Arthur gave his first Tea Party speech of the spring at the meeting hall adjacent to the Sleepy Hollow hotel in town.

"The government estimates that already 60% of all Americans now receive more in welfare benefits than they pay into it. When our forefathers wrote our tax policies, everyone was expected

to pay payroll taxes, but today only 47% of American households now pay federal income taxes, according to the IRS.

What is it that has caused spending by the government to increase so exponentially in the last two years? Overall, according to the Congressional Budget Office, Washington is spending 23 percent more today than it did two years ago. This is quite an increase given the concern about deficits, all the financial troubles of European countries and all the talk about financial responsibility by the administration. The directions of the increased spending have not caused the unemployment rate to lower. The increased spending can't all be attributed to the Iraq War which has tapered way down over the last several months, or the bank bailouts which we are told will be paid back.

It is time to revert back to some of the policies that built our country, investing in our small businesses, facing up to corrupt politicians and not re-electing them, and doing everything we can to create jobs that pay good wages for work that helps create a better planet. The lies and greed of big government and big business must be stopped. Federal legislation where the details are penciled in after the bill is signed isn't honoring the peoples vote.

Taxpayer dollars should not be spent to reward failed companies to advance America's lobbying interests. History tells us that infrastructure spending, such as Dwight Eisenhower's Interstate Highway System greatly stimulated the economy. Improving our infrastructure puts people to work. Safe roads and bridges lower the freight costs for business delivering products to market. Military research and development and incentives to small businesses are what helped develop the internet into the information super highway that it is today.

With all the information out there, our leaders are inconsistent on the notion of compassion, depending on how they feel that day about immigration, building a mosque near ground zero, gay marriage or helping our inner city school kids.

Instead of paying attention to all the media that is exposing us to Mel Gibson's rampages or whatever escapades Lindsey Lohan is doing, we should be watching the informative programs on public television such as Charlie Rose or Travis Smiley. These two shows broadcasts real educational news programs that entertain and make you think, thought about ideas that might contribute to making this a better world."

The audience was a small crowd, but they gave Arthur a nice round of applause when he was finished speaking and he got his feet wet speaking about politics and issues important to him. Looking at the piece of paper with all the notes he had prepared for his speech, he decided to fold it up and put it in his pocket to save as a keepsake. Not often in a political position to experience feelings of euphoria, a warm and fuzzy sensation crept through his body after delivering his first Tea Party speech without a hitch.

"Thanks you for your speech," said one elderly male attendee, walking with a cane.

"You did a nice job holding everybody's attention," said another middle-aged lady in a flowery dress.

"Are they paying you anymore yet?" said Justin. Arthur's little friend Justin was in attendance with his mom, Ruth, who at the coaxing of her son, took some time off from her busy administrative job at Christian Hospital to hear Arthur speak. Both of them sat in chairs in the back row so as not to distract Arthur or make him nervous.

"You're brilliant and they need to pay you more," repeatedly said Justin. Justin's mom remained quiet as her smiled widened across her face and her eyes stared at Arthur.

"This was my first Tea Party speech and the movement is about paying attention to politics and making sure our leaders govern in a manner which keeps our country great and makes our world a better place; it's not about making its members more money Justin."

"Yes, but you held the people's attention the whole time and made some very good points. You did great, and you are a much better speaker than most of the media people seen on TV or heard on the radio. Maybe not this month or next month, but by next year, everybody's going to want to hear you speak. You are going to attract a lot of attention."

"Well, that is very high praise, but thank you for your kind words Justin."

"You are going to have to get more organized and maybe you should set up a foundation to solicit donations and buy liability insurance to protect yourself."

Justin's ideas were getting to be a little too much for his mother and she had to set him straight. "Too much organization is not a problem for one teenager who I know that lives with me. Well anyway, thank you Arthur for allowing Justin to participate in programs at the community center. I enjoyed listening to you speak, but we haven't eaten yet, so I need to go home and make dinner. Thanks again for everything, as movements of Ruth's facial features seemed to assume three or four interpretations of the effects of how the day ganged up on her."

While Arthur had talked to Susie on a daily basis in recent weeks, he hadn't talked to Sandra in five weeks. Sandra was dating a guy who lived out in Blanchester, where everybody was rich, or at least where everybody tried to live an upscale life. Arthur was unaware that this guy had recently moved some of his tuff into Sandra's condo. This new boyfriend's name was Tommy Campbell. Tommy's parents owned a chain of sporting goods stores throughout the Midwest. Tommy was a good athlete in high school but only a mediocre student. After attending three semesters of college at the community college, he dropped out, partly due to struggling grades and partly because he had a family business waiting for him to go to work. His parents refused to subsidize his lifestyle if he wasn't attending college or working for the family business. Tommy was barely a C student and needed to do some growing up, while Sandra had always been an A student in core subjects and everything else she signed up for. Sandra failed to look for interests she had in common with Tommy at first, only realizing that she fell for his charmingly good looks. He was aware of her amazing intelligence right away, and he was challenged by the thought of converting her to some of his devious ways.

Tommy was determined to make Sandra a party girl, which was a shame, because Sandra was protective of her lungs and health for her entire life before she met him. On an early afternoon in May full of green foliage and colorful blooms about to open its doors to summer, they drove out in Tommy's tricked out Dodge 3500 Ram Truck to wine country in Herman. The newly formed couple was a hundred miles away from family and friends, away from any populace town for that matter. Tommy brought all the supplies to try and corrupt a young girl, cigarettes, two joints and a gallon of cheap wine. The idea was to get Sandra drunk and get her to lie down next to him under the moon in the back of his extended truck bed. Countless indecent suggestions by Tommy to try something new while you are still young convinced Sandra to smoke a cigarette, and then a joint, on top of the sample tasting both encountered at the small wine-making establishments located in the rolling hills of Ozark country. A cigarette, a whole joint and several samples of different wines felt like a massive amount of drugs to a girl who led a clean life up to this point in her life.

Sandra felt guilty about breaking rules, and though many young people try smoking pot at some point, she hated drugs and the wretched feeling about herself for giving in to a boy that she barely new. Because five hours of wine tasting and pot smoking made her mind fuzzy and her stomach nauseous, she new she had to stay still and try to contain herself and not give Tommy any mixed signals of passion.

"Are you doing OK?" asked Tommy.

"I am just fine, thank you. I just want to go home now," said Sandra.

"Are you sure you are fine?"

"Yes, I'm just not much of a party girl; can we just get in the car and start driving home?"

"That's fine; just give me a moment to get a couple of CD's out of the case in the glove compartment for the ride home."

Sandra liked country music, but the music Tommy picked for the ride home was loud rap and all the lyrics were about booty, dirty sex, mother-this and mother-that. Now Sandra had a headache to go along with her stomachache and dizziness. After riding in the car for about thirty minutes, Sandra asked Tommy to pull over on the side of the road.

"Are you Ok?"

"Yes, I'm fine, I just need to vomit, please give me a moment alone. Please pull over."

When all cars and trucks passed and there were no longer any vehicles in the rear view mirror for as far as he could see, Tommy gradually slowed down and pulled over onto the gravel shoulder. Sandra opened the front passenger door and walked bent over just a few steps to the back of the truck. Holding on to the top of the truck bed above the right rear fender with one hand, she vomited with such an uncontrollable force that her discharge splattered her shoes, her pant legs, the wheel well, the tire and the fender of the truck. Though all the muscles in her body ached from the explosive energy used to puke, soon the nausea in her stomach and the dizziness in her head subsided to a manageable level. Driving back home, with the Missouri wine country behind them, Sandra's breath, her shoes and clothes still reeked of vomit, but at least now she wouldn't have to worry about Tommy trying to force himself on her. She wanted to take a shower and brush her teeth. She just wanted to go home. Because the drive to her dad's house was shorter than the drive to her condo, Sandra told Tommy to take her there. Sandra already now knew Tommy was a jerk, but when dropping her off in front of the house on Hill View, he didn't even pull into the driveway; he just waited for her to open the door and get out in the street and then he sped off without saying a word. When Sandra opened the front door and walked into the living room, Arthur was sitting in his favorite leather lounge chair reading the newspaper.

"Oh no, not you too, what the heck happened to you?

"I'm sorry dad, I made a big mistake."

"You smell, is that vomit all over your clothes and shoes?"

"Yes, I made a big mistake."

"Well, get out of those clothes and go take a shower and we will talk about it after you get cleaned up."

It was true that Sandra was already punishing herself by going straight to her dad's house instead of going home to her own condo, but she needed someone to talk to. She came to talk to her dad instead of her mom because she didn't feel comfortable discussing her problems with Stuart staying at the Hobson house. Her dad had been making an extra effort with her because of all the new living arrangements, and besides he was the one person in the world she trusted. She was feeling remorseful and didn't like the effects of alcohol and pot and losing the ability to think with a clear mind. She certainly didn't like getting sick from using the stuff. She wasn't a party girl; she enjoyed getting up early in the morning to run two or three miles before going to work. She had made a mistake and was glad to have a friend like her dad to talk to. After showering and changing into fresh clothes, Sandra walked down the hall to the living room and sat on the end of the couch closest to the leather chair where Arthur was sitting.

"So, you know you have to pay attention to the whispers in life. Your body is reacting to the things you decided to put in it and trying to send a message back to you. In a parallel universe, isn't there enough crap in this world? Which side do you want to be on, the good side or the bad side? Every time you smoke a cigarette or a joint, drink liquor, or do drugs, you are wasting your money, harming your health and doing nothing to improve the world. On the flipside, refraining from these things saves you money, prolongs your health and allows you more time to do something productive."

"I'm sorry I disappointed you dad."

"I think you disappointed yourself. You go wine tasting with a guy you know little about, someone you just met and he is driving drunk. You don't know anything about him, his education, intelligence, marital status, or his compassion for others, his hobbies, career interests or his politics. Your entire assessment of this guy was based on his good looks. In our society, who is handsome or beautiful doesn't always acquiesce a definitive response anyway. It is important to stay aware and learn about the important parts of a person's makeup before going out on a date."

"It just all seemed so innocuous at the beginning."

"The right young man will come along someday, a young man who will want to see how you get along with your father first. An aware young man is more interested in finding out how a young woman treats her father, not just how fast he can get in her pants. Observing how a daughter treats her father allows a young man a window to see how he might be treated later."

"Again, I'm sorry I disappointed you dad."

"More than you disappointed me it sounds like you disappointed yourself. I'm not going to sit here and beat you up about the decisions you already made, but I do want to talk some more about recreational drugs and abuse of prescription drugs in hopes of helping you think about making better choices in the future. I haven't told you yet, because I just found out myself yesterday. Your Uncle Johnny, who has been living in Atlanta, is a heroin addict. He admitted to me on the phone that he has been using for two years and he lost his job about a year ago after many warnings by his boss for missing days at work. I have to make a choice. Do I devote all my time to campaigning and making a bid for the mayoral job, or do I help try to save Johnny from his own death sentence?"

"Wow, I'm so sorry dad, my ordeal sure came at a bad time."

"I just want you do know the seriousness of doing drugs and driving and drinking? Also, we are going to have to come together and come up with a plan to try and save Johnny's life because only about five percent of heroin addicts recover; most of them end up dead or in jail."

"Has it always been easy to get heroin?" asked Sandra.

"A generation ago, Americans watched the "Mob" and the motorcycle gang "Hells Angels" try their hand at drug dealing. Now our venerated lands have a decaying miasma of illegal immigrants and desperate Americans doing the dirty work. These drug cartels amassed such a large network that it made street heroin easy to find and cheap to buy in the suburbs of any city in America. Drug dealers today aren't just standing on street corners in inner cities; they are literally everywhere, selling their crack and heroin in small towns and every neighborhood of suburbia, working an angle and putting some communities on the verge of collapse. For some of these drug dealers, if someone was to tell them they could make money standing on a rooftop in the rain selling shaving cream mixed with heroin, the next day you would see them standing on a rooftop in the rain selling shaving cream with heroin," professed Arthur.

"You would think the life of a drug dealer is an emotional roller coaster because their time is consumed in earning a living from engaging in criminal activities," added Sandra.

"Too often the reality of the lifestyle is its sudden finality, death at a young age. Drug traffickers have become homeland terrorists in the minds of law enforcement officials and public perception. Because of the connection of the way the illegal drug trade funds the terrorists, from the cultivation of the poppy plant through the drug manufacturing process and to the distribution on the streets of our cities and suburbs, a strengthened fight by the DEA (Drug Enforcement Agency) is using all domestic laws in trying to assert maximum penalties to major drug traffickers," said Arthur, trying to drive home his point.

"Tomorrow is Sunday, so we have all night to discuss things," declared Sandra.

"Alcoholics will often drink beer, wine or hard liquor before meeting with friends so that it appears that they're drinking the same amount as everyone else—when, in fact, they're way ahead, and you were riding around in a car with this Tommy guy who was probably drinking all day long. Alcoholics want to appear to be successful just like their friends in public, but sober they can't admit their weaknesses. Their abuse of alcohol has built a tolerance that is much higher, so they have to drink a lot more. For people who drink too much, the escape is worse than the reality. They vomit at the end of the night, have hangovers in the morning and the cycle repeats itself every week, sometimes everyday and hiding most of their suffering from everybody else."

"Dad, you know I'm not a big party girl. This was the first time I caved in to my curiosities," said Sandra, staring at her father.

"Sometimes a conversation is too important for two people to wait to discuss a problem. Over time, people with drinking or drug addiction problems increase the quantity and frequency of their substance of choice, mainly because they are building up a tolerance. With a higher tolerance, comes more drinking or drug use. With more drug use is the revelation of how fast the face is damaged in just a short time of a few years. Because it is usually good to humanize stories about what really happens inside the drug culture, police are using disturbing before and after mug shots helping to start a new anti-drug campaign, with hopes that the photographs grab young peoples' attention by appealing to their vanity. Alcoholics and drug addicts who self-medicate to feel normal sure don't look normal. Faces which were once attractive metamorphose into tawdry toothless and scabby wrecks. This sub-segment of the population, who gives up on finding their way, needs to look for the smaller things in life to appreciate. It is time for these people to stop all the bullshit, all the trumped up bullshit, and look in the mirror."

"Is heroin easy to get in Atlanta?" asked Sandra.

"It is becoming easy to get almost everywhere, but Atlanta has become the hub for drug trafficking in the Southeastern U.S. because there are so many people living their lives one step ahead of the police and two steps from the grave. For the same reasons legitimate businesses like setting up shop in Atlanta, so does the drug cartels. This is one real cause Oprah could devote some time to if she was still on the air. The easy access to interstate highways that connect to other major cities makes redistribution of heroin and meth-amphetamine easy. The problem is that more people are dying at the end of a needle than at the end of a gun," Arthur stopping to take a deep breath, feeling worked up after raving and venting his frustration with the whole drug mess.

"Are the people dying usually long term addicts?" asked Sandra.

"Some people get addicted the first time they use heroin and some people die the first time they use heroin. Uncle Johnny has a major problem with heroin addiction and he needs help," said Arthur.

"So dad, Uncle Johnny always helped me when I was a little girl. I remember a story he told me about Jackie Mitchell, a woman who pitched for a men's minor league baseball team, the Chattanooga Lookouts, in the 1920's. Jackie wanted to quit baseball, but her coach convinced her to stick with it. She did and later signed a contract to play several seasons of exhibitions games in professional baseball. She struck out Lou Gehrig and Babe Ruth consecutively in one game against the New York Yankees. Johnny told me; needless to say, she had a ridiculous curve ball. So since we are not going to give up this time either, how are we going to try to help Uncle Johnny?" asked Sandra.

"It's complicated and I've been thinking about lots of things. Growing up in Rainbow Creek, Johnny was given many things as a child and he always was filled with assurances that later in his life he would have plenty of opportunities. The way a centerfielder runs down a fly ball hit over his head, the sense of where the hit ball might arrive at the same time he reaches up to catch it and instantaneously feeling the satisfaction of starring for the team, was the way he expected every facet of his life to go for the early years of his life. He dressed in preppy new clothes, kept his hair trimmed, and earned good grades in high school and college. But after returning home from the war, and he struggled to land the great job with one of the limited amounts of fortune 500 companies in or close to town, he lost some of his confidence and his troubles began to mount," Arthur continued. "For more than two decades he worked lesser jobs which underutilized his skills with few benefits and little chance for advancement. Then one day, after learning of a promising position working in the marketing department for a music production company located in Atlanta, Johnny applied and was offered the job. He moved to Atlanta, but the job only lasted one year and the company folded, no longer able to make payroll or defray expenses. Gripped by the anger of losing his job and the frustration of the music business, combined with too much free time, he turned away from his guitar and started using drugs. The culprit of his demise manifested from deep inside his soul, something not political but self destructive instead, like a man continuing to eat the same food at the same restaurant that caused him to suffer food poisoning every time he ate there. Only this time it wasn't food causing the poisoning; it was an addiction to heroin causing all the suffering."

"We have to help Uncle Johnny," repeated Sandra. "At a time in his life when he needs us the most, we should be remembered for doing the most we can for him."

"He is very confused right now. The middle class needs less confusion from celebrities and politically influential people. I remember Johnny telling me about a concert performed by Billy Joel and Sir Paul McCartney. McCartney sang "Let it be." Soon as the song and the concert ended, Billy Joel told the sold-out mega audience, 'Don't take any shit from anybody.' Johnny told me he was confused, and he asked me, 'What is it? Let it be or don't take any shit from anybody.' This advice sounded like the same advice used by many of our politicians, whatever makes them money or gets them reelected. The lesson for all is that if you are going to make money and give others advice, at least give some thought to how your work can help people."

Johnny Hobson's good looks, his five feet, eleven inches tall frame, baby blue eyes and his broad-ranged voice are qualities music producers look for in dazzling entertainers. Even before he taught himself to read music, Johnny seemed to instinctively understand the basic sounds and principles of playing a guitar. Johnny's music career could have been different. His transcriptions of concert masterworks provided a fresh and unique look at songs from top artists of the past, while his interpretations of works from the contemporary artists of the world were helping him break new ground with a few works of his own which showed promise. Though he probably would have never received international recognition as a singer, writer or composer, his musical and linguistic abilities could have afforded him plenty of work in North America and Canada. It was truly a shame that his drug use took over as precedence in the way just as he was coming into his own.

Atlanta politicians, like politicians in every other big metropolitan area in America, downplayed the homeless and hophead problems in their city. Johnny knew many of the characters who belonged to hophead streets in Atlanta. He was also aware of the scrawny dogs agitating for human affection and constantly searching for food on the streets. Hophead streets are firmly rooted in the real world, not solely because of the financial crisis and unemployment as some like to use as an excuse, but because of the powerful underground network of dangerous people perpetrating a drug culture on a predicated people. Johnny knew just where to go for a fix, camouflaged within the urban landscape, in the decaying buildings obscured by unattended foliage just beyond where the children played in the park on any given day. The inner circles of the drug dealing culture changed from week to week because of jail terms, overdoses, deaths and the rare cases where a person was saved because someone else cared enough to try to help. Johnny's best friend on the streets, if you can call him a friend, was an ex-barge deckhand named "Willie Mo". Willie Mo, a father of several children, had little contact with family members when he worked and none in the last ten years while using heroin. Willie Mo, once a cool battle-weary soldier with movie-star good looks and strong manners, was now much frailer and softer than a man should be at his age. Johnny and Willie Mo bonded after meeting each other during tours of duty fighting on the front lines in Vietnam and reunited on the streets back home when they met again trying to satisfy cravings for heroin. Under the spell of heroin, neither man realized the extent of their families' hatred of their drug use and the peculiar twist it assumed by disallowing a respect any Vietnam veteran deserved returning from war. Down deep in Willie Mo's soul existed a warm-hearted and kind man, but it was hard to imagine now if he would allow another person to see this side of him again, before it was too late. Then again, who knows what anyone is capable of down life's road of twists and turns? If either man was going to have a chance of turning his own life around, their relationship on the streets needed to end immediately.

"So how are we going to help Uncle Johnny?" Sandra asserting herself again wanted a direct and specific answer.

"First we have to get him into rehab to detoxify, which is very painful and uncomfortable, otherwise we won't be able to get through to him while he is still using heroin. I will call him first thing in the morning and make flight arrangements to go see him."

"Dad I want to go with you. I can cook meals and help in any way you need me to help. I have two weeks of vacation left at work. How long would we stay in Atlanta?"

"I think your help would be much appreciated. A three or four person intervention is much better than just one person trying to tackle this big of a chore. The trick will be to get Johnny in rehab as quick as possible, hopefully a 60-day program with a better than average track record. I would like to leave tomorrow because time is of the essence while we know he is off the streets right now. I know things could change by tomorrow, but with the grace of God, hopefully we can find a place with the right environment and skills to help him with his disease. When Johnny called me, I sensed his shame and it felt like maybe he has hit rock bottom, but ultimately he is going to have to want to help himself. Staying clean for one year is a big step because most addict relapse even after several attempts at rehab. It's getting late so we should probably get some sleep."

"OK, well, I'll call my boss at his home tomorrow morning, if you call about the flight itinerary, and we will go from there. Good night dad, I hope you sleep well. I am very sorry about everything that happened today and everything that is happening with Uncle Johnny. Today has been an eventfully bad day."

By 8 am the next morning, Sandra was at her condo gathering enough clothes to fill two suitcases. She was relieved to see that she wouldn't have to deal with kicking Tommy out of her home. He had already gathered his things and left. He even put his key on the kitchen table with a note saying, "Sorry things didn't work out between us." Her emotions not swayed one way or the other, she was happy the outcome allowed her to hide the rest of the details about her short term living arrangement with Tommy from her father.

Arthur booked a flight to Atlanta International Airport for him and Sandra, the plane scheduled to leave in just a few hours from St. Louis Lambert Airport at 1:45 pm. Arthur called and asked Johnny to meet him and Sandra between luggage carousels two and three inside Atlanta's International Airport at 5 pm. Johnny said he would be there, even suggesting a place the three of them could stop at for dinner on the way home.

With the twenty-mile-per hour winds behind the airplane during most of the flight, Sandra and Arthur arrived in Atlanta a few minutes sooner than expected. After a brisk walk from the arrival gate to the baggage area, neither Arthur nor Sandra spotted Johnny anywhere in the immediate area. After lifting their luggage from the spinning conveyor, both of them took a seat close to carousels two and three and waited. Soon it was 5:15 pm, then 5:30 pm, then 6 pm, and still there was no sign of Johnny.

Sandra leaped up from her chair, "Dad, how much longer do you think we should wait? Even if traffic was terrible, Uncle Johnny should have been here by now."

"What if you compared Johnny's addiction for heroin to a vampire's need to suck blood? Would you think he still had the power to stay away from his habit?" said Arthur.

"I know you are referring to the recent Twilight movie that so many girls went gaga over, because of all the cute boy vampires in the film. But in folklore, a vampire is a reanimated corpse that sucks the blood of sleeping persons and preys ruthlessly on others," said Sandra.

"So unless you're the type of person who believes in romantic vampire movies, you would more easily compare a vampire to a drug dealer, correct?" said Arthur.

"I think so, because vampires and drug dealers can never be trusted by other people. It's strange in a way and maybe even a little ironic, but Uncle Johnny is the one who taught me about a vamp. A vamp is a simple, short improvisation by a band when one of the musicians makes a mistake and the rest of the members fake their way through protecting the performance overall," said Sandra.

"Everywhere we look today there are movies and television programs about vampires and werewolves. It is time to warn everybody; never moon a werewolf and be extra suspicious of a vampire playing a guitar," said Arthur.

"Though your analogy is funny, I don't know if I like the comparison to Uncle Johnny," said Sandra.

"I don't have a good feeling about Johnny either, but I do have his address written down on a folded piece of paper in my pocket. Let's see, here it is. His address is 501 Central Avenue SW and he lives in a downtown apartment building between Woodruff Park and Hurt Park. Isn't it ironic that his address number 501 is the same time we should have been leaving the airport together? What do you say we wave a cab and go to his apartment? Maybe he just dozed off asleep or lost track of time, though my better sense of judgment tells me he hasn't lived responsibly for the past two years."

"Sounds good, I can see the sign pointing towards the curb where the cabs and shuttles pickup passengers waiting on the sidewalk."

All this time since Sandra and her dad left the airport in St. Louis, she had been thinking about making a good impression on her Uncle Johnny and trying to prove herself worthy of helping her father with whatever needed to be done. She wanted to make amends for the mistake she made with Tommy and try to understand why her uncle was making much bigger mistakes in order to help him fix them. Her thing for her Uncle Johnny went back to when she was a little girl. Uncle Johnny loved sports and traveling to different ballparks, and he bought Sandra her first softball glove, a left-handed Rawlings model she liked so much because it felt like it was custom-made to fit her little hand. During visits and holidays, she spent no more than a few hours per visit with him, but Uncle Johnny always went out of his way to make her feel special. When she thinks about the past, in some respects, the two of them had an ideal friendship, though admittedly less ideal now when she allows herself to think about all the bad things Uncle Johnny must have been doing for the last two years. All of those years as a little girl, Sandra remembered as happy times in her life, when everything just fell in place. She loved Uncle Johnny's big smile, his big muscles, his glistening blue eyes, and the attention he gave her. At her tenth birthday party, he showed up with a new ten-speed bicycle with a pink bow taped to the seat. Whether he was giving her some technical pointers about hitting a softball or a recap about some new singer who hit the country charts, the tone of his voice was always soft and sweet with her.

When the cab arrived at Johnny's apartment building, Arthur paid the driver and thanked him with a nice tip. Sandra grabbed her purse and two suitcases and hurried to the front door of the entrance to the apartment building. While holding the heavy metal door open with her right foot, she waited for Arthur to catch up with her. The trace up the five flights of stairs to Johnny's pad carrying luggage was work, but nothing like the work ahead for Arthur and Sandra. Sandra knocked hard on the dark green door of the apartment numbered 501.

"Knock again Sandra," said Arthur, now guarding his and Sandra's suitcases.

From the peep hole in the door, she could see a light on in the kitchen of the apartment, but she had to knock on the door five times, and the voice that finally answered was Johnny.

"Sandra, you made it here from St. Louis! Hello Arthur, he said. "I can't believe you guys are here. Did you guys have a good flight?"

"Why didn't you pick us up at the airport?" said Arthur, as bright-eyed Sandra stood still in her almost new Nike tennis shoes.

"I don't know, I thought talking responsibly on the phone sounded like the right approach at the time, but things have been crazy around here. You are my successful brother and I figured you would just take a cab here. Sandra, I apologize for not being there at the airport waiting for you when your plane landed."

Sandra was frowning, as she remained quiet.

"When is the last time you used, Johnny?" asked Arthur.

"Well, those are strong words for beginning a conversation with your little brother who you haven't seen in a couple of years and traveled so far to see?"

"Cut the crap Johnny, we are here for a reason and it is time to start telling the truth. It is time to quit using heroin and get your life together before it's too late. We don't want to have to identify your dead body after the police find it in a gutter somewhere. We really need to talk about how you can take better care of yourself. You have to start telling the truth about everything and start following some rules. You haven't been living a clean life. I swear to God, Johnny, we are not here to give you grief. Sandra and I are the two people in this world who care about you the most."

"Look, I promise I'll try harder and before I forget, here is the extra key to my apartment in case you want to do some sight-seeing or shopping during your visit. As if not being able to get inside your apartment isn't bad enough, not because I locked myself out, but because I once broke off the lock inside the lock and had to go to the manager's office to ask for help from the maintenance guy. One of the leasing agents sitting at her desk said, 'Do you live here?' I felt like saying, 'No, I'm just here to see if someone will help me break in to an apartment. I've had my eyes on one apartment and I think there might be something good inside it.' Well enough about all that, you guys must be hungry. How about the three of us walk to the diner down the street to grab a bite to eat? It only takes about five minutes to walk there and the food is excellent."

"OK, but first thing in the morning, all three of us are going to meet with some people from a treatment facility. I already contacted them on my cell phone when we were waiting for you at the airport."

"Fine, let's start walking to the diner. The food there is really good, I'm glad you both will have a chance to try it."

After a nice stroll down the sidewalk of five or six city blocks lined with big oak trees and light traffic, the threesome entered the "24-hr-diner." Johnny suggested a booth next to the big window with a view of the street and away from the bathrooms. Johnny sat on one side; Sandra scooted in on the other side, while Arthur was the last to sit down filing in next to his daughter. The waitress came over wearing a familiar white diner uniform and a hairnet on her head with pencil behind her ear and take-order pad in hand. "Hi Johnny, have you been behaving yourself? Who are these two lovely people?"

"This is my brother Arthur and my niece Sandra. My brother is a Tea Party guy; he likes to hobnail the provincial politicians in Rainbow Creek. He's involved in many domestic programs with the work he does at his local community center."

"Nice to meet both of you, my name is Gloria; I'll be your waitress tonight. A Democratic senator and his wife from one of the neighboring districts outside Georgia ate at our restaurant last month. I told the senator and his wife, 'Tonight's two specials are chicken almandine and fresh boiled shrimp with red sauce.' Each of them put down their menus almost immediately."

"The chicken sounds great, I'll have that," said the senator's wife.

I nodded my head and asked, "And the vegetable?" said Gloria.

"I will have a green leafy salad because it is food for the brain," replied the senator's wife.

"Oh, he'll have the shrimp," the senator's wife added. "I ordered for my husband because I am helping him to lose a few pounds," she added.

"I take it the senator's wife liked to joke about bottom feeders and brain-dead politicians," said Johnny.

"I'm starting to think the liberals think any workers who make above minimum wage are rich and can afford to pay for all sorts of new entitlement programs, blaming Republicans for not doing more for people sooner. Hopefully Republicans won't get blamed for the rainy weather we are supposed to get tomorrow. If the day comes when they start talking this extreme, they will probably tell the Tea Party members that they are a bunch of cockroaches and if it wasn't for this supplementary dousing of rain on top of them to keep them sustained, they would be placed on the endangered species list," said Arthur, ranting on a little too long.

"It sounds like you are a little disgusted with politicians, the same way I'm a little disgusted with them," said Gloria.

"When they call the roll at Senate House meetings, I wonder if the senators should answer 'present' or 'not guilty,'" replied Arthur.

"What can I get for all of you? The special for tonight is a turkey club with curly fries and a beverage of your choice. The meat is from a twelve pound turkey we cooked in a roaster, not the processed kind you buy in a package. Are you ready to order first Sandra?"

"The special sounds good to me. I'll have a diet Coke to drink. Thank you."

"How about you Arthur, what will you have?"

"I'll have the special too and give me an iced-tea with lemon please."

"And you Johnny, do you want the usual?"

"Yes, thank you."

Gloria walked backed behind the counter and placed the order with the grill cook. Johnny pulled out a couple napkins from the dispenser on the table and blew his nose. A tall attractive lady walking her two poodles on the sidewalk could be seen through the window.

"I need to go wash my hands before eating, I'll be back in two minutes," said Arthur.

"I should probably do the same," said Sandra.

"Go ahead, I'll watch your stuff," said Johnny.

When Sandra and Arthur returned to the booth, Gloria had placed their drinks on the table, but Johnny was gone. Sandra's purse, which Johnny vowed to watch, was still resting against at the end of the booth seat where the bench butted up against the wall. But when Sandra looked inside it to check her wallet, all her money was gone. Her Uncle Johnny had robbed her blind of the $400 she brought along to help pay for expenses while at the same time she was sacrificing her time to try and help him.

"Dad, I think Uncle Johnny took my money. While you were in the men's bathroom, did Uncle Johnny go there to wash his hands too?"

"No, I'm afraid not Sandra. I think we are starting to see the tragic consequences families have to face when dealing with a loved one who is a heroin addict. Johnny needed a fix and at this point in his addiction, when he wants a fix, nothing else matters, not even his brother and niece who he is sharing a meal with at a restaurant."

Gloria brought over the two large plate specials and a doughnut on a smaller plate with a cup of coffee for Johnny, his usual order. "Can I get you guys anything else?" she asked.

"Gloria, did you see my Uncle Johnny leave the restaurant?" asked Sandra.

"Yes dear, he usually doesn't stay long. Most of the time, he drinks one cup of coffee and takes a bite or two of his doughnut, but he always pays me and leaves a one dollar tip. I do worry about him though because of some of the people he associates with lately. When he first started coming here, he used to tell stories about how Asian chefs chop their vegetables top to bottom when they prepare dishes, but American chefs slice their vegetables from one side to the other. He was so charming then. That's why I thought it was so nice to see him walk in to the diner with two lovely folks like you and your dad. I will say a prayer for you and your family, dear."

"Sandra, eventually Johnny will come back in a couple of days, so let's eat our food and try to enjoy the nice walk back to the apartment," Arthur told his daughter.

The night did not end, as it should have, with a nice conversation similar to the ones in the old days when Sandra built such a loving relationship with her Uncle Johnny. She couldn't believe that he changed so much as to just leave her and her dad in a diner in a city they were unfamiliar with the surroundings. Sandra was filled with worry and vowed to pay closer attention and promised to follow her own rules better and not smoke any more pot or do any drugs.

After finishing their late meal at the diner, and after paying the bill and leaving a nice tip for Gloria, Arthur and Sandra walked back to Johnny's apartment and retired for the evening. Both were tired from the long hours of traveling and all of the commotion of the day. When Sandra was a little girl and she had an emotional crisis, she and her dad would walk to the ball field in their neighborhood for thirty minutes of batting practice to chasten frustrations, but besides being much older now; this situation was much bigger problem for her. No amount of walking or pounding balls into the outfield could make her feel better at the moment.

The very next morning before Sandra had a chance to discuss a plan with her dad to help her uncle, she looked in the cupboard and found a can of instant coffee, but looking in the refrigerator to hopefully score some orange juice, there was none. A can of string beans, a bottle of vinegar, a bottle of bleach, and a box of stale macaroni noodles were the only other four items in the cupboard and the refrigerator was empty except for one bottle of Budweiser and a moldy baloney sandwich in a partially sealed plastic bag. Sandra could only think about the dissimilarity between her dad acting as a good provider who always furnished his family with food, clothes, shelter, health care and maintenance to the house for nurturance, the granting of safety, security, warmth and a sense of "home", while she was starting to realize the empty life of an addict. She once heard that many meth, heroin and cocaine users get to a point of having no appetite at all. They then start getting compliments because of loss weight. Since weight loss is usually seen as a positive thing in our society, it is often overlooked as a symptom of drug abuse. Sandra redirected her attention to her dad as she saw him walk into the kitchen.

"Dad, did you sleep well?"

"Yes, I was very tired, though I recall having a very intense dream. The conflict in my dream was classic. The evil leaders of the world were bombing and crushing all the peaceful towns and cities in the world. The highest-ranking members of the Tea Party, along with my brothers Kevin and Johnny, and Susie and you, learned how to fly huge, robotic American eagles. In my dream, these robotic eagles, all of us discover, can become body parts that join to form a single giant armed cavalier called a Teagletron. The Teagle-tron, it turns out, can fire unlimited amounts of atomic hand grenades at evildoers and kick all kinds of ass. At just about the apex of all the fighting, I woke up feeling as if I was falling into a deep hole of dark energy. "

"I found some instant coffee and I boiled some water in the kettle on the stove, but you will have to drink it black. I hope drinking black coffee doesn't cause your mind to revert back into that dark hole."

"No it won't, thank you for making the coffee."

"Maybe your dream stemmed from worrying that someday there won't be enough good people left to restore American values and fight against the drug war once all the grownups are old."

"I think my dream was a way of telling me that all the problems in the world are bigger than anyone. All these confrontations have energies of their own and all of them have entered into the Zeitgeist. And all we can do is harness our own power and nudge it in certain ways to help give back, before evildoers take everything and there is nothing else left to take."

"There isn't any food in this house and when I looked in the silverware drawer, all the spoons are dirty with black stains from heating and dissolving heroin on them. Plus there was one bottle of Budweiser in the refrigerator, and that was it, despite all the empty cans lying around the apartment."

"Johnny must have visited a favorite taco joint four or five times per week for dinner, grabbing a small bag of those terrible tasting pita chips roasted in garlic and a handful of beef tacos, and eating much of each of these snack foods along the way as he strolled down the sidewalk back to his apartment at night. The leftover hot sauce containers, empty chip bags, and salt and pepper packets he managed to keep in jars stored in the kitchen cabinets. Before his drug use increased to a critical point, Bill Bryson must have been one of Johnny's favorite authors. Bryson paperbacks, *A Walk in the Woods*, *The Lost Continent*, and *The Life and Times of the Thunderbolt Kid*, are scattered around on the floor in his bedroom closet."

"I did notice Bryson's book, *The Life and Times of the Thunderbolt Kid*. The book is a story about a curious boy overcoming obstacles and growing up in Des Moines, Iowa. I read it several months ago and parts of the read remind me of growing up in Rainbow Creek. So how are we going to help Uncle Johnny?"

"The best way for us to help Johnny fight the drug war is to eliminate any alcohol, drugs or paraphernalia from the apartment, thus eliminating some of the demand. So let us throw away the spoons, the bottle of Budweiser and any matches that are lying around. Getting the upper hand against the drug gangs and dealers, many of which are engaged in bloody warfare fighting for selling turf and smuggling routes, is a big job that we are going to have to leave for a bigger army. But we can try to do our part with the hope that more and more people become educated from a grassroots approach on the signs of drug abuse, the financial consequences that work against families and the dangers bestowed upon our military and law enforcement officials."

"Dad, besides the spoons with burn marks, I also saw several boxes of laxatives in the cabinet behind the mirror and burnt foil gum wrappers on the floor near the small black trash can in the bathroom."

"I didn't say anything before, but during the short time we were with Johnny, did you notice the tracks on his arms and his constant itching and scratching of his extremities?

Did you notice how constricted his pupils were, like tiny pinpoints?

"I didn't notice his pupils, but I did notice all the itching and scratching he was doing."

"All these things are signs of an addict using heroin. The constricted pinpoint pupils, the vomiting, using laxatives for constipation, nodding-out after recent increased activity, weight loss, missing shoelaces used as arm tie offs for injecting heroin, bottles of vinegar and bleach used to clean needles, and bloody cotton balls lying around are all signs of heroin use. Female heroin addicts notice abnormal and dangerous cessation of menstruation."

"Dad, I do see the many terrible consequences of heroin addiction, they are everywhere in this apartment. I want to cleanup this apartment and maybe paint the walls. We can't give up on Uncle Johnny and I can't help thinking about all the good times we had in the old days."

"For anyone going through this dark hole of addiction, you can do your best to try to help the person, but the only approach with a chance to work is tough love. It usually results in prison time, but that is better than death. Treatment takes various forms and is only accomplished after detoxification. The driving force of treatment addresses the underlying causes of drug abuse and focuses on helping addicts become more self-aware, responsible, self-reliant and able to manage their own stress without the crutch of drugs. Johnny can blame his family, his friends, the cartels, the black market, the drug pushers and all other bad influences, but each individual has to take charge of their own life and say no to drugs in order to lessen the demand for them in the real world."

"I don't care what it takes; we aren't giving up on him. All your life, dad, you taught me to never give up and never stop fighting, even when you don't know where to turn because you are too emotionally drained," Sandra continues. I hate when others say it's too late to help people once they have gone to prison or once an addict is addicted to heroin or after a person steals jewelry from a family member. This sends an awful message. Material things can be replaced, but people are indispensible."

"The condition of this apartment is barely a step above living in a rusty boxcar, empty of any accessories, except for a few discarded desensitizing drug needles. I cannot help it, but I keep thinking about an interesting analogy I recently heard on television between youth and the corrugated cardboard box. Often, young children enjoy playing in discarded corrugated shipping containers. A common cliché is that, if presented with a large expensive toy, a child will quickly become bored with the toy and play with the box instead. Johnny certainly enjoyed playing with boxes as a young boy, using his imagination to portray the box as an infinite variety of objects. Johnny used a cardboard box for imaginative purposes from a playhouse, to a time machine, to a moving object, which he used to slide down steep grass hills around the neighborhood. I remember when the National Toy Hall of Fame added the cardboard box to its museum. Ironically, a child thinking of something as playful and innocent may think very differently about it as an adult. Living in a cardboard box as an adult is stereotypically associated with homelessness and drug use. It really scares me to think Johnny's life has possibly come down to drugs and living in a cardboard box. Youthful imagination is wonderful, but only men with years of experience making responsible decisions can shape a better future. History shows there is no other way besides capitalism to escape poverty. This is a certainty and any other means to rule are just ways for rulers to deceive its citizens, steal their money and shift the way it is spent, never addressing the real reasons for our problems."

In the bulls-eye of known drug trafficking in Atlanta, Arthur and Sandra continually put pressure on local police, meeting with a captain and a lieutenant three times each, in an attempt to ask for help in stopping the infiltration of heroin sales in the communities close to where Johnny lived. Seventeen young adults, who lived in a section of town where he lived near the new Atlanta Crossing mega-size shopping plaza, were hooked on heroin, including one couple's blond haired, blue-eyed sixteen-year-old daughter. The mother did everything possible in an attempt to keep her daughter alive. She told neighbors about circumstances putting her own reputation at risk, she drove around bad neighborhoods looking for her daughter and she even confronted a drug-dealer and was bitten by a dog at the front door of his home. The heroin-addicted girl's father took on two extra jobs to pay for various expensive drug treatment programs. Because of loving unwavering devotion from her parents, the daughter has a good chance of being one of the few who will beat this treadmill way of life. The Atlanta police lieutenant told Arthur and Sandra that the girl has been clean now for six months.

For several days, Arthur and Sandra continued their full-court press in an attempt to make Johnny's apartment look brand-new. Before either of them did any cleaning, Arthur set off a fumigating bomb to disinfect and kill any vermin lingering in the cracks and crevices in any of the rooms. He left the windows open to let in fresh air and take arms against the garbage smells of stale beer and living a trashy life of darkness. Arthur and Sandra stayed away from the apartment for twelve hours while the chemical compounds completed the process of quantitative easing. Sandra could not bare the thought of Uncle Johnny spending the entire summer alone in a drug-infested, roach-infested, dirty, and smelly apartment. She threw out multiple plastic bags of trash, washed and dried every dish, cleaned the kitchen countertop, mopped the floors in the bathroom, and scrubbed the toilet and the sink to a shine where you could see your reflection in the Tuscan calcite porcelain. Arthur, with approval from Ms. Lilly, the apartment manager, scrounged two gallons of semi-gloss white paint from a utility closet in the building and covered the smoke-stained walls and ceilings of Johnny's apartment with a fresh coat of sheen. Sandra and Arthur together made two visits on foot to a corner market for groceries because each of them could only carry two bags of needed items per trip. The ice box was now full, with ice cream, hamburger, chicken breasts, salmon and Atlantic Pollock fillets in the freezer, and milk, eggs, orange juice, lunchmeat, Swiss cheese, apples, grapes, butter, jelly, mayonnaise, two lemons and a gallon of pre-mixed iced tea in the refrigerator. All her life, Sandra refused to beg her parents for cash infusions to spend money on herself, but in this case, even though her uncle took her money, she easily was able to convince her dad to pay Johnny's rent for the current month and one month ahead.

Five days after robbing Sandra and sneaking away from the diner, Johnny came slithering back to the apartment in the middle of the afternoon looking terrible and smelling of body odor. The first thing Sandra did was drop down to sit in a chair and assess the immediacy of the situation. Arthur was upset and ready to jostle with his brother, pissed off and reacting like most men would to the situation when someone steals $400 from their child. The much stronger Arthur barged into the frontal space of his skinny younger brother and pushed him against the wall in the living room. Sandra was already visibly upset, tossing her hair with both hands and now walking small circles idly in place. She let out a scream of frustration when her frail Uncle Johnny fell to the ground hitting his head on a side table and unwilling to fight back. Arthur and Sandra lingered near the front door of the apartment, watching for a reaction from Johnny.

"Are you OK, Johnny?" said Arthur.

"I'm fine; fighting isn't part of my repertoire."

"You're bleeding, I will get a wet cloth," said Sandra.

Returning with a small white bathroom towel warmed from a rinse of hot water, Sandra knelt down and applied pressure to the forehead of her Uncle Johnny.

"The cut doesn't look very deep; I don't think you need stitches. Just hold this cloth in place for a few minutes and hopefully the bleeding will stop."

Arthur was in the kitchen talking on the phone with the director, Ruth Staley, of the Pleasant Grove Rehabilitation Center of Atlanta. He was giving directions to her so that the Pleasant Grove shuttle driver could immediately leave the Center's parking lot en route to pickup Johnny at the apartment and drive back to start treatment.

Sandra turned on the radio tuned to an oldies but goodies station. Since he did not have a car and often rode the bus to get to where he was going, listening to music was not one of Johnny's priorities anymore, as it was earlier in his life as she remembered. Sandra remembered how Johnny loved music and always had something knowledgeable to say about a new song or any genre of sounds. Sandra turned up the volume once she recognized Frank Sinatra's voice.

"Do you like this kind of music?" she said.

"I like Bing Crosby, Frank Sinatra, Perry Como and some of the old crooners. I guess basically yes, I like the smooth solo artists of the 50's big band era, the music my parents grew up listening to."

"Do you think the old crooners were nicer guys than some of the drug-addicted rock-and-rollers who came after them?"

"I don't know; it all depends. Sinatra won an Academy Award for Best Supporting Actor in the movie "From Here to Eternity." I had heard that Sinatra had to fight many of his own demons. Expelled from high school for rowdy conduct, he never graduated. He had a reputation as a womanizer and he drank a lot. His father was a former boxer, who after breaking both his wrists, became a Captain with the Hoboken Fire Department. While still working as a Captain, his downfall began after buying a tavern and becoming a heavy drinker."

"Doesn't that tell you anything about booze and drugs?"

"I guess it should, especially after getting knocked down by my brother."

"What else do you know about Frank Sinatra or Bong Crosby or Perry Como?"

"Supposedly, Sinatra's mother, known as Dolly, was an abortionist who ran the illegal business from her home. Bing Crosby seemed to have a better reputation, possibly from playing the roles of Father O'Malley in 'The Bells of Saint Mary's' and his portrayal of Bob Wallace, a World War II army hero and entertainer in 'White Christmas'. Perry Como seemed to keep his personal life out of the limelight."

"Did Walt Disney make many movies during those 'Rat Pack' years?" asked Sandra.

"At one point in American history, even before the 'Rat Pack' years, Walt Disney Company was the darling of all American businesses. Major motion picture studios made over five hundred movies per year in the 50's. Only about a hundred and fifty movies are made by major movie producers today. I bet many people, if asked today, would think those numbers are reversed. Everything has just become so expensive," said Johnny.

"Oprah could tell us about how expensive things have become, especially now that she owns her own network. By the way, speaking of Oprah, I was watching her give an interview the other night to Piers Morgan on his new talk show. He asked her, "What grade would you give the president at the two-year midway point of his term in office?" She answered that she did not pay enough attention to the curriculum to give him a grade. She then added that she believed the president has not done anything to disappoint the American people," said Sandra.

"I think President Obama's main problem is too many people are still out of work. I'm not sure Piers Morgan, even though he is from England, is qualified as a political pundit here in the U. S. if he doesn't ask her a question about the economy." said Johnny.

"Oprah told Piers she is not qualified to run for a political position herself, but I do remember when she professed on the national stage to endorse Barack Obama during his presidential campaign. Because of her popularity, she may have even influenced the outcome of the election," suggested Sandra.

Arthur hung up the phone and after making three glasses of iced tea on the rocks, walked back into the living room interrupting the calming conversation between Johnny and Sandra.

"I heard the end of the conversation you guys were having about Oprah. For Oprah to say she did not pay attention, but she does not think the president disappointed is a bit of a contradictory statement. You have to pay attention if you are going to give opinions. It is a bit contradictory to endorse a man for the highest position in the land and then not pay attention to his way of running the country," said Arthur.

"Dad, did you watch and listen to the interview too?" asked Sandra.

"Yes, I was really struck by the questions asked and the answers given by Oprah. She went on to say that, her brand is "Love" and her life isn't about having a lot of shoes and houses; it's much bigger than that. She went on to say that, she is only the "Messenger." I understand to be successful a person usually has to do some form of self-promotion. However, her brand of "Love" seems so spread out now it just does not feel genuine anymore. Money does not give you wisdom, experience does. One person cannot be an expert about everything. A television show, movies, her magazine, several product lines and now her own network have led her to see herself as the self-proclaimed 'Messenger.' One person can give opinions, but it might be time to take a step back when that same person giving the opinions starts calling herself the Messenger. Jesus Christ was the Messenger and like the rest of us, Oprah is still learning. I like Oprah, but I sure did not like her responses to the questions she answered in the interview that night. Oprah is right about understanding intuition. People in life are either with you or against you. If something doesn't feel right, it doesn't make sense to continue the strategy," said Arthur.

"While the Oprah Show did bring awareness to important issues, sometimes it felt like it was more about riding the coattails of the latest hot celebrity to build her empire. The shows were more geared towards women and it took the producers ten years to air a taping to honor the injured soldiers returning from wars in the Middle East," said Johnny. "The book *Three Cups of Tea* was endorsed by Oprah on one of her shows. The author, Greg Mortonsen, fabricated a story about getting lost on a dangerous mountain-climbing expedition in Afghanistan and being rescued by Afghan women. With book proceeds, he said he built eleven schools in a war-torn area, but that was discovered to be another lie. He made millions of dollars selling his book, but the story and his declaration were big lies."

"One person Oprah does often talk about is her friend Maya Angelou. Oprah is a marketer and when she likes someone or some product, it gets exposure. Angelou's book titled, *I Know Why the Caged Bird Sings*, talks about her experience getting raped by her mother's boyfriend. I read the book last year. The rapist only served four days in prison. Upon his release, Angelou's uncles kicked the man to death. Angelou blamed herself and quit speaking for five years when she was a young girl," said Arthur.

"The subconscious mind is like a security guard at the door of the conscious mind. Anyone who has had to endure a horrific experience or live-threatening illness, knows you can withdraw into your mind to try and disassociate yourself from what is happening for the time being, sometimes accomplished under the most despicable and difficult conditions. Any experience of horror ultimately buries itself deep into a person's roots and seldom is there a trust for people ever again. I've experienced similar feelings at different times since coming back from Vietnam, but some of the personal and career decisions I made were the wrong lifestyle choices to help my healing process," said Johnny.

"So, Johnny, how did you get involved with heroin?" said Arthur handing him and Sandra each a glass of iced tea.

"It started with a pill, a pain pill for an old knee injury. I then found ways to continue to persuade doctors to re-fill prescription meds like Xanax and OxyContin. The prescription meds were expensive and at the bars and on the streets I learned about heroin capsules which were just as good at dulling the pain, but were cheaper and much more available. People need to know that heroin is all over the place now."

"You have to get help to change your ways. You can't keep committing crimes and stealing money to support your heroin habit."

Before Arthur or Johnny could make any further comments, there were several loud knocks on the door to the apartment. Johnny swung open the door, a little surprised at not knowing the two people standing in the hallway.

"Hi, my name is Ruth Staley from Pleasant Grove Rehabilitation Center of Atlanta this is my driver, Harold. I am here to speak with Johnny Hobson and his family and help lead an intervention. Are you Johnny Hobson?" Of the three people within her vision in the living room, she knew which one was Johnny. She had enough years of experience dealing with heroin addicts to spot a serious user one hundred feet away.

"Yes, I am Johnny Hobson, but I never called anybody to lead an intervention. I guess you all think because I barely finished high school, I need to listen to all of you, while all of you laugh, smirk and wonder what me and my trailer park friends do to survive."

"It sounds like you have some intelligence and I promise to respect you and any strong viewpoints you express on a particular issue. It is admirable when any person can debate, banter, and yet walk away with a chuckle despite their differences with others. When all is said and done, all that matters is the good parts we take away from a conversation and use them to compartmentalize in our brains," said Ms. Staley.

"I had a difficult time concentrating on my duties when I was in the army in Vietnam, because all I could think about was playing my guitar and getting back to the states, but my music career didn't go as I had hoped," said Johnny.

"I certainly can certainly sympathize with your feelings," said Ms. Staley.

"Teens who grew up in Vietnam were involved in military conflicts for their entire childhoods and they were surrounded by adults who experienced deep economic woes. Despair resonated everywhere when I was over there. I hate when any politician softens the violence associated with war or makes the war exploitative to gain profits for a few of his jaded wealthy friends who live in the Capitol. The wealthy control everything now. The odds are ever in their favor. I don't have a lot and I'm not interested in being anybody's hero, but I think too many people have become desensitized to trauma and other's pain. I want more people to be happy."

"You tasted the dirt and bled the blood with your fellow soldiers, truly understanding what it means to fight in a war, and the drug war is no different, even when it is based on lies. A good soldier knows when something does not fit in a war story because someone is lying. It is time to make a deal at a soldier's level and stop the bloodletting. A drug dealer should not be able to override a man and his family, just like a politician sitting in an office should not be able to override a general on the ground in the middle of a battle. Let's get back to re-establishing the life of Johnny the musician, not the drug addict, by working to confront problems, not deny them," said Ms. Staley.

Arthur quickly interjecting, "Johnny, I called Ms. Staley. For five days Sandra and I have been working hard cleaning up your apartment and trying to help you clean up you life and your financial affairs. Take a seat Johnny; we are all going to give Ms. Staley the courtesy of listening to what else she has to say."

Arthur and Sandra sat on each side of Johnny, all three sitting close to each other on the sofa. Ms. Staley and Harold sat in separate chairs directly across from them.

"First of all, thank you very much Arthur for taking the initiative to call me. Too many people don't know where to turn or are embarrassed about what options they have to ask for help. There are rehab facilities with doctors and trained counselors that can help. Some facilities are better than others. The more the message gets out and the more help addicts and their families get, the stronger our recovery teams become and hopefully we will save more lives from this horrible disease. Johnny, you are lucky to have family members who love and care about you. Together as a group, we can conquer this addiction."

"Ms. Staley, may I get you and Harold a glass of iced tea?"

"That would be wonderful dear, thank you."

Sandra really was a special young woman, considerate and caring. She was not into bake sales or cooking contests, mainly because she did not have much experience in that area yet. If she decided to put her mind to a cause in the kitchen, anything was possible.

She was knowledgeable about healthy beverages to drink which she attributed to all the years she played sports and learned about nutrition, electrolytes, carbohydrates, proteins and phenylketonurics, which is the process of adding acids to drinks to extend shelf life. Because long-term use of these products can be damaging to the digestive system, Sandra offered to bring Ms. Staley and Harold each a glass of iced tea and a coaster instead.

"What does heroin actually do to a young person's brain," Sandra asked Ms. Staley.

"Life is a disaster for teenagers involved in illegal drug use. We now know that the brain's prefrontal cortex isn't fully developed until a person is in their late twenties, yet teenagers accept the opinions of their peers over the opinions of their parents and those in advisory roles who have more experience. The prefrontal cortex is the part of the brain, which is responsible for helping an individual organize plans and ideas, form strategies and control impulses. Dopamine, naturally produced by the body, is not yet at optimal levels during adolescent years either. Dopamine is the natural chemical messenger, which allows us to pay attention to our surroundings and help us make important decisions in our daily lives. Using heroin disrupts the natural growth process of our brains," explained Ms. Staley.

"That's scary," said Sandra.

"I'm not a doctor, but since I've worked so long in this field, trying to help addicts, I can explain what happens to the brain in the way it was explained to me by doctors who study the brain. Opiates (heroin) acts on many areas in the brain and the central nervous system. Heroin can change the brain stem, body functions and even depress breathing. Heroin changes the limbic system, which controls emotions to increase feelings of pleasure in the central nervous system. The drug diminishes the sensation to feel and blocks pain messages transmitted by the spinal cord to other parts of the body. Trying to understand the brain, doctors have enough work to do in the areas of depression, schizophrenia and aggressive behavior. Piling on with man induced use of opiates and playing Russian roulette with the neurons and genetic circuits of the brain is dangerous, unnecessary and foolish. The area of the brain where you find the heaviest concentration of opiate receptors is the corpus striatum. This part of the brain plays a part in how a person perceives information. Heroin use increases the number of opiate preceptors in brain and decreases regular brain function and the ability to think rationally. After ten years of heroin use brain function is about over. Many heroin addicts are dead by age forty. We should be bringing drug dealers face-to-face with mothers of murdered children. It is possible to stop some violent dealers from selling drugs, simply by talking to them. Everybody wants to talk about what can't be done, instead of talking about ways to fix problems. Insanity is doing the same thing over and over and expecting a different result," offered Ms. Staley in a manner that showed experience and knowledge of her field.

Arthur relayed another story. "I recently read about a homeless woman who was a regular with law enforcement across southern counties in Missouri. Her name was Carly 'Sunshine' Schofield. She had been arrested a whopping forty-three times since the turn of the century, with fifteen convictions, mostly for being drunk in public or trespassing after a heroin binge. Schofield's trip to a jail in Southern Missouri the evening of September 4, 2010, would be her last. The following afternoon authorities found her dead on the floor of her cell. Swanson was seriously ill when taken into custody, vomiting blood, but she never received medical treatment: She should have gone to a hospital. One witness who was in the jail cell next to her at the time, but who did not know Sunshine said she heard her crying to them to call an ambulance, and they went by her cell and said, 'Shut the hell up.' The official cause of death listed as a complication of chronic alcoholism and drug use. Many questions arose why police repeatedly arrested Schofield, without referring her to an alcohol treatment program or help her seek counseling. She was taken into custody as a victim of physical abuse perpetrated by drug dealers three times in the year leading up to her death, including one incident where she suffered broken ribs, but she never was taken to the hospital."

"It sounds like she never had a chance because no one ever took the time to help her. She died from alcohol and heroin poisoning," said Ms. Staley. "Imagine this headline around the world, maybe even printed in the New York Times, "The Taliban lead the world's economies." Only the brainwashed radicals would believe that. Since conservatives would realize how ridiculous the claim was, this is not what the media might report. Imagine instead the liberal media reports, "Peace did not bring economic development, the Taliban efficiently took over the mines and opium production." This type of reporting explains why so many people around the world get confused and even hate Americans. This has become a large problem because so many news reporters are eager to chase a sensational story that will bring in dollars to sell their story. Telling the truth is not a priority and a compromise of morals. America, the greatest force for good among nations is hated, and the Taliban, never a force for good gains new recruits and more heroin sales."

"Now I'm even more scared for Uncle Johnny," said Sandra. "However, there are young people who actually enjoy having sober adult conversations instead of getting plastered every night or every weekend. But I'm starting to understand how the dangers of alcohol and drug use should not be underestimated because its problems sneak up on a person like nothing else."

"In the US it now costs more to send a young person to jail for four years than it does to college. This is another good reason all of us should be doing more to help young people understand the importance of a good education, one that teaches them the dangers of drugs. Now is our chance and obligation, to fulfill our promise to the children of America," said Ms. Staley, her passion for the subject resonating from her voice.

"Why do young people have to feel like freaks if they don't cave-in to the peer pressures of using drugs and alcohol in order to belong? These kids surely do not need any illegal substances to confuse them even more. Most of the kids involved in alcohol and drugs will survive, but many of them will miss taking advantage of opportunities that could have written their success stories, because they wasted so much of their time inside the alcohol and drug culture, a recurring series of bad decisions in a circular pattern that lacks circumspection. More young people should want to make something special out of their lives," said Arthur.

"Fear of the unknown holds a person back. But doing heroin or any other drugs prolongs the fear. Fear of detoxification holds an addict back from seeking treatment. Heroin addiction is a vicious circle. I'm not sure when staying sober went out of style, but living life with a clear mind all the time is so much better than living life drunk or messed up on drugs," preached Ms. Staley in the loudest most caring voice any of the three Hobson's had heard since Margaret died."

"How bad is heroin traffic in Atlanta?" asked Arthur.

"Heroin use in middle-class suburbia has become epidemic in every city in America. First, the drug takes away a person's integrity and then it takes away their personality. It is not fear mongering to suggest that heroin traffic has increased ten-fold in Atlanta the last few years and is coming into the US through Mexico from South America and Afghanistan. Atlanta has become the hub for drug trafficking in the Southeastern US because there are so many people living their lives one-step ahead of the police and two steps from the grave. For the same reasons, legitimate businesses like setting up shop in Atlanta, so does the drug cartels. Oprah could devote some time to this one real cause. The easy access to interstate highways that connect to other major cities makes redistribution of heroin and meth-amphetamine easy."

"How many people are dying from heroin use?" asked Arthur.

"The problem is that more people are dying at the end of a needle than at the end of a gun. In the past five years, we have seen over five hundred deaths yearly from its use in each of the hub cities Chicago and Atlanta, and over a hundred deaths annually in St. Louis. Johnny, because none of us in this room want you to be one of those casualties, Harold and I are going to take you back to Pleasant Grove for a 60-day educational stay-vacation at our facility," exclaimed Ms. Staley.

"I never made arrangements to go to Pleasant Grove with you," said Johnny.

"This information I'm giving you is all true and hopefully this kind of knowledge will bug the drug users and inspire all the drinkers to become thinkers, to finally help you wake-up and see what you are missing in life, maybe for the first time in your life. It is time people, to get real," said Ms. Staley.

"Your free time is your own time to do what you want. In a corporate work environment where employees have to kiss a boss's ass, toiling to improve the bottom line so the company stock will increase a point, it's important to remember why people work. People work so they will have money to enjoy their lives during their free time. If you choose to drink, do drugs and smoke, you will significantly decrease the amount of enjoyable free time in your life due to poor health while living or a shorter lifespan because of early death. Living a joyful life is not about fighting against the values of teetotal ling do-gooders and fighting against their beliefs about sobriety. It's about having a clear mind, taking care of your health, and noticing and appreciating all the little things that life has to offer," said Harold, Ms. Staley's driver and assistant, mainly focusing his attention on Johnny. Looking directly into the eyes of Arthur and Sandra, Harold finished by saying, "The public service number for alcohol and drug abuse is (1-800-alcohol) a referral hotline."

"I'm Harold's boss. Now you can see why I like the guy so much. He speaks from his heart," said Ms. Staley.

"Johnny, you have to go because I want my old Uncle Johnny back," said Sandra with tears in her eyes.

"Johnny, it is time to end all the foolishness and all the suffering this disease is causing in all of our lives," said Arthur.

Sandra walked across the room to where Johnny was sitting, bent over, and gave him a long bear hug, begging him to take the headed advice of Ms. Staley. Everything Ms. Staley said up to this point made sense and it was obvious to Sandra that she was the one with all the experience who would have the best chance of saving Johnny's life. Sandra pulled back and looked directly into Johnny's eyes, hesitating for a moment, while Ms. Staley spoke.

"Smart people with sensible plans will try to help empower you to take your life back. It will take a good deal of audacity from you, but if you help with the plans, together we can take back our neighborhoods one at a time, one person at a time," said Ms. Staley. "The mayors of our large cities must do more to stop the street violence by raising public health awareness, talking about the dangers of drugs and helping individuals find the training they need to sharpen their job skills. The mayor of Atlanta has asked every small business in the metropolitan area to hire one person as a fulltime employee to help combat the high crime and jobless rates. When an individual is hired, a nice feature article in the newspaper publicizes the event and promotes the small business. In just a few months, the mayor is hoping the new program will help more people in Atlanta join the workforce," said Ms. Staley.

"Johnny, do you really want to be part of the rot that is infiltrating families and neighborhoods everywhere? Drug dealers bully people on the streets. Scared residents abandon their homes and flee to safer neighborhoods, businesses choose not to invest, and politicians allow the many foreclosed vacant properties bought up by city governments to rot," said Arthur.

"A trainer doesn't teach tricks to a killer whale in far away deep ocean waters. He lures the whale in a controlled large pool environment, so the whale can learn free from distractions but still in his element. I learned this from Susie," said Sandra.

"You can't help a drug user while he is still using, the elevator in his mind is broken, he is still wondering the streets, and the glass of his life he looks through is foggy. He isn't going to receive the message until he enters a program which offers a different path, a path to finding a job, because a real man isn't supposed to steal from family members, girlfriends, or complete strangers," said Ms. Staley.

"Johnny, please tell me you will leave today, right now to start your rehab program. Please tell me that you know it is the right thing to do," said Sandra wiping the tears in her eyes.

"OK, I will go," said Johnny.

Finally there was some hope for the Hobson's. Everyone stood up at the same time. Arthur vowed to keep in touch with Ms. Staley during Johnny's rehabilitation, though he already knew visitors weren't allowed during the first phase of the program. Harold put his arm around Johnny's shoulders and escorted him and Ms. Staley immediately out of the apartment, down the sidewalk to the Pleasant Grove shuttle van to start the difficult ride of trying to bring back the treasures of a man lost in a deep dark hole of addiction, knowing there are no guarantees. The first few days in rehab are the worst because of the excruciating pain and discomfort the patient endures during the natural detoxifying process of eliminating the drug from the body. Standing on the sidewalk, Arthur and Sandra waved good-bye as the shuttle headed down the oak-tree-lined street towards the entrance to the highway.

According to Arthur, Johnny had grown up living at the Hobson House and had his own bedroom in the remodeled section of the basement. Both grandfathers of the three Hobson boys were alcoholics, and many of the neighbors down towards the end of the road openly drank beer and smoked pot during get-togethers in backyards or in a nearby park. During his junior and senior years of high school, Johnny worked at a two-star hotel in St. Louis, cleaning rooms, making beds, and scrubbing bathrooms, exposing him to some of the seedier things which take place in hotel rooms, the drug dealing, the drinking parties and prostitution. This was in addition to helping his aging parents maintain the Hobson property, farming the crops, cutting several acres of grass, sealing the driveway, painting the outside of the house, trimming trees, making simple repairs and doing anything his father asked. His dad depended on his help because the older brothers had already moved away from home, leaving the family roost to pursue their own dreams. Johnny provided all this help in hopes of winning his dad's approval, but this was difficult because he did not share his father's interests of watching westerns and football games on television, hunting pheasant and fishing for bass and bluegill in the streams and rivers of central and southern Missouri. Despite working what amounted to a forty-hour-per-week full-time unpaid job at home and another part-time job at the hotel, Johnny learned how to cook from reading books and trying new recipes using the herbs and vegetables he grew and tended to in the garden on the side of the house. His grades in high school suffered because he worked so much, but he helped his parents and he helped take care of the property, while earning an income to pay personal bills. Like most young people, he had big dreams, but instead of pursuing them as his two brothers did, he kept his to himself. He did not like all the politics and competition it took to get ahead in the business world.

When it came to politics and competition, Arthur was fascinated by both subjects, especially in contrast to the stark two worlds lived by his brother Johnny and him. Johnny's drug culture life was earthy, but abusive and mentally manipulative. The world he knew in Rainbow Creek was affluent, comparatively speaking, except that his opportunities for musical success were limited. But before he would decide if he wanted to move back to his hometown, he would have to realize he had become a liability and a shattered soul, toggling back-and-forth between unsafe neighborhoods and the unsettling flammables he was creating in his whole way of living in Atlanta. The final fade-to-darkness parts of addiction he was learning at Ms. Staley's rehabilitation facility left him to interpret what had happened and what is still to come in his life. Ms. Staley did her best to convince him he needed to, "seek to understand before seeking understanding from others".

Ethical and moral issues have been a part of cultures since Adam and Eve ate apples in the Garden of Eden. Freedom of choice, gay marriages, the war on drugs and illegal immigration are confusing issues, but Arthur was a little surprised when he learned from Ms. Staley that so many nations, places like Holland and Nicaragua, did not consider the use of street drugs a crime. He was confused about how Americans can freely spend billions in illegal street drugs every year without a guilty conscious, while Mexico is paying the price of countless drug murders and ruined lives working for drug cartels. Arthur figured if more parents taught their children the old proverb, "When the image of your name is ruined, your life is in trouble," maybe the America's cultural relationship with Mexico would improve. Somewhere along the line, all these kids lost their way. Because of all the drug problems, there is less investment in Mexico, tourism is significantly down, schools are deteriorating and businesses are moving to other countries. It seemed such a shame to Arthur that in Merida, the vibrant capital of the state of Yucatan with one of the lowest crime rates in all of Mexico was not attracting visitors because of drug wars far away to the north. Hundreds of Mayan archeological sites, pyramids, temples, palaces and treasures that rival those in Egypt are losing out from attracting crowds of people from the tour buses, which should be rolling in from all directions. A traveler in North

America should not need a gun to mount a personal expedition anywhere in Mexico, much less a chance to scramble up the steps of a steep pyramid with a strong sense of adventure. Arthur wondered why politicians on both sides of the border between the US and Mexico were not using their resources to improve public relations and advertise the untapped treasures of both countries. Arthur could not believe his ears when he heard a black Republican presidential candidate announce that he wanted to build a fence with an electric wire on top to kill illegal immigrants trying to cross the border. If given the power, how could a man running for president, especially a black man who understood civil rights issues, confess that one of the first things he wants to do when the tables are turned is practice mind-blowing politics against another ethnic group? Arthur thought it was time the younger generation stepped up to the plate. He felt the same kids who vacationed in Mexican resorts during spring breaks during college, were now old enough to help build relationships and create jobs and partnerships with Mexico. To Arthur, the only way both countries have a chance to find an alternative for these kids selling drugs for the cartels, is if someone reaches out to them. He thought to himself, wouldn't it be nice if for once an inexperienced younger generation helped fix a problem, instead of camping out on public land protesting and complaining about every inconvenience they must endure and every entitlement they think should be handed to them, while they sit in tents, wait and do nothing to help any situation?

Back at Johnny's apartment, Sandra cleaned out the refrigerator and discarded all the perishables inside it. Arthur called the Yellow-Cab taxi company to secure a ride to Atlanta International Airport so he and Sandra could catch the next flight back to St. Louis. Arthur wrote a letter to Johnny and put it in the big blue USP mailbox at a nearby street corner before a cab arrived for him and Sandra. He hoped that Johnny would read the letter at a later date upon his return to rehab.

Dear Johnny:

I debated whether to write or not, because I know that scolding a drug addict just makes him or her mad, but you do have to face the truth sometime. The one thing that makes me mad is how you have played your family over and over. From what I know, you have been using heroin for a few years now. Half a million drug offenders are in prison in the United States. Using heroin for a period of five years causes many scars and permanent brain damage. Ten year users are usually dead by the age of forty and you are already passed that age.

I don't feel sorry for you, because everyone in our family has tried to help you. At least while you are in rehab, we know that you are still alive. For the last few years, you have had a hard time figuring out who the good people are that care about you and those that are just using you.

The last few years have been hard for all of us, mom and dad's deaths, my separation with Jane, college expenses, and all the other struggles of everyday life. But as a family, we deal with it and help each other. Mom made it (though we walked slowly and took a number of breaks) to the top row of Busch Stadium for a Cardinals game before she died, pretty good for someone who had five by-passes and a heart valve replacement. In a strange way, I think by her example, she was trying to tell you to fight harder to get back to the top.

It will not be easy for you, but giving up and excuses are for losers. I know that you are strong enough and tough enough, I just hope you are smart enough to make the needed changes in your life. It probably seems that your family doesn't want much to do with you right now, only because that is the truth and you have broken all of our trust. Things can get easier with time, but first you will have to set short-term and long-term goals for yourself. If you can stay clean for an entire year, you will start to turn routine into habit and learn to appreciate the important little accomplishments in life without all the senseless drama and craziness of living a life surrounded by drugs.

This letter has been written in hopes that you will channel more of your thoughts thinking about how your parents raised you and how Sandra and I want you to stop chasing the distorted but very temporary feelings of heroin. We are tremendously hurt because we are having a very difficult time getting through to you and heroin is twisting your way of thinking. When you are using heroin, you are missing life's experiences because you abuse your mental faculties and deny your brain from understanding the whole picture of what is happening. If you do not change your behavior, before you know it, the heroin will have irreversible effects to your brain and body. Eventually, the heroin will not even help you with the ability to feel good. Drugs are a downward spiral to a hole that gets darker and deeper.

Your choices affect the entire family. They affect your nieces, more than you know. Some self-doubt creeps into their minds and it affects their self-confidence when they see their uncle not knowing the difference between right and wrong.

Life is much better without the extreme highs and lows. I will try not to patronize you by talking about the criminal, financial, social and psychological aspects of heroin. However, the most important part of living our lives is to prepare ourselves for our maker. Recently you have fallen down, but now it is your time to step up to the plate and do the right thing. I hope and pray that you are strong enough to change your situation.

Sincerely,

Arthur

With real love from your family

Nearly an hour after dropping the letter in the mailbox, Arthur and Sandra were comfortably sitting in seats 11A and 11B four-thousand feet up in the air, and hoping their recent efforts made a difference for Johnny. If he had hit bottom, if he took his rehab seriously, and he did want to turn his life around, at least he had a clean apartment to return to in sixty days.

"Dad, after all the attention we focused on trying to help Uncle Johnny, how are you doing?" said Sandra as she adjusted the back rest of her seat as the airplane was now leveled-out and at cruising speed.

"I'm doing OK, but I will continue to worry about Johnny. Hopefully we did enough and the people working with him will get through to him."

"You are still talking about Johnny. I asked how you are doing."

"How are you and Mom doing? Are the two of you doing OK since the divorce? You guys have been apart for some time now and Stuart has been living with mom for several months."

"I have been thinking about this more than you know. As children, boys and girls are taught to determine their worth in comparison with others. If we were smarter than, prettier than, better dressed than, stronger than, faster than or get better grades than, then we were validated and we had worth. This worth causes some to want too much power and control to the extent that their behavior causes problems in social interactions with family members, co-workers, friends and others, but especially with a spouse who threatens their authority. We were taught to focus away from who we really were as an individual. At some point in life, we were taught to focus on accumulating property and material things, and to marry to determine if we have worth. All the time we would have been better off just being ourselves, just being human, making mistakes and finding out what makes us happy," said Arthur.

"Do you feel you weren't allowed to be yourself and you weren't happy?" asked Sandra.

"People in general have a need or craving for love, but men and women are so often disappointed in the opposite sex. Even when their own happiness level is nothing to brag about, one spouse may perceive that it is appropriate to inflict the norms of their own live on the other spouse. There are so many pressures on middle-class Americans, when negotiating for anything, some women and men too, take the role of the martyr type or the other extreme role of determination in seeing the bright side of everything. Both strategies are unnatural and don't allow for real growth and expressing true feelings in a marriage. Love is a verb, and to preserve it and keep it fresh, both partners have to work at it. Trouble is, often times one or the other or both partners don't feel staying together is worth the effort," explained Arthur.

"I remember watching *Seinfeld* one day with mom and Jerry said, "Single men are playing wiffleball, while married men are fighting a war in their own home." He was using humor to explain what it feels like to be married after living so many years as a single man," recalled Sandra.

"People often talk about the past with exaggerated fondness. Sometimes aspects of life were better in the old days; life was easier and less complicated. There were fewer roads, less cars and less traffic, less things to worry about. Incomes rose almost every year for five decades after World War II. The US had a vibrant middle class for half a century. Manufacturing was robust as interstates and bridges were gradually added to our infrastructure. But to tell the truth, the social stigmas of divorce portrayed in the *Leave it to Beaver* television era had as much to do with lower divorce rates as people deciding to stay in unhappy marriages on their own accord," said Arthur.

"Dad, I must admit I think men reason differently than woman, but when talking to you, you always offer something new with a perspective I hadn't considered before," said Sandra.

"A woman is the only one to have the choice of deciding if a baby is born or not, no matter what the man wants, and assuming of course whether the woman is pregnant or wants to get pregnant in the first place. To some women having an abortion means preventing overpopulation in their world. To other women having a baby is their world. For the most part men do most of the other heavy lifting. Men usually mow the grass, trim the hedges, shovel snow, paint the house, haul firewood, re-model the basement and do other backbreaking chores, but it is never enough and it is never exactly, what the wife wants. When a man is up at the plate, with bases loaded and two outs, and the count is 3-0, he does not want to swing at the next pitch. In other words, you do not keep demanding more work and casting aspersions on an unsuspecting man, when has already done enough. Men and women have equal amounts of creativity, but generally, men are more labor intensive, while women are over the moon about colors, fabrics and picking out wallpaper. Couples negotiate almost everything else to find common ground. Where to live, what items to buy, what cars to drive, what to eat for dinner, what color paint to use on the living room walls and what bills to pay first are all things to negotiate," said Arthur.

"Did you ever have this conversation with mom?" asked Sandra.

"Hundreds of times, but when two people live their lives in such close proximity, one sentence, one phrase or even one word can setoff the other person and any communication ends immediately right there," said Arthur, starting to feel like the conversation he was having with his daughter was the kind of talk Johnny was having with Ms. Staley at the rehab facility.

"Maybe you should have bought two airplane tickets to somewhere and you and mom would have been forced to sit together and work out your differences and have a nice discussion like you and I are having now," said Sandra.

"I don't know if our problems could have been solved so easily. The airplane may have had to make an emergency landing to the nearest runway. It is hard to explain, but in a difficult marriage, the love a father has for his children is different than the love he has for his spouse. Maybe it has something to do with a child sharing the same blood of their parents," said Arthur.

"Did you and mom fight about money?" asked Sandra.

"When one spouse controls the checkbook and that same spouse always decides what meals to eat or which television programs to watch, a marriage becomes stale. When one spouse comes home from work and lies on the couch for the rest of the night, a marriage becomes stale. When one spouse refuses or shows no interest in sex, a marriage becomes stale. When one partner gets tired of bargaining for too many negotiations or the other partner stops bringing anything interesting to the relationship, a stale marriage often develops into divorce. Each of us had our faults. Just make sure you have a lot of common interests and that you are truly in love before you get married Sandra?" said Arthur, trying to offer meaningful fatherly advice.

The captain's voice resonated over the telecom. He told the passengers that the current temperature in St. Louis is seventy-six degrees with partly cloudy skies, but only a slight chance of showers for the evening. The stewardess working the front end of the service cart stocked with beverages rolled down the isle to row 11 and looked directly towards Sandra.

"What can I get you dear?"

"I'll have a cranberry juice, please."

"And you Sir, what can I get you?"

"Make it easy, I'll have a cranberry juice, also, thank you."

"Two cranberry juice drinks coming right up."

The stewardess filled two clear plastic cups with ice cubes and placed them on the trays pulled down over the laps of Sandra and Arthur. Next, she handed each of them a napkin and an unopened 12-ounce can of Welch's cranberry juice.

Sandra continued asking questions and Arthur continued answering them. He couldn't help thinking how mature she had become since high school, impressed with her ability to use repartee without second-guessing the other person.

"And after everything we experienced in Atlanta, how are you feeling?" Arthur asked Sandra approximately twenty minutes before the plane was to land in St. Louis.

"I'm fine, mom is supposed to come over tomorrow to help me bake some cookies to take to work Monday. Going back to work and getting paid actually sounds nice, but I am glad we did everything we could to try and help Uncle Johnny."

"I couldn't be more proud of everything you did to help make fast decisions in difficult circumstances for the past two weeks. We accomplished a lot in a short amount of time."

At the end of a long two weeks for Arthur and Sandra, the plane landed and taxied to the gate without any waiting or other incident. Arthur and Sandra grabbed their luggage at carousel two and walked the long airport corridor to the lower level garage where Arthur parked his Buick.

On the drive home from Lambert Airport, Arthur had to slam on the brakes to avoid an accident. A man driving a red Ford pickup thought Arthur was following too close. The man gave no warning about what he was going to do, before abruptly stopping his truck in the middle of the road. After braking hard and skidding three car lengths to avoid a crash, Arthur heard the front license plate of his car tap the rear license plate of the man's pickup, once both vehicles were at a halt. Arthur checked and saw that Sandra was OK. Then he backed up and drove around the pickup, so he could pull his car to the side of the road. The pickup, still on the road, rolled up alongside Arthur's car. The man pushed a button to lower the passenger window and threw the remains of a Burger King fish sandwich he had been eating at Arthur. Because Arthur leaned back to avoid the thrown object, the fish sandwich hit Sandra. Splats of ketchup checkered Sandra's white blouse and shreds of lettuce covered her lap. The bun and the wrapper ended up next to her feet on the floor mat. The man in the red pickup pounced on the accelerator and sped away. Gazing into each other's eyes, Arthur and Sandra burst into laughter. Almost home and after all of the tumultuous events of their trip, there was nothing left to do, except try to laugh.

Arthur drove Sandra to her condominium, helped her carry her luggage inside, and gave her a big hug. He thanked her once again, ending their conversation and the longest period of time spent with Sandra since the family was intact together. Driving back home, he was tired and anxious to return to sleeping in his own bed. Once home, he walked straight towards his bedroom, took off his clothes and flopped himself on the bed, ready for a good night's sleep. He jumped back out of bed, walked over to the light switch he forgot to turn off, pulled the curtains on the window a little closer so they overlapped, grabbed an extra blanket and laid down on his bed with one pillow between his knees and another puffier one under his head. He hoped sleep and darkness would be the combination to offer some relief from a difficult trip that put him in a state of flayed mental fatigue. Within a few minutes, he was asleep.

★ 9 ★

Adjusting to the Real World

The next morning, asleep for only five hours, Arthur felt a magnitude 5.5 earthquake centered over the city of Sullivan, one hour away from Rainbow Creek. The event shook the lamps on the tables, the dishes in the cabinets, and the books on the shelves, wakening and startling him from a deep sleep. Not able to fall back asleep, he decided to start addressing all the things a person falls behind on when away from the house for an extended amount of time—unpacking luggage, doing laundry, paying the bills, and catching-up on e-mail messages.

After writing checks for the utility bills and loading the washing machine with light-colored pieces of clothing first, Arthur checked his e-mail and found a message from Susie.

Hi Dad,
It is with great regret that I write you this letter. To avoid burdening you with the expenses of a large wedding, my boyfriend and I decided to elope. Even though my boyfriend wears a nose clip, ear piercings, body piercings, a beard, and several tattoos, he is a good man. I feel free when I am with him, and now that I am trying to get pregnant, he says he will take care of me and a baby. We will be living happily in a trailer in the woods outside of Columbia. We already stacked enough firewood for next winter. My boyfriend and I like to smoke marijuana to relax. In the meantime, pray that our doctor will be able to remedy our venereal diseases. But don't worry about us, Dad. I'm twenty years old now, and I know how to take care of myself. Someday, we will come visit you.
Love,
Susie

P.S. Dad, none of the content in this message is true. I'm up early, heading over to the library to study. I just wanted to remind you that there are worse things in life than having divorced parents. I love you. Sandra sent me a message before she went to sleep last night. I hear Burger King serves a mean fish sandwich.

When the sun came out, Arthur walked outside in the backyard noticing that a mole had burrowed tunnels along the foundation and wrapping around the side of the house to the front yard. He followed the paths of the mole tunnels to the front of the house, encountering Karen Anderson, who was up early snatching the newspaper from her driveway.

"Hey, honey britches, haven't seen you around the neighborhood lately!"

"No, Sandra and I were in Atlanta visiting my brother Johnny the past couple of weeks."

"Well, you picked a good time to take a trip because the weather here was horrible while you guys were away. One thunderstorm produced baseball-size hail that damaged roofs and the hoods of cars throughout Rainbow Creek. Never in my life did I see hail that large; it was scary. Listen, do you hear that noise coming from the big Bradford pear tree in your front yard?"

"Yes, what is that?" asked Arthur.

"Those sounds are coming from the last of the cicadas. They have been here for over two weeks. At one point, almost every tree in the neighborhood was full of the loud, annoying insects buzzing about in everybody's business," said Karen.

"Did the cicadas fly away or die?" asked Arthur.

"Some died, but many are still here," said Karen.

"They are annoying," Arthur agreed.

"Yes, but I think they're a bit enthralling too," intimated Karen. "There was a report about them on the news the other night, they've been such a nuisance. Turns out they like heat and do their most spirited singing during the hotter hours of a summer day. They have a thirteen-year life cycle and live underground as nymphs for most of their lives. The nymphs feed on root juice and have strong legs for digging. In the final stages of their lives, they construct an exit tunnel to the surface and emerge. Then they shed their skins on a nearby plant or tree for the last time and emerge as an adult, ready for mating. Isn't that romantic?"

Just then, the sound of Victor's mint-condition 1966 dark blue Mustang with brand-new tires and a recently added duel carburetor could be heard roaring down Hill View Avenue. After parking his classic ride on the right side of his two-car garage, Victor walked over to join his wife and Arthur for a little friendly conversation. Usually Victor talked about the weather or bragged about a great shot he made during a recent golf outing. Today he wanted to talk about baseball.

"How are you doing, Arthur? I haven't seen you for at least a month."

"I'm doing OK, just returning from a trip. I'm a little tired, that is all. How are you?"

"You know, retired guys just do what they feel like doing. I was watching a Chicago White Sox game on TV a few nights ago. Did you see that play Mark Buehrle made? I haven't had a chance to talk to you about it."

"No, I didn't see the play. What happened?"

"Maybe the best play ever in the history of baseball occurred that night. It was the highlight of opening day for the Chicago White Sox and they showed it on the highlight reel for days. Buehrle kick saved a line drive back to the mound with his left foot. The baseball ricocheted into foul territory on the first-base side, halfway between home plate and first base. Buehrle sprinted to the spot and as he was falling down to reach for the ball with his glove, he scooped it backward between his legs. The first baseman, in a completely stretched-out position on the foul side of the first-base bag, caught the ball with his bare hand, just barely nipping the runner as the umpire flashed a thrilling 'out' call to the crowd," explained Victor.

"Sounds exciting. I'm sorry I missed it. My daughter Sandra and I just got back from visiting my brother in Atlanta, and before that, I was busy with work and political stuff, so I haven't kept up with all the baseball games lately. The sports channels will probably show the play again. I'll look for it, I promise."

"You should. Like I said, it was the best play of all time."

"Thanks for the chat, Karen and Victor. I need to get back to work now—you know, still catching up on everything after being gone for two and half weeks. Have a nice day." Arthur was not sure if Karen was making a move on him, with all the talk about cicada nymphs, root juice, and finding a mate. All he could think about was this new focus on everything moving and tunneling under his house, the earth's plates sliding over each other, cicada nymphs and moles digging tunnels underground on his property. Change was everywhere.

Before Arthur left with Sandra for two weeks in Atlanta, he had the post office hold his mail. Now that he was home, one of the first things he wanted to do was to read his mail. He drove his Buick to the Rainbow Creek post office and the clerk behind the counter retrieved a small box full of letters, bills, and ads for Arthur to take home.

For several years, print ads and TV ads have shown retired couples sipping piña colada's sitting in lawn chairs on the beach and enjoying watching the waves crashing in from the ocean, all possible because these people planned ahead by contributing to their 401(k) plans. In reality, most of these plans have ripped off the people who are now at retirement age and sitting at their kitchen tables, worried about paying increasingly higher bills. Workers, still going to their jobs every day, worried if they would stay employed.

Now that sex pill companies like Viagra and Cialis advertised on stadium walls directly behind home plate, they assaulted American families watching at home behind a dinner plate. "Why do all these types of television commercials always show a naked man and woman lounging in separate bathtubs outdoors, on top of a hill, and next to a lake with mountains in the backdrop?" wondered Arthur. The ad made him marvel about these elderly people, portrayed as having lots of sex, and if they were, where are all those outdoor bathtubs located? Arthur wondered if he was the only person who even thought about this.

"What is with all these imposing concerns about erectile dysfunction supplements?" thought Arthur. He opened a white business envelope with no mention of a company in the return address. Inside the envelope was a brochure explaining all the benefits of another erectile dysfunction supplement called Instarise. First there was Viagra, then Cialis, Extenze, Tostorall, Megamax, Rock Hard, and now Instarise. Instarise announced in the brochure that their product increases your testosterone as proven by clinical studies out West. Instarise does not mention where out West. However, they do mention the product to be the only all-natural erectile dysfunction supplement, whatever that means. This amazing new testosterone lifter shoots up your sexual performance, strengthens your heart, increases your energy, helps you lose weight, increases your strength, and relieves your prostate problems.

"Wow, Instarise makes you a superman," thought Arthur.

Arthur read on. *You will keep suffering from the following problems until you start using Instarise: less sexual desire, fatigue, declining motivation, weight gain in the belly area, loss of muscle strength, less self-confidence, prostate problems, loss of bone strength, loss of memory, heart problems, sagging facial skin, and premature aging. You will continue to suffer from slower thinking, thinning hair, a weakened immune system, aches and pains, irritability, loss of height, anxiety, and bad mood swings.*

"Damn, it's time to go buy some Instarise right now!" thought Arthur.

For an erection that lasts more than 4 hours, call your physician.

"Did the Instarise folks ever consider that men might want to sleep for more than four hours?" thought Arthur. "In four hours, a man could eat a nice meal, watch an entire baseball or football game, and still have time for a drink or a cup of coffee."

Your body is a vacuum cleaner that gradually sucks the life right out of you. You can only take one of two roads now. One road leads to worsening health, the other to better health. If you ignore this important news, you are choosing worse health for yourself. Here is the great news. New studies in the West prove the pills eliminate or greatly reduce your health problems when you restore your low testosterone level back to the level you had when you were younger. With higher levels of testosterone, men have improved sexual performance and more interest in sex. They feel more energetic, vigorous, and alive. They feel better, enjoy their lives more, and have a better outlook about life.

"Could this possibly be true?" Arthur thought. "I'm sure there's more to this story." Instead of readying yourself to buy some Instarise, if you are curious like Arthur, you do your research and discover something else.

So Arthur did some research. Searching the Internet he found that Medicare has paid thousands in bogus claims for products associated with erectile dysfunction. A few weeks after a five-city bust, officials in Miami discovered that Medicare paid thousands in bogus claims for penis pumps to treat erectile dysfunction in women. This discovery does not help the credibility of the industry. Medicare needs to change the way they do business. Criminal background checks come to Arthur's mind.

Arthur read more of the lengthy Instarise ad. "Harvard Medical School is not associated with this product and they do not endorse it. Doctors are conducting more medical studies in the West. Instarise has been shown to reduce heart problems, decrease visceral fat mass in the belly area, decrease cholesterol, improve blood pressure, and improve blood sugar levels. When you take Instarise daily, you can end or prevent common prostate problems. Stop waking up at night to urinate three or more times. Stop being tired during the day from broken up sleep. This product will help you lose twenty or more pounds faster and easier than you can imagine because its use will increase your aerobic metabolism rate."

Instarise was starting to sound pretty good again to Arthur.

"Using Instarise means putting an end to those embarrassing 'senior moments' of forgetting names, dates, or other things."

"Maybe it puts an end to 'senior moments' because you are concentrating on something else and embarrassed about walking around with a huge erection for four hours, stupid," thought Arthur.

"Here's the best news of all. The exciting news is really about your opportunity to spend the rest of your life healthier and happier. Now with Instarise you can have great health for the things that really make you happy. This product's literature is about showing any man how he will be able to run faster, jump higher, and lift more weight if he uses this pill. Spend more time with your kids and grandkids. Go fishing. Do what you love more. Go play golf."

"A big boner getting in the way of swinging the golf club, now that's embarrassing. Are they kidding? Who wants any of this?," thought Arthur. He was confused. Maybe the pill gives a man a four-hour erection only if something is wrong. Maybe that signals a major health problem and if that happens, the man using this product is supposed to see his doctor immediately.

He did more research. Instarise has not been evaluated by the Food and Drug Administration. The FDA says this product does not diagnose, treat, or cure any diseases. Since doctors are still working on clinical studies somewhere in the West and the final verdict is not in, Arthur was convinced men should not buy this product.

"Are they kidding? This kind of mail would make great fodder for writing material to be used by late night comedians. Instarise makes you think long and hard," said Arthur. Realizing the moment, "Holy crap, this stupid ad has me talking to myself."

With all the money spent on advertising for the multitudes of different sex pills, Arthur started to realize that the public notices geared toward a younger market the same way cigarette companies try to hook young people to smoke. Young people are confused enough about sex, he thought. Now they have to watch old people naked in bathtubs on tops of mountains and that will just confuse them some more. Never is their any mention of safe sex, unprotected sex, AIDS or venereal disease in any of these TV ads. These products are all about making money with no real intention of making the world a better place.

During the early years of their marriage, Jane and Arthur watched Saturday Night Live actors introduce many skits dealing with sexual behavior, sexual dysfunction, women's appearance, men's appearance, and baldness. Admittedly, Jane and Arthur both thought one of the funniest skits of all time was the one promoting the "Bosley Hair Treatment" procedure. In this skit, technicians bent behind white sheets supposedly pluck hairs from patients' pubic areas and implant it in the bald heads of the men and the thinning scalps of the women. When the procedures are all completed, the camera pans over to the happy patients, focusing on the curly hair patches on the tops of their heads. Seeing these patches of pubic hair on the heads of a blonde, a redhead, and a brunette, it was impossible not to laugh.

On the golf course, in the gym, and away from the shadows of women, men often inject too much talk about sex, sometimes debasing a solid discussion. For several years now, they have joked about all these brands of sex pills flooding the scene. Though Arthur never remotely considering using this type of product, he thought ads were conning men into believing these companies could barely keep up with the demand for their pills. He was sick of all the false advertising and all the lies to the public. In spite of all the nonsense, he tried to laugh more, still hoping for an increase in honest business partnerships in Rainbow Creek. He hoped that someday government and big business would stop trying to screw each other and make putting the unemployed back to work a priority. Policies that squeezed out a few more pennies from ideas that worked was no longer acceptable, because then these ideas can become ineffective. New policies needed to address large wasteful spending programs that were lining the pockets of dishonest men.

At last setting the Instarise brochure aside, Arthur opened his final piece of mail, an announcement from the Rainbow Creek Athletic Association declaring the schedule for fall and winter meetings for board members, coaches, and interested parents. Like every coach, Arthur had suffered through plenty of the politics associated with coaching kid's sports, but even on his worst days, he felt it most important to teach young players sportsmanship. As a kid himself, all Arthur wanted to do was play baseball, because the game was something he knew well. As a grade-schooler and high school player, he was a very good baseball catcher. His daughters, Sandra and Susie, held their own as softball players too, but very few athletic organizations ran their programs with fairness. By high school, the girls whose fathers donated the most money to the school or the girls whose fathers were friends with the softball coach garnered the most opportunities.

Finished with spending days with his daughters at Rainbow Creek Athletic Association, Arthur had flashbacks of his coaching days when the team was all that mattered and any personal concerns before the game started were set aside. Arthur studied learning disciplines in college and did his best to stay informed about what to look for when teaching kids in the classroom or on the playing field, but there were always parents or other coaches who thought they knew better than he did. Asking parents to turn to the same page when it came to their children was like asking them all to simultaneously pronounce, "Ask asterisk, clam cram a clean cream cinnamon can, scissors sizzle, thistles sizzle, un-sifted thistles for thistle-sifters," five times in a row without making a mistake. Even with all the challenges and difficulties associated with coaching young athletes, Arthur finished out every season no matter the team's record, hoping he made a difference for at least one family.

Arthur studied the seven basic teaching styles that coaches and teachers should consider when giving instruction to children. Professional educators called these styles *spatial, linguistic, auditory, kinesthetic, mathematical, interpersonal, and intrapersonal.* He handed out copies of his work and research to parents if he thought the material might help to maximize practices. He enjoyed when others commented that the concepts were new to them and they thought they might use the teaching styles to pay attention in other areas of the daily lives of their children.

"*Spatial* is a visual teaching style involving the use of diagrams and images to further special understanding." Arthur used this approach at the first practice of the season each year. He brought coaching manuals and books with artwork, photographs, video, planning designs, and navigation tools used to enhance learning. Arthur told his players, "Spatial learners become artists, architects, photographers, designers, filmmakers, navigators and strategic planners."

"*Linguistic* is a verbal learning style involving the use of words in speech and writing," Arthur told the team at indoor practices held inside the community center when it rained.

In the same way his mother coached him to be a better listener and choose his words carefully, he coached his players to understand the biggest, loudest speaker isn't necessarily right. He used simulators of written words on a big screen and recordings of famous coaches' speeches to enhance learning. Arthur brought a different approach to coaching and teaching at most practices, hoping his players learned something new. "Auditory is a learning style involving sound and music," he told the parents before getting started, in the hopes of livening up an early Saturday morning practice. "Listen to the sound of the bat at practice today, and you will be able to hear if the ball was hit hard." *Auditory* learners become musicians, conductors, composers and sound engineers.

"*Kinesthetic* is a physical learning style involving using your body, hands, feet, and sense of movement," said Arthur, on a beautiful sunny July day of practice with the temperature in the high 80s. "Activities, movement, and hands-on lessons are used to enhance learning." His players who were in good physical shape enjoyed the faster pace of practice and the extra running drills he arranged, but some of his players complained. Players from each extreme of the curve made comments such as, "Now I understand" or "I can't get a grip on this; practice is too demanding." He told his players that kinesthetic learners become mechanics, technicians, construction workers, laborers, athletes, actors, dancers, and guitar players.

"*Mathematical logic* is a learning style using reasoning and number systems," Arthur told his players. He coached his athletes advanced techniques of exploring systems, following processes, and analyzing procedures used to enhance learning, when he decided they were ready. He listened to players' comments to understand which players wanted to learn more details about techniques and game strategies. He understood that most players did not like to just go through the motions, and they were more interested in exploring the links between different approaches and systems. "Your brains may protest at first when something is illogical or irrational, but you will have a good chance of recalling it later," Arthur told his players one week before the start of the first game every season. He taught his players the infield fly rule, how to keep a scorebook like the pros, and an advanced software method of keeping statistics to monitor their progress. "Interpersonal is a social learning style where students prefer to learn in groups or with others." Working with others in groups or working on understanding why each person has different viewpoints about strategy by using role-playing activities, Arthur tried to enhance the learning curve of his players. "Sometimes learning takes place just from seeing mistakes of others," Arthur told his team toward the end of a season every year. He made comments such as, "Our team must work together to turn double-plays," and "Let's pull together to discuss strategy," and "Let's get groups together to explore our options." Arthur heard some of his players making comments such as, "Will someone please tell me what they think?" and "Help me understand this play." Interpersonal learners become counselors, teachers, coaches, sales clerks, and politicians.

In the big picture of life, Arthur saw too many lesser politicians following along with the separate agendas of their party, throwing too much money at fads and oversaturated markets, with little chance of bringing increased returns and pro-growth policies. Just as he tried to get his young athletes to work together as a team, he wanted Congress to encourage proven plans, instead of all these new risky ideas that allow too much room for corruption. He was sure most of these powerful men never heard of any of these learning styles. How could they possibly learn from each other, when they never learned these strategies themselves?

"*Intrapersonal* is a solitary learning style where students prefer to work alone by doing self-study. Some students may not like learning in groups. In self-study, students spend time with a coach or a teacher to clarify information they haven't been able to clarify by themselves," professed Arthur, hoping that all his players would someday work toward self-sufficiency in sports and in real life. He asked all his players to research a topic of their choice, something related to softball or team sports, and present their works to the rest of the team. When the girls made their presentations, they made comments such as, "This is what I think or feel about that," and "I'll get back to you on that," when asked a question they did not have the answer for yet. Intrapersonal learners become authors, researchers, entrepreneurs, park rangers, and inventors.

"Each athlete prefers different learning styles and techniques. Everyone uses a mix of learning styles," said Arthur. He liked to summarize all his strategies on the last day of the season. "There is no right mix to fit all people. It is best to use multiple strategies, but some coaches or teachers still use one learning style and mislabel those students who use that style well as 'bright.' Never given the chance to use other learning styles, sometimes coaches and teachers brand players and students with negative labels. Interlinking concepts by using different academic disciplines and coaching styles increases a student's ability to understand any academic subject." Arthur did not care so much about winning games as he did about making sure his players improved and played smarter. He figured the winning would come later. He also figured few players become professional athletes, but the players who learned to express themselves had a better chance of success in their careers.

Arthur was convinced that any learning style used by coaches and teachers will lose its luster if educators aren't trained in noticing the basic warning signs of students with learning disabilities. He told parents, "Too often our culture teaches us to walk away from problems. Too often students that need help are entrenched in our public school systems without getting a proper diagnosis and they do not receive the help they need. Teachers and coaches are asking parents to be more proactive in helping students who need help. This has become increasingly more important as school districts cut more teaching jobs, because it is thought teachers' salaries have become too expensive due to union bargaining agreements. If my mother, Margaret Hobson, were still alive, she would certainly side with the teachers. She would have endorsed exceptionally educated and devoted teachers who have sacrificed for years studying to earn their master's degrees and paying out-of-pocket education expenses all along, bettering themselves and deserving a pension, especially when they do not receive Social Security benefits when they retire."

Social Security was set up to keep elderly people out of poverty. That mission evolved into a multitude of overburdened welfare programs, each started to gather votes in elections. To many teachers in places like Rainbow Creek, it felt like Republican governors were leading an assault on teachers, and every other organized segment of American society, including police, firefighters, and unions, making them scapegoats for our country's financial problems. This was one area the Tea Party, Democrats, and Republicans needed to compromise, because of the importance of these occupations. Down deep, Arthur didn't believe unions were being attacked; he believed Republicans were attacking deficits. However, he did believe if teachers, firefighters, and police are required to accept salary and pension cuts, so should government employees. "You may not think these policies about jobs apply to you, but when your livelihood is the next one targeted, you may start to pay more attention," Arthur told friends and neighbors. He understood that honest people who are self-aware know that the focus of all the national government budget cuts should be on the white-collar crime infestation that exists in our political environment and our financial systems, not on our classroom teachers, our protectors, and our minimum-wage workers. Some people Arthur talked to thought he rambled on at times, but he was on a much bigger mission than most others were willing to spend the time on. He wanted fairness for the middle class.

As a boy, when Arthur went to a baseball game with his dad, the sounds and smells he witnessed at the stadium made him feel part of the pulse of the city, part of a collective heartbeat. To him, the game was about heroes, villains, and fools. Players won and lost, making errors, striking out, falling down, getting hurt, getting humiliated, and for once, it was not him. For any small boy seeing his favorite star player for the first time, it really did feel like baseball heaven. For a few hours, all his stress, all his problems, all his pain, and all his fears went away as he rooted for a victory by the home team. Baseball reinvigorated him. The players worked hard to make opportunities and create their own luck. They usually knew what fundamentals mattered most and they tried to do the right thing.

Like the Constitution, the baseball rulebook has kept the words from its original presentation, with only a few amendments. A bat, a ball, an umpire, and bases are necessities of the game. Three strikes are still an out and three outs still end a half inning for the team at bat. The outfield fences are still over three hundred feet from home plate. The rules of the game have changed very little over the last century. However, for Arthur, baseball is no longer Americana, along with Chevrolet and apple pie. To him, "take me out to the ball game" has become "pay too much for my ticket, parking, and concessions" because the experience is no longer affordable for many fans and their families. To Arthur and many others from his generation, salaries of the superstars were pushing fans away from the game at a time when jobs were hard to come by and mortgages were hard to pay. The game still played the same way, but the business of baseball had changed and become too expensive. For Arthur it became difficult to root for double-digit multimillion-dollar athletes with sports agents and expert lawyers who keep them out of prison when they commit serious crimes, and greedy owners who milk society of their hard-earned dollars. This culture of make as much money as you can, as fast as you can until someone catches you doing something wrong is so prevalent in business and in sports today, he doubted fans would see any immediate changes in their favor.

For several months, Kay Applebaum spent most of her days fielding complaints from Rainbow Creek and other Missouri taxpayers forced to approve the financing of sports stadiums for wealthy team owners.

Citizens asked, "Why do politicians allow this to happen when taxpayers didn't have a chance to vote on this issue?"

"Maybe the owners and politicians are afraid that people just might wake up to the nonsense, because we all know the politicians and the wealthy business owners fill each other's pockets with money," Kay would tell them.

These multibillion-dollar owners insisted that fans build and pay for stadiums or they would threaten to move their teams to another city if authorities failed to meet demands. With all the controversy created by threats, Kay and Arthur concluded that the team moving just might not be such a bad thing. A billion dollars of taxpayer money could go a long way in fixing infrastructure, making transportation better, improving our schools and other services important to repairing the decay in our cities. Kay and Arthur thought about all the fixes that people could benefit from every day, if instead of spending so much money to witness a few scheduled baseball games fans spent their money on practical things.

Arthur was interested in just about everything, but not so much in sports anymore. He caught the final scores on the late evening news, but he did not watch entire games of baseball, football, hockey, or basketball like he once did, annoying Jane, when he was still married to her.

When he started working at the community center, he did whatever it took to help to build relationships and make the experience for visitors better. He was not just a middle-level executive or an office worker. He buffed floors, stacked chairs during big events, unloaded and loaded trucks at the dock at the rear of the building, cleaned bathrooms, cut grass, and striped the parking lot—anything to help the services and beautification of the community center. As a young man, he was trying to connect with his friends and neighbors, but as he grew older, the plan was more about building his platform as he made his plans to run for mayor. Arthur was tired of listening to politicians who thought it easier to answer the tough questions with a defensive rebuttal when the work was not finished to a sufficient extent to fix a problem. An answer that addresses the reasons for failure gives a clearer picture to why the problem was not resolved yet. So many people criticize others for the way they handled something, but offer no substantial new ideas to find a solution. Arthur tired of individuals wanting to pry into everybody else's business, but never offered any information about personal information to help others.

Arthur had vowed to remember a remark a woman made after he finished his first short speech to a small gathering of people at the beginning of the Tea Party movement. Her statement incensed Arthur and made him want to work even harder. "Look, there is no doubt you have to have a platform of work before you can give a speech and address the public with any credibility," said the woman.

"I appreciate your perspective, but surely you believe our country cannot afford to lose the middle class. This is an important issue," said Arthur quickly.

"Any thoughts or ideas for fixing this country relate to a platform, and a well-developed platform draws an audience and gives us a sense of forward movement, that is, a sense that you are taking us somewhere in our thinking and learning. Your speech struck me as a random essay and I just do not see citizens turning to you for commentary on these diverse topics. You need a substantial platform to carry off something like this," she said.

"Let me ask you this? Who better to talk about the middle class than an intelligent, hardworking middle-class man with a well-thought-out plan put together after thousands of hours of research? I will take your advice by continuing to work toward building my platform, but I do not think that celebrities and rich people should be the only ones to write books, make speeches, and pass laws and voice opinions, which affect all of us. It is wrong to always equate wealth with fairness and intelligence," said Arthur, keeping his cool.

"Well, maybe you are on your way to establishing your platform," she said.

"Tyrannical forces are working against mainstream middle-class culture. My talk here is the beginning of a chronicle to get the discussions started about spreading awareness so people pay more attention to the truth about relevant issues of politics, creation of jobs, education, drugs and alcohol, professional sports, the environment, and how they are all influenced in Rainbow Creek and other communities in America. My objective is for people to refine their own beliefs and make changes to make the world a better place for all of us. We have celebrated the one hundredth anniversary of Mark Twain's death and are nearing the one hundred and fiftieth anniversary of the deaths of Abraham Lincoln and Charles Dickens, and paying attention to social reform is even more important today," said Arthur. He figured this was a good place to end his one-on-one discussion with the woman. The woman must have felt the same way, or possibly she realized that maybe she was a little overmatched by Arthur, the man she accused of not having a platform moments earlier. She shook her head and walked away.

At the beginnings of the Tea Party movement, thousands of people organized their little rallies, during which they mainly protested against any increase in taxes. After gatherings in Los Angeles, writers and comedians joked, "The new movement should be called the Green Herbal Double Decaf Party, not the Tea Party." Jay Leno joked on the *Tonight Show*, "At the UN, President Obama called on other countries to help track down and eliminate radicals and terrorists. They told Obama, 'Hey, the Tea Party is your main problem now, friend.' These Tea Party groups are very conservative. In fact, 58 percent of the Tea Party members now believe Joe Biden is a Muslim." Early critiques by liberal cable TV networks accused the Tea Party of negativity because followers only listened to the voices in the back of the room making the most noise. Inaccurate Tea Party edicts and public decrees were surfacing everywhere. Most Tea Baggers wanted less government or to keep the status quo. Those who wanted the government to stay out of people's lives heard some liberals say that they are anti-American and should send back their Social Security checks and their Medicaid card. They were told, do not call the police or fire department, do not visit the library, and do not send your kids to public school. Liberals told citizens the Tea Party deserved all the unfair comments directed at them, when all they wanted was to keep more of their freedoms. The Tea Baggers believed our ancestors initially set up the government to help the elderly, the sick, and the young children who are not old enough to become full-time wage earners. Moreover, just because a person questions an issue does not mean that person is not patriotic. As the movement grew and the media noticed the passion and energy of the Tea Baggers, a clearer understanding of the issues they were advocating for became visible to more people. The Tea Party did not trust our leaders and a midday discussion over lunch was not going to supply the answers to all their questions.

To get away from their work for one day, Arthur, Frank, Victor, and Gary played in the annual golf tournament at Sunset Valley Golf Course, sponsored by the Rainbow

Creek Chamber of Commerce. The four friends laughed and joked, happy about relaxing for a few hours, enjoying the game of golf. The foursomes in front of them moved along smoothly every hole, until the eighteenth hole, where there was a bottleneck. Arthur and his friends stood at the final tee waiting for the group in front of them to finish putting. The eighteenth hole was a par three requiring an iron shot over a pond to reach the green. The men conversed as they waited.

Arthur: "Gary, you're a single man. Have you been dating anyone recently?"

Gary: "Well, last week I was walking to my car in a parking lot. This attractive woman riding toward me on an old Schwinn bicycle, the kind with the baskets attached on both sides of the rear wheel, stopped to adjust something in one of the baskets. We started talking. Eventually I asked her if she wanted to go to a Cardinals-Cubs game during their last home series of the season. The woman said she didn't like baseball. She said she was into extreme sports."

Arthur: "How old was this woman?"

Gary: "She looked about fifty. I guess I was struck by the contrast of the old bicycle and this fit, modern-day looking woman."

Arthur: "What the heck would a fifty-year-old woman be doing, still involved in extreme sports?"

Gary: "She said she was into mountain and rock climbing."

Arthur: "There aren't any mountains in Rainbow Creek. Maybe she was trying to be polite."

Gary: "Why can't women just be honest with you? I'm a big boy and I react to honesty better anyway. I figured the heck with it, so I got in my car and drove away. I did wave good-bye to her. I guess I'm no 'Art Hob the heartthrob.'"

Frank: "Hey, 'Art Hob the Heartthrob,' why don't you hit first. The group in front of us is off the green."

Arthur hit his iron shot off the tee. It went over the pond and over the green, then hit the roof of the clubhouse on the fly. The ball rolled back down from the roof, hit a picnic table on the patio, and took a high bounce into the air, before rolling down a slope onto the green, hitting the flag, and dropping straight down into the hole. Arthur had hit his first hole-in-one. Though it wasn't pretty, it counted.

Gary: "That's what I call extreme sports."

Frank: "Maybe that shot is a sign of good things to come. Way to go 'Lucky.' If the story gets out about your shot, maybe it will help propel a campaign run for mayor."

Arthur: "Let's not get too carried away."

Victor: "When we get to the clubhouse, I'll buy lunch to celebrate Arthur's hole-in-one."

One Saturday afternoon two weeks into the fall semester, over lunch at the Student Center at the University of Missouri, Arthur and Susie had a memorable father-daughter talk about Susie's career plans. Susie liked science and research because the studies lifted people out of unemployment and cured diseases in humans and animals, not only in America but also in places like Haiti, Africa, and India. Later she could decide which specialty she found most important to continue to study, whether veterinary studies, horticulture, medicine, or animal food science. Humans are curious by nature and like to explore and Susie figured by studying science exploration, she could inspire others to get involved. She learned from her father that more involvement creates more capacity for action and taps new discoveries for growth. To her, nothing was all doom and gloom. If people just get involved in good causes, they can fix any kind of problem, and all of us must feel it is important to make a difference in the world. She learned from her grandparents and parents the impact of groundbreaking work by middle-class people who have earned rather than inherited their money should exert a powerful influence on our attitudes and on society. She was looking for new places to explore and the hope for new adventure and the anticipation for something better to heighten her college experience. The only true barriers to finding new adventures were just a matter of her stepping out of her comfort zones. Whenever Arthur, Sandra, or Susie found something they wanted changed bad enough, a fire inside them started burning with a desire to organize and put up a grassroots fight to go after it.

Arthur was not the only person in the family trying to build a platform. Susie loved animals and she was leaning toward working in the area of biological or veterinary sciences. Her current transcript consisted of a number of AP credits and a GPA above 3.5, but often even for students' earning a bachelor's degree with decent grades acceptance into veterinary school was more difficult than medical school. Most of Susie's classes thus far had been taken to meet basic requirements and fulfill elective credits. The degree of difficulty of the classes in the fields of science is higher than in most other areas of study.

"I just hope you can handle the workload and still stay true to yourself," said Arthur.

"What do you mean, Dad?" said Susie.

"You are away from your family and have to use your wits to handle all the demands placed on you at college," said Arthur.

"Well, at least I don't have to hold down a full-time job like many of my classmates," said Susie. "I have more time to concentrate on my studies without holding down a job too. Thank God for my scholarship. I also have four thousand dollars left in my checking account, money I saved while working at the restaurant back home."

"Money goes fast when there isn't any money coming in, so you have to learn to live on the cheap when you are in college," said Arthur, sounding like a preacher to Susie.

"Dad, I know all this," said Susie, a little irritated by the turn the conversation was taking.

"I believe you can do anything you put your mind to. Just remember, the professors say you need to study two hours for every hour of credit you take. So since every week you are sitting in classrooms about fifteen hours, that means you should be studying another thirty hours, either at the library or at your apartment. You are going to arguably the best university in the state. Walt Disney, Samuel Clemmons, General John J. Pershing, and Otto Frederick Rohwedder were born in Missouri and, during your studies, you will learn more about these great Americans. Walt Disney made some of the best children's movies and Mark Twain wrote some of the best literary works of all time. General Pershing was in charge of the entire command of Allied military forces in World War I. We can't even fathom what responsibilities he handled and the decisions he had to make for the best interest of the United States. Rohwedder invented the bread slicing machine," said Arthur, barely taking a breath in between his sentences.

"Dad, you are rambling on just a little too much for my tastes right now. Please don't make our conversation one-sided and our time together annoying," said Susie, already annoyed.

"Well, just remember to ask me if you need anything, because parents worry about their children no matter how old they get," said Arthur.

"That is sweet for you to be concerned about me, but this isn't the Stone Ages anymore. I hope I'm not offending you, but I will be all right. The professors have assistants to help students who have questions. The library has the latest technology linked to other campuses, and my computer tablet is loaded with books and software used in class. I'm still finding my way and I promise you I will try my best."

"Well, just remember the whole reason you are here in Columbia is to get a great education."

"One last thing, Dad. Will you give me fifty dollars worth of *quantitative easing* so I can buy a parking pass for the campus lot?"

"Now you sound like a politician. Do you know *quantitative easing* was supposed to inject a half trillion dollars into the economy? The Democrats and the Feds must think, 'The suckers fell for it again.' They told us Treasury rates would stay low, but they didn't tell us the value of the dollar would lower, housing would be slow to recover, spending would continue to increase, more corruption would eat away at our money, and the economy would slow even more. They burned taxpayers' money in the sand the first time, and now they want to wash it away a second time."

"Dad, I promise I won't spend the fifty dollars frivolously. First thing in the morning, I will walk directly to the cashier's office on campus to pay for my parking pass."

"I know you will."

Susie smiled. "I have to tell you a story one of my biology professors told me. It's about making difficult decisions, but the end of the story is the result of decisions made by ocean marine biologists, not politicians. I now have a better understanding of the ramifications of difficult decisions we sometimes have to make in job situations and in life. Right after the Exxon Valdez oil spill in Alaska, marine biologists worked frantically to save the seals. The average cost of rehabilitating an injured seal caught in a major oil spill is about eighty thousand dollars. At a special ceremony, two of the saved seals were released back into the ocean amid wild cheers and applause from a large group of bystanders in attendance. Just one minute after the seals were released, in full view of all the bystanders, a killer whale came crashing through the water and ate both of the seals. If masculinity asserts that there are things worth dying for and femininity asserts that there are things worth living for, then this story is a metaphor for the decisions all of us must decide concerning what is worth saving in our future lifestyles," said Susie.

"Realizing there are no shortcuts to safety, success, hard work, hustle, and perseverance are still attributes that we don't have a substitute for in our lives. I remember the one thing residents of Valdez, Alaska, realized after the cleanup efforts was that they couldn't count on the politicians or the executives of the big oil companies to clean up the mess. All they could count on was themselves," added Arthur.

Susie was a good student but her academic limits had never been tested to the degree college professors push their students. Only time would tell if she could cut the muster at the Division I level and pass the hard science classes such as biogenetics, microbiology, physics, and advanced chemistry. After lunch and an afternoon of shopping with Susie at the campus shops in downtown Columbia, Arthur dropped her off at her apartment, hugged her good night, and began the hour and a half solo drive on the interstate back to Rainbow Creek.

As Arthur drove deeper across the state at the evening hour, the setting sun and the remoteness of the scenes brought out an appreciation of the colors of the brawny forestation and the less marred hills off in the horizon. Before the sun set on clear weather evenings, the vast landscapes on both sides of the interstate provided picturesque views for drivers, especially this time of the season, with the leaves starting to change hues, some of the summer fence repairs and barn paint jobs visible, and the yellow and purple wildflowers still yielding a bounty. On Arthur's drive across the eastern half of Missouri, every ten miles or so, the interstate offered a small section of land bulldozed and chain-sawed, tree trunks stacked and ready for use as telephone poles in their second lives, possibly used close to where they sit, next to the roughly graded stretch of dirt and gravel and stumps. All this done in the name of progress, they say.

10

Planning for a Bigger Platform

Without his realizing it, paying attention to professional baseball, talking with his two daughters, having discussions with his friend Frank, and getting involved with the Tea Party had vastly refined Arthur's views about politics. He now understood how the rules, regulated and evolving over time, allowed powerful men to gain wealth, seldom increasing the ambition of less fortunate citizens. The efforts of the middle class always get squeezed. From a personal perspective, he saw his brother Johnny using heroin as a resource in his life, instead of using resources to live as a hero. Looking at the big picture of the country, he saw little being done to reward the people actually doing the work. He hoped politicians would overcome the idea that everybody is the same, and start realizing that educated minds are the real weapons for fixing the problems of society. He wished more parents would teach their children to stand on their own feet.

Everybody plans for things in their life to some degree. People plan their grocery lists, trips to the bank, their kid's activities, and special days like birthdays and weddings. Most people do not plan enough and do not give enough thought to picking a career that will make them happy and keep them interested throughout their working years. Private thoughts are flexible and people can happily change jobs when new opportunities arise. When the government creates a plan to create jobs in a certain sector, people who benefit from the newly created jobs form a special interest group to ensure that the jobs stay intact, no matter how costly the jobs are to society as a whole. Jobs with a rigid job description and not open to suggestions and new ideas do nothing to spur creativity and create more jobs.

At the start of the twenty-first century, for every retired person in Rainbow Creek, there were five others still in the workforce. Twenty years in, there will be only three workers for every retired person. Programs rooted in the twentieth century no longer meet twenty-first-century realities because robots and computers have replaced more than three-quarters of the workers at the manufacturing facilities in town, many already replaced by machines. Just in the past year, three manufacturers in Rainbow Creek closed their doors forever, all for different reasons. The owner of Jake's Machine Shop, Jake Morehead, decided to retire, and his business went idle because he could not find a machinist in town skilled enough to run the equipment he used to make small appliance parts. Another manufacturer, a maker of fenders and side panels for automobiles, moved its operations overseas for cheaper labor and materials. A lightbulb manufacturer closed down because their standard incandescent bulbs became obsolete compared to the newer longer-lasting, light-emitting diode bulbs made in California that now were flooding the market. Americans everywhere were feeling a need for more work to fix the problems in our country, before fixing all the problems in the other one hundred ninety five countries on our planet. Arthur started talking to his mayor, congressional representatives, local businesspersons, and a local union representative about a fair playing field, a balance between union and business, a balance between government and the private sector, much better control of our welfare programs, and much stricter penalties to corrupt officials, politicians, bankers, and business owners. He hoped that in another decade or two, there would be more opportunities for young people, if not for attrition of the workforce alone. However, for now, he wrote letters to his representatives, telling them, if a company moved jobs overseas, he didn't think it was fair for them to get the tax benefits that living and working in America provides them. Following is one letter Arthur wrote to his local congressional representative, Mr. Timothy Erhardt:

Dear Mr. Timothy Erhardt,
No matter your feelings about union or right-to-work issues in this country, the American middle class was built when unions were growing, and the economy weakens when unions were in decline, during the Great Depression and now today. Working middle-class people united so they could get decent wages, health benefits, and a pension. Company executives were unable to pay themselves outrageous multimillion-dollar bonuses and perks at the end of the year, insidious money from the sweat of labor. The knock against unions, while they help workers receive equal pay for equal work, they don't protect against workers who receive equal pay for doing little or no work. Government workers usually vote for tax increases because in most instances more taxpayer money flowing into the national budget assures them job security. In the US, there are 7.9 million government workers in the public sector and 7.4 million union workers in the private sector. New York is the highest unionized state and North Carolina is the lowest unionized state in the country. Some groups of union workers are becoming considerably smaller. Think about the jobs that used to pay a comfortable wage plus benefits. From

manufacturing to auto workers and postal workers, these jobs are going away in America, getting downsized or simply being replaced by technology and robots in the private sector. Big Labor is always in favor of a union.

Instead of politics to the left or right, wouldn't it be nice if we had politics that worked toward solving the problems of the people in our country? Just like people have problems, companies have ups and downs and it is important to study the reasons why. Tariffs on exports, changing weather patterns, gasoline prices, value of the dollar, emerging markets demands, disruptions in foreign countries, healthcare costs for employees, and inflation have huge effects on the bottom line for companies. Too much legislation and too many other forces are working against the businesses in Rainbow Creek. We have too much corruption.

Middle-class culture in the United States rests on the morals of human capitalism; in the past, those who went to work learned skills on the job and made enough money to care for their families, and they were rewarded by the market. These morals now seem shakier than before because too many people are relying on the government to take care of them. No wonder spirits and incomes of workers are sagging. We have to find ways to be more competitive and regain jobs we lost in the manufacturing sector. The government paying for training laid-off workers seems like a better use of funds than just handing out unemployment checks through the welfare system. It is better to teach people how to earn money instead of giving away money with nothing expected in return. The United States is becoming a welfare state. Our politicians continue to throw money at lower income people who are the least qualified to use the money to create long-term fixes, businesses or jobs.

Best Wishes,

Arthur Hobson

The Hubble Space Telescope has helped astronomers try to pinpoint the universe's age and understand the evolution of galaxies by finding planets outside the earth's solar system. The Hubble has helped astronomers discover dark energy, a force that seems to be pulling the universe apart at an alarming rate, maybe more concerning than the accelerating rate at which the force politicians are pulling apart people. While the forces of the solar system were out of politicians' control, Arthur wished they would just start working together. He was realizing that the focus for creating jobs was going to have to be more on local citizens and local businesses. Founding Rainbow Creek citizens focused on creating a better existence for their families by focusing on the available materials, the needs of the people, and the land near where they lived. Rugged and self-reliant men and women built the railroads, laid the bricks to form the walls of the first colleges and universities, built the roads and highways, worked the ranches, farmed the fields, dug the coal mines, manipulated machinery in factories and operated heavy equipment to develop terrain. It was time for the mayor of Rainbow Creek to bring administrators, executives, manufacturers and business owners together to train new workers, bring back some manufacturing jobs, and expand in the areas where improvements are needed in the community.

The family makeup of the middle class in Rainbow Creek today took all forms and shapes. Traditional families are just one segment of the population. Children are being raised by single mothers, single fathers, gays and lesbians. The feminist movement pushed for equal opportunities and equal pay for women as breadwinners, not taking into account that some women valued their biological urges of staying home and raising their children. If allowed, a lot of the men in Rainbow Creek would love to stay home and care for their kids, but the reality was the dream just costs more now and it usually took two incomes to pay for it.

Susie was home from college for the weekend partially because she had been missing her dad, but mostly because she was already nearing a month ahead of her budgeted fall-semester spending. At college she didn't want to be known as the party girl who did multiple Jell-O shots at the bar, when she new she was supposed to be devoting extra time in science labs. She didn't want to look like a freeloader, borrowing things from other girls, either. So when her food and supplies neared the bare minimum, she drove home to visit her dad, so she could offer to help him with a trip to the grocery store.

Arthur and Susie were in line at the A & P with a full cart of fresh fruits, canned vegetables, ground beef, lunchmeat, two whole chickens, one bag of Pollock filets, two cans of salmon, two gallons of skim milk, several boxes of cereal, a case of bottled water, and a case of diet Coca-Cola. The line wasn't moving, and finally Susie noticed a commotion between a female customer named "Margie Mae" and the lady clerk up front at the cashier. The clerk new her name, possibly from previous run-ins at the grocery store.

Susie: "Dad, what is happening up at the front of our line?"

Arthur: "I don't know, but it looks like the customer has a bunch of food stamps and coupons in her hands."

For the past several months, the new reality TV show *Extreme Couponing* had been airing on national networks teaching shoppers how to use coupons to save money at grocery stores across the nation. Though the stores where the extreme shopping trips were filmed didn't play by the same rules they enforce for the rest of their regular customers, many viewers weren't aware of this discrepancy. The stores bent and broke the rules by doubling and tripling coupons in order to enhance the made-for-TV illusion of incredible savings when the cameras were rolling. Margie Mae was one of those shoppers who didn't understand that what viewers saw on TV was entertainment, not reality, about as far from reality as you can get.

Margie Mae: "I am on government assistance for food and I want my coupons applied toward my food stamps. I don't have any extra cash to pay for groceries. I am tired of facing the same issues every time I shop at a grocery store."

Clerk: "Margie Mae, many customers use coupons to stretch their food stamps at the supermarket, but you have to pay the taxes on the coupon items in cash."

Margie Mae: "I called the Department of Health and Welfare to ask them about paying taxes and they told me it was against the law to charge tax on food stamp purchases."

Clerk: "It's true that shoppers who use food stamps are not supposed to be charged tax for grocery purchases, but unfortunately, coupons are not tax free on non-grocery items, so you owe us $3.84 in taxes for the coupon items."

Margie Mae: "My budget is already stretched to the limit and I am not carrying any cash to pay for taxes."

To put an end to the frustration of the confrontation, the clerk finally just reached into her purse and paid the $3.84 in taxes out of her own money. Margie Mae went on her way.

Susie: "That was very nice of you to pay the taxes for that lady," she said to the clerk.

Clerk: "The problem begins after the coupons are scanned and the method of payment is entered as a tax-free food assistance program. Most stores will correctly note that no tax should be charged. But some stores, like ours, separate purchases into two categories: products with coupons applied and those without. The register automatically charges tax on the couponed items. In short, the scanners view coupons as cash payment and determine that the tax on couponed items must also be paid in cash. If the shopper uses no coupons and just relies on their food assistance money to pay, they are not charged tax."

Susie: "Dealing with the public is difficult sometimes."

Clerk: "I don't know what people want. Using coupons with food stamps gives people a greater savings, even with the tax they have to pay out of their pocket. Using coupons also makes their grocery money last longer. Some people try to make things easier by using food stamps for food items and only using coupons for non-food items, but not everyone thinks to do that."

The clerk was very good at doing her job and at the same time carrying on her conversation with Susie, but after Arthur paid for his and Susie's groceries with his credit card, he had to voice his opinion, temporarily holding up the line again, making sure others could hear him.

Arthur: "This whole food stamps thing is sad, really. The program is a good example of how something created with good intention has turned out to be another reason for what is wrong with our country. I understand in difficult times, people need a little help sometimes. But to me, it just seems every time a welfare program is created, people learn to milk the system. Not only did Margie Mae receive a free full cart of food stamp items and more free items with coupons, she didn't even think she was responsible for the taxes on all the free items. Food manufacturers make no money on her purchases, if you call

all her free items 'purchases.' The store makes no profit, even if they are reimbursed by the government some discounted money. And hardworking middle-class families pay the extra costs of higher prices at the grocery store to support these programs. Is it no wonder our economy is in the tank. I just want to hear someone say, 'I just started a new job; I don't need food stamps any longer.' Now that would give us all something to celebrate."

Susie: "Look at this, Dad. I just typed in 'Middle Class Task Force' and did a Google search on my cell phone. Then I clicked on the first listing and typed in 'poverty' on the search line at the website. Vice President Joe Biden's 'Middle Class Task Force' is the name of his website; and besides having his name attached to the site, he talks about another legislative act passed to increase the food stamp program by $20 billion. Information reports the site apparently is transmitted from 1600 Pennsylvania in Washington, DC."

Arthur: "This is very interesting, Susie. The name Middle Class Task Force gives the impression that work is being done on behalf of the middle class."

Susie: "But the website is not about protecting or passing legislation to help the middle class. They call it the "Middle Class Task Force," but it's just another website discussing welfare programs. The website touts the speeches and latest ideas of Vice President Joe Biden. After reading it, you understand that the verbiage is about mandates to promote mobility for disadvantaged families. It's about targeting efforts to subsidize programs and give assistance to needy people, putting more money in their pockets so they can rise closer to the ranks of the middle class without any additional effort."

Arthur: "Sounds like it is just another program where the middle class is told this is a good thing because these folks will spend the money, creating a ripple and multiplier effect leading to more economic activity and jobs. Hello, giving all this money away for free without people having to do anything to earn it just causes fewer people to search for jobs and more money out of the pockets of people who do work."

Susie: "It all sounds sneaky to me. Dad, I think I'm starting to understand why you're always telling people it's about time politicians recognize that the middle class must shift back toward a capitalist economy."

Arthur: "Everyone needs to work. Balancing time at work and with the family is what causes the real heartache for people in America. The government has too much influence over the private sector. This influence has caused too many people to become dependent on government welfare programs, which puts increasingly more pressure on the people who do work."

After loading up the groceries in the backseat of the car, Arthur started the engine and pulled out of the parking lot, hoping to enjoy the rest of the day and evening with his daughter. Susie was in a talkative mood, anxious to tell her dad about some of the interesting things she had been learning in her science classes at college.

Susie: "Blue Fin tuna is way too expensive, but did you notice I threw a bag of Pollock filets and two cans of salmon in our cart? I can make those for dinner this evening, if you want me to."

Arthur: "I will help you with dinner. I can make the salad. We have plenty of lettuce, tomatoes, and other garden vegetables in the crisper."

Susie: "I learned some pretty cool stuff this year about salmon, the Blue Fin tuna and Pollock fish."

Arthur: "Oh yeah? Let's hear it."

Susie: "Since women make a majority of the purchases in the United States, part of the answer to bringing back the economy is making available more products and services that appeal to women."

Arthur: "When you talk about the economy and how to create jobs, you are talking my language. I'm already interested in what you have to say."

Susie: "In one of my classes, I'm learning about how some companies are combining science and business to create new opportunities for young women. The Salmon Leather Company is an example of a unique business with a success story. The company makes a type of leather from discarded skins of mature salmon bred in fish farms. Once the skins were considered only waste scraps and the only part of the fish used was the salmon meat that ended up on dinner plates. But now the salmon skins are subjected to extensive treatment, including tanning, to help remove any trace of a fishy smell, to make a type of leather."

Arthur: "Is salmon leather as strong as cowhide?"

Susie: "Salmon leather has the same strength as sheepskin and is very similar to leather made from shark skin. It can be dyed twenty different colors and cut in various styles. This strong fabric is becoming popular on walls, furniture, and accessories in salons and restaurants and office buildings."

Arthur: "What is the connection you first mentioned about the company and women?"

Susie: "Well, the salmon leather is considered the ecologically sound alternative to exotic and endangered animal and reptile hides, so women are becoming aware of its important use in the making of purses and accessories as a purchasing option."

Arthur: "I see. I'm catching on. I know lifestyle changes and healthy beverages like vitamin-enhanced water sold by franchises owned by women have done very well for growth in beverage companies. It sounds like more companies should be listening to their women customers. An emphasis on promoting entrepreneurship by women would definitely help create more job opportunities at a time when we desperately need them. Now, go ahead and tell me about the Blue Fin tuna."

Susie: "Sushi is the fatty red meat of the belly of the Blue Fin tuna. Cheaper versions of sushi come from Yellow Fin or Big Eye tuna. At the rate fishermen are catching Blue Fin tuna, the fish will be extinct in a decade. The best Blue Fin catches sometimes command over one hundred thousand dollars per fish at auction. A generation ago, people thought the sole purpose of the Blue Fin tuna was to grind it up and serve to cats."

Arthur: "I didn't know that. What other interesting fish stories have you been learning about?"

Susie: "Safety and finding fish are the two main priorities of ocean fishermen, obviously. But the underwater continental shelves abruptly fall thousands of feet below the surface in the Bering Sea off the Aleutian Islands of Alaska. Though the fishing is dangerous there, the location is one of the most plentiful fishing areas in the world."

Arthur: "What kind of fish is most plentiful there?"

Susie: "This is what I was about to tell you. If you eat a fish sandwich at McDonald's, chances are the filet you eat was made from the Pollock caught in this area of the ocean off Alaska. Jobs were created because courageous Alaskan fishermen engineered structural ways to take advantage of the terrain surrounding the island communities. Until recent years, the Pollock was also considered a trash fish because of its bland taste. But the plenteousness of this fish and the melding of great seasonings and breading created a demand not seen at fast-food restaurants since the combination of hamburger and French fries."

Arthur: "I had no clue where the fish on a McDonald's sandwich came from."

Susie: "If I was one of the managers at McDonald's I would teach the employees what I learned about fat in the fish sandwiches in hopes of improving the product. Their fish sandwiches have 18 grams of fat, 3.5 grams of saturated fat, 40 grams of cholesterol, and 650 milligrams of sodium. The buns are made from white flour. With a few subtle changes, McDonald's could offer a much healthier fish sandwich and revenues would go up. By cooking the filets in low-fat olive oil, using 10 percent less seasoning, and using buns made from wheat flour, they could dramatically cut down on the fat and salt without sacrificing the taste."

Arthur: "Sound like the professor broke down the scientific and caloric values of the fish sandwich for you and the rest of the students in class, but did you learn anything about the harvesting, manufacturing, or shipping process?"

Susie: "There's more. Only 2 percent of Pollock hatchlings live to be four-year-old adults, so Alaskan officials restrict fishermen to catching 1.4 million tons of Pollock in the Bering Sea each year. The workers on the top hull of huge fishing vessels manage the nets to catch the fish, and the bottom deck inside the ship employs one hundred workers to operate all the automated processing machinery. Even skin, fish heads, and guts are baked, dried, and ground into fine particles to later be used as fertilizer. The whole operation is about efficiency."

Arthur: "It sounds like, true to the tradition of the Alaskan spirit, no parts of the fish are wasted in the entire process. The government could learn a valuable lesson here when thinking about creating new jobs. We need to find more ways to use materials that were once considered just waste."

Susie: "Even the fish eggs, collected at one important step of the operation, are sold as caviar and eaten as a delicacy in Japan and high-end restaurants around the world."

Arthur: "I'm proud of you, Susie. It appears that you are paying close attention in class and learning a lot in your field of study. Stay on course and you will eventually find your path to making a valuable contribution to society."

Susie: "Dad, this is probably a good time to ask your approval for me to apply for a summer study program aboard a scientific shipping vessel. The program last for seven weeks, leaving a port in San Francisco en route to Hawaii and doing ocean studies along the way. Once arriving in Honolulu, students participate in environmental studies on the island for several days before returning to the States."

Arthur: "What kinds of studies to students get involved in with this program?"

Susie: "If I am accepted into the program, the three professors involved in the program are all in charge of different studies, but twenty students will get the chance to help with all three studies and earn eight college credits for their participation in the program. The studies deal with topics about sailfish, trash in our oceans, and recycling for a better environment."

Arthur: "It all sounds very interesting. My main concern would be your safety."

Susie: "The shipping vessel is huge, almost as big as a cruise ship. Students have a chance to earn enough money to pay for the trip by working in the kitchen and helping to prepare meals. Other universities have had an affiliation with the program for ten years, without any major problems. Universities have a lot at stake, so with safety in mind, a group of specially trained security officers are also on board. It's a great opportunity."

Arthur: "Just do your research. Talk to some of the girls who took the trip last year or the year before and if everything checks out and you get accepted, then I think it will be OK if you go on the trip to help with the studies."

Arthur had discovered in just a couple of shopping and dinner conversations, that Susie was learning more about oceans, fish, animals and the roles they play in relationship to human beings than her father realized in just one semester at college. She was much more aware of all the comparisons people made of crazy human behavior to normal animal behavior. She was reading about studies which suggest that all bears are left-handed and that bats always fly toward the left when exiting a cave at night. She didn't know yet if anyone would miss the Guam Flying Fox, Laughing Owl, Palestinian Painted Frog, Tasmanian Wolf or the Rogue Chico de Salmor Giant Lizard. These five animals are now extinct and all were lost in the last one hundred years. The Guam Flying Fox was actually a small fruit bat and was hunted as a food source, probably what led to its extinction. The loss of its habitat is owed to World War II, and predation by brown tree snakes didn't help its survival rate. The causes of animal extinction in all cases during the last one hundred years are traced to loss of habitat due to weather conditions and human activities, hunting, and poaching. Susie's studies already convinced her it is high time people understood that human beings are part of the ecosystem and any alterations to it are invariably going to affect all of us. With all the concerns about government and all the worries of people today, she believed maybe more of us miss the Laughing Owl than we are willing to admit.

More than anything in life, Arthur wanted his two daughters to receive a great college education. Jane wasn't always so single-minded. Jane's parents never neglected her, but they never encouraged her to plan financially or to follow the dream of a promising career, the way many parents today do. Arthur thought it was pathetic for anyone in their forties or fifties to still have that sense of entitlement and to still accept parental or government subsidies because they never gave the effort necessary to achieve some kind of success. Even worse for Arthur, he thought it extremely unfair for any slacker with a lazy attitude to have it better than anyone who was brilliant and extraordinary. It was a nice surprise, even without encouragement from anyone else or any formal planning, when Jane began spending almost all her time fixing up the Hobson House. She was growing into a pretty good interior designer. The great thing about Arthur is that, even though he and Jane had been separated for quite some time now, he wished her well and hoped she was happy.

Arthur started spending more and more of his time supporting worthy Tea Party causes, mostly at the local and state level, but always paying attention to events publicized in newspapers of large metropolitan cities across the nation. Arthur believed that the Tea Party movement at its core was a worthy cause with a checks and balances agenda trying to keep the Democrats and the Republicans honest, forcing a more responsible dialogue about what contributions are best for straightening the spine of America. He understood that as a Tea Party sympathizer, it was wise for him to keep his cool so the dingbats, dirt bags, know-nothings, troublemakers, fanatics, pathological liars, ignoramuses, nerds, and flip-floppers didn't turn political gatherings into charades. Many of the worthy Tea Party followers are people out of work, nearing retirement, or frail senior citizens. Arthur hated it when politicians insinuated that they had the right to tell senior citizens with serious medical conditions that their voices only represented their own enlightened self-interest. The Tea Party Patriots wanted a healthcare plan and a government with a deficit-reduction plan, one that eliminated waste and abuse for the majority of taxpayers, not one designed for the aristocrats with whom politicians have grown much too cozy. Because American taxpayers have been supporting corrupt politicians at the local, state, and federal levels for many years now, the Tea Party was finally saying, "Enough is enough." Creating jobs, fighting illegal drug use, stopping Medicare abuse, cutting spending, and voting out corrupt politicians who have nearly bankrupted the United States, became the most important mantras to Arthur and many other Tea Party followers.

Arthur split his time between the community center and working to advance the Tea Party movement. He explained to Kay Applebaum that one of the members of the Tea Party invited him to Heartland for a lecture devoted to exploring health care, education, energy use, and job creation. All these services, Arthur endorsed as mainstream free-market industries that government leaders turned into Marxist-run businesses and taxpayers took for granted. Medicare—government run—needed a major house cleaning to take back control of a program jammed with fraud. He believed free markets were good for economic growth and a GDP of 2 percent or more was a good thing, but any kind of expansion had to be done in a way that didn't destroy the planet by polluting its air and water.

"The Tea Party," a visitor to the community center named Addison said. "Is that some kind of club where a group of old ladies gathers around to drink green tea?"

"No," Arthur said quietly. "It's a group of people who are challenging some of our government policies, but your reference to the word green wasn't too far off base, because the Tea Party is interested in technology, energy, and issues that improve the economy and keep the environment clean. People want to stop all the waste, corruption, and damage to the planet.

"What else does the Tea Party stand for?" asked Addison.

"The Tea Party is about ordinary Americans who haven't abandoned their values and now have skepticism toward the way our country is being run. Over the last two years, at Tea Party rallies and marches, and in a few raucous town hall meetings that politicians increasingly fear to hold, citizens have demanded that politicians justify their actions and practice what they preach in terms of fiscal responsibility. Citizens want to trust politicians to spend their money wisely and efficiently," said Arthur.

"I thought the main objective of the Tea Party was to uphold the rule of law in our country, the Constitution?" probed Addison.

"It is the main focus and over the past couple of years, the Tea Party has distributed more than six million free copies of a pocket-sized book that includes all the original printed words of the Declaration of Independence and the Constitution," bragged Arthur.

"I guess the demonstrators in Egypt and some of the Middle Eastern countries could use a Tea Party too?" said Addison, reaching for a chocolate bar at the large opening at the bottom of the lobby vending machine.

"The Tea Party is all about awareness and voting for the right people at elections. The US provided more than forty billion in aid to Egypt over the past thirty years, roughly equivalent to the personal fortune possessed by Hosni Mubarak when he was driven from power a few months ago. Why are US taxpayers forced to bankroll brazen foreign crooks such as Mubarak? A real leader doesn't care about the political ramifications of things to gain votes, he cares about the truth. He doesn't sell out his own people for his own financial gains," said Arthur.

"Happiness is in the hands of all of us," said Addison, chewing on her chocolate bar.

"Did you know that employers in California, with operations on the Ivory Coast, hire child slaves and sell them to farmers to work in the fields and spray dangerous chemicals on cocoa trees? Once the coca beans are ripe, the young workers pick them by hand for pennies per hour. Human trafficking used to be the number one crime in Eastern Europe. How close behind is the US in the number of human trafficking crimes committed by American companies?" asked Arthur.

"I feel guilty for eating that chocolate bar now, and I don't mean just for the reason of indulging in a few extra calories. I will pay more attention to how products I buy are made and where they come from," replied Addison.

"See, that's what I'm talking about. The Tea Party is all about awareness and making more responsible decisions and seeing the big picture," declared Arthur, as if he were standing behind a podium announcing his candidacy. "Because of technology and Super G air flight, we are all neighbors no matter the distance on our planet. Once you become aware, you see more in the dark than some will ever see in the light."

"What do you think of all the baseball dads and soccer moms out there driving their big gas-guzzling SUVs, buying candy bars at concession stands, always in a hurry at McDonald's or Wendy's, and living materialistic lives trying to keep up with their neighbors?" asked Addison.

"It is time for baseball dads and soccer moms, married or divorced, to take down the walls and show a little emotion by venturing out from their cocoons. At the upper end of the snobbish spectrum, some of these highfaluting parents treat young fast-food workers and retail clerks as lesser human beings than the faces on billboards. Although parents tell their children they know a lot more about life, maybe their children just do not know it yet that their parents are wrong in some regards. If parents let children see some of the real world they know, maybe later they will deal with the real world in a better way. It costs parents very little to let their children and the young workers in the world feel important and useful in helping find ways to solve problems within their family arrangements. They will realize that the material things in life aren't the important things in life," said Arthur.

What bothered Arthur much more than the behavior of any of the baseball dads or soccer moms was the portrayal of all the self-absorbed money-mongering women on television. Arthur never quite understood the phony lifestyles of the privileged white homemakers who dwelled in the cloistered world of devoting most of their time shopping at only the best stores. He hated how they met for regular brunches at fancy restaurants with their other high-society cosmetically enhanced friends, taking private tennis lessons, driving expensive cars, trashing the Junior League, gossiping about others, and complaining about anything that upsets the natural order of their day. He did not understand why they did not seem to have at least a small secret side hiding a real ambition for some kind of important project. To Arthur it seemed too many people in this world just want someone else to take care of them. For many of these women, only plans that elevate their images as important socialites are approved and scheduled to fit their personal time frames. They have no time for others. "Arthur, are you a woman hater?" said Addison, somewhat unexpectedly.

"Of course not. I just like women who aren't afraid to get their hands dirty, do a little work, take a little salt from the earth, and fight for a cause. I hate when women make a personal choice to keep all their true feelings about humanity private and dampen relationships just because they or their sugar daddy has more money. Watching these phony women is little like watching the Democrats and the Republicans, with opposing views about the issues, trying to harness their own power at a Senate hearing, knowing they really don't want to listen to or congregate with the men and women on the other side of the aisle," replied Arthur.

"I'm not particularly familiar with all the causes of the Tea Party, but you have been talking about some interesting ideas and you certainly have an alluring perspective on some of the problems on our planet," stated Addison, pressing on in an attempt to possibly coerce the beginning of a relationship with Arthur.

Arthur, not seeing the real intentions of the questions asked by Addison, continued talking. "The whole reason we need the Tea Party," he said, "is that a levelheaded conversation about the economy is going to have to begin outside the regular political process, because President Obama's change just isn't getting the job done for the middle class. Somebody has to be the resonant voice for the people who do the majority of the work in the country; otherwise, the elite are going to turn the US into a third-world country."

"You seem to have a lot of ideas about spreading the word and increasing opportunities as a disciple of the Tea Party," said Addison, gushing now.

"Real people don't feel good about themselves when they are given everything they have. They feel good about themselves when they have the opportunities to earn things for themselves," said Arthur, finally coming down from his soapbox.

Addison, with her eyes focused on Arthur and a big smile on her face, was listening intently as she sat on the plush padded armchair in the lobby of the community center. There was no place in the world she wanted to be right now than in Rainbow Creek talking to Arthur. She was already thinking about how she could help Arthur build his platform so he could help the middle class.

"Would you like to stop for a beer after work?" Addison asked Arthur.

"I quit drinking twenty years ago," said Arthur. Arthur was not used to women inviting him out on a date, but he liked the trend of equal women's rights, especially when it benefited both sexes.

"It doesn't have to be a drink. I know of this out-of-the-way Italian-American restaurant where the food is great and the patio is open on nights when the sky is clear and the stars are plentiful. I realize not everybody wants to be inebriated, revolting, and rude. I really just wanted to invite you out for more adult conversation, instead of going straight home to do the ordinary, watch television."

"Thank you for the invitation. To me, at my age, every time I see a person drinking beer, drinking liquor, smoking a cigarette, doing drugs, I see a person wasting money, harming their health, and doing nothing to improve their surroundings. Refraining from these things saves money, prolongs a life, and allows a person more time to do something productive."

"Good cooks put their souls into their food. People can get to know each other and work out their differences when breaking bread together. The restaurant I mentioned uses only the best meats and ingredients in their dishes.

"I will accept your invitation to dinner because almost everyone knows it is wise to take time to eat some healthy tomatoes, herbs, and pasta, helping make sure we treat more animals humanely, and hoping later more people will treat others like they want to be treated. Besides, eating a good meal sounds a lot better than lining up in separate tribes and throwing rocks at each other."

"You make me laugh, Arthur."

Before Arthur could say anything else, his cell phone began to beep. He flipped open his phone to say "hello" and right away he recognized the voice on the other end as Ms. Staley from the rehabilitation facility in Atlanta.

"Arthur, I'm calling to give you an update on your brother Johnny. Do you have a few minutes?"

"Sure, go ahead. How is everything?" Arthur stepped to a quiet corner to listen.

"It was a rough start, Arthur, especially the detoxification phase during the first few days. Ever since Johnny started feeling better and his body rid itself of all the bad chemicals, we have been making steady progress. The other patients seem to like Johnny, and did you know he was such a good singer and dancer?"

"Yes, he certainly didn't learn those skills from me. He was always close with my daughter Sandra and he shared his love of music with her. Along the way, he learned to dance at the clubs and on the streets. I know he likes Latin Jazz."

"Latin Jazz is just a small part of it. He is good at dancing the salsa, the samba, the meringue—some very advanced stuff for a white boy who grew up in the Midwest."

"He is a talented musician and dancer. As a teenager, all he wanted to do was play guitar and listen to music."

"I have some other good news too. Many times drug addicts show up at rehab facilities without insurance coverage and no other means of paying for services. For all the things Johnny was doing wrong, he kept up on his health insurance payments. With the plan he chose, 90 percent of his expenses are covered while he is here."

"Great. Last night I was watching Charlie Rose press Nancy Pelosi about the Healthcare Reform Bill just passed. Rose asked her, 'What is one important proposal that Republicans wanted included in the bill?' Initially she did not answer and when Rose asked her again, she avoided the question and waffled around the subject, talking about what Democrats were able to do. She soon went on to Change the subject. She was better at discrediting anything the Republicans tried to say or do. If Tea Party conservatives call something grass roots, she calls it Astroturf. This whole healthcare thing is turning into a big mess for a lot of people."

"At least Johnny's care is covered by insurance."

"I'm glad things are going in the right direction for Johnny."

"Well, we aren't all the way there yet. Addicts who relapse usually end up in prison, then after doing time, the warden releases them to compete for jobs and their lives play out against the menacing backdrop of the shadows of their felony records. They are at a disadvantage, mentally enfeebled by a prolonged use of drugs. Johnny has people skills and musical talent. He should be doing something with his life. Even something as simple as one piece of music that an addict listened to when getting high can trigger a psychological cue to desire heroin again. For some addicts it can be the smell of a certain food they come across that starts the craving. We must continue working with him to do everything we can to ensure he makes lifetime behavioral changes. I will keep you updated on his progress."

"Ms. Staley, you are an amazing woman. You must see some unbelievable stuff. How do you do it all?"

"It helps to keep a sense of humor.".

"Thank you, Ms. Staley. Please call me if you think of anything Johnny needs from home or anything I can do to help your organization. I appreciate what you are doing for my family."

"Just keep up-to-date with educating yourself about addiction, so you can continue to help Johnny. Remember treatment is not a one-week, thirty-day, or sixty-day matter. It is a chronic matter and it requires a lifetime of lifestyle changes. Staying clean is a full-time job for the entire family."

"Thanks again, Ms. Staley, I will try to stay alert to the matter. Have a nice evening."

At some point after admission to the treatment facility, Johnny finally realized his old way of living was not working. On the outside, things may have become difficult to manage—at home, on the job, socially, legally and financially—but he realized he could not maintain a normal life crowding out his days by using alcohol, heroin, or any other forms of drugs. However, the real pain that existed was on the inside. Feelings of resentment, hopelessness, anxiety, and fear began to creep into every waking moment because of his addiction. His harsher, stronger, and faster life when he was young was now softer, weaker, and slower as he was growing older. Johnny was tiring of taking to the streets to fight his own unnecessary war. He was realizing there was less pain and suffering in his life when he stayed clean. The thought of taking a good look in the mirror never crossed his mind while he was drinking and doing heroin. He had not been honest, hopeful, or accepting of himself and he had needed help for a long time.

Arthur came to understand that everybody has some kind of sorrow to carry throughout their lives. He determined we all have missing pieces to the puzzle, some worse than others, and blessings where others have gaps too. Now, however, Addison saw Arthur as a complete package, lacking no obvious parts. Arthur not only knew about the Tea Party, he had a well-rounded intellect and easily expressed himself; he could draw, write, and fix a leaky roof and he took good care of his car, which meant he was a good catch for any available middle-aged woman.

"I would love to see where you grew up in Rainbow Creek," said Addison, walking to the car in the restaurant parking lot arm-in-arm with Arthur after he had paid the bill.

Arthur wasn't sure that was a good idea. "Don't worry. Your childhood home has to be more interesting than my childhood home. I lived in a one-bedroom apartment surrounded by other apartment buildings without a nice view in any direction. So how about you show me your childhood home. I want to see it."

"OK, but I've been divorced for a while, and my daughters' mother has lived in the house with her boyfriend ever since my parents died. We can drive over there and I'll show it to you from the street."

The comment about divorce and his daughters' mother occupying the old Hobson House did not seem to bother Addison. After making the pleasant jaunt and parking his car at an angle a few hundred feet away from the front of the Hobson House, with Jane's and Stuart's vehicles parked toward the foreground of the long driveway, Arthur saw that the exterior looked great from the street. He explained to Addison how his family maintained all the wooden floors over the years, Jane updated the kitchen with modern stainless steel appliances, and the living area was full of bookcases stacked with reading materials and books about everything from adventure books to books about politics and philosophy to self-help. Arthur described his childhood bedroom, telling Addison about the Little League baseball and soccer trophies that filled a corner display case. From the street, it was easy for Addison to imagine all the games played when children roamed the huge backyard and the curiosity seeking that occurred in the woods and the creek surrounding the old estate.

In truth, all the manufactured changes in living arrangements and scenery at the Hobson House were sobering to Arthur. In the past, his marriage to Jane sometimes felt like two pit bulls chained to the same tree, always butting heads about something. When an owner chains one pit-bull to his own tree doing his own thing and another pit-bull to another tree, the pit bulls get along fine. After a few years in a marriage, many people everywhere figure this out and stay married, continuing to live separate lives, instead of admitting they played a bad hand, but Arthur and Jane were not like other people. Their marriage did not look so bad from the outside, but the living quarters on the inside felt far away from fantasyland and both partners wanted something different.

Outside the car, rain started coming down hard. Arthur began to think about how happy he was a decade ago when he knew his two toddler-age daughters were asleep at night, while he sat in his favorite leather lounge chair reading the evening newspaper, and listening to mild thundershowers off into the distance of the night. In those instances, in his mind, everything in his little world was safe and cozy. Now, inside the car, he and Addison were whirling with lust. Arthur had showed her a personal side of his life and she took it as a sign that he wanted more from their relationship.

"So this is where I spent my childhood years," Arthur said. "This is where I lived the good times and the bad times."

"The property is beautiful," said Addison.

"The only things still growing on the eleven-acre property are the few garden-variety vegetables my ex-wife oversees. At one time, the land overflowed with rows and rows of crops: tomatoes, cucumbers, lettuce heads, string beans, pumpkins, and strawberries. The strawberries were a good source of income for my family. My mom and dad worked hard on hot days in the summer, crawling around on the ground to pick the strawberries. My brothers and I would sell them roadside at a plywood stand my dad built one weekend. Though my brothers and I helped our parents with the farm, all three of us knew we didn't want to make a living working in the fields."

"I love how the estate sits on top of a rising mound and overlooks the wooded area and the entire stimulating community," said Addison, luring at Arthur.

"I'm not sure what you mean by that, but it sure sounds sensual," said Arthur.

"I was trying to flirt with you," said Addison.

"A man needs to protect from bulges that balloon into cracks and elevate the temperature inside the home. One hundred percent silicone is the way to go, especially to prevent leaks in the insulation that can affect the electrical wiring in the bedroom, on top of the washer and drier, and in the basement. Impervious to any damaging conditions, proper handling of silicone prevents shrinkage and moisture leakage in the crack. Silicone is best for the long haul, unlike acrylic, which can crack or shrink over time. Make sure you keep the surface clean, prep the tube and seal the proper size. Insert the gun at a forty-five-degree angle and use constant pressure to keep a tight grip. For a great finish, use your fingers or a wet smoothing tool within two to three minutes."

"That's the sexiest thing I ever heard in my life. That was hot," said Addison.

"I wasn't finished. Use mineral spirits to clean up. What did you think I was talking about, Addison? I was talking about using caulk to winterize the outside seams on the house," said Arthur.

"Whatever you were trying to say, your words sounded like some kind of hot sexual advance you might use on a woman in hopes of making a right-wing hookup possible," she said. Addison did not care what else Arthur said at this point. She pushed his seat back in the car to a more reclining position, climbed over, and straddled him with her posterior resting on the steering wheel.

"Did you ever date a guy who used Instarise?" Arthur asked.

"What? Now I am confused," said Addison.

"Never mind," said Arthur, quickly yielding not to ask any more dumb questions.

"Kiss me," she said.

He did, and it was better than questioning why he should not or why she had chosen him to have sex with right there, right now. At that moment in the evening, as the rain was steadily falling and the sun was setting behind the nimbus clouds on the western horizon, with the car windows partially open and the breeze billowing through, they laughed and made love with blitheness. They perspired, laughed some more, held each other while out of breath and after pausing to listen to the whistling of the leaves in the trees, made love again. Having sex in the car and being on top the whole time was not exactly the most comfortable place for Addison, but she was well satisfied and she lauded Arthur. Before this evening, she had only romanticized about an uncomplicated sexual interlude with a kindly mature intellectual man. One giant lightning strike seemed to signal the end of the lovemaking session for the evening. The cracked vinyl of the leather seat left claw marks on her kneecaps. Putting her clothes back on, as if she were applying medicine to a wound, she realized she would remember this evening forever. For one of the few times in his life, Arthur felt more like the pursued than the pursuer; that there was a kind of ease he felt just being himself without needing to work overtime to achieve a goal. He adjusted his seatback, started the ignition, and drove Addison back to her car at the community center parking lot. He was not the kind of man who would do a disappearing act after having sex with a woman, and Addison was not shy about assuring him that she wanted to see him again. Before getting into her car, she slipped him a torn piece of paper with her phone number and she kissed him good night. She needed someone to love and he was open to a relationship as long as she did not want to vie for all his time. Both of them had met enough people who turned out to be only bottom feeders, bed-post notches, liars, screwups, damaged friends, and dangerous antagonists to the rest of the world.

The next morning, Arthur started researching and preparing for his talk at a rally announced by the Heartland Tea Party Coalition and scheduled later in the month. He was living his life like he had just found out his time on earth was limited and he did not want to waste it living by someone else's lousy rules and drowning out his inner voice. More than ever before, he was building up courage to follow through with his agenda. He was tired of the privileged telling the less fortunate how blessed they were, while all the other poor bastards in the world are just going to have to suffer whatever consequences come their way. He dreamed that he would someday do something important enough where his life and the lives of others would never be the same. Even when Arthur was wrong or sounded brilliantly terrible, Addison or Sandra or Justin was there to tell him how proud they were for working so hard and taking the steps to accomplish something of worth.

Arthur had a strong desire to treat other people nicely, but a sour taste always built up in his mouth when he saw other men acting fake with women. He never acted fake with his own two daughters, even if it meant they would not speak to him for extended amounts of time. Susie was away at college and had not spoken to her dad since he forgot to call on her birthday the weekend before Columbus Day. After a brief attempt by her father to apologize one week later, Susie still was in no mood to talk. Arthur waited another week and tried calling her again on his cell phone.

Arthur: "Are you still not speaking to me? I am just wondering how you are doing. How long is this estrangement going to last?"

Silence.

Arthur: "Are you finding your classes interesting? Are you living a healthy lifestyle?"

More silence.

Arthur: "You know what you're being? You are being disrespectful. This is a bunch of baloney. I call to see how you are doing, and this is how you treat your father?"

Susie still did not speak.

A car engine can break the stillness of the night and an unopened letter found behind couch cushions can rekindle communication, but Arthur was struggling to convince Susie to talk.

Arthur: "If you're waiting for me to apologize again for forgetting your birthday, I'm sorry. I did not do it with any intention of hurting you. I don't think you should continue ignoring me, blaming your problems on me, and lamenting about everything the older generation has done to cause the world to turn rotten. I never, ever intended to hurt you then or anytime before in your life, but I just can't take the silence anymore. It is time for you to act your age, not your shoe size. If you think the answer to any of your problems is not speaking to your father, then you can leave it at that. I look at it as a sign of more disrespect."

More silence; Susie did not speak.

Arthur: "I was hoping by taking another step to call, you would somehow be willing to forgive and forget. It appears you are still mad about things. If you feel like talking and you think we could try to figure things out, please call me sometime."

More silence; Susie did not speak.

Arthur: "I'm not some bum father who ran away from his problems and is hanging out on street corners drinking beer from cans draped in paper bags, and I know you're not a bag lady with mental illness," he said trying to warm to Susie's state of mind. "I am your father and I will always be part of your life as long as I am alive. I think I deserve a little more than the nothing you have been giving me. I know you have other things on your mind like boyfriends, classes, homework, and what to make to eat when you get hungry, but nobody is ever too busy to make a four-minute phone call every two or three weeks just to let your family know you are OK."

Finally, Susie spoke.

Susie: "I thought when you ponder the paramount things in your life, everything has to come from your soul, or otherwise it doesn't matter."

Arthur: "Yes, I always tried to teach the essential qualities of life to you and Sandra."

Susie: "First you forgot my birthday. Then you tried to make up for it by sending me one of those generic 'happy-face" birthday cards. Are you too cheap these days to buy me an appropriate card with a handwritten note, something more special? You taught me to ignore twisted words used by many of our politicians. I guess I was looking for some words of encouragement from my father. Sometimes a girl just wants to feel special."

Arthur: "You're right, Susie. I'm sorry. When I was in sales, I sent those 'happy-face' cards to customers on their birthdays thanking them for their business. The shoebox where I kept those cards is almost empty. Now that you gave me this new information, nobody will have to worry about receiving another 'happy-face' card from me. Maybe we both can breathe a little easier."

Arthur probably deserved the repression, maybe from pushing too hard and due to the hundreds of mistakes he had made in loving his two daughters too much. Susie was feeling like her father slashed her in the face with a belt, even though she was unwilling to admit that she baited her dad into feeling worse by repeatedly ignoring his inquiries. Arthur was feeling like he had failed his daughter. If Susie still wanted a dad who could teach her things like he did when she was a little girl, if Susie just realized how hard her dad tried, if Susie knew how much her dad really loved her, if Susie just understood that parents have feelings too, she and her dad would get along great. There were no real conversations between Arthur and Susie during the rest of the first semester she was away at college. Since not all things concerning the matter with Susie immediately became clear to Arthur, he focused on his work, trying to build his platform, while Susie hardly seemed to miss her father, concentrating on her college classes and campus life. What really was happening was that Arthur was becoming more Arthur and Susie more Susie.

Arthur and Susie both felt a little awkward talking to each other about sex, but like any good father, he made his concerns known. Arthur wanted his younger daughter to realize the dream of graduating from college and not ruining it by getting pregnant or leaving campus early because some flaky shining knight in armor whisked her away. The lamentable truth for Arthur, even after considering the sexual escapade with Addison, is that sex was not as satisfying and urgent as it was in his earlier days. There just always seemed to be something else he should be doing. By no means did Arthur consider himself an expert, but he was not naïve about sex either. However, one night will forever remain in his memory. At age twenty-four and not in a relationship, he met a girl a couple of years older at a local sculptor's exhibit set up as a makeshift art gallery in the banquet center of a Hilton Hotel. She was the most beautiful woman he had ever seen. She struck up a conversation with him and one thing led to another. They walked around admiring the artwork together, then ate dinner at the hotel, and after that, drank a few light beers at the hotel bar. In reverse roles, the woman invited Arthur back to her hotel room for a one-night stand of aggressive passion combined with safe sex. She even supplied the condoms. When the alarm on the nightstand sounded at 6:30 a.m., the woman had already showered and was finished getting dressed, while Arthur was still trying to wake up.

Woman: "Good-bye, Arthur."

Arthur: "Are you leaving? Do you have time for coffee or breakfast?"

Woman: "I had a lovely evening."

Arthur: "Will I ever see you again?"

Woman: "Arthur, I have to flag a taxi to the airport and catch a flight. I will check out at the front desk, but you need to be out of this room by 11 a.m."

At that moment, the woman left and Arthur, not knowing what hit him, never saw her again. He knew that men walked out on women all the time, but it felt weird for a woman to leave him so abruptly and so early in the morning.

Arthur had his memories of younger years, his sex with the most beautiful woman he ever saw, and mistakes he made in his life, but he kept most of these memories to himself. He wished his relationship with Susie was better, but he needed to give her space to grow right now, and he hoped things would get better later. He hoped in the future, talking on the telephone with Susie would not seem like working a customer service job trying to get the person on the other end to stay on the line. Sitting in his office at home, the phone rang. It was Addison.

They said their hellos and then Addison brought the conversation to the topic of politics.

Addison: "Why can't politicians think about how all their self-centered ways of living are affecting all the people they are supposed to represent?"

Arthur tried to adjust his thoughts away from thinking about the most beautiful woman he ever saw and Susie not wanting to speak to him.

Arthur, playing devil's advocate: "Things are never what they appear. Didn't you ever do something that was wrong and no one ever found out about it?"

Addison, surprised and a little taken aback: "Yes, I wrecked my dad's car and let my brother take the blame for it without telling anyone that I was the person responsible."

Arthur: "I didn't mean to change the subject. We really do need politicians who want to make a difference and aren't afraid of being held responsible."

Addison: "I hate when governors or the president takes all these vacations and spends taxpayers' money on concerts, golf outings, parties, celebrations, basketball games, family vacations, and trips overseas when citizens here are without jobs. Aren't politicians who get elected supposed to represent the voters?"

Arthur: "I agree with you. There is plenty of time for vacations and parties after these men and women finish their term or terms in office. They will have plenty of free time and money to spend after they write their memoirs. Shouldn't the few years they spend in office be all about working as hard as possible to make sure the country is headed in the right direction?"

Addison: "Instead of these liberals telling us ways to spur growth and create jobs, it feels more like we just want them to curb the spending. If they keep creating more ways to spend our money, the day will come when they tell us that the light at the end of the tunnel is going to have to be turned off because no money is left to pay for the electricity to keep it on."

Arthur: "To me it feels like when the oldest son or daughter, acting as a guardian, makes the very difficult decision to take away the keys from an aging parent. The guardian witnesses their elderly parent driving erratically, yet the elderly parent does not recognize they can no longer manage driving, and they do not want the privilege taken away."

Addison: "I know good governments cut wasteful spending, but how can the government create jobs?"

Arthur: "The government doesn't really create jobs for the majority of people, because tax dollars from private-sector jobs pay for government workers. The government needs to create incentives for businesses and lower the corporate tax rate from 35 to 19 percent, the average rate paid by companies in Europe and Asia. The United States is not like Russia with limited resources. It is time to roll back the government and reduce the inconsequential regulatory burdens placed on business. There are great American companies, like Thomas and Betts, Genuine Parts, Donaldson, General Mills, and Kellogg's, which will hire people if taxes go lower. American citizens do not need any more speeches from the president about broad principles. Out-of-work individuals want to hear about specific plans that will create real incentives to help businesses hire and get people back to work."

Addison: "I love the way you explain things. I'll see you at the community center soon."

Arthur and Addison were becoming great friends. Arthur knew many people in Rainbow Creek, but he enjoyed talking to Addison more than anyone else, especially after she left messages on the answering machine wanting to meet to sit down somewhere to talk about politics. Today, people seldom sit down and have a sustained conversation. It seems this problem is everywhere. Addison agreed with Arthur that text messages, abbreviated words, initialed words, throwaway products, cheap cookie-cutter buildings, and chain developments are causing all the unique things, authentic things, and honest things to die off. Intellectually and environmentally, too many politicians and too many citizens just follow along like a leaf floating down a stream, only reacting to the latest trend or fad.

As the car rolled into the driveway on Hill View, at the end of a relaxing evening out on the town for dinner and a movie and a sleepy but focused drive back home, Arthur and Addison quickly noticed Johnny sitting and waiting on the top step of the front porch. An old large black vinyl piece of luggage was resting near the front door behind him.

Johnny: "How are you, Arthur, and who is the beautiful young lady with you?"

Arthur: "I'm doing okay. This is my friend Addison. We have been seeing each other for a few months now."

Addison: "Hi, Johnny."

Johnny: "That's great. It's nice to meet you, Addison. I hope I'm not intruding on you, Arthur, but I would really appreciate it if you would let me stay with you for a few weeks while I look for a job and try to get back on my feet."

Arthur: "First let's all go inside to sit at the kitchen table and talk. You must be starving. Help yourself to anything you want to eat or drink. There's leftover fried chicken in the refrigerator and plenty of snacks in the pantry too."

Johnny: "I appreciate the hospitality and I am hungry. I had just enough money to buy a train ticket to St. Louis, and from there, I hitchhiked to your front porch."

To Arthur, Johnny was more than just his brother. He was also the kind of real person that rollicking filmmakers told stories about and whose outsized actions seemed tailor-made for a Hallmark movie. Not only could Johnny be highly entertaining telling tales of his life, but a person could also feel genuinely sorry for him once they realized his dreams got too big. It bothered Arthur when he thought his brother overstepped his freedoms, wondering if he only came back for the fried chicken and free rent.

Arthur: "Johnny, if you are going to stay here, you will have to help out around here. I've been thinking and I would like to ask a favor from you."

Johnny: "Sure, what is it you need, Arthur?"

Arthur: "With the midterm Senatorial elections in two weeks, the Republican mayor of Rainbow Creek, Wade Armstrong, and a couple of Tea Party representatives will be speaking next week at a rally inside the Captain's Ballroom, which holds about two thousand people. Before the event starts and after the speakers are finished with their talks, we still need some additional background entertainment to help make the whole thing a big success. I was wondering if you would be willing to play your guitar and sing or maybe teach some of your dance moves to volunteers on stage."

Johnny: "Well, this is Rainbow Creek, right? In rehab I worked hard to learn to play "Wish Me a Rainbow" on my guitar. I think this song would be fitting for the event, don't you?"

Arthur: "Fantastic! Then can I tell the event planners to pencil you in on the schedule for next Tuesday evening? You have to be there by 6 p.m."

Johnny: "If you introduce me to the public, I will be there."

Arthur: "Great! I'm not one of the scheduled speakers this time, but I don't see any problem why the mayor wouldn't let me introduce you to the crowd."

Johnny: "So it's set then."

The general fund was the main topic of discussion on the annual report as Mayor Joey Langwell of Heartland and Mayor Wade Armstrong of Rainbow Creek presented information on the state of the economy and other financial concerns in their jurisdictions to kick off a special two-district rally. The information was fairly stated in all material respects in relation to the financial statements as a whole, even though capital improvement expenditures and payments for debt services were higher than the actual revenues in the general coffers of both communities. The park and sewer funds showed revenues held in accounts were less than the amounts held in previous years in both towns. Street repairs dominated the last half of the town hall rally held by officials of the city of Rainbow Creek. Details were described to inform residents of what they can expect from road workers repairing potholes and striping lanes through tax initiatives, at an estimated cost of $911 per household. Representatives from the Rainbow Creek and Heartland departments of planning, fire, police, highway, and traffic were on hand to support the initiative, needing a majority vote for approval. Residents of Heartland were concerned about how the streets, most of which were built between 1947 and 1963, would be fixed. Officials told the residents that the most traveled streets downtown would be replaced, while less traveled roads would require less costly fixes such as hot patches to potholes. A statement was read that not all the streets need to be fixed all at once and that a three-to-four-year plan would be implemented as a reasonable length of time to bring the streets up to accepted standards. The mayors recommended that city officials from each city set up some type of oversight committee to make sure citizens know how money is spent in the various accounts. The oversight in Heartland and Rainbow Creek could be as simple as proofreading copies of statements from the bank and reviewing reconciliations on a monthly basis. Because of the financial crisis of 2008, these types of city recommendations made sense to Arthur, but he wanted to see more done to develop a formal investment policy that addressed interest rates, credit risk, custodial risk, and the creation of jobs. The boards in Rainbow Creek and Heartland had already voted unanimously to enter their mayor's respective reports into the record.

For the first time in Rainbow Creek and Heartland, people were bringing homemade signs to town hall meetings and the number of people attending was more than the usual audience. A balding middle-aged man held a sign that read, "THE WORKING CLASS IS TOO BIG TO FAIL." A young working woman dressed in business attire, puffy shirt, and pants suit, held a sign that read, "OBAMA BAILED OUT WALL STREET AND THEN HE SOLD OUT MAIN STREET." An elderly retired man held a folded grocery bag high in the air with words written on it in black magic marker stating, "GREED IS UN-AMERICAN." Another sign read, "END CORRUPTION IN RAINBOW CREEK AND HEARTLAND."

Mayor Armstrong's remarks about regulations and the economy marked one of the few times Arthur agreed with the mayor's politics. For a change, the mayor was making a lot of sense. Mayor Armstrong said, "Any brain-dead economist knows that regulations and higher taxes cost jobs. Politicians who have never worked a day outside the political arena don't know how to make a payroll or equalize a balance sheet or understand the problems a business faces. The plight of the economy is very reactive to bad policies and when a local, state, or federal government piles on more rules and regulations, the economy takes more hits. We can't solve problems by using the same kind of thinking we used when we created them."

Changes to policies were emotional for some of the people who had lived in Rainbow Creek since the fifties. In the fifties and sixties, Rainbow Creek was a typical suburban, middle-class, baby boomer community of young families raising their children. Folks enjoyed backyard barbecues, fish fries, and neighborhood celebrations. When Mayor

Armstrong told residents the city will never return to the old days, some of the oldest citizens didn't like the rhetoric.

At least Mayor Armstrong stayed away from blaming the boomers for everything wrong in his town. Arthur was tired of hearing the "boomer generation" taking the bad rap for the bad economy and blame for everything else that is wrong with the world today. Life wasn't always black and white for boomers, just like it wasn't for generations before them and it won't be for generations after them.

Baby boomers believe in education and worked hard to send their children to college. They are clever and resourceful, independent and self-reliant people. Boomers grew up during an era of reform, but they had the courage to question authority systems and challenge the status quo in the sixties and again as part of the recent Tea Party movement. Nearly eighty million baby boomers will exit the workplace in the next decade. These employees are retiring at the rate of eight thousand per day. This unprecedented loss of a skilled workforce will have to be replaced.

"If we're going to continue to take care of the major problems of our city, the money to pay for things has to come from somewhere to maintain a high level of government, and the only place I know it could come from is through new taxes, more taxes," Mayor Langwell said. "I don't keep secrets from residents, and my role as mayor is to give you the information and the facts, substantiated facts backed up by proof and evidence."

After the two mayors were finished speaking, Arthur took to the microphone, quickly introducing his brother. "We want to thank you guys for coming to the rally," said Arthur. "Now my brother Johnny Hobson would like to play his rendition of the song "Wish Me a Rainbow," a hit with tunes and words by Ray Evans and Jay Livingston." Johnny walked on the stage with an electric guitar strapped around his shoulders, and almost immediately, every young female in attendance wanted to get closer. Before he began singing, he tried to inspire the young people with a promotional plug for his favorite guitar company.

Johnny: "Martin Guitar Company has been creating the finest acoustic instruments in the world for a long time, even before the days of Abraham Lincoln. They continue to innovate and they introduced the techniques and features that have become industry standards including X-bracing and the 14-fret guitar. Martin guitars are hand-made by mostly women who use skillful techniques taught to them by the founder of the company, Christian Frederick Martin. Martin guitars are the choice of musicians around the world, from the icons of rock, country, folk, and bluegrass, to those just beginning to play. You can see Martin guitars across all segments of pop culture, including on the television shows *American Idol, Glee,* and *the Voice.*" With that, Johnny turned up the acoustics and turned up the excitement by rousing the crowd with his strumming and singing.

Johnny's singing voice wasn't quite elevated to the level of Nat King Cole or Frank Sinatra, but his guitar playing ability made up for it and he definitely entertained the crowd. Johnny then belted out a song he wrote himself: "While we need a new beginning, we must kick out all the finks, because a government which is run without the consent of the people stinks. We want to keep our treasures in Rainbow Creek, and because tomorrow depends on jobs today, stop the wasteful spending that has reached its peak, quit blaming others and enact policies that help businesses show us the way. May we all awake to the delusions of political tweaks, and may a rainbow appear on every rainy day." Though the two mayors were no longer standing on the stage, Johnny was sure both men were still near enough to hear the music and the participation by the people. The Tea Party was spawning a new genre of protest music that was becoming the soundtrack for the political movement's gatherings. Johnny found it particularly amusing when people said they didn't pay attention to politics, but most of the music they listened to was all about the issues of the day.

Memorable music has always sprung from people protesting change, from the slave days in the South and the union uprisings during the Depression to the issues of civil rights in the sixties and the protestors of the Vietnam War. Music has even had a role in converting some of the hippies who supported liberal ideas in the sixties to a more conservative right of the Tea Party today. Many Tea Baggers are over fifty and they can remember listening to the liberal protest music of Bob Dylan, Woody Guthrie, Pete Seeger, John Lennon, and Patti Smith. Dylan's "Blowin' in the Wind," Guthrie's "This Land Is Your Land," Lennon's "Give Peace a Chance," Smith's "People Have the Power," and Seeger's "If I had a Hammer" topped the charts a half century ago.

Conservative protest music clearly depicted what a liberal life is like, criticizing liberal hypocrisy and fascism, chastising people for accepting the mainstream media's version of events and not paying attention personally to politics. The liberal press can't stand it when conservatives propose things that prove they are intelligent enough to sort out their own financial strategies, without the help of Washington. Songs about patriotism and standing for America in the name of freedom celebrate the people and all the good things about living in the US. The songs tell citizens to stay away from liberal excess and illegal acts in order to be a positive influence for the next generation.

Newer songs continue a conservative political theme; The Infidels' "Liberalism Is a Mental Disorder" clearly attacks liberal values. Linkin Park's song "New Divide" depicts a typical scenario of conservatives having to defend themselves from unreasonable liberal attacks and the ever-widening divide between the two ideologies in search of the truth. Taylor Swift's song "**Mine**" relates how her parents stooped to liberal values and divorced, and how she doesn't want that to happen with the guy she marries.

Johnny listened to all of these songs for motivation in his own life as he tried to build a platform for his musical career. Listening to music became a small piece of Arthur's life too. Whenever he was tired and just wanted to relax or when he needed some inspiration for a speech he was writing, Arthur found comfort in borrowing albums and CDs from Johnny's collection. The music helped him reinforce his beliefs that Americans needed to get back to working hard, saving money, and starting real capitalist enterprises, and stop letting elitists and Wall Street steer the country in a dangerous direction, by stealing people's money. Listening to all the music assured him of having no illusions about forty years of financial inertia that has seen brokerage firms, hedge funds, and the credit card industry skyrocket to nearly half of the national GDP. The songs spoke for the people. In between verses, Arthur heard words telling us, if our leaders keep on this course financially, in a few years the government will be able to dip into private individual bank accounts to pay down the national debt without our permission, and we will not be able to do anything to stop them. The songs made him think Rainbow Creek's real chickens were all the unfunded promises, bankrupt welfare entitlements, and real inflation coming home to roost when the town was finally out of money. The liberal media hated the idea of the Tea Party trying to write its own song about their vision of limited government, low taxation on businesses, free enterprise, and the right to express opinions and promote ideas. Listening to all this music with Arthur and Johnny inspired Addison to take out a half-page ad in the *Rainbow Call* newspaper to promote the Tea Party movement and Arthur's bid for mayor.

The Tea Party is about getting back the respect citizens once had for their government, which paralleled the land of opportunity and celebrated hard work to earn a good living. Clearly citizens across the nation are angered at those who did well but earned their money unfairly. But it isn't fair to discredit the companies that played by the rules, destroying their reputations by politics of envy just because they did well. Misguided leadership makes mistakes when it sets a dangerous tone of painting all successful Americans with the same broad strokes, as if all millionaires, billionaires, and all hardworking wage earners who have income over a certain amount are bad people. Right now, our town and our country are in dangerous territory, because our leaders have no idea what they are talking about and they are misleading people. Vote for Arthur Hobson in the next mayoral election. He supports businesses and will do everything he can to create a better environment for small businesses in our town.

Like old times, Arthur and Johnny were brothers having fun and working together for a cause greater than either could accomplish alone. Drugs, violence, government corruption, pollution, global warming, oil spills, environmental disasters, nuclear radiation leaks, and other problems have led concerned people to ask, "Will humans step up to the plate to help before ruining the earth?" Arthur believed the planet could be transformed into a paradise and any day he worked to teach others how they must improve ways of doing things responsibly to qualify to live here was a great day. He told locals that the way we treat our planet has a direct impact on the lives of all people living on it, including each individual and their loved ones. Just as Johnny was trying to find balance in his life without using drugs, Arthur hoped government and business leaders could find a balance between the creative side and the environmentally safe side of the entrepreneurial spirit.

One week before Arthur was to give his speech at the rally in Heartland, Jane entered in a vegetable garden contest at the Freedom Festival in Fieldcrest, celebrating the century and a half milestone of the founding of the small community just down the road from Rainbow Creek. What better way to celebrate the event than with great food and great gardening ideas and entering a contest, she thought. All throughout the weekend celebration, fairgoers enjoyed great summertime treats like funnel cake, kettle corn, hot dogs, hamburgers, bratwursts, toasted ravioli, chicken wings, and apple pie, watermelon, and ice-cream cones. One fenced-off area at the fair offered a full sit-down dining experience of hand-made, great tasting, Italian-style pizza cooked in a wood-fired outdoor oven. The toppings were fresh and the pizzas cooked in just ten minutes. Each year the festival had its share of dichotomy too, while one group was selling fried things on sticks, people at another stand might be passing out health and wellness information.

One stand, a regular lobby for heart wellness and awareness at the entrance of the festival each year, raised money for the Rainbow Angels for Kids, a foundation helping children with heart problems. A yellow halo, blue wings, and red heart of love combined to make the Rainbow Angel logo. The volunteer group helped families deal with hospital bills by passing out pamphlets with information about the heart and accepting small contributions from citizens. The small individual donations of money collected at the festival and other gatherings, such as craft fairs, football games, basketball games, bake sales, and flea markets, added up in big ways to help the families with hospital stays during the year. A good portion of the donations went toward trying to stop the greedy companies hoarding vital medications from kids with heart problems, and then marking up the prices by six times, before selling the remedies to desperate families and medical facilities.

The American Red Cross arranged for some of their area volunteer staff to staff a booth offering tips for emergency preparedness. The staff encouraged families, businesses, schools, and organizations to take steps now to become better prepared for the next emergency or disaster. People living in the tornado alley of the Midwest know that power outages, water-main breaks, and severe weather can strike at any time, so the Red Cross staff asked Rainbow Creek citizens to make a renewed commitment emergency preparedness. So many at the fair were happy to make the commitment.

A group of volunteer growers set up their booth in the same patch of grass and shade every year at the festival, secure in their belief that healthy eating will save lives. During early hours of the festival, the volunteer growers working the booth handed out strawberry tarts, blueberry muffins, sliced bagels, fresh-picked organic apples, and paper cups full of fresh-squeezed orange juice and hot tea. Some years the volunteers dealt with wind and rain, but storms never blew away their spirit and their hospitality never wavered. Working the booth took a lot of effort, but the people doing the work just wanted the job done right.

The ambassadors and board members of the chambers of commerce from Fieldcrest, Heartland, and Rainbow Creek greeted fairgoers and told them a little about what their organizations did for their communities. Many fairgoers wanted to know more about charity events, breakfast meetings where attendees exchanged business cards, and the annual fishing and golf tournaments. For several years, the Chambers had been trying new ways to build their membership with some success through drives, booths at fairs, trivia nights, reward programs and hiring a sales representative. During the early-morning hours of the first day of the Freedom Festival, the three chambers of commerce helped forty-eight visitors and talked to two dozen business representatives. Seventeen prospects requested chamber information from the Rainbow Creek ambassadors alone.

Festival organizers arranged contests for growers with entries in the categories of vegetables, fruits, and special exhibits. Almost two hundred entries underwent the scrutiny of a panel of nationally accredited judges as fairgoers and contestants watched in suspense. The vegetables and fruits categories were all about size. The special exhibits category featured a wide variety of subject matter related to gardening and keeping a nice lawn. The exhibits included lavish displays about how to kill moles, how to recycle food wastes, and how to use fresh and dried plant materials to design creative floral designs for the home.

When Jane heard her name announced as the blue ribbon winner for the largest tomato entered in the contest, she was not sure if she won the vegetable category or the fruit category, but she did not care. All she knew is that she won first place and she was excited. The skin of her tomato was flawless and it was the size of a grapefruit. She could hardly believe that she beat all the professionals, the commercial farmers and the members of the Fieldcrest Garden Club. After the other winners were announced, Johnny turned around the guitar hanging on his back and started strumming and singing another authentic tune:

"Apple Butter, Apple Juice, Apple Trees,
Apple Pies, Apple Tarts, Applebee's,
Mutsu, Braeburn, Honey Crisp and Northern Spy's,
Our women bake the best American Apple Pies,
And at the end of each Freedom Festival, fairgoers sing this song,
All about apple things, and again next year, everybody will sing along."

The fairgoers and contestants sang the verse three times, as Johnny strummed his guitar, and everyone was happy. After several days of working on his notes and running ideas by Addison, Arthur drove to Heartland accompanied by her, to give another Tea Party speech in front of several hundred people who showed up at the far end of the Walmart parking lot. He was the second speaker after the Republican mayor of Heartland, Mr. Joey Langwell. After a brief statement and an introduction from the mayor, it was Arthur's turn to speak.

It is in our DNA to have a healthy skeptical view of our government. Democrats, Republicans, and Tea Party organizers are all guilty of misidentifying the facts and their lists are short on how to fix things. Once a politician labels lies as the truth in a speech, can voters trust him to speak the truth afterward? The reality of the facts must address the complaining and yelling at each other or we will not fix things. The government has to submit to some oversight in order to protect Americans so that in the future, we are presented with fair mortgages, safe food, safe medicine, good business practices, quality goods and services, smart environmental policies, and a strong military to protect against others who threaten us. We have to keep an open mind about deciding our issues; otherwise we keep the same assumptions we have always thought, without any room to grow. We have to listen to both sides and remain willing to research and learn more even though we feel compromised by ridiculous concerns and lambasted with unfounded complaints. All politics is local.

The United States used to be a country ruled by reason and common sense. Socialism cannot work here in this country. Americans want an opportunity to earn an honest income without sacrificing their dignity and freedom to pursue their own aspirations, not the ones prescribed by the government. Americans desire to live in a country where success depends on people's efforts, not on what a bureaucrat decides or wants. People should base relationships with others on voluntary agreements, with safety the only requirement. Laws should protect our earnings, not allow them to be excessively taxed and spent by greedy politicians and wealthy officials. In the name of justice, the economy is rigged. Middle-class Americans have been screaming from the rooftops, trying to get politicians to pay attention and focus on the work at hand. We are tired of this feeling that politicians have a very different way of doing business and instead of assuming that everything is OK, we are looking back and finding out that it is not. We must send a loud message to our government leaders by voting for candidates who will listen. Stop the runaway spending, stop taking over our businesses and farms, stop mortgaging our children's future, and help create real jobs where people produce goods and services that make our planet better. The Tea Party is against any more debt or any more bailouts that force responsible taxpayers to pay for other people's irresponsible behavior.

Small businesses in the US created two-thirds of the net new jobs during the past three decades. Small businesses in Rainbow Creek returns sixty-eight cents of every dollar spent in locally owned stores back to the community through taxes, payroll, and expenditures. If you elect me mayor, and even if you decide not to vote for me, I would like to ask all our residents to commit to spending a majority of their monthly shopping budgets in locally owned businesses. The bookstore on Heritage Street, the music store on Nottingham Lane, the pet store on Elm Street, the bakery on Canter Leigh Street, the shoe store on Main Street, and the garden shop on Woodlawn Drive, all contribute to our community without public handouts or tax increment financing. These stores give back to our community and they invest in our neighborhoods. They partner with Rainbow Christian Church to provide turkeys, stuffing, vegetables, cranberry sauce, pumpkin pies, apple pies, cookies, and other goodies to mark the beginning of the holidays with a free meal for anyone interested in attending the Thanksgiving celebration each year. If you would rather eat your Thanksgiving dinner at home, stop by anyway to thank the small-business owners for what they do for the community or find out about special discounts, gift wrapping services, or Christmas shopping ideas.

If we support our small businesses and we help create jobs, then we avoid some of the sad occurrences like the story of the couple one county over arguing about their finances. Recently, the police reacted to a call by a woman who complained about a high level of noise and a possible assault in a house next-door to her. A forty-seven-year-old man said he had argued with his wife after getting up from a nap and finding her screaming about finances and him not having a job. The woman said her husband choked her and threw her cell phone, while the husband said his wife had hidden his wallet and his false teeth. The police took the husband to jail. I guess her plan to save money and cut the food bill worked. At least now, the man will eat while in jail, but taxpayers will foot another bill. Thank you for your time.

Arthur felt good about his speech in Heartland, but others felt he expected too much and he hoped for too much. Arthur continued to fight on for what he believed in because he wanted his country to become a more realistic place for the next generation. There were political realities in the past as there are in the present, that preclude blind faith and that discourage people from thinking that everything will work out favorably. He believed that major difficulties had always been overcome in the United States and such things will eventually get worked out. Worked out not because of an overload of regulations and laws, but because great leaders used common sense and common decency. Even in places other than Rainbow Creek, in places like New Orleans and Joplin, though the government worked slowly and disasters were difficult to overcome, people eventually came together with the help of great leaders.

Addison: "I always feel inspired after listening to one of your speeches and paying attention to the reactions of the people in the audience."

Arthur: "When giving a speech, my focus is on the words, not the people. I just hope my message is making a difference."

Addison: "Well, you always make me feel better about current issues, like protecting earnings, creating jobs, and stopping bailouts."

Arthur: "I could go along with the bailouts of the financial institutions to save the economy, until I found out the same men who erected this mess are still in power running the banks."

From the frequency of their meetings and from the eloquent ways Addison talked to him, Arthur finally got it in his head that he was falling in love with her and she was more than just a receptive friend to him.

Addison: "Arthur, how does the American public know where campaign contributions are spent? Where do politicians spend all the money? Do they spend some of the contributions on food, entertainment, or personal needs and wants? Maybe some of the money goes into the personal accounts of the candidates. Maybe it is time to appropriate a special tax on all campaign contributions, paid for by the political candidates who benefit from it."

Arthur: "Those are very good questions and concerns, but right now I'm starving. Do you want to go get something to eat?"

Addison: "Sure, can we eat at the same restaurant we ate at the first day we met?"

Arthur: "That sounds good. Let's go. But after hearing the story the biologist told me today, I don't think I want to order fish."

Addison: "What happened?"

Arthur: "A biologist caught an elusive seven foot sawfish in a river in Missouri today. He was perplexed about how to explain how the sawfish resurfaced in Missouri waters. The fish had thirty-nine razor sharp teeth projecting off its chainsaw like bill. The biologist spent most of his career trying to catch one of these creatures, which scientists thought to be near extinction, because for decades the long toothy snout caused the sawfish to lose many battles caught in commercial fishing nets in other parts of the world. These consequences made the sawfish especially slow to recover from overfishing. The fact that the females bare live pups with semi-hardened rostrum covered with teeth, made it easy to understand why they produced at low birth rates."

Addison: "I think women would produce at much lower rates too, if they had to pass younglings with thirty-nine razor sharp teeth protruding through a membrane when giving birth. Maybe you would understand better if I told you giving birth might feel similar to your male membrane being set on fire, partially disintegrating and then eventually falling off."

Arthur: "I get it. And speaking of producing, all we really are talking about here is that life is really about people, planet, and profit."

Addison: "Yeah, but without two sawfish reproducing, none of this other talk about the three P's would have mattered and we would not be having this conversation."

Arthur: "Yeah, and if my penis burned, disintegrated, and fell off, not much else would matter for me either."

Addison chuckled. The restaurant was the halfway between Heartland and Rainbow Creek. Finally sitting down at their favorite booth, Addison noticed that some of the items on the menu had changed since their last visit.

Addison: "I've been reading this book about life in America prior to the Civil War. Before the 1900s, women were dedicated to saving themselves for their husbands. At least that is what generations of women who followed them told us and most of them may have been telling the truth. The word *hooker* derives from earlier practices of prostitutes during Civil War times. General Hooker's Union Army Division allowed women followers to help soldiers with mending uniforms, cooking, cleaning and nursing needs. They helped with a little more than just those needs. Many of the soldiers sought out prostitutes. Venereal disease was rampant in a camp built between the White House and the Capitol Building; two in five soldiers became infected. Women could not join the military. Doctor Peters assassinated Confederate General Earl Van Dorn for having an illicit affair with his wife. Before Peters shot him, the General confessed that wine, woman, and song had ruined him. Do you think my wine drinking, my tastes in music, and I are ruining you, Arthur?"

Arthur: "Of course not, but I will say a few things. Your story makes me want to forget everything I ever learned about the classic negotiating approaches of compromise, collaborate, accommodate or withdraw. Maybe by working smarter, we can develop some new strategies for the future."

Addison: "Speaking of smart, I think ordering our old standbys was a smart move. My cod tastes great. Is your food good?"

Arthur: "Excellent. At one point in my life, I was happiest with a beer in one hand and holding a freshly baked loaf of French bread sliced in half to accommodate the addition of deli meat and Swiss cheese in the other hand. This was the way I ate until I realized the dangers of drinking too much beer and not eating enough fruits and vegetables."

Arthur now had two daughters who he loved, a new girlfriend in his life who cared about politics, and a brother recovering from drug addiction whom he watched out for. He was interested in politics because he had a vision for the middle class and he wanted to do his part to help build the bridge to the twenty-first century for others. He thought national leaders in government needed to stop their bickering and give up on ideas that do not work and ones that have not been tested in other states yet. To him, it was time for the country to be great again and time for the leaders of institutions to govern in noncorrupt ways again.

Because Arthur was determined not to be separated from his children in the same way other divorced men are, he went out of his way to show particular interest in his two daughters, whom he felt to be genuinely good souls, even when they'd rejected his earnest questions about their favorite writers and any interest they may have in boyfriends. Though Jane could have wished for her daughters to be more like her, spending her hours of the day as she pleases and having a man come home from work with the sole purpose of attending to her needs in the evening, she was content. She was very proud to have daughters who were college educated and wise to the modern trends of the world.

Arthur would never give up on five things: his two daughters, his brother Johnny, his writing, or his politics. He once heard that even John Grisham, who has sold a quarter of a billion copies of his books worldwide, was turned down by thirty literary agent naysayers who sent him rejection letters before his first novel, *A Time to Kill,* was published. Even for the best writers in the world, they know it takes time to build a platform, so he did not give up on his writing or love for politics. Arthur kept a file of any rejection letters he received from publishers or e-mails he received from angry citizens who disagreed with his politics. He did this to stay humble, but he also thought that one day his time would come. When he did write, often there was a baseball game on the radio in the background, because this relaxed Arthur and brought him back to sitting in the bleacher seats at the old Busch Stadium talking about baseball and politics with his father. He and his father were baseball purists back in the days when fans packed the stadium in St. Louis to watch Bob Gibson pitch against Sandy Koufax or Don Drysdale of the Los Angeles Dodgers. A key bunt or a stolen base along with a hit might be enough offense to score the only run needed to win the game. The game is surely different now, and ever since the steroid era, Arthur was not as big a supporter of seeing all the focus directed on the long ball, as most other fans seemed to appreciate nowadays.

Arthur was much more focused since finalizing his divorce. He realized there are always three sides to every story in a marriage: his, hers, and the truth. A whale off the coast of California can communicate with a whale off the coast of Hawaii, but a man cannot communicate with a woman in the same house, often because their interests turn in opposite directions or they no longer care what the other person needs. During a verbal fight, Arthur wanted to go to the merits of a respective argument, not straight to the hurt and the emotional sides of things like Jane did. When Arthur became stressed, sick of all the crazy reasoning and all the trying to understand, he got frustrated and then shut down. When Jane felt stress, she became angry and then got emotional. With every additional argument, their marriage qualified less, and when two people are going in different directions, a marriage is secondary. Every disagreement in Arthur and Jane's marriage felt like trying to pass new legislation. Every argument felt like a bee sting, a tetanus shot, itchy poison ivy, and a snakebite all at once.

A century and a half ago tough men rode horses, hunted to put food on the table, spoke their minds and were in charge of their families. Today men feel oppressed by traditions of modern Western society to some extent and people only notice when there is a conscious effort to study it. Men have to act and speak politically correctly to a degree that they seem overly influenced by women. Men and women are different and they can only coexist when they can find common ground, and Arthur and Jane really struggled to find theirs.

Like every man, Arthur had a dream for his family. He mainly wanted his daughters to be happy and healthy. Just because he became divorced didn't mean he wasn't going to continue being a great father. Like any good man who is divorced with children, he believed a man with children is a father before anything else. Unfortunately with some men, a key risk of divorce is that it seems to disrupt most friendships to other married friends, but luckily this wasn't the case with Arthur. Maybe some couples think divorce is a contagious disease. More important than any kind of arrangement in his divorce was the long-term well-being of his daughters. Sandra and Susie were now old enough to know when they had been fed lines, and no matter what, Arthur or Jane were willing to do anything for the best interest of their daughters. Children usually side with their mother on most issues; this is natural, especially since the children live with their mothers in most circumstances. Arthur had to get used to the idea that when reaching out to his daughters, they sometimes rebelled for no apparent reason or there was a conflict with their schedules. He had to realize that one parent never knows for sure what the other parent is telling the children. He was thankful his children were older, because younger children of divorce can become very good at manipulating one parent against the other and they sometimes hold a grudge. On one side of the coin, older children fighting for their independence don't want to have much to do with one or both of their parents most times anyway. On the flip side, it becomes the parents' fault when something goes wrong. Parenting is a balancing act of progressively letting go of the apron strings but always being there for their children if they need them. Arthur and Jane tried to allow their daughters to make trivial mistakes in order to learn not to make big mistakes without squelching their daughter's dreams or letting them underestimate what they could accomplish. The idea of America passed along from generation to generation in the Hobson family wasn't just about going along with everyone else; it was about aspirations of each individual bringing something exciting and new to the experience of living free.

When talking to his daughters about divorce, staying neutral was important to Arthur. At the community center, he had witnessed other divorced fathers who tried to turn their children against their mothers, but the antics of talking bad about mothers always harmed the children emotionally. He understood that when you trash a child's mother, you are trashing a part of the child. Jane is Sandra's and Susie's mom for the rest of their lives. Arthur and Jane vowed to each other to be responsive to the needs of their daughters. Of all the deep nasty talk that got stirred up in the past, certain things said can never be forgotten, but if either of the exes is a bad person, the children were sure to discover it on their own. Arthur hoped his and Jane's goal to raise their daughters to grow up to be trustworthy, honest, loving, hardworking individuals who treat others as they themselves would like to be treated, would stay the same; then the world benefits too. And it's OK to aspire to a better life, but Arthur wanted Sandra and Susie to follow in the footsteps of the good people in history who only took what they earned, because this is what they were taught, and soon it will be their turn to pass on what they believe.

It was becoming a routine for Arthur to relax in his favorite chair reading a book, while Johnny sat on the sofa reading the newspaper with his feet propped up on the ottoman. Soon after Arthur finished reading the story of William James, a well-rounded man who taught medicine and psychology at Harvard in the late 1800s, he started a conversation with Johnny.

Arthur: "The prevalent fear of poverty among the educated classes is the worst moral disease from which our civilization suffers, according to William James. What James meant was that an educated person is trained in many areas and should draw upon that knowledge and further develop it to be successful."

Johnny: "I think I know what you are getting at, Arthur."

Arthur: "James treated thinking and knowledge as instruments in the struggle to make a better life. He analyzed in terms of consequences to any action that leads to the truth. He applied this doctrine to the analysis of change, chance, freedom, variety, pluralism, novelty, and even applying for a job. I worry that you might have a difficult time finding a job because of your history of using drugs."

Johnny: "I am trying to decide which of my skill sets to pursue in looking for a job. I like to work with my hands, I love music, and during our high school years, I'm sure you remember Mom always asking me to help her bake things in the kitchen. Not knowing at the time, I guess I was filling in the space of her not having a daughter."

Because Johnny stayed single all his life and he spent a lot of time in the kitchen, his talents as a baker grew to a professional level. But because of his drug addiction, he squandered away opportunities in this field earlier in his life.

Next morning, Johnny arranged with Jane to pick fresh apples from a tree at the back end of the Hobson House property, and with them he baked several homemade pies to pass out to neighbors so he could become more acquainted with them, but nobody believed he baked the tasty treats himself. The pies smelled and looked so good, the neighbors just assumed he bought them at the bakery in town. He was finding out that reputations take a long time to repair when they only know about a person's mistakes. Some of the newer residents credited Johnny's wife or mother for the fantastic-smelling pies, not knowing that he was single and his mom had passed away a few years ago.

Arthur was concerned about Johnny. How was he going to find a job? Arthur hated it when he heard about aristocratic business owners who cut the salaries of their employees just to safeguard their own wealth and line their pockets, losing the trust of workers. He believed if corporations used the money from these salary cuts to hire a few new employees, the investment would go a long way in bringing down unemployment and stimulating the economy. But they don't use the money this way, and laying off workers isn't the answer for fixing the economy. He believed that by letting go of workers, an environment is created where there is less money being spent to circulate through the economy. Eventually the managers doing the laying off become victims of unemployment themselves. For Arthur, a better solution is to make a better product or service and to create more demand at a fair price without getting greedy. Too many times the bottom line changes the focus of the real purpose of trying to make our lives easier and our planet better. He often told family members and those down at the community center, "Greed is the desire to have wealth you didn't earn."

Arthur: "So, Johnny, are you ready to look for a job or start your own business?"

Johnny: "I've been giving it a lot of thought lately."

Arthur: "One of the things we have to realize is to say there is something profoundly wrong when the top one percent has more wealth than the bottom half of all workers in the United States, when the CEOs of large corporations earn ten-thousand times what their workers make. This is not what our country's founders had in mind when they wrote the Constitution. Some of these CEOs are making money by paying themselves absurd bonuses, milking the tax system, and just flat-out corruption. Some of that money could have been reinvested in more equipment and training, which in turn creates more jobs, but many of these executives decided to squeeze the turnips of a generation, fully knowing that another generation of technically savvy employees is entering the workforce. You might find that you are competing against a lot of talented younger people."

Johnny: "I realize that I face much difficulty in securing a job with a good company because background checks will uncover some of my difficulties with drug use. This is why I am thinking about starting my own business, working as a self-employed businessman. To keep things interesting, I've been thinking about doing a little something different each day of the week. If I design a brochure on the computer and talk to enough people around town, maybe I can sign up enough customers to give it a go."

Arthur: "You mean build a company? Both of us would sort of be doing the same thing, building our platforms."

Johnny: "On Mondays, I could mow lawns and do landscaping for the elderly home-owners in the neighborhood. On Tuesdays, I could paint trim on the outside of houses, because as you know, most people don't like to paint. On Wednesdays, I could plant shrubs around air conditioners and heat pumps to form a shade barrier in the summer-time and a windbreak during the winter, to help homeowners and commercial businesses save money on energy. On Thursday evenings, Latin dance night, I could teach lessons at the studio in town. If I could find a gig playing my guitar or giving lessons close to home that would pretty much take care of the entire workweek."

Arthur: "It sounds like you have been giving it a lot of thought."

Johnny: "I'm trying to be more thoughtful, like you, Arthur."

Arthur: "While it is true that every man and child has a national duty to make an honest effort to contribute to society, an uneducated public will be the weakness that causes our government to fail. We must remember the reason our ancestors came to this country. They came here for freedom and justice and to get away from the tyranny and disconnect of dictators. They came here looking for economic prosperity and a chance to better themselves. The president and his family, senators and their families enjoy many privileges, including eating great food and traveling to some exotic locations during their terms in office, while making decisions about how the rest of us should live. We want to enjoy some of the niceties of life too. I tire of these policies negating the real headlines and promoting false hopes by pushing conformity and equality over excellence and genius. What would our ancestors think of the disconnection between Washington, DC, and the rest of the people in our country?"

Johnny: "They would probably turn over in their graves. Instead of listening to our leaders telling everyone, 'We have a dire situation concerning the economy, jobs, and racism,' as we were told before, they should tell us about new ideas using American inge-nuity, instead of rearranging the pieces of a shrinking American pie."

It was getting close to the end of November in Rainbow Creek. In the Midwest, some winters are worse than others. One year it may only snow two or three times during the entire winter season. Other years ten or more snowstorms may blanket the ground for most of the three-month winter cold spell. This year it hadn't snowed yet but the weather was turning much colder. Arthur and Johnny brought inside a few oak logs from the woodpile in the backyard to make their first fireplace fire of the season.

Johnny: "It must be extremely rewarding to write something or say something that affects other people in a good way."

Arthur: "It's the same feeling you get when a musician plays something or sings something that affects other people in a good way. I was so proud to call you my brother when you did your thing at the Freedom Festival and the rally in Heartland in front of all those people. And I'm so proud that you have continued on with your life free of drugs and alcohol. Too many times when people do attempt to quit using, others aren't there to support or congratulate them on their lifestyle changes."

Johnny: "Thank you, Arthur. I have been trying much harder to live a better life with more of my focus on God. I was mowing the grass yesterday for a commercial customer who owns a retail plaza, and the gas line on my riding mower started leaking badly. The plastic tubing, which connects the gas tank to the carburetor and allows the gas to flow freely, burst and cracked due to wear and tear. I was ready to quit for the day, but as I was walking to the other side of the parking lot to fetch my truck and truck ramps to load up my broken-down riding lawnmower, mysteriously, I found lying on the asphalt, a piece of plastic tubing which was longer and fit more snug than the broken piece did before it became cracked. How do you explain things when they happen this way? When no other fix or no other human being is near to help, only a higher power can come to us in times of need."

Arthur: "Be careful of your use of the word fix."

Johnny: "You know what I mean."

Arthur: "Let me ask you a political question. When contemplating which politician to vote for, do you put more emphasis on listening to the candidates who give a great speech or reading and researching the track records of the candidates to see what they have accomplished?"

Johnny: "A politician with a track record of legitimate accomplishments or anyone who has built something with their own two hands feels the satisfaction of accomplishing a goal every time they finish a project. Otherwise, talk is just a lot of rhetoric without any results."

Arthur: "I like your explanation. This is why I like writing, to feed my creative side, and working at the community center, to help pay the bills and face the reality of life."

Johnny: "I like singing and playing guitar to feed my creative side and building my business to help pay the bills. I guess I'm trying to face the reality side of life in a similar manner as you."

Arthur: "It is profound how events in life work out. Sometimes we have to think differently or completely reverse our thinking to make the connections and figure out remedies to problems. However, most of the time, hard work and an honest desire to make things better is usually all that is needed."

Johnny: "Why does the government always seem to pass legislation that benefits the billionaires or the poor?"

Arthur: "That's a great question. Maybe if legislation was geared to protect the middle class, more people would aspire to greater successes and less of the population would flounder. Those who do flounder at least might be able to hold jobs that require fewer responsibilities."

Johnny: "I know a little bit about working the earth to create new opportunities. If you are stuck in a hole that is too deep, you stop digging. It's not enough to just call something by another name. This is what seems to be happening with the liberals who now call themselves progressives, stimulus is now called an investment, and tax increases are now disguised as tax reform."

Arthur: "Maybe someday we will live in a world where spontaneous applause for great teachers is heard regularly, instead of all the noise we hear from politicians with the loudest voices drowning out all the most intelligent ideas. I don't want to go back to the sixties, but the 'I have a dream speeches' sounded a lot better than the current 'I have a scheme speeches,' as far as I am concerned."

Johnny: "I read a synopsis this morning about a bunch of scared people who lost their jobs at a solar panel company earlier in the week. I think a more detailed account of what happened was discussed on the radio and some of the cable TV networks."

Arthur: "I heard the story on the radio the other day, that the half-billion-dollar stimulus given to the American solar panel company to create jobs was a complete failure. Exactly one year after receiving the stimulus money, the company filed for bankruptcy and blamed cheaper Chinese competition for their failures. Where did all that money go?"

Johnny: "I remember when President Obama visited the solar-energy company on national TV, gloating about the stimulus strategy and his policies for green technology. He touted the company as a model of a government and business partnership."

Arthur: "Yes, I remember that too. His words could be construed as the perfect metaphor for what's happened to the economy of our country."

Johnny: "Didn't the president say, 'We're all in this together,' while pushing his jobs bill?"

Arthur: "I don't think his half-socialized, half-corporatized policies fit the notion of freedom. We're only 'all in this together' if a federally favored company goes belly up, sticking the middle-class taxpayer with the tab. When do taxpayers share the profits when these companies do well?"

"If we want a return to our Constitution, its principles of limited and separate power and its emphasis on *We the People*, how can we support TIF or eminent domain powers given by our governments to corporations over homeowners without the authority from us or Congress as the Constitution requires?"

Johnny: "The Tea Party Patriots come mostly from the conservative politics wing that is fed up with politicians that continually side with the wealthy business executives, right?"

Arthur: "This is one issue the Tea Party has right, and the Republicans and Democrats can learn from, if they pay attention. How can we have a free market when our government keeps giving all the advantages to a select group of our largest institutions? No matter their size, every business should pay their fare share of taxes used to make our schools stronger, more competitive, and better at preparing students for a world economy."

Johnny: "People need to support small businesses. It's that simple."

Arthur: "We should be more concerned about the mom-and-pop retailers in the community. When making policy for the times we are living in, we must remember human conditions of the past. As long as big-box businesses are allowed to shrink the middle class by running the mom-and-pops out of town, the slide in education will continue too. Because the employees of the big-box stores don't make enough money, education becomes secondary for their families' day-to-day lifestyles."

Johnny: "I heard when a person shops locally, a large percentage of each dollar spent stays in the local economy."

Arthur: "That's right. By shopping at mom-and-pop stores, customers who spend money there guarantee that two-thirds of every dollar returns to that local economy and they won't have to fight big crowds while getting better service."

Johnny: "When a company specializes in one thing and their employees continue to improve on that one thing, then the company earns all the success deservedly coming their way. Take, for instance, Scott's Lawn Care Treatments. Their products are simply the best in the industry and many Americans already know this. No matter how hard competitors try to match their product, they can't. But this is OK, because Scott's earned all of their success without stepping on the toes of other companies, trying to dominate every niche."

Arthur: "Antitrust laws are supposed to keep large corporations from dominating all sectors of any industry. Any dictator, government, or large corporation that tries to control all rules of the game, hurts the general good of the middle class, breaking their spirit and chances for success."

Millions of Americans think like Arthur and Johnny Hobson and know America was founded as the "land of the free and home of the brave." Freedoms are what make America great and there are still plenty of opportunities for individuals who choose to take advantage of an idea by pursuing their dreams, inventing something, creating a business, or starting a new job. There are no limits in America and this is why Conservatives want a limited government in our lives, so Americans remain independent, not dependent on an institution, a government agency, or a bureaucracy. The Tea Party was trying to bring awareness to individual freedoms by exposing policies where the government conspires with large corporations to gain an unfair advantage over smaller businesses. Because of the dangerous environment of the world we live in today, Arthur was sure the main role of government was to help the Defense Department protect its citizens.

Arthur believed the family environment was the place where dependency should be encouraged the most, and in effect creating a codependent Big Brother society at a lesser level. According to Arthur, too often a Big Brother government is taking from the people who work hard to take care of those who don't want to work or are looking for handouts. Like millions of other people, Arthur saw too big of a government as a money-grabbing machine, politicians taking money from workers and spending the money foolishly to buy their votes and keep their "cushy" jobs in Washington. These types of power-hungry selfish ambitions is what keeps stirring the Tea Party, the people who used to be the silent majority, to stand up and speak out, much to the disdain of the liberals in power. Older Rainbow Creek citizens were aware that four of the past seven governors of their neighboring state of Illinois ended up as convicted felons.

Paul Revere rode through town to warn, 'The British are coming' to alert Colonial militia of approaching British forces before the battles of Lexington and Concord. His 'midnight ride' on the night of April 18, 1775 is a legendary part of United States history. Revere was a prosperous and prominent Boston silversmith, who helped organize an intelligence and alarm system to keep watch on the British military, who wanted to control the lives of the settlers.

The Tea Party was sounding the battle alarm against forces again. The Tea Party was spreading across the country and larger groups of Patriots were becoming more aware of the politicians who were corrupt, ineffective, or not upholding the values of the Constitution. While extremists exists in every large group of society, the Tea Party had generally worked peacefully as an organization: no riots, no burning of buildings, no looting, and no violence as was witnessed during the civil rights era when protestors started fires, looted businesses, destroyed property, and fought with police. But when a man shot nineteen people and killed six more at a political rally in Tucson, Arizona, President Obama put his spin on the tragic event hinting that Tea Party followers and the general public helped cause this act of total disregard for the civility of politics. The president's remarks offended Tea Party Patriots because they thought the shooting had nothing to do with civility of politics and everything to do with mental illness. People working for the Department of Mental Health were all too aware of patients going untreated because of recent mental health budget cuts. The shooter had a long history of mental illness. Democratic State Representative Gabby Giffords was holding a constituent meeting called, "Congress on Your Corner," at the Safeway supermarket parking lot when the shooting occurred. Dorothy Morris, a retired secretary, John Roll, a chief judge of the US District Court of Arizona, Phyllis Schneck, a homemaker, Dorwan Stoddard, a retired construction worker, and Gabriel Zimmerman, a community outreach director for Giffords, were all shot and killed at the gathering.

After hearing the bad news, Arthur decided to drive west to Columbia to visit Susie for an overnight stay and on the way there, he could refine his thoughts about politics and whether he thought it a good idea or not if a developer is approved to build a Walmart in Fieldcrest, the neighboring town to Rainbow Creek. Arthur felt alive anytime he was multitasking, and by re-establishing his relationship with his daughter Susie and taking advantage of the quiet travel time in his car, he was doing just that. Susie was already preparing dinner by the time he arrived at her apartment and she vindicated herself as a gracious host as soon as Arthur walked in the front door. Arthur helped make a salad while she did the cooking and set out her fanciest dinnerware: two Steak-n-Shake glasses, two folded paper towels substituting as napkins, and plates and silverware that didn't match but did the job. It was as if he and she both had been waiting to see an old friend so they could vent their feelings about the shouting incident months before and talk about their plans for the future.

Susie: "Try not to pay attention to the hodgepodge of dining utensils; it's going to be fine."

Arthur: "Do you mean the food or our father-daughter relationship?"

Susie: "You know, when a girl has a big personality, there can be big dramas. It takes time for her to work out the idiosyncrasies of her individuality. It's kind of like receiving a short-term economic stimulus check from Uncle Sam and trying to figure out the best way to spend the money. For you and me, we just have to figure out how to speak each other's language."

Arthur: "Gosh, Susie, the college experience is making you scholarly."

Susie: "Well, maybe some of the wisdom comes from having parents who still actually read books, teach their children to read books, and think about how to make things better."

Arthur: "I'll take that as a compliment, thank you, Susie."

Susie: "We have been studying the presidents in my American History class."

Arthur: "That sounds like a class I would enjoy sitting in on."

Susie: "Andrew Jackson didn't seem like a very good president. Why is his face on a twenty-dollar bill?"

Arthur: "Contrary to popular belief, I wasn't around when the government decided to use Jackson's face on the printed paper bills. Lots of things our government does happen under the radar when citizens choose not to pay attention and only care about the immediate needs of their personal lives. I know Andrew Jackson was the seventh president of the United States."

Susie: "I learned in class that President Jackson was a polarizing figure who destroyed the national bank and relocated Indian tribes from the Southeast to West of the Mississippi River. His enthusiastic followers created what is now considered the start of the

Democratic Party. Jackson studied law in Salisbury, North Carolina, and though his legal experience was scanty, he convinced enough people to vote for him in the rough-and-tumble world of the frontier. Even though he was a rich slaveholder, he appealed to the common man politically by denouncing the aristocracy as close-minded undemocratic people."

Arthur: "Wasn't Andrew Jackson the president responsible for expanding the spoils system to strengthen his political base? The Whigs and moralists denounced his aggressive governing style of enforcing changes in almost all laws concerning land or money."

Susie: "The spoils system is the term used for when a newly elected president gives jobs to people who helped him secure votes during the campaign, right?"

Arthur: "Correct. The term was derived from the phrase 'to the victor belong the spoils' by New York Senator William L. Marcy, referring to the victory of the Jackson Democrats in the election of 1829. After the election hundreds of government officials and post office workers lost jobs, but Jackson's friends were appointed posts in top positions."

Susie: "Knowing about the spoils system helps me understand why some states are trying to install the 'Pay for Performance System' in public school systems. During bad economic times, schools lay off young bright enthusiastic schoolteachers, while keeping some older, lazy, ineffective teachers only because they have tenure."

Arthur: "School systems need more harmony. I think there are instances where some older public school teachers, after all those years in the classroom, become disgruntled over some of the things they see."

Susie: "In class we learned that at the beginning, the Indians were a peaceful people who attempted to live in harmony, along with the new immigrants of our young nation. When asked to leave their homeland and relocate out West, the Indians argued their case to the Supreme Court, which found in their favor. But President Jackson ignored the court's decision and forced thousands of Indians to relocate."

Arthur: "So many lives were lost during the extreme winter journey on the Trail of Tears. The history lesson should make us want to rethink what is going on at the US-Mexico border today, don't you think?"

Susie: "Yes, because we all want the same things. Every person wants to smile, wants a job, wants to make a living, and wants to enjoy life during their leisure time."

Arthur: "True, but every person has to pay attention long enough to ensure local and federal politicians don't abuse our liberties or enact policies that stunt growth, steal workers' money, and lessen opportunities for job creation. But I agree with you, if it was done right, the US and Mexico could establish a great partnership, similar to the one we have with Canada."

Susie: "Isn't it true that most of the problems we have with illegal immigration along the border stems from people needing jobs? Too many desperate people get involved in selling drugs and other illegal activities."

Arthur: "Corruption of officials put aside, the states of California, Arizona, and Texas have to find better solutions for immigration matters. Since federal agencies and the administration don't want all fifty states doing their own version of immigration law, it makes sense that US officials and business leaders would want to meet with Mexican officials to try to generate ideas to create more private-sector jobs."

Susie: "The people of Mexico would stop coming into the United States illegally if they had employment and a safe place to live in their home country. If they had good health care, women in their ninth month of pregnancy would stop buying airplane tickets to go to hospitals in the US to have their babies."

Arthur: "Mexico is run by too many kingpins, though former President Vincente Fox did try hard to fight massive fraud by dissidents who formed the National Democratic Front of Mexico. The corruption infected every layer of government. If the government was respected, businesses would attract investors, and stock purchases of companies within Mexican boundaries would help build the Mexican economy. It's as if an electromagnetic pulse was released by a nuclear weapon detonated in the sky and it devastated all the businesses along the northern border of Mexico. It is time the leaders of Mexico paid attention to Mexican lore and history and take control of problems imposed on citizens with a less deceptive and simpler structure which enforces the laws."

Susie: "When did Mexico become such a dangerous place? It seems it's only getting worse."

Arthur: "A vast majority of the guns in Mexico come from the States. The same routes of transporting drugs to Miami, New York City, Los Angeles, Chicago, and Atlanta have been allowed to continue without any massive attempts to put a stop to it. This tells us that we can't point the finger at Mexico for all our immigration problems. Most Americans are unaware of the beautiful land and wonderful culture inside the rural towns of Mexico. Guns and drugs are jeopardizing the continuation of cultural traditions. The beaches, canyons, caves, lagoons, lakes, mountains, peninsulas, plateaus, rivers, volcanoes, waterfalls, and wetlands are underutilized as tourist destinations. Marketing the strengths of Mexico is compromised when safety is a major issue. Mexico becomes underappreciated. Developers with the right vision and honorable intentions could possibly turn some of these destinations into paradises. Mexico needs some new faces running things."

Susie: "Relating a phrase from my biological science studies, 'Crocodile Politics' is a good way to describe what is happening there. When a crocodile is hungry, it waits under the water and watches the first time it sees prey. Then the crocodile stalks the prey to see if there is a pattern in where it approaches the watering hole. Once a pattern is established at the watering hole, the crocodile closes in and pounces, putting a spin on the prey to make a killing. It sounds like there is too much corruption everywhere, and people are just tired of it."

Arthur: "We will never end all of the corruption, but it is probably more important to listen to a candidate's views during a primary election than the general election. Voters will hear more truths about policies and what politicians will do when they are competing with others from their own party. During the general election, candidates tailor their strategies to get votes. Once politicians are elected, often changes are made fast and furiously, without enough thought given to possible dangerous outcomes. To arrive closer to any truth, voters need to pick candidates based on track records, not promises or rhetoric. Mexico and the US need some new faces running things."

Susie: "I'd be happy to see someone else's face on our twenty-dollar bills … not that I've seen many twenty-dollar bills lately. I'd like to see an accomplished person on our twenty-dollar bills, maybe someone like Steve Jobs, a job creator."

Arthur: "I agree with you; business owners create jobs. The wrong government intervention and too many regulations on companies prevent businesses from hiring more people. There's always been a kind of disconnect between citizens and politicians, but it definitely is much worse now and we need to close the gap. Once fraud is detected in the president, his cabinet, or anywhere else in his party down to the local level, an imperial system creates discomfort in the population, and inside the government the president's power is no longer absolute."

Susie: "I think young people are naturally curious, but when votes are being counted and tabulation systems are known to mysteriously shut down, their distrust of politics is stronger from the very beginning. Fraud does nothing to calm fears of violence and it fuels more questions about the electoral process and the people in power." It was a nice evening for Arthur to see through Susie's eyes, how she'd matured in just one semester on her own. From one hundred and twenty-five miles away, it was difficult for Arthur not to worry about her, but with his previous failed attempts to rectify the childish arguments with her now behind them, he could see that here in Columbia, Susie was leading a safe and adult life. Here he was in her kitchen having an adult conversation about important issues, and he loved it.

Because Arthur worked so hard, often opening the community center early in the morning and staying until closing time late at night, Kay Applebaum allowed a flexible schedule and covered for him when he gave talks or needed time away to visit with one of his daughters. During the early years of his twenty-year career working for the Rainbow Creek Community Center, a division of the Parks and Recreation Department, Arthur picked up litter on county-owned grounds and emptied trash receptacles at parks and recreational facilities. Arthur wasn't just a white-collar manager with a gift to gab and a tremendous drive to diplomatically instruct others to do things better; he buffed floors, stacked chairs, unloaded and loaded trucks, carried equipment to storage rooms, cut grass, striped the lines on the parking lot; he led by example and did whatever it took to help his community and build relationships. He knew how to work, plan, make connections, and build his platform.

When Arthur's two daughters were young, he was working so hard trying to give them a good life that the family didn't take many vacations. It didn't sit well with him when he witnessed presidents and senators taking numerous vacations with their families on taxpayers' money, playing golf every week, attending a multitude of concerts, and hosting countless numbers of parties during their terms in office. He hated when politicians started off their speeches with "Look" or answered inquisitions with "No doubt" because the first word was patronizing and the latter words always appeared overused because very few things in life are absolute. Generations of Hobsons believed that because officials in public service elected to terms of two or four years made salaries paid by taxpayers, they should be working as hard as they can during this short period to make things better by enforcing the laws of the land and obeying the Constitution. Vacations are absolutely necessary to reinvigorate people reaching for higher standards in their lives, and by taking a cruise or settling into another region of the world for a couple of weeks, you are able to delve deeper into the cultures and landscapes that interest you most; but when elected officials are vacationing to excess instead of completing their public service duties, citizens get angry because they figure politicians will have the rest of their lives to take vacations.

Returning from a wonderful weekend spent with Susie, Arthur walked into his house only to find Johnny lying on the sofa bundled in extra blankets and a big pillow from the bed under his head. He wasn't feeling well and Arthur could tell right away.

Arthur: "Did the president make you sick to your stomach today with his comments about the national debt and his ideas on creating jobs?"

Johnny: "All week I've been fighting flu-like symptoms and I was just hoping they would go away. The symptoms seemed to get worse, so I've been lying here on the couch most of the day."

Arthur: "Rest should do you good. You know, on the ride home from Columbia, all the reporters on the radio stations were talking about some of the comments the president made today about the national debt and the economy. He said that 80 percent of small businesses and individuals are OK with tax hikes, when all the polls show that roughly only 34 percent of those polled think tax hikes are acceptable with all the problems surrounding the state of the economy. When did it become fashionable to totally fabricate numbers and tell such flat-out lies to the people? Something is very wrong with this type of rhetoric."

Johnny: "I don't know. We've gone from an economy where we make things, to an economy where we make things up."

Arthur: "I'm sorry for talking about this when you don't feel good. I'll leave you alone. Get some rest and both of us can talk in the morning. Hope you feel better tomorrow."

Johnny: "Thank you, Arthur."

The next morning Sandra, on one of her days off work, came over to visit her dad and her Uncle Johnny. The first thing she did was look in the refrigerator and the cupboard to see what food items were available to make breakfast. Though the sun had been over the horizon for about two hours, Johnny was still in bed. When he did finally emerge from the guest bedroom in sweat pants and a sleeveless T-shirt, his eyes were glazed and he still looked a little shaky. Arthur was still reading the paper at the kitchen table and enjoying a second cup of coffee.

"Mind if I grab myself a cup of coffee?" asked Sandra.

"Of course not, dear," said Arthur.

After pouring a cup and taking a sip, Sandra explained, "This cup of coffee tastes good, but you know coffee can be ruined at any step along the process. If the soil absorbs too much moisture, coffee beans absorb greedy odors and contaminants. Too light of a roast, produces undeveloped bitter tasting coffee; while over-roasting coffee produces a taste resembling charcoal. Coffee stables quickly sitting on a hot plate, reducing the finest brew to a stale cup of bile."

"Yesterday as I was driving thru town, and for the first time ever, I saw a motor fuel carrier truck exiting on to the highway, but it wasn't filled with gas. The truck was filled with coffee and big bright red letters spelling out the word C-O-F-F-E-E were painted on the sides of its stainless-steel tank," said Arthur.

"Who the heck drinks that much coffee?" said Johnny.

"I don't know," said Arthur.

"A man trying to get elected mayor isn't supposed to say, 'I don't know,'" said Johnny.

"An honest one does," said Arthur. "I can only speculate who drinks that much hot coffee."

"I know the motor fuel carriers have multiple compartments for different grades and types of fuel, and once the compartments are filled, the fuel is delivered to multiple locations. Maybe different types of hot coffee are pumped from different compartments into giant percolators at such places as large corporations, universities, truck stops, or other places where there is a large consumption of coffee," said Johnny.

"Scrambled eggs and turkey bacon, maybe some hot coffee, Uncle Johnny?" Sandra said cheerfully.

"Sounds pretty good," said Johnny.

"I made coffee, but I can squeeze some oranges if you'd rather drink juice."

"Coffee is fine, thank you, sweetheart."

"It's simple enough to make you a toasted English muffin, too, if you want one to go with your eggs and bacon."

"OK, thank you again, sweetheart."

"Maybe all this increased coffee consumption is good for America. If people dispose more of their grease, cooking oil, and fats into empty coffee cans, we could solve a lot of our sewer overflow problems and backups of raw sewage into basements," said Sandra.

"If you ask me, a house on top of a hill should be worth more money than the same house in a valley, because the first floors or basements of homes on tops of hills don't flood from water or sewage backup even a fraction as often as the houses built in low plains," said Johnny.

"So we have a deal then: no one is allowed to pour grease or oil down the drains," said Sandra.

Johnny and Sandra genuinely cared about each other, and their friendship was back to where it was before the years of drug abuse and all the confusion that wackiness caused for each of them. Once she had everything ready, Sandra brought over Johnny's breakfast and joined the two men at the kitchen table.

"What do you two guys have planned for the day?"

Johnny: "This morning I have to mow three lawns in the neighborhood and later this afternoon I have to start building a retaining wall to fix a drainage problem for Sandy Hendricks over in Fieldcrest. I took a Tylenol earlier and maybe if I sweat for a while, I'll get rid of this virus."

Arthur: "We have the chamber meeting tonight to talk about Walmart's move to town. I'll be home after that."

Sandra: "Dad, if it's OK with you, I'm going to stay here today. I brought this great book I've been reading and maybe I can finish it by this afternoon. The book is called *Zeitoun* by Dave Eggers, and it is a national bestseller. I'll have dinner going by the time you guys get home. Hope you feel better, Uncle Johnny."

The chamber meeting at the community center was the first hearing for residents to air their ideas about preserving the municipality's feel as a small town operated by family-run small businesses. Opinion in Rainbow Creek was evenly mixed between those who favored a developer's plan for a new Walmart superstore and those who were against it. Reasons for opposition ranged from a general hostility toward granting tax abatements to rich developers to objections by citizens because of a lack of details furnished about the plan. Proponents saw a Walmart superstore as a way to shop for consumer staples at cheaper prices. Bobby Rankles, a retired autoworker, was the first person to speak the day the interested parties and citizens arrived at the chamber meeting to discuss the planned development.

Rankles: "It is common in society today, for baby boomers to drive their foreign-made automobiles to the bank to use the drive-through lanes to cash their checks. They then motor on to Walmart to buy items produced overseas by workers who contribute nothing to Social Security."

Shelly Buckley of Rainbow Creek was the next resident to walk to the podium to express her opposition to the developer's plans.

Buckley: "One of the highest-paid professional baseball players of our time is not satisfied with the free-agent deal proposed to him. and he wants more than the twenty million dollars per year over a seven-year contract. The owners of our region's professional baseball franchise are Walmart executives, and they write the checks to pay the players' salaries. Meanwhile, Walmart pays its store employees a wage below the poverty level for a family of four, and half of their employees can't afford any form of health insurance. It is doubtful whether the player or his agent ever thinks about that, but both men should before a new contract is signed. Is this really where we want our taxpayers' money to go, paying for stadiums and lining the pockets of Walmart executives and multimillion-dollar athletes playing for the teams owned by these same executives? Let the wealthy executives pay for their own supercenters and sports stadiums."

The collective billionaire owners of Walmart promised to build a ballpark complex for a new rookie-league professional baseball team in Heartland, complete with restaurants, offices, and parking garages to gain support for taxpayers' money to build a Walmart supercenter. The value of the professional organization increased tenfold since owners purchased the team for twenty-five million dollars two decades ago. Now they wanted the taxpayers to subsidize paying for the new ballpark when they had plenty of money to pay for it themselves. The press and politicians essentially gave the professional baseball organization a free ride on any initial contractual obligations, but seven years later, the land was still vacant. Landscapers cleared rubble and planted grass to present the project as a more desirable location for the developers instead of an eyesore to residents a few years ago.

Perhaps the best argument of the day came from a little elderly lady from Rainbow Creek named Mary Whitaker. Mary raised five boys with big appetites on one average paycheck per week. She knew how to stretch a dollar.

Whitaker: "The Walmarts of the world should be allowed to build their stores, but they should do it with their own money. Why does the biggest retailer in the world need assistance? They always come to the party with both their hands out. We should be more concerned about the mom-and-pop retailers in the community. They are the ones who make this city what it is." After some applause for Ms. Whitaker, Stanley Sutherland, representing the developer, greeted the concerned group of citizens at the community center to a mixture of jeers and cheers. He set his briefcase down on the floor and placed a pad full of notes on top of the podium. An overhead projector reflected a schematic of the site plan on the wall behind him.

Sutherland: "Products purchased through the Internet on Amazon.com are not taxed. The company set up a warehouse in Texas as a subsidiary, creating a loophole in the physical presence rule. Why should a customer have to pay taxes for a book purchased at a brick-and-mortar superstore, but not for a book purchased online? Rulings get complicated and not everyone is happy no matter who wins. The courts will ultimately decide the issue. If the outcome is in favor of the online retailer, nothing will change and schools will lose out on additional tax revenues. If the ruling goes against the online retailer, the possibility exists that the company could move operations overseas. The same thing could happen with the Walmart organization. If developers aren't allowed to build new supercenters, new jobs won't be created and their headquarters could move overseas."

It was Arthur's turn to speak next. Opposing the development, he greeted the people first and then comfortably walked around the podium and looked out into the audience without any notes in hand. He was a professional speaker. During previous speeches when citizens asked him a barrage of questions, even when others berated him with a cross-examination of questions he already spoke to, he always answered candidly to the best of his knowledge. This time his speech was different, because he wanted citizens to see the big picture as he saw it, and he wanted to confront Sutherland head-on.

Arthur: "There are reasons why cities and towns prosper and grow. Some have tremendous growth by proximity to employment, valuable housing, bike trails, nice parks, enforcement of restrictive air-quality standards, and other amenities. Rainbow Creek, a fast-growing municipality in middle America, is an example of a very successful community with elements of small-town charm. The downtown section is full of nineteenth-century brick buildings and dozens of shops and restaurants, most of them locally owned, like the fittingly eccentric sweet shop called Mom's Candy and Popcorn. Local taxes from these shops support the public school systems, parks, and roads, making sure their public amenities don't decline or decay. But even though Rainbow Creek has all of these charming attractions, the biggest reason families give for deciding to live there is the great school system. If we allow a supercenter in our town, everything will change and many of our shops will be forced to close their doors, leaving abandoned buildings all around town. That is not safe for our children and will not help our town prosper."

Sutherland made one strong argument that stuck in Arthur's mind. Sutherland raised the question, "Why aren't all municipalities collecting sales tax on Internet transactions?

These are taxes owed and could easily be collected. Collecting this sales tax would raise revenue for the community and support local businesses that were at an 8 percent disadvantage because they collect sales tax." For many of the concerned citizens in the audience who understood that municipalities have to create some new ways to collect revenue, this Internet sales tax made sense; otherwise local government might continue to cut jobs, school programs, health programs, highway repairs, and programs for seniors. Twenty other states in America already tax Internet sales and they are raising hundreds of millions of dollars doing it. Arthur wanted more answers from the developer and though he thought this man made a point about Internet taxes, this argument had little to do with whether or not Walmart should come to town.

Arthur: "Mr. Sutherland, a company can supply an unlimited number of jobs, but if the employer of these people doesn't pay for healthcare and the employees can't save enough for a house or their kids' education, then the problems of the economy aren't addressed. If Walmart comes to Rainbow Creek, how would you take care of the citizens in this community?"

Sutherland: "It is a mistake to look at just one thing. Poverty is a complex issue."

Arthur: "I'm not looking at one thing. When I asked you the question, I addressed jobs, housing, education, and health care. We have to address all of these issues in an integrated way or we're just kidding ourselves. If you don't address all these challenges, you won't get results in this town. The largest and wealthiest corporation in the world needs the local and state government to subsidize its employee health care, not to mention getting tax breaks from communities that it builds in. Are you kidding me? The hypocrisy of big-business developers and politicians goes back to the Prohibition days. While telling voters they wanted to keep their counties dry to please constituents, they were living their personal lives wet. Today wealthy developers tell consumers to conserve on energy while they fly around the country in their personal jets and live in huge mansions with enormous monthly electric bills. Big-box company executives pay little in the form of wages and benefits, then ask workers to support government-subsidized health care programs, while they give themselves bonuses and increases in salary and stock options."

Sutherland: "I will be glad to talk to you individually at the conclusion of this chamber meeting. Thank you for your concerns, sir."

For the first time Arthur was dead set on entering his name in the mayoral race, no longer just contemplating it. He was unimpressed with the developer and how Sutherland shoved off answers until a later time, not addressing them in front of the larger audience. He was even less impressed that Mayor Armstrong didn't find the chamber meeting important enough to attend. He thought his hometown possibly was one vote away from anarchy and tyranny. This Sutherland guy was the slickest person Arthur had ever met. He was sure this man had the money behind him to do anything to push his way passed the people. When journalists or citizens challenged Sutherland, he barely flinched and attacked them back. Arthur wondered if William Randolph Hearst, Rupert Murdoch, the Republicans, the Tea Party, and organized religion combined, was big enough to slow the Walmart movement. He was so disillusioned by the whole mess at the end of the meeting that he barely said good-bye to anyone before walking to his car and driving home.

"I cooked a pork roast for us," Sandra told Arthur when he arrived home.

"I had a rough day listening to all the nonsense the developer was throwing at the audience. A nice meal will definitely put me in a better mood," said Arthur.

"I don't want to worsen your mood, but if you didn't see it already, Irvin Shelby said something very strange on a television infomercial on a local network. He told viewers that if they voted for him in the election for mayor, they would receive a set of steak knives and a container of Oxiclean."

"That doesn't bother me. It sounds like Shelby was just trying to be funny. What I am thinking about is the smell and sizzle of the pot roast you are cooking."

"Remember that tongue-twister with the word sizzles in it, and you tried so hard to teach Susie and me to say it fast."

"Yes, I do. It went like this: 'scissors, sizzles, thistles, sifters, un-sifted thistles for thistle-sifters.' Say that five times real fast."

"That's pretty good, Dad. You still remember."

A few seconds later, Johnny came walking in the front door with mud in his hair, mud on his shoes, and dirt smudges above his eyebrows with his sweaty shirt sticking to his body.

"Hey, I heard you guys trying to repeat that old tongue twister. I have a new one for you. 'Annihilation, litigation, taxation, regulation, castration.' Try saying that five times fast. It may happen to more people than we think, before they have a chance to say it."

"That's so funny, Uncle Johnny, but sadly, I think the definitions for those words are related," said Sandra.

"Americans are so tired of the government spending money that we don't have for programs we don't want," said Johnny.

"Sandra, ask your Uncle Johnny to tell you about the guy wearing muddy shoes when he worked at Stix, Baer and Fuller in his younger years," said Arthur.

"What about the guy wearing muddy shoes at Stix, Baer and Fuller, Uncle Johnny?" asked Sandra.

"I was working as a shoe salesman at Stix, Baer and Fuller back in the early seventies. This guy walked inside the store and wanted to buy a pair of size 11 black patent leather dress shoes. We were out of that size, but a box with a pair of size 12 shoes was sitting on a shelf in the stockroom. Kiddingly I told the man, 'Sir, we are out of stock in your size, but if you want, I can sell you the pair of size 12s and you can walk across the street to buy a small bag of cotton balls at Woolworths. If you stuff a few cotton balls in the toes of both shoes, then the size 12s will fit your feet. The guy bought the shoes and twenty minutes later, after walking over to Woolworths in the rain, the man returned to my department to tell me how great his shoes fit. 'My shoes fit like gloves,' he said, even though his new shoes were muddied on the outside and the toes were filled with cotton balls on the inside."

"That's funny! You always could make me laugh," said Sandra.

"The employees in the shoe department laughed about that incident for a long time too," returned Johnny.

"How's the retaining wall looking?" Sandra asked Johnny.

"The retaining wall is definitely going to help drain the rainwater properly. It will be a big improvement to the functionality and appearance of the Hendricks' backyard."

"How much longer do you think it's going to take to complete the project?"

"In two or three days, the wall will be finished. Later in the week I teach my dance classes."

"It is nice to see your businesses coming along so great in such a short amount of time. Well, anyway, get cleaned up because dinner will be ready in about fifteen minutes. I'm making pork roast."

Though Sandra had her own place, the house on Hill View still felt like her real home because of all the childhood memories she shared with her younger sister while growing up there. She loved coming over occasionally to fix dinner for her dad and her uncle. Comforting evenings spent at the dinner table over a great meal and interesting conversation somehow made this setting her favorite place in the world. She felt genuinely loved and appreciated by both men, and she enjoyed keeping tabs on their work by listening to their interesting tales.

For the next two weeks, a crew working under the direction of Mark Sutherland planted a Bradford Pear tree on common ground next to the street and in front of each house in the Rainbow Creek neighborhood to try and promote goodwill for the contingency pushing the Walmart development. Whether to spite him or by coincidence, the Sutherland crew planted a real pear tree on the common ground in front of Arthur's house. But Arthur didn't care, and five months after taking root, the tree started to bear fruit. He loved the sweet-tasting pears and picked several bagfuls to pass out to his neighbors.

11

Recognizing the Whispers
of Support

Arthur was the kind of parent who wanted his daughters and other kids in the neighborhood to earn the things they got. If he witnessed neighborhood boys stealing a case of soda pop out of a neighbor's garage or making fun of the elderly, he confronted them. If he witnessed girls out front at the movie theater cussing as if they were imitating sailors out at sea, he asked them to try to talk nicer. His point did not always make its way through to them and sometimes they redirected the cussing at him. At the other end of the spectrum, if he saw a teenager mowing the grass for an elderly neighbor, he brought the teenager a plastic cup filled with crushed ice and cold lemonade. He did the same for the trash man and the mail carrier on blistering warm days in July and August. He did it mainly because he knew how it felt to labor in the extreme elements from all the years he worked outside when he was younger. From Arthur's vantage point, the citizens and small-business owners in Rainbow Creek were optimistic people, but they were frustrated by the past several years of politics led by Mayor Armstrong. To their delight, Mayor Armstrong announced that he would not seek re-election at the end of the year. The day after Mayor Armstrong made this announcement, the phone at Arthur's house was ringing off the hook and messages filled his answering machine.

"Run for mayor, Arthur," was the first message, left by Addison.

"Run for mayor, my friend," was the next message, from Justin at the community center.

Even Ruth Staley of the Pleasant Grove Rehabilitation Center in Atlanta called to leave a message. She was an avid deliberator of mayoral issues around the country and she was a strong woman who paid attention to political changes which affected the way she tried to battle the illegal drug trade.

"Run for mayor, Arthur. Cities need leaders who will tell them things and stay true to the word and will not do something completely different. Make the connection for the people and tell them how more regulations and more control by a small group of people causes a loss of jobs, which causes more desperate people to sell drugs and more addicts roaming the streets," Ruth said, as the answering machine ran its course, out of room for longer winded messages.

Acquaintances from Tea Party rallies left messages in hopes of inspiring Arthur and reaffirming his decision to put his name in the hat for the next mayoral race. Kay Applebaum called to offer her support for him to take on the extra municipal activities. Kay had always allowed Arthur to blend his day job with his other civic interests, and it was no different this time. She did not see him carving out part of his workday for the community center and another part of the day for the office duties of the mayor. As director of the community center, she understood how things just become blended, and whenever they overlap, they overlap. She knew what it was like to be a problem solver, meaning much of his work done by e-mail, conference calls, telephone calls, and remote computer access from anywhere, had a way of working itself out. Knowing Arthur, she just figured his working hours would increase a little.

Thirty-five individuals had held the office of mayor, the chief executive and the most powerful man of town government in Rainbow Creek. Only four men, John Powers, Francis Fletcher, Willy Garrett, and Vince Tucker, served nonconsecutive terms during all that time. The longest-serving mayor in the history of Rainbow Creek was Henry Clements, who served office a total of twelve consecutive years and eleven days. The shortest-serving mayor was Calvin Jones, who died in a fall down a flight of steps nine days after taking office. Rainbow Creek incorporated as a city and changed its governance to a mayor-council format six days before Christmas in 1943. John Powers was the first mayor elected under the new political system.

To some of the old conservative war veterans in town, the town's strongest and most patriotic men were overseas fighting wars for causes in other countries and too many liberal types of council were acting like pansies, passing excessive laws and taking advantage of women and the future of children. To the elderly old guard, not enough men were standing up to the increased prices of everything and all the new rules causing more aches and pains in their daily lives.

One of the reasons Arthur was set on running for mayor was that he was tired of politicians constantly creating new laws and regulations with strings attached, always quickly passed after people have lost everything in the wake of another disaster. Every time there was a storm, flood, high winds, or a fire, new ordinances were passed. Whenever a driver lost control of his car and ran over a sign or a pedestrian tripped on a sidewalk curb, a new ordinance was passed. To him it felt like trying to cash in by selling a coin collection when only six buffalo-head nickels make up the assemblage. Personally, he thought he had game, but soon he would have to show he was willing to lay it all out there for others to judge if he deserved a bigger platform.

Weighing heavily on his mind was the issue of unemployment in his community. Arthur wondered if he could really fix the true unemployment problem, which is much worse than the local government was reporting. He knew this was a fact and if anyone questioned him, he relayed the following comments: "In Heartland, seventy-eight people recently applied for a single janitorial job paying fifteen dollars an hour, plus benefits. In St. Louis, an estimated six hundred people waited in line at the local employment office, some camping out on the sidewalk for as long as three days, to apply for ten mechanic apprenticeship positions." He read about other stories in other communities too.

Almost one hour after listening to all the messages on his answering machine, Arthur called Sandra, Susie, Addison, and Johnny on their cell phones and asked them to meet with him at home to get their feelings on what he was planning to do. That evening he discussed the pros and cons of the job and asked if they would help with his campaign.

Arthur: "I just want to give a small briefing on what we are doing here. With all the data collected on almost all of us, our government should be able to analyze our likes and dislikes, purchases, opinions, and finances. Corporations, small businesses, market research companies, and political campaigns tabulate e-mail addresses, personal information, phone numbers, credit scores, and surveys of our opinions. The average person in Rainbow Creek uses seven passwords as credit agencies monitor their debt from information about them scattered on thousands of databases. With the politicians attempting to get wiser, it is even more important for citizens to stay informed of the issues affecting our lives. If people start to consider their virtual community an acceptable replacement for real ones, they will lose the sense of what truly is important in our lives. There is a time and place for cell phones and computers, but our use of them should not take for granted talking with citizens, friends, or relatives. Most importantly, we must keep any personal information we hear as confidential."

Addison: "We got it. What happens in Vegas stays in Vegas, we promise."

Arthur: "Our community is not growing jobs, because the local government makes it harder and harder for small businesses while giving all the tax breaks to conglomerates. As mayor, one of the priorities I would work to change is to help small businesses. With the current regulations imposed on our small-business owners, our community will never experience the type of growth necessary to dig our citizens out of the holes their in."

Addison: "What kind of help do you want from me?"

Arthur: "I want you to act as my campaign manager. It means working evenings and long weekends for the next eight months to promote our message."

Addison: "You know I like politics and I like to talk. I would love knocking on doors to hand out buttons and brochures and talking to our neighbors. I'm sure I could persuade many of them to let us put signs in their front yards."

Sandra: "Dad, I could design a brochure on the computer for the campaign if you tell me what you want it to say."

Arthur: "Great, that would be terrific."

Susie: "I can work hard for a couple of months during the summer until I have to go back to school."

Arthur: "Sure, Susie, I wouldn't want it any other way. Your education is our number one priority. I am just thrilled that you are part of this."

Johnny: "I can make phone calls at night to help you spread your message and solicit donations for the campaign when I get home from work on nights I'm not teaching at the studio. Did I tell you that Jake's Jazz Studio hired me to teach a beginning class on how to play the guitar on Friday nights, starting next week?"

Arthur: "That's terrific, Johnny."

Thank you, everyone. Doesn't anyone have any questions or complaints about privacy or issues about our future working environment?"

Susie: "College students know how to live on the cheap, so just keep us fed and supply us with plenty of flavored bottled water and we will be OK."

Arthur: "Almost all of the rising costs of starting a business in the last decade are not from higher labor costs. They come from higher taxes and regulatory charges, which other nations simply do not impose. I will not be able to pay anyone wages, but maybe we can run our campaign as an example of how to start a small business. So we keep our energy levels high, having plenty of healthy food items and bottles of water on hand will not be a problem."

Johnny: "When I was fourteen years old, I couldn't believe how dumb my father was, and by the time I turned twenty-one, I couldn't believe how much my father had learned. Do both you girls think in the same terms about your father, now that he is running for mayor?"

Sandra: "Uncle Johnny, I am a Missourian and I know Mark Twain coined that phrase and I think you told me that when I was fourteen."

Johnny: "I was just testing you to see if you remembered."

Susie: "Well, Uncle Johnny, I never heard that before, so I am glad you said it again."

Arthur: "Didn't Mark Twain write about and question why kids put so much faith in their peers who barely have any experience with making serious decisions in life?"

Johnny: "Yes, he did, and in *The Adventures of Huckleberry Finn*, he teaches young readers many lessons about when and when not to listen to peers. I know one peer we do not need to listen to in our town. Arthur, did you hear the latest thing Irvin Shelby has been telling voters?"

Arthur: "No, what has he been saying?"

Johnny: "He's been saying the Tea Party is responsible for the financial meltdown and the economy getting worse. His Tea Party bashing is just a miserable dithering attempt to undermine you and all the good work you did at the community center. Shelby never seems to understand the big picture about anything. It's no wonder he never professes anything about civic responsibility."

Arthur: "That kind of argument makes me feel like a buck lost in the fog standing in the middle of the road during deer season. The last and current administrations are the only people who can be blamed for the irresponsible fiscal policies imposed on the citizens, lessening the chances for job growth in which unemployed workers ostensibly need now."

Johnny: "When I was living in Atlanta, I got that same sick feeling in my gut when I saw a small-town mayor picking up a single tar ball on one of Georgia's beaches in front of a TV cameraman and a reporter. The mayor said, 'This is an example of the tar balls people have been talking about.' Filming a politician picking up one tiny tar ball gave a false impression about the extent of the damage caused by the BP oil spill in the Gulf of Mexico."

Arthur: "Some things in our lives are just out of our control."

Johnny: "You are right about that. Who would have thought music, even if in a purposely misdirected way, played a role in the lives of the scum of the earth terrorists imprisoned at Guantanamo? Nudity, water-boarding, and loud music played continuously were interrogation techniques used to extract intelligence from prisoners. Whether these techniques work or not, I think you have to use empathy and knowledge to connect with the other person you are interrogating. Mom always taught us empathy is a vicarious emotion and honesty is always the best policy. Then again, neither Mom nor you nor I was there to know the truth about how it all went down."

Arthur: "Mom definitely tried to teach us to pay attention. She didn't want her sons walking around in a daze all the time. I'm sorry, Johnny. I didn't mean that as a personal attack."

Johnny: "I know you didn't. Speaking of walking around in a daze, I'm getting tired of walking around and stepping in dog crap in the front yards of the customers where I do lawn care and landscaping work. You did say honesty is the best policy, right. I think I'm going to send out a letter to all the neighbors."

Arthur: "If it really is a big problem, there is nothing wrong with sending out a letter."

Johnny worked on his letter the next day. Within two days, he mailed seventy-five copies of his letter to neighbors of whom fifteen were customers. He wrote:

Dear resident,

I love dogs. I think every family should have a dog. I just do not like stepping in dog crap, then walking around for the rest of the day working and smelling the obnoxious odor coming from the bottom of my shoes. I routinely step in dog crap in my customer's front yards and I can assure you I am trying to catch the culprit so I can give the pet's owner a manual with instructions on how to pick up after their pet. Inverting a newspaper wrapper over your hand is one idea that works well for picking up the waste. Then all you have to do is pull the bag back over your hand, tie a knot in the end of the bag, and throw it in a trashcan. If you walk your dog, please pick up after your animal. If your children walk the dog at night, please ensure they pick up after the animal too. Don't be 'That Person' that leaves piles of crap laying around in neighbors' yards for other people to step in, because people are getting hostile about it when they call me. I do not think this is what our government had in mind when Congress passed the stimulus bill hoping to create some shovel ready jobs. If you need a little inspiration before taking on this dirty job, listen to the song, "Taking Care of Business" by Bachman-Turner Overdrive, before you walk outside. I do not want to belabor this issue anymore, but I do think it is important for everyone to take care of his or her own pet's waste. So please take care of the messes so neighbors can smell the roses instead of the foul odors. Vote for my brother, Arthur Hobson, in the mayoral election, because he will help us take care of our town's bigger messes.

Thank you,

Johnny Hobson

Two weeks before the deadline, Arthur went to the courthouse to file his application as a candidate for the next mayoral election in Rainbow Creek. The main reason Arthur decided to enter his name in the race was that incumbent Mayor Armstrong decided to retire. The final straw for Arthur, however, was when he heard that his opposition, Irvin Shelby, was in favor of the Obama administration's socialist decision to print more money to devalue the dollar by 14 percent overnight. The Democrats believed this would make it easier for needy people to afford their debts. In reality, in Arthur's mind, all this did was steal money from anyone who had savings and make them poorer overnight, giving away their money for free and making everything that is purchased much more expensive in the coming years. For the country as a whole, Arthur was sure all this decision did was to continue one of the worst economic decades in American history.

Shelby campaigned mainly on promises to fix the struggling public school system and extending unemployment benefits for people out of work. Former council member Shelby ran against Mayor Armstrong two years ago and received two of every five votes. Rainbow Creek was one of those old communities that held steadfast to voting for its mayor every two years instead of every four years. Arthur was hoping he could garner enough support from citizens to defeat his well-financed opponent. Shelby supported the proposed Walmart development, a program to rid the city of lead paint, and another one, which would bring in a consultant firm to recommend fixes for the school district. Arthur figured all of these projects probably somehow returned kickbacks to Shelby.

Arthur was more interested in trying to lift the spirits of all the citizens in Rainbow Creek, because he believed his hometown could be a greater community if its civic and political leaders worked together, to improve the quality of life in the neighborhoods and create growth opportunities for its small businesses. Businesses needed more sales, not more regulations. Arthur was adamant about spreading the word to tell residents that they must know the importance of investing time and money in their own neighborhoods. Mom-and-pop retailers, restaurants, unique shops, and public education all need exposure and support from the community to keep the job market strong.

Addison and Sandra collaborated on mailing out a letter that had three purposes, to tell citizens about issues important to their candidate, to ask for help in the coming election, and to ask for their votes. The campaign was a long and hard fight for relatives, friends, and volunteers dedicated to trying to bring victory to conservative principles and values. Arthur knocked on hundreds of doors, Johnny made thousands of phone calls, and Addison and Sandra mailed a letter to nearly every address in town. The Hobson team did its best to share the message of creating jobs, balancing the budget, ensuring Second Amendment rights, fighting the illegal drug trade, supporting public schools from a grassroots approach, fighting the regulatory changes that hurt small businesses, and campaigning on a mostly conservative agenda. Frank Lambert even stopped by the unofficial campaign headquarters on Hill View Avenue for several hours to help make phone calls, fold letters, and apply stamps to election postcards.

Frank: "Arthur, I don't mind helping make phone calls during election season, because I enjoy giving my opinions about politics, but how do we stop the darn scam artists from calling us all the time. Every day I get a call at suppertime from an automated phone messaging service that starts, 'Hello, this is Rachel from credit card services.' I complained to the phone company, the FCC, the ABC, and the XYZ. Nothing seems to work."

Arthur: "I don't know how to fix this problem, but if I'm elected mayor, maybe I can add it to the mayoral agenda."

Frank: "You'd think that with today's technology, the large local telephone companies could get a handle on the scams people are complaining about, especially the ones where unscrupulous individuals try to steal Social Security and credit card numbers. The state attorney general says that for every fifty calls the thieves make, one person actually divulges their personal information to them."

Arthur: "If one phone company blocks their calls, the thieves start using a different phone service."

Frank: "I'm on the 'Do Not Call List,' but why have laws if people don't have to abide by them? I just don't think enough is being done to catch these crooks, and I'm tired of taking time out of each day to answer these stupid calls."

Arthur: "I agree with you 100 percent, and it's probably time an alderman or someone from the mayor's office talks to the executives at Ma Bell and their competition."

Frank: "Every time you call a phone number about a product or a question about service, you talk to someone with broken English or an automated answering machine. First by recording, they tell you how very important your phone call is to them, but not enough to let you talk to another human being. Then you get a bunch of options, generally pressing any of the numbers one through nine, meant to cover any problems you might have experienced with your product or service. The problem is that most of the time the options presented do not cover the problems you are having. Therefore, you hang up the phone and start over and you are back to the same set of options from your previous call. Maybe you can add fixing this problem to your agenda too."

At any event where Arthur spoke, he told the audience that he wanted to increase the percentage of the tax revenue used for education by 5 percent and decrease the welfare dollar by 5 percent. He also told the people he wanted to decrease the salaries of elected officials, judges, prosecutors, and public defenders by 3 percent.

Sandra and Susie, considered the two thumb texting marketing officers of the Hobson campaign, dovetailed their efforts to strategize with all channels of modern politics. Bloggers in town relied on the girls' tracking the kinds of devices people used to access e-mail and websites as the voters helped customize the campaign platform. The girls understood that the time had arrived for successful political entities to transmit political newscasts on mobile devices. Arthur's support team worked tirelessly to read relevant social network comments from residents of Rainbow Creek and e-mail campaign letters asking them for their votes. The message was simple.

Dear Friends,

I hope this letter finds you well. This letter is a request for your vote in the next Rainbow Creek mayoral election. As a community center executive, I have done my very best to spread ideas that will allow our community to prosper. With enough votes from citizens, a bigger platform will allow me to continue to work for the benefit of a larger base of citizens in Rainbow Creek, where families can prosper and businesses can grow. Please consider supporting my election campaign. Together, we can achieve great things for the Rainbow Creek region. Let us focus on what works and do not let any more negative talk about the economy fuel more pessimism. Nobody ever *made a dime from panicking. Please join us at Grant's Lodge in Rainbow Creek on Saturday, September 18, at 4 p.m. for a raffle, soft drinks, and light appetizers. Admission is $10 per person to cover food and beverage expenses.*

I hope to see you on September 18.
Thank you,
Arthur Hobson
Candidate for Mayor

Irvin Shelby secretly started using Arthur's slogan of "Great things for Rainbow Creek" to annoy voters. He taped Arthur's message and then used it during an auto-mated telephone campaign, by calling residents between midnight and five o'clock in the morning, waking people from a dead sleep and hoping to irritate them enough to sway vote toward his own junta. It was late in the evening on a Friday night in early September when Arthur, Addison, and Sandra divvied up what was left of the alphabetized list of names, with corresponding addresses of residences that had not yet received a letter. Arthur took the longest list, naturally, but he retired to bed first. Addison was tired and took her list home with her. Sandra took a diet cola to her room and sat listening to the sounds of Carrie Underwood and Kelly Clarkson as she folded letters, licked stamps, and wrote names and addresses on envelopes. Not until it was nearly midnight did she venture out of her room to look for snacks to eat at the table in the kitchen. Johnny, already seated and not feeling well again, turned sideways with his face resting on his arms folded over on the kitchen table.

Sandra: "Uncle Johnny, are you feeling sick again?"

Johnny: "Yes, I'm feeling the same symptoms I felt last week. The symptoms went away for a few days, but they are back again this evening. I should probably make an appointment to go see a doctor in the morning."

Sandra: "I'll ask Dad to write down his doctor's phone number for you and you can call him first thing in the morning. I think most doctors' office hours start at 8 a.m."

Johnny: "Thank you, Sandra.

Sandra: "I'll sit here with you for a little while and we can wait for some chicken soup to boil. If you feel like eating a couple of crackers and sipping on my chicken soup, I'll share a midnight snack with you."

Johnny assented, though not in a very energetic way. Sandra was worried and sensed something was wrong, but she did not want to ask more questions, which might frighten her uncle. Instead she buttered a few crackers and poured the hot chicken noodle soup into bowls and brought the light meal over to the table. She was such a strong woman and lately her short-term plans focused on helping her father try to win the mayoral race. But now, she was worried more about her Uncle Johnny. She did not want her father sidetracked from his important work with the campaign, so she took it upon herself to make the appointment and take Johnny to the doctor's office the next morning. Her new plan now was to find out what was making Johnny sick.

The Grant's Lodge campaign event came and went. Joey Russell, a history teacher from Heartland, won the raffle, winning a new flat-screen digital television. Almost three hundred people showed up for the celebration, some enjoying the free food, some attending because they wanted to hear what Arthur had to say. Arthur, while standing at the podium, kept his message short, telling attendees he wanted to spend much of his time helping families prosper and businesses grow. During his speech he told the people he would do everything he could to find and create job opportunities, so all citizens of Rainbow Creek could earn a living and make enough money to turn back the clock and afford a bit more conveniences on their free time. Another reason he cut his speech short: his colon was acting up again, and he needed to use the bathroom. The prominent part of his speech went as follows:

For too many years mayors in this town have written legislation that is too long and not transparent. Many times the new laws only benefit the ones writing the bills and no one else knows what is in it. Why do Americans put up with this deception that all these bills will create jobs? We deserve more and a prudent government is something the Tea Party is trying to fight for across the country. So many areas of society make it easy for government, big banks, investment firms, big businesses, entertainment, and professional sports teams to steamroll over the middle class in so many ways. Like a disappearing act in front of our eyes, the Tea Party is helping to convince citizens not to accept everything told to us by politicians, while at the same time we continue to work harder and receive much less in return, and they and their cronies benefit. We cannot keep listening to excuses by politicians. We can't lose any more of our people in Rainbow Creek from the middle-class base.

For much of September, Johnny had a persistent fever and cough. At first check, Dr. William Hegarty determined Johnny had some kind of infection, but he needed to do blood work and other extensive tests to determine what was wrong. Pathologists would relay the results of the tests back to the doctor's office when they were ready in a few days. For now, Dr. Hegarty prescribed a weeklong round of antibiotics and rest. However, this did not make Johnny feel any better. In fact, he started to feel worse, and more symptoms were noticeable, including headaches, night sweats, chills, shortness of breath, and some weight loss.

On a cool evening in early October, weak and sitting in the brown leather La-Z-Boy in the living room and covered by multiple blankets, Johnny waited for Arthur to walk in the front door. Finally about 10 p.m., he did.

Johnny: "Hi, Arthur, you worked late tonight."

Arthur: "Yes, you know how it is when crunch time arrives."

Johnny: "Yes, in Atlanta, every time I should have found a job, gone back to college, or volunteered for something, my drug use seemed to get in the way. The wrong things are on the plates of people who do heroin. Caring about things takes a leave of absence from their lives."

Arthur: "I cherish the times I have with you and the girls, especially times like Parent's Weekend with Susie at the University of Missouri, sharing a ride with Sandra and Addison to a cultural event, or talking music or politics with you."

Johnny: "Chuck Berry and Johnnie Johnson created songs together for many years, but Berry made the royalties because Johnson did drugs and drank too much and didn't take care of business. "Maybelline" and "Johnnie Be Good" were huge hit songs. Down the road, when Johnson finally tried to sue Berry, the judge ruled too much time had passed by to go back and determine a monetary settlement. I just hope my drug use hasn't screwed up your chances to win the mayoral race."

Arthur: "Hey, just as Johnson got sober and he and his old friend made a movie about the earlier times playing music together, you quit drugs and the two of us have been busy building our platforms. If I lose, it will be because we did not spend as much money on the campaign as Shelby and because many married women will not vote for a divorced male candidate. They think all divorced men are out chasing women most of the time and won't devote their energy to their jobs."

Johnny: "Well, there's only so much you can do about those people. You just have to keep getting your message out there. It's not like you're in it for the money."

Arthur: "No, I'm not in it for the money. The president of the United States oversees all the nation's catastrophes and the most important affairs of our country, and the postmaster general oversees hundreds of billions of on-time delivery of mail in all fifty states each year, yet both jobs pay less than the salaries of every player on the New York Yankees major league roster. But I guess the president and the postmaster general make up for lost salary in the future when they write their books and speak on their lecture circuits."

Johnny: "I just hope you do not lose the mayor's race because of me. I hope nobody in Shelby's camp tries to make a connection between you and my criminal past involving drugs."

Arthur: "I'm just glad we both decided to really go forward with neither one of us worrying about receiving any sissy remuneration for injustices of the past. I wish more people would start to realize they have to create more opportunities for themselves. I am glad you overcame your weaknesses and became a good citizen. The way I could tell was not just your decision to stop using drugs, but just as importantly, your conscious effort not to brag about real or unrealized accomplishments. To a certain degree, 9/11 already changed all of us, but some of the high-ranking members of the federal administration and local politics are too young and too inexperienced to understand all the lessons this and other parts of history should have taught us."

Johnny: "I remember when a fireman found only bones of a dead child underneath the rubble at the World Trade Center site, and with his hands cupped and holding his findings, presented them to the medical examiner saying, 'Please help me, this is my dead son.' We Americans must never forget."

Arthur: "Johnny, you are intelligent and sensitive. That is a good combination. Everyone feels battered by life and the outside world, but you should not feel that way at home. When it is all over, all that matters is that we turned our lives in the right direction and when we look in the mirror, we can say we did something worthwhile. I love you, man."

Johnny: "I love you, too. It is strange how a man's inner peace seeps out slowly over the course of a lifetime as he gets to know himself and understand his bonds of kinship with his brothers. Even in the unruliest of troubled areas, a man can learn to save only what is important, just as a creek bed accepts the shift of gravel after floodwaters run through it during a torrential rainstorm. My background of self-destruction sometimes haunts me by what might have happened or what might happen next, but I'm happy that the conflicting dominions of my life have wandered closer to the truth."

Arthur continued with his campaign work, though the worry about the health of his brother was always on his mind. For a few days, Sandra and Addison made sure Johnny took his medicine. Both women tried to get him to eat light and healthy warm meals, which usually amounted to his taking just two or three bites because of difficulty keeping anything down. He was still losing weight and now his hair was losing its sheen. By the end of the week, Johnny was taken to Christian Hospital, the result of fear and last resort for Sandra and Addison. Johnny became a resident patient on the floor run by doctors specializing in infectious diseases, but still in the care of Dr. Hegarty. The special team of doctors found that their guitar-playing patient had a buildup of fluid around his lungs and an elevated white blood cell count, a possible indication of a very serious infection.

During the course of his medical history interview with Dr. Hegarty and again with the specialized team of doctors and nurses, Johnny only casually mentioned his past drug use. In today's society, the first question the admitting doctors and nurses ask a patient is, "Do you smoke, drink, or use drugs?" Once the doctors discovered Johnny had elevated white blood cells and drastic weight loss and loss of hair, these were signs to start asking him questions about stranger things. "Have you ever shared drug needles, are you homosexual or bisexual, have you ever had oral sex with another man before, have you ever spent the night at a crack house or a heroin den?" The more medical history questions Johnny answered and the more diagnostic test procedures he endured, the weaker he seemed to get.

Waiting for the doctors' diagnosis, Arthur spent his visit to the hospital walking the long hall on the fifth floor and looking out the large picture window. He did mental tallies and recalculations of the most popular color of cars in the parking lot in the two hours since the orderly wheeled out his brother from his semiprivate room, private at the time, because he was not currently sharing space with another patient. At last count, he estimated that ninety-five white cars, eighty-nine silver, seventy-nine black, sixty-four red, and fifty-seven blue cars filled spaces in the parking lot. He considered trucks the same as cars for counting purposes, but the numbers were not scientific, only approximations as vehicles either left or entered the parking lot every minute or two. An orderly walking in the hall passed by Arthur, noticing him pointing his finger and counting cars under his breath.

Orderly: "You know the Model T was only available in black, because back then, black paint dried faster than any other paint. Then they started painting cars white, because the white paint was easier to match when a car needed body repair after a wreck. Now cars are available in all sorts of colors, but it's still a common misconception that insurance companies charge higher rates for red cars. People make the assumption red cars are more likely to get ticketed by police officers."

Arthur: "You named three of the five most popular color cars in the parking lot. It sounds like you and others have already contemplated my pass-the-time type of calculations."

Orderly: "Hospitals are busy places. About once a month, somebody standing in the exact spot you are standing, counts the cars or makes a remark about the most popular colors of cars in the parking lot. Silver and blue are the only colors you did not mention to me. At one time, silver was the most popular color ordered by new car buyers. From your calculations, is silver still one of the top five colors?"

Arthur: "Yes, you know what you are talking about. I counted eighty-nine silver cars, give or take."

It was getting on toward five o'clock and Arthur was worried about his brother. Dr. Hegarty consulted with a colleague, Dr. Charles Landau, who worked in the infectious diseases department at the Centers for Disease Control and Prevention in Atlanta. For Dr. Landau, a specialist who spent a lot of time flying to far-flung places around the world to study diseases, it was nice for him to hear from his old doctor friend from Rainbow Creek, whom he had met in medical school. However, for Johnny, his health seemed to be rapidly deteriorated during his last hour in the hospital. To the end, the doctors and nurses did everything they could to make Johnny comfortable. Never an easy part of a doctor's job, Dr. Hegarty walked out to the waiting room to tell Arthur and Sandra the bad news.

Dr. Hegarty: "I'm sorry, Arthur and Sandra, but Johnny passed away a few minutes ago. We tried everything we could to keep him alive."

Arthur: "Oh no! How did this happen so fast?"

Dr. Landau: "The process happened slower than you think. The disease was working against Johnny for a long time, but his heroin use was acting like a painkiller before, masking his symptoms until they showed up again. Somewhere along the line, he contracted HIV. Here at the end, the effects of full-blown AIDS on the body and an expeditious weakening of Johnny's immune system caused his death."

Sobbing, Sandra broke down in the arms of her father. "He was doing so well. He quit doing drugs nearly seven months ago and he was working hard to build up his business."

Arthur: "Thank you, Dr. Hegarty and Dr. Landau. I know this kind of bad news is never easy for anyone. This is difficult for our family, but particularly for my daughter Sandra and me, because we both were very close to Johnny."

When Arthur called Ms. Staley to relay the tragic news, she professed her desire to start a program in Johnny's honor. She wanted to train police officers, paramedics, and rehab staff to treat drug and alcohol abuse from a disease approach instead of a criminal approach. She believed spraying people with mace and locking up people without educating them did not address the problem. Maybe being tired of all the terrible outcomes and senseless deaths had a lot to do with the way she felt. In short, Ms. Staley did not think the laws in America were protecting the citizens from the increasing danger of criminals who perpetrate drug violence and intimidation as a way of life. She felt it was incumbent on our national leadership to stop being oblivious to the drug culture and find a way to fix the prison system. She believed that American ingenuity could discover better ways to deal with the problems of drugs and nonviolent criminal behavior while still minimizing violent crime and large-scale gang activity, because everybody in America deserved to live in a safe environment made better by such changes. She continued her work in drug counseling because she still had hope.

A few days later, Arthur gave the eulogy at the funeral, speaking to a small gathering of people who came to pay respects to Johnny and the Hobson family. Ms. Staley flew in from Atlanta to attend the funeral. Kay Applebaum, Karen Anderson, Frank Lambert, Gary Bordeaux, Larry Bordeaux, Justin, Jane, and Stuart came to lend support to Arthur, Sandra, and Susie. Addison was right by Arthur's side. Kevin and Shirley took the first flight to St. Louis and then a swift taxi ride to join family and friends. Many of Johnny's landscaping customers and a few of his musician friends stopped by the funeral home to pay their respects too. Arthur stepped in front of the podium in the corner of the room and told the gathering he wanted to say a few words to eulogize his brother Johnny.

"This morning I was standing on top of the hill overlooking the Hobson House estate where my brother Johnny and I ran around playing when we were little boys. The big oak tree in the front yard showed her leaves blowing in the mighty morning breeze, many falling to the ground. For many decades, the tree has been an object of beauty and strength. I stood and watched at length, reminiscing about the idyllic childhoods Kevin, Johnny, and I spent together, until the tree was almost bare of all her magnificent colors, different shades of red, yellow, orange, green, and brown. All of a sudden, the leaves were gone. Gone where, you ask. The leaves were gone from my sight and they were only a memory in my brain of hanging out on its branches of life. Johnny stayed strong to the end, never complaining when he was sick, and staying committed to earning his way by using his muscles to rake leaves, carry landscaping stones, and bear the load of running his business. He made amends with his mistakes of the past and readied himself for his eventual better destination. Though his disease diminished his size and reputation, he no longer feels pain. We feel the pain. Just at the moment when we say, 'He's gone,' there are angels watching and saying, 'Here he comes!' There are always people on earth who can tell you exactly what is in God's plans; remarkably enough, God's likes and dislikes always seem to match their own ways of thinking. They can always tell you exactly what is on God's mind. Most of us believe in some kind of God, but to know whom God is exactly flies way over all of our heads. I do believe that in the same fashion the mighty breeze took all of the leaves from the oak tree, God took all of the good in Johnny's soul today. Thank you, everyone, for giving your support and praying for our family."

Feeling so much grief in the days that followed the funeral, Arthur had to force himself to tie up the loose ends of Johnny's financial matters and notifying his landscaping customers that he had passed away. All of Johnny's clothes, Arthur gave to Goodwill.

Johnny received a notice in the mail with a return address from Portland, Oregon, one week after he died. The notice stated he might be included in a class action settlement impacted by a derivative involving Idex Mutual Funds investments. Johnny had about five thousand dollars invested in a handful of Idex Mutual Funds and listed Arthur as the beneficiary in case of his death. The notice stated that lawyers reached a settlement in the class-action suit in which the plaintiffs alleged the company facilitated improper market timing, late trading, and excessive trading in certain Idex mutual funds. At first, the defendants denied they did anything wrong. Then the two sides disagreed on how much money, if any, to pay. Finally, the class-action suit was resolved out of court and the defendant was told to pay money to eligible holders of the mutual funds, which included Johnny.

Arthur spent about an hour reading the settlement information and filling out the six pages of the claim form in order to receive a settlement payment. He folded up the completed claim form, put it in a return envelope, and mailed it off.

At a recovery rate of .0002 per share, the defendants paid out a total of $2,604,700 to all eligible mutual fund holders. Because Johnny had just started his retirement plan, he only owned six shares of the Idex Fixed Income Fund. After the settlement was granted, he should have received a check for $.01 (one penny), except the settlement formula only paid those entitled to a distribution of fifty dollars or more, and though Arthur was looking into this matter only for the possibility of transferring benefits to his two daughters and closing out the final responsibilities of his brother, he received nothing from the settlement. He was out a stamp and the lawyers made off with almost one-fifth of the $2,604,700 settlement, which was a $500,000 commission. Idex may someday be a good investment firm, but Arthur was discovering a firsthand reaffirmation of his personal belief in how class-action suits are usually a sham for the individuals they represent. Lawyers create lawsuits where they should not exist, creating too much of a litigious society. When Arthur called his friend Frank to tell him about his class-action experience, he received another honest opinion, just as he always relied on from his friend. After explaining his class-action situation, Frank offered his take on lawyers, Congress, Wall Street, and the Occupy movement that was sweeping the nation.

Frank: "Investment companies send out booklets containing notice of joint annual meeting of stockholders and a proxy statement that supposedly provide you with information you should review before voting on proposals that will be presented at the meeting. You receive these proxy materials because you own either shares of a fund's stock or shares of beneficial interest in a fund. As a stockholder, you have the right to vote for the election of directors or trustees. Trouble is you have no idea who these people are."

Arthur: "From all this paperwork, it looks like Johnny had the right to vote on various proposals concerning his investments in this new fund. But how could anyone have any idea of the true meaning of the wording of the amendment proposals?"

Frank: "As a shareholder, you have to decide whether to vote for, against, or just abstain your opinion. Half the time the proposals remove limits on the directors' authority to take action that would benefit the funds. It is not clear who benefits from the action, the investment firm or the shareholders, but there is a good chance the benefits go to the firm. The firm asks shareholders to vote on fee measurement periods, reimbursement of administration expenses, charter provisions, laws in other states, reclassification of fundamental investment objectives, and all sorts of provisions that seem worded to confuse or have relevance only to those writing the proposals."

Arthur: "To me, all these proposals just look like special deals between directors, boards, fund managers, banks, trustees, lawyers, and politicians."

Frank: "You are right. Getting to the core of understanding all the arrangements is nearly impossible or at the very least, a full-time job for a consumer advocate group. The amendments are written in a language full of lingo that really doesn't tell the investor anything,"

Arthur: "I looked at the dollar figures reported in the fine print of the booklets sent to me, and it looks like accounting firms are paid exorbitant amounts of money for auditing fund accounts once each year."

Frank: "If you meander through all the pages in the proxy statement, stock firms tell shareholders to consider all the voting proposals for the proxy meeting routine, even though they allow Wall Street firms to make up products to invest in. For all the investors who do not take the time to vote, the New York Stock Exchange rules allow stockbrokers to vote for their clients, further stacking the deck. What a racket these folks have going! The kids occupying Wall Street aren't as wet behind the ears as our Republican officials say they are, and the Democrats are using them to get what they want, more legislation."

Arthur: "The Occupiers deserve more credit for their sacrifices than the liberal media is allowing them."

Frank: "At the end of the day, the Occupiers don't want the Fed's actions or Wall Street's actions to be the only thing driving business markets. More important is the actual financial performance of companies, their ability to generate revenue growth, and their ability to keep expenses in check. If companies are successful in delivering goods and services, the Occupiers want to see evidence of jobs created to satisfy their demands. It is a bad sign if a stockbroker offers advice to an unemployed person to buy stock in the Bank of Timbuktu, ownership in Nigerian barges, or shares of real estate in the Swamps of the Everglades."

Arthur: "You make a lot of sense, Frank, and I think the Occupy kids make some valid points too. Trouble is, many people only see the protestors as trespassing on public property and littering the parks. Some people worry more about who is going to clean up the trash than who is going to clean up the mess Congress, Wall Street, and their lawyers are creating."

Frank: "These class-action suit lawyers steal from society, just as members of Congress align themselves with Wall Street executives to steal from investors. The Occupiers camping out in American cities feel Wall Street has corrupted America's financial system, shipped jobs oversees, stripped research and development, and made up products to invest in. To the Occupiers, much of America's money put into Wall Street accounts is just financing another form of a giant casino."

Arthur: "I think 'Occupy Wall Street' should be renamed 'Occupy Congress,' because those on Wall Street just do what the government allows them to do, until awareness of shareholders forces them to pass more laws to rein in the crooks. Most of the Wall Street executives and the high-level politicians are in cahoots anyway. When well-intentioned men founded Rainbow Creek, pigs were native to the town. Over time the larger pigs made their way to Washington to take advantage of better opportunities to feed."

Frank: "Sounds like you think the country was once in better shape. It's the lying high-level politicians who have put our country in this mess."

Arthur: "It never occurs to these guys that the middle class makes sacrifices every day for the future of their families. We worry about financial freedom, family values, personal growth, helping others, and acting as role models, paying taxes, and trying to have a little fun along the way. They are only interested in how they can influence power grabs in the here and now."

Frank: "Sorry, Arthur, my other line is ringing; I'll talk to you later."

After making another phone call, then transferring several times through the Idex investment phone chain, Arthur was finally connected to Benjamin Zank, a man who spoke in a down-to-earth manner to his clients. Arthur's first impression of this man was one that made him feel like he was talking to an honest man in a not so honest industry.

Benjamin: "Hi, this is Benjamin Zank of the Idex Investment firm. How can I help you?"

Arthur: "Hello, my name is Arthur Hobson and I would like to cash out my brother Johnny's account. Johnny passed away and I am named as the beneficiary on his investment account."

Benjamin: "I'm sorry for your loss. Your brother's name is Johnny Hobson, correct?"

Arthur: "Thank you, sir. Yes, it is."

Benjamin: "Please give me just a few seconds to pull up the account. … I am also sorry to tell you that the account is down about 10 percent from his initial investment distributions. In general, stocks have had a poor run for over a decade now. If we really want to try to find out where things went wrong, we just need to follow the charts of the companies your brother chose to invest in recently. The sad fact is that most American corporations no longer recognize or treat shareholders as true owners. Even as the economy struggles to climb out of the worst recession in more than seventy years, many of their profits are soaring. Yet the bulk of these earnings, as in the decade just past, are not finding their way to investors. Instead, firms divert these rivers of cash toward empire-building acquisitions, dubious share repurchases, and obscene executive pay packets. Total profits for the companies that make up the S&P 500 could top one trillion dollars in the upcoming year, yet the average stock in this group yields only a two-point dividend, half of the historic average.

Some of our best-known, best-loved companies get away with paying no dividend at all. I apologize for rambling on in your time of grief, but I was just hoping I would have a little better news for you, especially since your brother died."

Arthur: "What stocks did Johnny invest in?"

Benjamin: "It looks like he was investing in a group of Chinese stocks that promised higher dividends without disclosing much information about their financial statements."

Arthur: "Sounds risky to me."

Benjamin: "Yes, but he wasn't the only person sucked in to buying little-known Chinese real estate, technology, and utility stocks. Many Americans investing in Chinese stocks are discovering reasons for disappointing performances. Financial filings the Chinese companies make with the SEC are often very different from those filed with the Chinese government, by drastic amounts. When analysts visit the corporate facilities in China, the operations are much smaller and much less impressive than shown in brochures and presentations. Old investors and young people alike must pay attention to the schemes of dishonest businesses and trading partners around the world."

Arthur: "Corruption, wherever it manifests, always bothers me."

Benjamin: "China's government and growing middle class is using its purchasing power to invest in companies and products in the United States. The Chinese are buying huge stakes in Coca-Cola and Johnson & Johnson. They are buying real estate in vacation destinations like Branson, Missouri, and Las Vegas. They are collaborating with other buyers to lessen their risks and draw less attention to their investments around the globe. The Chinese, aware of their image did not want the media to report a similar story that they are taking over; "Made in China" is becoming "Owned by China." The Chinese know that Fort Knox is far from being the largest depository of gold in America; the Federal Reserve Bank in New York takes that honor."

Arthur: "Where else is the Chinese government investing its money?"

Benjamin: "China has been investing overseas in assets like copper, gold, timber, oil, and iron than it puts into US treasury bonds. The Chinese currency, the yuan, undervalued against the dollar by such a wide margin really bothers me. The strategy of the Chinese is to design their government bolstering the value of the yuan by only small increments each year, to delay catching up with the greenback, by investing in hard assets now. Annual interest payments on US debt to China have become an old-style investment strategy and easily outweigh concerns of the lessening value of the dollar, partially caused by the Fed's insistence on printing money."

Arthur: "I guess the Chinese are optimistic that investing in hard materials will hold their value and even increase in value over time. Won't this help influence an economic strategy by China to put pressure on the US to raise interest rates, causing a more difficult recovery?"

Benjamin: "American investors are safe for now, because the Chinese government knows they must maintain a balance of wise investments and making sure the US remains able to afford Chinese products. In fifteen years, if the yuan catches up with the dollar, China's expansion of its own market and smart purchases of enough raw materials around the world could lessen the importance of exports. The SEC in the US probably will not make much of a regulatory effort for investors who tie up their money in Chinese stocks. For quite a while, the SEC has been warning us about the expense of probing overseas businesses, because of the danger of prying into relationships between foreign governments and the businesses they regulate, especially when agencies such as the SEC cannot subpoena evidence from China."

Arthur: "From outside China and looking in, despite all the government control and differences in rules, it seems commerce is freer than ever. But with the Chinese people more aware of markets than ever before, our politicians probably need to wise up to all the rules causing an unfair playing field and working against us, so they learn to protect American money."

Benjamin: "I agree with you."

Arthur: "I know the balance in Johnny's account isn't a lot of money, but when you get a chance, could you send me a statement and the papers to sign in order to close out the account? In return, I will send you a copy of Johnny's death certificate."

Benjamin: "There will be a small processing fee and once we receive the death certificate, we will send you a check. Again, I am sorry for your loss."

Arthur: "Thank you for your help, Benjamin. I will make sure his two favorite nieces split the money. This is how Johnny would have wanted it, even though my name is listed as the beneficiary. Have a good day."

Arthur appreciated hearing Benjamin's point of view. He got angry when he thought about investment executives giving themselves multimillion-dollar bonuses, especially after receiving bailout money when so many small investors saw their homes foreclosed on or they lost their jobs. The executives fly to lavish vacation homes in private jets, drive luxury automobiles, play golf at top PGA golf courses, while investors feel robbed of their money, homes, and livelihoods. He had no doubt that policy makers were siding with and joining the investment crooks, making sure they benefitted from the rules they made, taking more money from the middle class.

Scary things happened during the days of the old Wild West, when cowboys stole everything from the Native Americans. The West is still a scary place because there will always be a subsegment of the population willing to take advantage of the elderly or rob from the middle-class base. Arthur now had a better understanding of the financial crisis, the greatest banking collapse since the Great Depression. It occurred while compensation with bonuses and benefits at Wall Street banks and securities firms climbed to record levels. In this modern-day Wild West financial environment, investing exclusively through stockbrokers who use a buy-and-hold strategy is usually counterproductive in achieving any long-term financial goals. The reality is that investment earnings will not grow as rapidly or as consistently as they once did, meaning flat earnings levels in the stock market. Just one conversation with Benjamin and another with his friend Frank convinced Arthur to see the stock market in a new light. All this global competition with everybody fighting for the same things was causing stagnation in stock prices with increased short-term volatility. In recognition of this fact, Arthur concluded the type of investing strategy done in the future will be different from the buy-and-hold strategy of the past. Strategies will still include buying stocks of well-run companies, but trades will involve carefully buying shares at sale prices on a cyclical basis and sold on short-term upticks, similar to betting on the Super Bowl. Changes in interest rates already appeared similar to point-spreads, valuation levels of the broad market similar to analyzing the playoff teams, and the psychological state of the investing public betting on the home team, will play big parts in future investments in the West.

"Far-reaching legislative changes will mean less disposable income for the middle class according to US forecasters," Arthur read in the quarterly Franklin Templeton report. "The world will see a steep decline in the number of American and European middle-class consumers to five hundred million by 2025, and an actual explosion of the Asian middle class to three and a half billion. Asia's sevenfold advantage in spenders will drive a majority of the world's sales for products like clothing, mobile devices, appliances, jewelry, and automobiles, creating shortages for retail items and higher prices in commodities." Reading this report did little to relieve any of Arthur's worries.

The death of Johnny surely permitted Arthur time to wallow in self-pity. Four days after the family buried Johnny, he found notes of a song Johnny was working on about patriotism, written to and about troops, honoring them for their service in Iraq and Afghanistan. The song didn't have a title yet, but the words went like this:

You know the Democrats and the Republicans never get along very well,
In addition, for you, it is not a very good time for delay.
Too bad the politicians are always the last ones to figure things out,
While in spite of all of the dismay, our brave soldiers continue to fight.
We all want America's representatives to get the politics right,

To realize when bullets are flying past the heads of boots on the ground,
The best decisions to protect the best of the best we must make quickly,
Because our heroes can't be left waiting for an eternity of unevenness,
While we are praying they make it home safe and sound.

Johnny knew what politics felt like as a soldier fighting in a war. Many times he and other young infantrymen had to face the realization of seeing friends shot dead by North Vietnamese hiding in the weeds or blown to pieces by roadside bombs. After the battles calmed down, they had to witness their fellow soldiers lying still in a bag on a slab of wood with an American flag laid over them, and when the bugler started to play taps, there was not a dry eye in sight.

Arthur tried to overcome some of his grief by looking at old black-and-white photos of some of the happier times he spent with his brother. He looked at pictures of him and Johnny playing with their dog, playing catch in the backyard, and making funny faces at a neighborhood friend's birthday party. Another newer digital photo showed Johnny laughing with Sandra and Susie, all three of them holding glasses of eggnog and sitting on the firm brown leather sofa at the Hobson House during the Christmas holidays more than five years before. With all of his problems, many self-induced, Johnny tried to soften some of the worst blows that life delivered through laughter, no matter how painful the situation, in order to make it survivable. Too much of Johnny's life felt as if the company he worked for moved overseas and he scurried wondrously about while his home lay empty, the weeds grew high, and the landscaping went unattended all summer. Then when the brutal winter weather hit, the storms damaged the roof and knocked down the trees, making things worse, he never quite feeling able to climb out of the mess.

He came across an old photo of himself and his first girlfriend, Christine. He was ten years old and she was nine.

When Arthur was just ten years old, he went on a camping trip with his godparents, who did not have children, and another family that were close friends to them. His godfather was a Korean War marine veteran and his godmother a homemaker. A little girl named Christine was a member of this other family. Arthur thought Christine was the cutest girl he had ever seen and he soon found out she was nearly the same age as he was. During the weeklong camping trip, the two new friends played catch, fished, water-skied, talked, told jokes, and hung out together. Christine was the coolest girl Arthur had ever met. After a week of innocent frolic and fun, with the end of the camping trip nearing, Christine pulled Arthur aside and kissed him on the lips. This was the first time a girl kissed him. She handed him an oversize envelope with a postcard inside and told him to read it on the way home.

Each family worked steadily to fold the tents and pack belongings, food, and supplies for the long ride home. Once everything was loaded into the cars and everybody said goodbye, the two families headed for home. Arthur could not wait to read the postcard. With his godfather driving and his godmother sitting in the front passenger seat, Arthur tried to get comfortable in a fully packed backseat with less room than if he had two adults sharing the space next to him. Once his godfather reached the interstate and most of the small talk quieted, he reached for the postcard stuffed in his back pocket. It read:

Roses are red,
Violets are blue,
I love you,
Hope you love me too.
  Christine

When his godfather finally steered the car into the driveway at the Hobson House, Arthur grabbed his stuff and jumped out of the car with a big smile on his face. He thanked his godfather and godmother and waved good-bye. He ran inside to his bedroom and placed the postcard in the bottom drawer of his small wooden desk. The bottom drawer was the sacred place where only his most treasured items were stored, his baseball cards, his dad's dog tags from the Korean War, his Stan Musial autograph, and his postcard from Christine. On the wall above his desk was a framed certificate with the following words of encouragement from America's first president.

A primary object … should be the education of our youth in the science of government. In a republic, what species of knowledge can be equally important? And what duty is more pressing … than communicating it to those who are to be the future guardians of the liberties of the country?
  —George Washington

Ten-year-old boys are curious about things and stay busy occupying their time at school with playing sports, working on hobbies, and running around in the woods. They don't know how to carry on with romantic relationships, but Arthur did know that Christine was the first girl to make his heart skip a beat, a feeling he never experienced before and a true innocent love which seldom ever is experienced again in life.

Christine had the unsettling kind of beauty that outshone everything around her. Her thick strawberry blond hair was long and shiny, but she often kept it in a ponytail, which hung out the backside of a baseball cap. Though she liked to wear baggy clothes, oversized T-shirts and flannel sweat pants, the way she moved was far from concealing her coordination, long hair, freckles, and bone structure. Pictures of her did not do her justice, making all her features smaller and minimizing her perfect complexion. Even with all her outer beauty, Arthur took more notice of her good manners, manifested in her patience with people who had a lot less going for them. When they were together, he was painfully aware of his habit of staring stupidly at her whenever she was looking the other way or off in the distance. Arthur was discovering a new understanding of the world, based on his own feelings, without decades of careful experimental study in striking accordance with the inductive principle of most young boys. His infatuation with Christine seemed to indicate that his thought process and taste in women was unscientifically on track.

Whenever Arthur talked to adults about Christine, they told him he would meet many girls in his life and he was too young to understand love. What if she was his dream girl, all these other people were wrong, and this was his chance to really connect and begin to share a happy life with her? His feelings for Christine were not those of a mentalist, illusionist, or magician. His feelings were real and maybe someday he would understand their capacity. Is every move of a person preordained or is every move in life supposed to be a surprise? These questions Arthur was too young to answer.

Two and a half years after the camping trip, on a Friday night, Arthur's father drove him and his friends Frank and Gary to the only outdoor ice-skating rink in Rainbow Creek. During the previous two winters, the boys skated on frozen ponds whenever they iced over. They were not great ice-skaters, but they were getting better and their ice skates were now broken in and comfortable. Arthur was the first to lace up his skates and the first to pass through the thick wooden gates opened to the skaters entering the ice rink. After a couple of quick laps around the rink, there Christine was, tightening the laces on one of her skates. Arthur's heart instantly started fluttering and after circling around the rink one more time and now struggling to catch up with the twelve-year-old girl speed skater, he decided to just stop and wait for her to circle around again. As she approached him and their eyes met, both girl and boy yelled out at the same time.

Christine: "Arthur, how are you?"

Arthur: "Hi, Christine!"

Christine: "Fancy seeing you here, Arthur. How have you been? It's been a couple of years."

Arthur: "Yes, I'm fine and it's great to see you."

Christine: "It is great to see you too! Well, let's get going before we get run over."

She grabbed Arthur by the hand and the two of them circled the rink repeatedly, talking, laughing, and smiling. Arthur's buddies watching in the wings were a little stunned at the turn of events, Gary saying, "Holy shit, Arthur is holding hands and skating with the hottest chick on the ice and we have only been here for ten minutes." Christine was a cool chick. To Arthur she was interesting, funny, nice, cute, and so easy to talk to. He did not know what it all meant at the time, but he was in love with her.

Over the next four years, Arthur and Christine met at the skating rink every winter Friday night they could convince their parents to drive them there. As young teenagers still trying to establish who they were as individuals, ice skating became their common bond during the winter, but they never saw each other during the other three seasons of the year. Since they were too young to drive initially and their homes were thirty miles apart, there was a limit to how often they could see each other. By the time Arthur was a senior in high school, he asked Christine to be his date to his prom. She accepted and it did not bother her at all that she did not know anyone else there accept Arthur. At the prom, the couple danced, listened to the band, and talked about their plans. She was strong willed and he was too. Though each of them did not know it at the time, this was one of the last evenings they would spend together. Two months later, they would leave to attend different universities.

Arthur knew that the young woman he once cared so much for loved him too. He knew this for certain, but it was all he knew for certain, then or now, because so much about her the last three decades remained unknown. Was she a good cook? Was she happy most of the time? Did she take enough time to smell the roses? Were there things in her life that happened that may have surprised him? Whatever the details of how she spent most of her days, most of them would have to remain in far remote and unsettled places of his fantasies about her.

Early in the morning, just one week after burying his brother Johnny, Arthur picked up the newspaper from his front lawn, walked back inside, and sat down with a cup of coffee at the kitchen table. In the obituaries, he noticed a special article about a woman who had passed away peacefully at a hospice center about an hour's drive from Arthur's home. The article stated doctors diagnosed her with breast cancer only three months ago and that she fought a courageous battle. It said she was the longtime director of development and civic affairs at the outdoor municipal theater in Heartland. She also served on the board of the Learning Disabilities Association and volunteered with Big Brothers and Big Sisters. The article also stated that during her life she loved speed skating and walking in Woodlands Park with her dog Lucy.

Reading this story reminded Arthur of an odd experience he had had about four months earlier. Arthur had been sitting in his car one late evening at a traffic light parallel to the walking trail at Woodlands Park when he noticed a woman walking a dog. She looked very familiar. Though it was starting to get dark outside, the woman looked back for a long time, even turning her head and staring at him as he stepped on the gas to pull away, as if she recognized him too. Now he could only imagine if maybe on this evening, thirty-eight years since he last saw her, he was looking at Christine one more time before, at age fifty-six, she died. Of all the people Arthur met along the journey up to this point in his life, she was the only person who always made him feel extraordinary and sure about his convictions. He remembered her as a summation of all the right parts, where nothing needed added and nothing needed taken away. For the past ten years of her life, Christine was divorced, but Arthur did not know it. He did not know a son named Max survived her either.

The deaths of Johnny and Christine weighed heavily on Arthur's mind for several weeks as he struggled to get back to doing the necessary things to compete in the mayoral race. He soon realized that the best way to honor his brother and friend was to celebrate the years they had together instead of wallowing in the pain of the losses. Because Arthur was a strong person and he was adamant about his feelings that any man or woman running for mayor must know the importance of investing time and money in neighborhoods throughout the community, he was able to slowly bring himself out of mourning and fight for causes, which connected him to the souls of Johnny and Christine. He talked about ways Rainbow Creek citizens could help support the job market and deter the illegal drug market. He fought for education at the local level and he talked to health care providers who truly understood compassion, needing to make sure they did business with honest vendors and government agencies that operated under the principles of a smart business model. Just as Christine was a shining example of a person with compassion and honesty, he wanted the people working in education and health care to keep both traits high on their list. As addicted as Johnny once was to the rules of the street instead of his future, Arthur became serious again about plans for a better Rainbow Creek, fighting street drugs, fighting back crime, reversing the impediments that the local and federal governments imposed that were impossible to deal with on a daily basis. He was irritated every day he saw rules and regulations made by bureaucrats who knew nothing about running a business. He wanted the bureaucrats to realize that too many of these changes were unnecessary because they cost too much money and stifled growth and opportunity. If the people making the rules for businesses took more time to understand business models, shop owners would not have to deal with more legislation by working more hours and letting employees go. If they considered two out of three Americans worked for small businesses, they would see a new approach of less confusing red-tape and an adjusted business model of lower taxes might make a big economic impact.

Arthur hated when the president and the Fed chairman together devised a scheme to print more money, causing the value of the dollar to lower so the government could pay for social programs. To him all this meant was that the men and women who work hard to earn their money now could only afford to buy less. Becoming the mayor could not control any of the networking at the federal level, but Arthur believed there were plenty of causes to fight for at the local level. The federal government had pushed stimulus and fiscal policies to the limit, and citizens had lost confidence in their leaders. People do not want to see the instruments of government used as weapons, and the Tea Party was trying to inform citizens to watch for politicians at every level who seemed interested only in getting reelected, not in making the US great again, a monument to the rest of the world. Bank customers were now aware of the failed leaders of big banks who helped create the financial mess, and who continued to work in the same corporate positions after receiving government bailout money. After the fallout, many Americans lost trust in the government to fix the problem, because many of those responsible still worked in high-level positions.

Rainbow Creek's incumbent Republican mayor decided to retire, and Arthur's Democratic opponent in the mayoral race, Irvin Shelby, campaigned on promises to fix the struggling school district, remedy the homeless problem, and increase unemployment benefits. Former council member Shelby ran against Mayor Armstrong four years ago and received 40 percent of the vote in an unsuccessful bid. Arthur was hoping he could get enough support from the community to defeat Shelby's well-financed campaign again. Shelby supported the Walmart development in Rainbow Creek, a program to rid the town of lead paint, and another program that would bring in a consultant firm to recommend fixes for the local school district. Arthur was more interested in trying to lift the spirits of the citizens in Rainbow Creek. He believed Rainbow Creek could be a great community again if its civic, commercial, and political leaders worked together to improve the quality of life in the neighborhoods and create growth opportunities for its small businesses. The main theme of his economic plan focused on telling voters, "Businesses need more sales, not more rules and regulations. More sales create jobs." Arthur thought any attempts to raise local taxes to pay for more new social welfare programs was a bunch of baloney, because the middle class worked hard for their money, and for years they paid for all the problems of the wealthy and the poor with a devalued dollar. He wondered why some politicians thought the middle class did not work to earn a living to take care of their own issues, as if they never got sick or had other issues to deal with on a daily basis. He wanted his local government to apportion more of the tax dollar toward education and less toward social welfare programs. He wanted business leaders to employ at least five workers for every one million dollars of revenue companies generated. His campaign focused on "Balance," and for every dollar of import product that came into the community of Rainbow Creek he wanted to export a dollar of product. Arthur figured that after a fair assessment, some money needed to be spent on technology, infrastructure, and the appearance of the community, because in the end, these things would bring prosperity and growth to Rainbow Creek.

One windy morning in late October, with the upcoming mayoral election on the minds of most Rainbow Creek residents, a woman approached Arthur as he was putting gas into the tank of his car at the local Shell gas station.

Woman: "Hi, Mr. Hobson, my name is Tammy Hatcher. I am a supporter of Irvin Shelby and I want to know, why are you trying to stir the pot? Irvin Shelby has more experience than you do in Rainbow Creek politics, and he knows much more about the ways in which we have always done things around here."

Arthur: "I mean no disrespect, Tammy, but while those ways might have worked well in the past, newer technology may very well be a more efficient way to complete some tasks around town in half the time. Over one hundred fifty years ago, people rode in wagon trains from the East to the West to travel thousands of miles and it took months to reach their destinations. Today the same trip takes a couple of days in a car or a bus, or just a few hours in an airplane. Progressive liberals are so hell-bent on change for change's sake, but I promise I will not use technology to cut jobs. There is plenty we can do to make our community better. I want to use technology to expedite the process. Our roads and bridges need repairs and our schools need updated restorations."

Tammy: "Irvin Shelby is my second cousin and he has always tried to take care of his family and friends. I would never vote for anyone running against a friend or family member."

The truth of her thoughts finally revealed itself. Just as if she never gave a single thought to how the gas she put in her tank at the gas station was recently stored at a nearby terminal, she did not care about local politics, as long as her relative won the mayoral election and she benefited from it. She did not care that other individuals and businesses needed raw crude, diesel, aviation fuel, propane, butane, kerosene, and heating oil, as long as she was able to pump gas into her car whenever she needed to drive to the bank, pick up groceries, or visit a friend. She did not care about the dangerous work accomplished to extract the oil a mile underground or to build the thousands of miles of pipelines in extreme weather conditions. She did not care about how men managed the large storage tanks holding millions of gallons of gasoline, or the risks motor fuel carriers deal with every day to deliver the different types and grades of fuel to gas stations. Arthur was tired of all the dishonest politicians and campaign tricks and favors they promised friends, taking advantage of the financial crisis, the housing meltdown, and the wars in the Middle East. He wanted people like Tammy to care more about how a certain kind of dishonest politics made life difficult for everybody else. He longed for politics, which could summon the country to greatness again and face our common challenges. Though he knew his comment probably would not do any good or change anything in her mind, he could not help himself, as he flung one last left jab Tammy Hatcher's way.

Arthur: "It is time to vote out any of our representatives who have proven to be dishonest. Whether our politicians believe they should keep the status quo or vote for change, their most important quality is honesty. Honesty doesn't require a high IQ."

Tammy Hatcher was typical of those who did not want to devote a lot of extra time to studying an issue, so she just walked away when anyone started talking too much for her taste. She had a preconceived idea of the way things were and nothing anyone else said was going to change her mind about anything. For her the possibility of a better social activism, better capitalism, better ideas, or a better candidate for mayor did not exist. She stopped listening long ago and for her, changing back to the other political party would just make things worse. Tammy was a confused child of the Vietnam era, never quite understanding if she should support the military or the protestors, and she did her best to avoid the feeling of backing into a corner when it came to having to make a real character decision. Maybe this is what she had in common with Irvin Shelby.

Arthur knew Irvin Shelby ever since he was a young boy. This man running against him was not everything he tried to tell voters he was, and Arthur had plenty of dirt about him, but he did not want to win the mayoral seat by lowering himself to running a smear campaign. He kept all the dirty secrets to himself, knowing that as a teenager, Shelby set a barn on fire in Rainbow Creek and stole fellow students' money from wallets in the pockets of folded pants put in unlocked lockers during high school gym classes. He poured lighter fluid on toads and lit them on fire just to watch them jump until they became lifeless, threw a black dog over a fence and breaking its leg, and nearly stoned to death another boy when he banged him over the head with a large rock during a fight on a creek bed. Shelby was not a person who always showed a good sense of character or who had a reputation for making the right decisions, and Arthur noticed more bad decisions mounting. Arthur realized that great catastrophes or fatal errors do not ruin the happiness of most people. A repetition of slowly destructive little things usually ruins happiness for people, and he wanted to win or lose the mayoral race by just sticking to the issues. The passion that drove him was everything to Arthur. He hoped that when citizens saw Shelby bite his lower lip during speeches when trying to emphasize a caring position to the public, they would find the gesture to appear phony.

Before driving home, Arthur stopped to see his friend Frank Lambert, the owner of The Right Car for You Corporation, now in its twenty-seventh year. His company oversaw a large fleet of rental cars and served the business-to-business and residential customer base mostly to people living within a half-hour drive of Rainbow Creek. About one-third of the company's customers lived in Heartland. Arthur knocked on Frank's office door and walked in.

Arthur: "Hey, Frank. Long time no see. How is everything?"

Frank: "I'm doing great, staying busy, can't complain, except for what some guy I never met did last night. It's nice to see you."

Arthur: "What happened last night?"

Frank: "Some idiot contractor illegally dumped sixty-two large plastic trash bags full of leaves and debris behind our office building. I guess the person was avoiding paying a disposal fee at a landfill, but it aggravates me that people think they can just take advantage of others this way. This morning I put a few of the bags in the large trash bin that sits in the corner of our property, but I had to pay an arm and a leg to have the rest of the mess hauled away."

Arthur: "It's a sign of the times. We live in a different world from the one we grew up in. A busload of people, only by happenstance, was listening to speakers at a Tea Party engagement I attended recently in Cape Girardeau. In route from Memphis, a Greyhound bus driver stopped at a restaurant in Cape so the passengers could take a bathroom break and get something to eat. After the passengers walked inside the restaurant, the bus driver disappeared and he left the bus unattended in the parking lot. After one passenger called the police department about the problem, a female dispatcher suggested the passengers walk down the street to an auditorium to listen to the Tea Party speakers, killing time while she tried to find a substitute Greyhound bus driver. When the Tea Party event ended, the passengers walked back and sat in the idle bus for five hours before a substitute bus driver finally arrived to take over at the wheel. There is this group called Citizens for Responsibility and Ethics, and Melanie Sloan is the director of the organization. I think the contractor and the bus driver could learn a lot by listening to what Melanie has to say about life."

Frank: "What brings you to this neck of the woods?

Arthur: "I just wanted to stop by and thank you for helping me with my campaign for mayor. In case you haven't heard already, it looks like the election is going to be close."

Frank: "Sandra already called to give me the scoop on what the latest polls. I have already told a few dozen friends and customers to consider voting for you, but the one thing scaring me is that Shelby has so much money behind him. How is that guy going to negotiate large complicated infrastructure contracts for labor workers in this town when he doesn't even know how to address the different trades by their proper names?"

Arthur: "Even if you find Shelby a little appalling for his lack in knowledge and the experience department, there is a real chance this guy may become the next mayor of Rainbow Creek."

Frank: "Shelby tells citizens to vote for him so he can put the diggers back to work. He does not call the trained heavy equipment workers, highway construction workers, or the hardworking restaurateurs by their proper names. He wants to put the people who fill the baskets with curly fries and cook the chicken fingers in oil back to work. The way he sees it, I guess rainbows will envelop this town while his cronies and members of city hall rejoice by dancing in the streets, because they are so happy he is their mayor. They are rejoicing because they know Shelby will take care of them later. Maybe he will promise to buy all the homemakers in our town a Slice-O-Matic with a deluxe chopping blade included. Then they can all chop mountains of onions, carrots, and celery together. Then Rainbow Creek's housewives will make enough soups, stews, and stir-fry to feed the world and life will be perfect."

Arthur: "Your metaphor reminds me of when the first lady told all the school children to eat healthy fruits and vegetables and then a short time later, told an audience of older adults that French fries were her favorite food. Any other good stories you can tell me about your business since the last time I talked to you?"

Frank: "Yesterday morning, a little elderly woman returned a rental car and she said the car started shaking and rattling when she drove it on the highway. We finally found out the cause of the car's bad handling after doing some diagnostic tests and road tests. When the elderly woman looked at the all-weather radial tires on her rental car, she thought they looked low on air. You know how most new radial tires look flat with the bottom sides bulging when a car is sitting still. Without a tire gauge handy, she just decided to fill the tires by herself until they looked like they had enough air pressure. It is amazing she made it back to our shop without the tires exploding, because each tire we tested showed 116 pounds of pressure! If we can find a way to pay her enough, we are thinking about asking the little elderly woman to make a TV commercial with us. If she agrees that viewers would find her story funny, not just laughing at her expense, maybe she would become a local celebrity."

Arthur: "Wow, I guess we can give thanks the woman was not involved in an accident. It sounds like you are staying busy. Are the sales and leasing departments doing OK?"

Frank: "I can't complain. I've been telling people during test drives to vote for you in the election."

Arthur: "Thanks, buddy. Tell me, what do you think about the president's plan to create jobs in this country?"

Frank: "All I can give you is my own perspective from what I see running my business. Do you want the long version or the short version?"

Arthur: "I have time for the long version if you have time to tell me."

Frank: "OK, here goes. When a person walks into my office for the first time to pick out a car, I put a written plan in place. The customer is assured the license plate on the car is current, tires are in good condition, interior lights are operable, windshield wipers work, oil levels are satisfactory, the horn sounds, radio works, seat belts click, defroster melts away access, tank is full of fuel, and the vehicle is clean. We want to know that the driver has enough experience and is at least twenty-one-years-old, able to show proof of insurance, and has a clean record as evidenced by a background check."

Arthur: "In a similar fashion, the Tea Party is trying to force politicians, during their terms in office, to adhere to the safety checks written in the Constitution."

Frank: "When someone rents our car, we ask the driver not to smoke or overuse the mirrors, use turn signals to avoid making sudden lane changes before crossing through an intersection, check left, then right, and left again before proceeding. We ask the driver to pay attention to all traffic signs, watch for low bridges, use off ramps when needed, watch for canopies at banks, and maintain a minimum of four seconds between the driver's car and the person driving in front of them."

Arthur: "I can tell you have given a lot of thought to how the policies made at the White House affect the small business man. Go on."

Frank: "When the driver returns the automobile after finishing the rental term, we check to make sure all passengers are safe, no dents are visible on the exterior, the cargo area is clean, the fuel level in the tank is returned to full, and the tires are aired to the proper pressure. The driver returns the car to the space in the parking lot, in the same shape as the driver first saw it—no leaks, no damage, and no pressing wear and tear. Otherwise, if the driver does not comply or lies to us, the driver will not be allowed another term behind the wheel due to the disrespect of the office. By sticking to these policies, the company grows and the people are safer because of them."

Arthur: "Very good, Frank. You are a flash of genius."

Frank: "If I remember correctly, we nicknamed you 'Flash' in high school for your ability to quickly come up with plays in the huddle to stop the run from the defensive side of the ball."

Arthur: "For thirty years our country has been unable to stop the run on outsourcing of jobs."

Frank: "Yes, we need more qualified workers, but illegal immigrants keep crossing the boarder into America, taking some of the trade jobs. I guess you might call this in-sourcing. Corporations have been outsourcing jobs by moving much of their operations overseas to avoid paying higher taxes. It's time for some 'middle-sourcing,' where politicians and business owners are more interested in bringing back the middle class, instead of lining their own pockets or making deals with and for other countries."

Arthur: "No one ever questions candidates about their reasons for wanting a political career. They never ask them, 'Do you ever think about what's in it for you or do you really have any specific plans about helping people help themselves?' The business leaders smart enough to have already realized this are finding that Americans heavily endorse their policies, products, and services, more than they ever dreamed possible before. I think your company is a perfect example of this way of thinking, providing good customer service and a product that helps people."

Frank: "I totally agree with you, Arthur. Too many business leaders just go along, put their heads down, don't want to rock the boat, shut their mouths, and kind of give up, beaten up by the politics of running their businesses to conform to all the compounding legislative rules placed upon them."

Arthur: "I needed to hear some thoughts from a trusted friend to gain some insight and inspiration. I really enjoyed visiting with you. You are the best; keep in touch."

Frank: "Nice to see you too, Arthur. Good luck in the election."

Throughout the campaign, Susie and Addison were the most technologically skilled workers helping to spread the word about Arthur's stand on issues and the fastest when it came to sending text messages to a large base of friends and then asking these recipients to relay the messages to their base of social media friends. Arthur preferred a more personable, old-fashioned way to connect to voters—making personal calls—because he remembered the days when people got excited when the telephone rang at the house. At one time, not too long ago, it was exciting to answer the telephone and see who was calling the house through the magic little black machine hanging on the wall. Sandra and Susie's generation did not have the same affection for answering the telephone because so often in recent times the callers on the other end were annoying, unsolicited, and unethical telemarketers using unscrupulous ways to try to convince people to divulge personal information or credit card numbers. Like most of the young people from their generation, Sandra and Susie loved to send text messages. Though texting was an effective way to ask people for their vote, Arthur worried that young people were speaking less these days and because of this they were being required to think less and clicking on icons to meet many of their daily needs. He thought social media was stealing away from young people the kind of relationship Arthur and Christine once had. He worried that this system of communication would just get worse every time the next better computer chip became available.

Deciphering journalistic reporting about what others said about him demanded more attention then Arthur previously prepared for, to filter out the angry and shallow opinion mongers to find the truth for the citizens. At one time in American history, newspapers with reporters who checked acquired facts, was the sole source of every town for dependable information, and readers counted on the delivery of them to their doorstep every morning. Now Arthur could relate to how celebrities felt when hounded by the paparazzi, because in a similar way, bloggers were writing anything they wanted to say about him on the Internet websites without anyone checking the sources before the information launched. Arthur became particularly irritated when he read a blog referring to his opponent as a political genius. He called a meeting with his family, friends, and other volunteers to vent his feelings about the blog.

Arthur: "Does anyone think it is political genius when a candidate uses his oratory ability to say things that will sound good to people who have not followed the issues in any detail, regardless of how obviously fraudulent what he says may be to those who have?"

Addison: "Too often the slick technique of shameless audacity ends up becoming a huge political asset, especially when used against the uninformed voter. Sometimes nothing Shelby says is the truth and everything coming out of his mouth is fabricated just to fit his own agenda when talking to a certain group of people."

Arthur: "I don't know if anyone else has noticed, but Shelby shamelessly uses words such as 'fair' and 'balanced' without ever talking about pinning down any details on how to make things better. At the heart of his political game he takes credit for things he never had anything to do with and he puts blame on other people when things he micromanaged didn't work out."

Sandra: "Dad, I remember when you said your involvement with the Tea Party wasn't about working with other people to ruin politics. You said it was about a grassroots effort to try and give a conscience to politicians and keeping them accountable for their words and actions."

Arthur: "Not too long ago, individual rights of certain classes of people were impeded by states' administrative regulation of society. Legislatures declared women unfit to vote, unsuited to practice law, and some of them declared that any woman who worked outside the home, weakened the white race. There was a time when labor unions influenced state legislators in Michigan representing male bartenders to pass a law banning female bartenders. In 1926, a Georgia state law was in effect to disallow black barbers from cutting the hair of white women. In 1935, Jim Crow laws forbade blacks and whites to fish together. As recently as 1965, politicians could not spend state money in Louisiana on black schools. Though America's politics today still have a long way to go, I am glad my daughters did not live back then during any of those times. And I'm glad I have the women around me that I do to help me with this campaign."

Sandra: "Tell me more about the Jim Crow laws."

Arthur: "Between the years 1880 and 1960, there was legislation on the books now called the Jim Crow laws. The laws promoted "separate but equal" rules for blacks and whites. How can anyone be separate and equal at the same time? These laws were clearly favorable to whites, and always gave them privilege over blacks. Richard Wright, a black man, told us of his story when he applied for his first job over three-quarters of a century ago. He stood up straight and said "yes, sir" and "no, sir." Obviously, he could not be himself back then. After a short while on the job, bosses fired him for something he did not do and they gave him just one minute to leave the factory. When he told his parents, they told him that he must never again attempt to exceed his boundaries. Racism caused history and politics to move slowly back then. Back then, there was not all this soap-on-a-rope or potpourri either."

Sandra: "So are you are saying racism exists to a much lesser degree today, than it did for a very long time, and history will move slower if we go back to racist practices and do not resolve all our political issues in fair ways?"

Arthur: "Yes, I think that is a good assessment."

Working to help her father with the campaign, Sandra had been giving more thought to political issues in the past several months than she had the previous part of her entire life. She was becoming more aware than most young girls were her age of the issues important to the citizens in Rainbow Creek. She was starting to understand that local business owners could not make long-term plans based on so many rules and regulations made by politicians in Washington thousands of miles away. She understood that unemployment was a problem, not because of racism but mostly because corporations decided to move jobs and plants overseas due to so many restrictions and high corporate tax rates in the United States. She learned from her father that small businesses and private sector jobs bring in cash, while taxpayers' dollars generally considered on the spending side of administrative budgets paid for government jobs.

Sandra: "Dad, do you think there is still a formidable level of racism in American politics today?"

Arthur: "Sweetheart, I'll give you that there are still racist bigots out there and it goes both ways, but to say that people are protesting our president because he is black is obscene and racist in its own right. Were people protesting George Bush because he was white? Why can't citizens criticize our current president as all the ones before him were? People are protesting mainly because of the socialist agenda and they want all the spending slowed, especially the wasteful spending. Your generation will be living under a mountain of debt."

Sandra: "I've learned that one of the main focuses of the Tea Party Patriots is that they don't want to continue spending when the government doesn't have enough money to pay for the programs we already have on the books."

Arthur: "Your Uncle Johnny believed that US households paying no taxes needed to pay something to help. He didn't think it was fair for any family to be protected by our military for free. He thought every family, especially ones with no member in the family serving, should have to pay some amount of taxes to support the military. To him, too many people living in the US, with no skin in the game, as they say, reap benefits, but never pay for anything. This really bothered your Uncle Johnny."

Sandra: "I have to agree with him. I sure miss Uncle Johnny."

Arthur: "There is a tendency of late for conservatives to portray anything the government does that they don't like as socialism. On the other side, it has become the standard shield for liberals to claim 'racism' anytime someone opposes a black politician, with their hope being that others will believe them and automatically discredit the opposition or that opposition will back away for fear of someone branding them a racist. It's absurd and inaccurate to imply that race is the common motivator behind disagreement amongst voters."

Sandra: "To me slanderous lies like these are far worse than the bigotry people try to portray."

Arthur: "I agree. If a person can't win an argument based on facts, then it is time to abandon the fight, instead of continuing on and looking like a deceitful fool afraid of an honest debate."

Sandra: "Children don't have a voice. They are too young to vote. All this government spending is unsustainable and irresponsible. The impulses of our politicians are out of control."

Arthur: "Your generation has to start asking the important questions."

Sandra: "People have the choice to vote for the politicians they want in power who will do the most to least offend them."

Arthur: "Confucius is credited with saying 'He who takes offense when none is intended is a fool. He who takes offense when offense is intended is a bigger fool,' but I think I actually like your last comment better, Sandra. You are a smart girl."

Sandra: "Well, I do love to read, but I'm not sure I'm ready for comparisons between Confucius and me, yet. I would like to see more done in schools where students are lagging behind in reading skills and they are not learning the technology to prepare them for the modern-day job market. I do understand some parents are finally jumping on this bandwagon, and a few states have actually passed 'Parent Trigger Laws' to fight for these ideas."

Arthur: "Your grandmother would have been proud of your support of children and their reading skills."

Addison: "Instead of the back-and-forth slander that insults our intelligence, it would be nice if we could read about ideas from skilled politicians, instead of listening to attack ads. Whom can we believe anyway? Those ugly, slanderous postcards that arrive in the mailbox at election time point out terrible things that candidates supposedly did or said, empty rhetoric that has been heard before."

Sandra: "Dad, a harmless Twitter feed is fun for anybody. Do you think I could send one last tweet about how you struggle every time you have to do a dietary cleanse to prepare for your colonoscopy exam?"

Arthur: "If you did that, I bet you would have to use spell-check to tweet the word diarrhea."

Addison: "Sandra, maybe you could also tweet how uptight your Dad looks in his plaid shirt, orange pants, and tortoise-shell reading glasses. I guess we are lucky he doesn't smoke a corn-cob pipe."

Arthur: "The rims of my eyeglasses might be a little wide, but I have never worn orange pants in my life. The pants I'm wearing are rust brown."

Sandra: "Is that what you call it? I didn't hear any rebuttal about your plaid shirt?"

Arthur: "Are you two women trying to warp my expectations and make me feel self-conscious? Maybe if I ordered a bobble head of me with a built-in wire-tapping device, I could listen to what both of you say about me when I'm not here."

Addison: "You know we are just trying to have a little fun."

Arthur: "I think it is crunch time and we need to tell everybody we talk to that they should vote for the person whom they think shows true passion, not the person who has been groomed in politics his whole life. Vote for the person who truly has ideas on how to make our community better, not the person with limited ingenuity who has never managed a business."

With just eleven days to go before the election, in one last big push to get the word out to try to secure more votes, Sandra, Addison, Frank, Justin, and even Jane and Stuart made lots of phone calls and mailed boxes full of flyers promoting Arthur's promise to work toward Jobs Creation. Sandra, who took the death of her Uncle Johnny particularly hard, barely left her condominium on most days, except to help with the campaign for a couple of hours each afternoon, because she needed time alone to mourn. During those difficult days, she created a small memorial on top of an end table in her bedroom to remember him. The memorial included old photos of Johnny playing his guitar, a gold-plated cross Johnny gave her, a holy card from the funeral parlor, a laminated copy of the obituary, and a few funny Hallmark cards Johnny sent to her on her birthday over the years and on other occasions for no reason at all. Whenever Sandra walked in to Arthur's house and saw the rest of her family and friends making phone calls, folding flyers, adhering stamps, and wetting envelopes, they all greeted her with hugs and kisses. The continuation of working on the campaign helped her through her grief, and a decision by the committee let her place campaign signs in yards where homeowners gave approval to do so. Sandra felt connected to her Uncle Johnny by doing this because many of these same yards she placed signs in were yards he mowed or landscaped when he was still alive and working his business.

All his life, Arthur tried, but most of the time he thought he could have done better too. He was his own worst critic. His Little League team came in second place five years in a row. His daughter's softball and basketball teams came in second place each year he coached. He was second in regional sales when he worked as a manufacturer's rep for a firm based in New York. He was the second born son in the Hobson family. Making a run for the mayoral seat, he worried that he might come in second place in the election when first place is the only place that matters.

Working hard right down to the end, Arthur gave his last speech before the election. He spoke at his home base at the community center, with Kay Applebaum, Frank, Gary, Larry, Sandra, Susie, Justin, Addison, Karen, Victor, Jane, Stuart, members of the Rainbow Creek Chamber of Commerce, and many other friends and acquaintances Arthur met during his life and on the campaign trail in the audience.

I think job creation should be the main focus for the next mayor of this town. I just want to give an example of why I think the current policies of shared politics aren't working in this town and many other places in this country. Here is a good example of how men from three different camps are reacting to the current policies of shared politics in this country today.

The first man holds two full-time jobs because he is ambitious and wants to support his family. He takes college classes at night to improve his marketable job skills and personal self-worth. His gross annual salary is between $50,000 and $70,000.

The second man is content working one job. He is single and makes enough money to pay his bills and have a little left to pay the gas to put in his small motorboat, so he can spend some time on the lake on weekends during the summer. His gross annual salary is between $30,000 and $50,000.

The third man has no ambition, does not hold a job, and does not look for work. Though he is healthy enough to work, he depends on welfare, unemployment checks, food stamps, discounts on his utility bills, government-sponsored health care, handouts from local churches, donations from charities, and free food from food pantries. He makes no effort to seek better skills through education or job training, and the only effort he exhibits is to find more entitlement programs.

Though these examples are simplified and every person's situation is different, most of us fit one category or the other to a certain degree. A small percentage of the population considered the wealthy and another segment of sick people are far beyond fitting into these three categories. Under shared politics, policies are legislated to level the playing field. The man working two jobs pays higher taxes. The man in the middle might pay higher property taxes while his wages are frozen. For the third man, the government gives an extension of his unemployment benefits, a cost-of-living raise on his food stamps, and a larger discount on his utility bills. All these policies the government administers under a guise of democratic, fair, and balanced labels. Is it fair to keep taking away from men who give their best effort, so we even the so-called playing field for men who do nothing? Middle-class workers have not had a raise in thirty years. I will do everything I can to put people to work. Job creation will be my focus. Please hop on the 'Hobson bandwagon' and vote for me at the polls. Thank you for your time.

Arthur lived an honest life and he was optimistic for the middle class, who always seemed treated as second class by the aristocrats. Just one time before he died, he hoped he would feel what is was like to be the best at something, but if not, he thought, he still had his friendship with his pretty assistant Addison, who was helpful in redirecting his disappointments, like a magician presents his legerdemain to misdirect the attention of the audience.

It was hard not to notice all the support from the gay community that poured out first to Johnny when he was sick and now to Arthur as Election Day neared. Food, sympathy cards, flowers, supplies, and gifts flowed in, delivered to the front door of the house on Hill View Avenue. Though Johnny was not gay, the gay community was excessively familiar with drug abuse, AIDS, and all the suffering involved with both diseases. A man named Roberto, who managed a regional Goodwill store in California, flew in overnight an ambitious supply of nearly new towels and smaller-sized shirts and pants in Johnny's memory, so Christian Hospital outpatients with AIDS would have clothing that fit after their weight loss. Roberto had a heart the size of a lion and over the years, he had helped thousands of men and women with health issues, never asking for anything in return and making donations to AIDS patients his life's work. Whenever government programs became unwieldy or life zapped the spirit and drive out of its citizens, Johnny's family and friends found it nice to know that there are individuals like Roberto to pick up some of the slack in places like Rainbow Creek.

Never in the history of the United States has corruption been so rampant in government. The government needs more leaders who are mindful of how hard it is to earn a living, and how precious our tax dollars are to voters. Voters want leaders who will spend the dollars flowing in wisely and the wishes of citizens treated with respect. Arthur definitely understood this reality. He was afraid that politics no longer equated to a better life because too often failure and corruption by leaders was lessening the chances of success. Something is wrong when a program that historically has small problems over a long period, suddenly has big problems over a short period. Arthur could not understand why the public would want to reelect any federal officials who let the national debt double in a matter of just a few years. He did everything he could to try to convince voters to vote for him, so that Rainbow Creek could operate as a successful business with an honest balance sheet and at least a small surplus of money to invest in the community at the end of each year. He was sure people did not do enough to voice their opinions and tell all politicians that voters are tired of this "take it or leave it" politics that just did not make sense.

Addison, Sandra, and Arthur gathered in the privacy of the house on Hill View Avenue on the evening of the election to watch the results come in on television. Susie was back at college, but she called her dad on her cell phone every two hours for the latest updates.

Addison: "The votes are very close and it looks like this election will go down to the wire. I know you, Arthur, and you don't worry about your own level of individual prominence about what you have achieved."

Arthur: "Well, whatever the outcome, I only worry about if the individuals I have tried to help become more ambitious and better people."

Addison: "When we see other candidates acting in an abusive, arrogant, or demeaning manner toward their opponent, their behavior almost always is a symptom of their fear of losing. But sometimes by putting someone else down to feel good about themselves, they win anyway."

Arthur: "It is important to think about the metric by which your life will be judged by God, and make a conscious decision to live every day treating others as you would like to be treated yourself, so that your life will be judged a success."

Sandra: "I think everyone on the campaign staff has become a better person from working together for this cause. We have learned humility from each other."

Arthur: "Generally you learn humility only if you feel really good about yourself and want to help someone else meet a goal or fight for a cause."

Addison: "Your opponent 'Shady Shelby' never did present a plan for a budget, and when you talked about specific ideas to address economic problems, more money for education and less money for entitlement programs, he shot down everything you said in hopes you would pay a terrible political price."

Arthur: "Addison, hopefully voters will understand that our side is trying to find solutions to our problems and our opponent is more interested in just getting elected. All my life I have been chasing my dreams. Win or lose, I guess I accomplished my biggest dream after all. I ended up with you. Maybe this is our moment. Thank you for helping me during this wonderful adventure," he said. Tears rolled down both sides of Addison's face.

Arthur had this long backward perspective of "where he had been and what he had done." He now knew what he could let go of and what needed his attention. He was ready for the third act in his life, the spiritual growth, emotional growth, and becoming wiser about the bigger picture whether he became mayor or not. He was now who he was and it was probably too late for any more serious life reviews or major changes in his beliefs. He lived a life experiencing and learning the truth about jealousy, anger, rejection, survival, success, love, competition, confidence, self-reliance, sorrow, pain, heartbreak, failure, curiosity, and bad and good choices. To him all of these sensitivities are God's ways of manifesting the truth about things.

By midnight, with all but 1 percent of the votes counted, Arthur lost the election in a very close race, receiving 48 percent of the ballots cast. Despite the outcome, despite the fact that his opponent spent ten times the amount of money as he did on the campaign, everyone who voted for Arthur or worked on his campaign knew he was a winner. Fate can be a strange thing. If this was Arthur's fate, he accepted it and he did not whine about his loss, because he knew people who give their best effort for many reasons do not always reap the rewards. Though it would have been very cool for Arthur to be the mayor, running around town with a nice title, receiving free tickets to sporting events and concerts, never paying for meals at local restaurants, a good salary and a furnished luxury car, the high-profile job and the benefits went to Irvin Shelby. Now Arthur did not have to worry about people blaming him for problems in the schools or complaining about problems at the police department, of which mayors have little control. Because more of the citizens of Rainbow Creek were genuinely worried about the future of their town, he hoped the new mayor and other officials would start finding solutions rather than inventing slogans, while residents held them to more accountable.

Immediately following the final election results, Arthur recognized that he would no longer have to worry about mustering enough energy to stay fully involved in the daily grind of politics, and he now had more time to spend with Addison and his two daughters. He did still worry that many times only wealthy people and popular celebrities seem allowed the platform to voice their opinions, even when their words are not well thought out and express no sense of forward movement. Though Arthur was a born leader, born leaders do not win all of the time. Though Arthur thought he needed the political world, the truth was the world needed more people like him, but most people just did not know it yet. He would continue to work at the community center and help people that way. Without the burden of politics, he realized he may be able to help even more people than he could have as mayor.

Though he lost the election, Arthur received hundreds of letters from voters expressing their disappointment with the outcome. One elderly black woman named Ellie Washington wrote Arthur saying, "I followed your campaign and you opened my eyes to some of the issues facing all people in our town. I did not agree with everything you said, but if we are supposed to be prospering in the richest country in the world, it is time for all American citizens to do their part so we can continue to afford to live here. If all we do is take away money from one group of people and give it to another group, how is America going to prosper and grow? I pray for you. Please let '*Jesus take the wheel*' just like Carrie Underwood sings." Arthur answered Ms. Ellie's letter, saying, "Thank you for your thoughtful letter of concern. Like the lyrics from the Bob Dylan song, I too am tired of all the "Blowing in the Wind" and due to the advice from Fleetwood Mac, I will "Never Stop Thinking about Tomorrow" because everyone of us must remain a "Free Bird," but not only because Lynyrd Skynyrd told us this back in the 70's. So often it feels like we are, "Starting All Over Again" (Petula Clark), but maybe one of these days we will "Get it Right the First Time" (Louisianna's LeRoux). Tea Party Patriots want more exploration of alternatives that will address our problems. Legislation with too much complexity is impossible to enforce honestly. You do not have to agree with everything the Tea Party stands for, but holding out for something better, something that will help balance our budget and take hold of the national deficit is a good thing for everybody. Try bringing your friends and joining some of the house parties Patriots across America are holding to show others there is a choice between individual freedom and government takeover that reshuffles our money and our lives. Our leaders need to stop apologizing for Americans and start believing in people and free markets. History has shown that if you give Americans the facts, they can be depended on to meet any national crisis."

Even though he lost his bid for mayor, the experience made Arthur realize that he reached people he never would have without the campaign. Women like Ms. Ellie and Addison taught him he could joke around to have a little fun, yet still be serious about his politics. He was sure he did not want to live in a country where the leaders were so serious they wanted the government to own everything, but nothing works.

Frank Lambert and Gary Bordeaux were disappointed their friend lost the election. Both men knew Arthur would be feeling a little down after spending so much time and energy working toward something he wanted so badly, but was unable to attain in the end. Frank and Gary drove to Arthur's home in hopes of cheering him up some.

Frank: "How are you doing, pal?"

Gary: "Are you OK, Arthur?"

Arthur: "Maybe it's a good thing I lost the election. My colon has been acting up lately. Can you guys imagine how the local press would've teased me about my extra bathroom breaks if I had won?"

Gary: "Don't be ridiculous, man. Even if they would've teased you, you are still the man, Mr. Almost Bathroom-Break-Dancing Mayor."

Arthur: "Thanks a lot. I'm not sure I like that inference. There was a senator who spent his break time in the men's room."

Gary: "Stop the confusion, that's not what I meant at all."

Arthur: "After everything my family has gone through these past couple of years—the divorce, my brother dying, and me loosing the election—I just hope my two daughters don't start thinking hard work doesn't pay off."

Frank: "There's no chance of that happening. Your daughters already know what a great dad they have and they know they are lucky to have you as their father. Everybody goes through tough times at some point in their lives."

Arthur: "Well, its times like these when a guy finds out who his real friends are, this is for sure. I do appreciate the two of you coming over, and though I have been sad lately about Johnny and disappointed in losing the election, I will be OK. Gary, give me one of your baseball analogies to explain what's happening in my life."

Gary: "Its like Frank said, you're a great father, and you're a great friend to Frank and me too. You are just living through a string of a few bad days. It is similar to a good ballplayer that just has a couple of bad games during the course of a season. Remember Milton Bradley? He was an above-average outfielder who played for the Chicago Cubs. Maybe the worst inning of defensive play in the history of baseball occurred on Friday, June 12, 2009. It may as well have been Friday the 13th. Bradley had his worst day in the outfield ever. While the generous scorer only gave him one error in the game, Bradley could have been responsible for a couple more. Early in the game, Bradley was caught napping on the bases and was called out by the umpire for the base-running blunder, picked off at first base. This was just the beginning of a bunch of mental mistakes. The ball always seems to find the player whose head is not in the game. In the next inning, he misjudged a fly ball he lost in the bright sun of a cloudless sky in this afternoon game at Wrigley Field. The ball fell several feet in front of him. Things were not going well for Bradley, but the play later in the game is the one that will go down in infamy for baseball fans. In the top of the eighth inning, with runners on first and third, and just one out, all-star Minnesota Twins catcher Joe Mauer hit a routine fly ball to Bradley, who made the catch. Pleased that he caught this fly ball, he flashed a Heisman trophy–type pose for the jeering crowd for a few seconds before throwing the ball into the outfield stands. He did this not realizing that making the catch meant that there were now only two outs. All the base runners scored. One lucky fan may have been happy to receive the souvenir baseball, but the other thousands of fans packing the Wrigley seats were incensed over the costly error. Cubs manager Lou Piniella was not happy either, because he knew this type of game could make the wrong kind of a legend. The Minnesota Twins went on to defeat the Chicago Cubs 7–4."

Arthur: "Oh no! Are you saying my life is going in the same direction as the Chicago Cubs?"

Gary: "No, I'm just saying if people wanted positive comments all the time instead of facing reality, what would be the incentive to keep listening to the game and keep pulling for a guy. I do not like people who are always happy, warm, and fuzzy, and who walk around thinking a rainbow encompasses their head. Life is not always that way. If you were like that all the time, I would think the zombies and the aliens took control of your mind and body. Johnny never sang about make believe zombies or aliens; he faced real life guerrilla tactics of war used by the enemy against him and the other American boots-on-the-ground, when he served in Vietnam."

Arthur: "Gary, thank you for your kind words. I always admired Johnny for his service to our country. He was one of the lucky ones to come home from Vietnam. What stuck with me the most about Johnny, after he returned home from Vietnam—he still bore so much of the effects from the war. Many of the young men drafted into the war and forced to make decisions about how to stay alive were at the same time trying to figure out who the hell they were as adults. This is as true now in Iraq and Afghanistan as it was in Vietnam."

12

Johnny's Notes Listening
to Ms. Staley

Low-life drug dealers charge teenagers double the price when they see them drive up in their parents' car. Male and female teenagers pay for their thousand-dollar-a-week habit by selling other drugs, burglarizing homes and cars, and even stealing from their own relatives' homes. A costly struggle against teenagers hooked on heroin rages in comfortable homes in suburban neighborhoods everywhere, and it seems everyone inside the homes is losing. Parents try to keep money and valuables, anything that may trade for heroin, on lockdown. One week the user is in court facing felony possession charges and the next week they are out on the streets using again. It is a war with no victory in sight.

A snapshot of heroin abuse and the story that surrounds it can be found in all socio-economic conditions, including middle-class municipalities where streets are lined with trees, bicycles lay idle on the front lawns, and American flags flap in the breeze. More and more of the young adults from these same neighborhoods are getting locked up for nonviolent drug offenses, while dangerous drug-dealing gangs are hemming in against our police force. Though the prison terms get drug offenders off the street, the stigma diminishes their lives and the billions of taxpayers' dollars spent on legal expenses could have been used for productive purposes.

Some of the young people are going to attend college and some are going to end up in prison. The taxpayers will help support all of them, but a college-educated worker will help stir the economy, while a prisoner sitting idle in a cell drains our financial system with no guarantees in the future.

Dangerous forms of organized and sometimes deadly gang activity have permeated our country to the point that no town is immune. If we want a prosperous economy, we have to rid our streets of drug trafficking. The weapons and tactics used to distribute drugs are of the highest order, and the bloodshed is spilling over into our neighborhoods. Administrators of hospitals and their doctors communicate an alarming spike in heroin overdose deaths. Parents, drug counselors, police, and the courts are overburdened with heroin drug cases, once deemed an obscure activity of longtime addicts in inner cities. Families are being destroyed all across America, the mayhem causing them to lose their homes and test their limits.

Because of the evils of drug addiction, items around the house disappear. Checks are missing from the checkbook. The need for money to pay for the addiction makes anything fair game. Coin collections, jewelry, antiques, and tools disappear from the house, Family heirlooms are taken to a pawn shop. But the addict never gets fair value trading these items, always settling for whatever they are offered to get enough cash for the next fix. Addicts show no morals or remorse because the drugs take over their ability to think rationally. They'll sell anything just to get the cash to buy more drugs.

Enablers are not responsible for an alcoholic's drinking problem or an addict's drug problem. But if enablers are not educated or aware of the particulars of the disease, their actions can delay solutions to overcoming the problem. The enabler is often a spouse, parent, best friend, or boyfriend or girlfriend of the chemically dependent person. It is the person who is closest and most depended on by the dependent person. As the illness grows, so does the involvement of the enabler, and the problem is exacerbated. With the increase of the illness comes the increased repression of the feelings of both the dependent and the enabler. The enabler in the family tries to take on a role of control instead of sharing responsibilities. As the dependent person increasingly loses the respect he craves, he resists and uses or drinks more, the enabler making more choices to compensate for the dependent person's lack of power.

There are patients at this drug treatment facility who have been using for thirty days and some who have been using for thirty years. An overdose can happen anywhere along the line. In general, drug users usually do not live very long. It does not help when a drug user relies on a scapegoat in the family to bear the blame of past mistakes. Not wanting to work as hard as other family members to achieve success do, often the scapegoat and drug user pull away from the family and look for satisfaction elsewhere. Because of all the anger and repressed guilt both the scapegoat and drug user feel, their fast and destructive ways draw lots of attention. Often, it is in refusing to join in family gatherings, unable to hold a steady job, frequent moving, keeping drugs and alcohol handy in the house, or just being stubborn and withdrawn. The scapegoat provides distraction from relatives and provides protection for the drug user who is dependent on the substance of choice. Instead of giving the dependent money to bail them out from problems, letting the dependent face their own financial mess is usually a better solution. Money or a place to stay for a couple of days just reinvigorates the addict and prolongs the agony of everyone involved, because it gives the addict another out, instead of dealing with the consequences or spending time in rehabilitation. Unfortunately, some dependents stay in the spiral until it is too late; they are dead. Because early death is the consequence of this spiral, each individual at this rehab center needs to stop pointing the finger, stop the blame game, and take responsibility for their own actions.

Substance abusers make great use of the "divide and conquer" strategy, manipulating family members by telling one thing to one person, something else to another. They may be honest with one family member about one thing and honest about another thing to someone else, but no one family member will know everything. The family starts to feel like a web tangled up in lies and half-truths. Credit cards go missing, friends and family members are owed money, and possessions are sold at the pawnshop.

From 1960 through 1980, most of the heroin reaching the United States originated from the Golden Triangle region of Southeast Asia, which included regions of Burma, Thailand, and Laos. This is why some of our Vietnam vets came home with a drug problem. From 1970 to 1990, the major heroin supply came from opium poppies grown in Mexico. Changes in the political climate of the different regions producing the opium poppy have shifted the main supply source to Afghanistan. Drug lords in Afghanistan control heroin trucked through dangerous routes to Iran and Turkey, before it ships to ports and cities in Europe and North America. Opium is the number one cash crop in Afghanistan, financing the Taliban. This part of the world is a quick study on the connection amongst illegal drugs, illiteracy, corruption, and the force for which these perplexing matters cause despair for people. However, much of the heroin trafficked today in the United States still arrives trucked in over the Mexican border or flown in by private airplanes. Just a few years ago, much of the drug supply was trucked in from Tijuana into California. Then it moved through Ciudad Juarez, Mexico, into Arizona. With more and more pressure in Southern California and the staunch fight for immigration reform in Arizona, a large percentage of the drug supply shifted east, with Laredo, Texas, and Atlanta, Georgia, as hot spots.

Street drugs are rarely pure. Fifty years ago, very little of a heroin mixture was heroin. Most of the content of a heroin bag back then contained powdered milk, powdered sugar, or ground up granules from the bark of a cinchona tree. The cinchona is a readily available tropical tree, and when the bark is ground, the resulting bitter-tasting white dust, called quinine, mixes well with heroin. In 1965, the average bag contained only 4 percent heroin content. Criminals have always used third-world techniques to extract the essential opium from the poppy plant. A handmade wooden screening contrivance, filthy wire instruments, unregulated chemicals, dirty water, and unlabeled powders step down the process to the finished product.

The strength of heroin doses over the past decade has progressively become more deadly. In towns and cities across America, doses average between 60 and 70 percent heroin. At these elevated levels, daily use over a two-week period is sufficient time for a pusher to hook a new customer into becoming physically dependent on heroin. Once this acquisition phase is accomplished, the heroin addict is then compelled to continue taking the drug for its euphoria effects. It soon becomes abundantly clear to the addict that severe withdrawal takes place when trying to stop the drug.

In one instance, drug lords looking for an addict who crossed them, inadvertently went to the wrong house and killed thirteen people and injured sixteen, all attending a teenager's birthday party in a small Mexican town on the border. Two dozen gunmen in seven vehicles opened fire on one house. By mistake, they went to the wrong house. However, in the aftermath, two adults and eleven teenagers were dead.

American soldiers travel halfway around the world to solve century-old problems, but our government does little to understand ways to solve a drug crisis crippling our country and our neighbor to the south. The US should encourage a regional balance of power with Canada and Mexico. Before this can happen, government must diminish the illegal drug industry and enforce the laws of our country. The success of North America depends on an honest flow of commerce and trade. As the dominant power, the United States must take the lead in enforcing the laws of the region. Citizens need to individually act responsibly and help manage the power, by refusing to buy or use street drugs. If the public chooses to act oblivious to our power, then our country will continue to feel like a herd of buffalo is trampling over our economy and everything else in the way. People living in safe environments accomplish extraordinary things. A safe border, void of lurking dangers created by drug cartels, would mean more partnerships with large businesses willing to expand in Mexico. Too many families left behind continue to have to deal with the heartache.

The talented author, the businessperson, the professional athlete, the movie star, the man across the street, the girl next door, the stay-at-home mom, the college student, and the teenager are all at risk for a dependent life of substance abuse. The more problems a person has in other parts of his or her life, the more susceptible this person is to substance abuse. With a little help and a lot of awareness, a change of course is possible and a plan of action can manifest itself before it is too late. The number of deaths or the degree of violence isn't a real indicator of who is winning the drug war, because drug traffickers, law enforcement officials, and innocent people are dying. Many blame Americans, because a large portion of the illegal drugs grown and manufactured elsewhere ship across the border into the US for consumption.

You feel like a "star" when you abuse drugs or get drunk, but the other people in your life take a backseat. Doing drugs gives a person a false sense of control of their circumstances. Success and confidence stems from achievement, not from getting high. By doing drugs, you are just throwing away your money, and most of you have plenty of experience at that. Whether you agree with me or not, that roughly one in six Americans have a problem with drugs and alcohol, we need to help our country prosper again. Do you want to be part of the problem or part of the solution? While so many people are living idle lives and watching the planet on the verge of destruction, wouldn't it be better to stay sober and help make the world a better place, instead of just making it through another day with drugs and alcohol? You will find out you are more alive living the life of a teetotaler than living the life of an addict or drunk. We cannot fix all the world's problems, but we can start by doing a better job of governing our own lives. If we do this, maybe the people in power will start to realize that we understand our own problems better than someone from the outside does.

What we believe and how we feel effects all the choices we make on a daily basis. Young people see what is on the surface, without the years of experience growing older and watching every facet of their lives go through expansion. What we once heard the world was like when we were young transforms to something completely different when we are older. When we are young, an hour seems like an eternity, but when we are old, an eternity seems only an hour away. Young people are never preoccupied with the uncertain future, only old people are. Once a person reaches a certain age, they understand the desire for security, no longer wanting to waste their time, and occasionally thinking about their own mortality.

Walking in a nearby park, strolling along a beach, and taking a hike in the mountains are just a few ways to connect to the world around us. Smelling the air when driving by a bakery, finding a twenty-dollar bill on a parking lot, reading a handwritten letter sent from a friend the old-fashioned way, or just lying in bed listening to the raindrops hit the roof are some of the little things in life worth taking time to appreciate. Small discoveries remind us that life is worth living and we should embrace the journey.

It is wrong when a program makes things so easy that there is no reason to do anything and if you try to do better, those same programs punish you by taking the benefits away. It is wrong for politicians to preach and sponsor dependency instead of encouraging independency. If promising more social welfare programs gets a politician elected, wouldn't that politician benefit by gaining votes from growing numbers of people without jobs, people working for companies receiving bailout help, and increasing numbers of substance abusers?

On your deathbed, you will try to open your eyes to look around, but it will be no use. You will begin to wonder what is next. Your entire life will flash before your eyes. Have you done enough to help make the planet better than you found it? Did you only take what you earned in life? Do we want our legacy characterized by the greatness of our mistakes or by the greatness of our achievements? We must pay attention; it is compli-cated, but it is all connected.

Ms. Staley's talks made a big impression on Johnny. Johnny knew all the names for the finished products of his drug of choice: horse, smack, big H, black tar, caballo, and eight ball. His drug abuse sank to a depth of searching for the eight ball version laced with crack cocaine. He supplemented his drug addiction by drinking at taverns because he felt like his music career was a failure, but he failed even more because of his addictions. He now understood there would be nothing worth knowing about him if he continued spending the rest of his life high and drunk.

13

Arthur's Health Care Letter
to the President

Dear Mr. President,

Al Gore once tried to tell Americans that he invented the Internet. It is time for politicians to stop all the lies and slander. It is disappointing when you see a biased individual campaigning for legislation, but he or she is talking about just one facet of an issue, thus presenting a slanted view of it. A hidden agenda with a conflict of interest exists when all the facts are not presented and arbitrary numbers are used to twist the outcome. It would be better if politicians and their campaign members presented all the facts and just let voters decide the issues. Our leaders spend too much time on rhetoric and not enough time on solutions, followed by sneaky ways to slip legislation through the House and the Senate. Once the health care reform bill was presented in writing, the senators and representatives did not have time to read the 4,000 pages of legislation before voting day. The bill was passed by a partisan Democratic support on your advice and as a favor to you. Any bill that is 4,000 pages ling is cheating the public.

Nancy Pelosi's "victory" speech when the health care bill passed was distressing. Instead of speaking to the possibility of dialogue to fix what is wrong with one of the most debated bills in history, she threw the win in the faces of the members of the Tea Party by carrying an oversized gavel into a meeting with Senate and House members. Citizens would have preferred to have been informed as to what exactly was in the bill, more of the details of 'change.' Citizens want their politicians to work together.

After closed meetings, ignored requests, and insulting attacks, Democrats and Republicans seem incapable of compromising or problem-solving any important issues, causing a polarized political system. This looks really bad when we have American soldiers losing their lives in Iraq and Afghanistan and twenty-three million people at home are unemployed. You tried to convince American families earning less than $100,000 a year that they can have health *care that costs 50% less than Canadians and Germans pay, without anyone paying a dime in additional health care insurance premiums. In reality, we both know this statement is a pipe dream.*

You reported during your national address to the people in the early spring of 2010, "Health care is expected to add $10 trillion to the national debt spread out over the next decade." Almost no one questions that the impact of health care will drastically affect the future of young people. They will be the ones footing the bill.

Despite the "soak-the-rich" rhetoric of your administration, the tax burden for expanding coverage of health insurance, as it does with everything else, will fall where it always does, on the middle-class taxpayers, because they are the ones who work to earn the money. Hardworking people who pay the majority of the taxes in this country are tired of providing a never-ending supply of cash and free services to the increasing hordes of slackers, those who manipulate the government system by taking help, sometimes from several welfare programs at the same time, for selfish reasons, when they really could be self-sufficient.

Health care reform is seeing a lot of changes. And with most government changes, there are always added expenses. One thing for sure, we must insist that bureaucrats are not in charge of medical decisions rather than doctors. Americans deserve the best efforts of politicians to achieve the best health care reform that meets their needs; and it is time more is done for the middle class. In nearly all of your changes, the middle class has taken it on the chin and in the pocketbook.

Readers of the stimulus and health care reform packages have to get through 600 pages before they can start to realize the concept of rationing and the appointing of a national coordinator to oversee decisions made by doctors and physicians. Doctors and physicians that don't enlist in the new government health care reform system and abide by the rules are subject to receiving fines. Our country might see an abnormally high number of doctors deciding to retire early in 2013, when many changes go into effect. Many doctors feel that rationing care is the change we will get from your health care plan. With so many people who aren't paying insurance premiums added to the health system, doctors say this is the only possible outcome.

The White House let another big promise go unfulfilled, a promise made during the campaign, to let CSPAN cameras film negotiations of the healthcare bill. Your administration backed down with no explanation to the people. However, the reason probably stemmed from the lack of support from Republicans because most reports say their ideas were nixed from the proposal. Of the main Republican proposals, only one made it into the final bill—to increase payments to primary physicians under Medicaid. It is arguable that you could have foreseen the outcome and you were making a quick public-relations decision to keep arguments out of sight from the people. Democrats will have a couple more years to mend bridges if they choose, before and if the changes go into effect. Tea Party Patriots are saying many of your reforms are un-Constitutional.

The Patient Protection and Affordable Care Act represents a new frontier for people who do not have health insurance coverage. The bill will increase insurance premiums, especially for the young and healthy. It would have to without any additional taxes and a large increase in people needing coverage and not dealing with how to handle malpractice yet. If government runs health care instead of insurance companies, then taxpayers pay for malpractice instead of insurance companies. During your campaign, Mr. President, you made a bold statement about increasing health insurance premiums. You announced, during a March 2010 press conference to a television audience, you would give federal authorities the power to block unreasonable rate hikes. Yet when Democrats presented the final body of work for their health care plan, this power to block was no where to be found. There is the worry that government will have too much control of other aspects, such as denial of coverage for preexisting conditions, raised taxes, more poverty, and more people with a higher dependence on government. In Canada, the average wait for surgery or treatment by a specialist is eighteen weeks. This wait increases the patient's risk of death or the risk that his or her injuries become irreparable. Do we really want a public plan that decreases the quality of care for everyone?

Basically, working Americans will pay for health care for those who don't have coverage, households whose members don't work, are retired, or already receive other income benefits from the government. The public plan for health care is a proposal that seeks to prevent denial of care. Under every instance, insurance companies would no longer be able to deny coverage on the basis of annual and lifetime limits on coverage. The public plan does not place any age limits on receiving care, although rumors are floating around to the contrary.

Today, on average, because of a high unemployment rate and a shifting of an older work-force into retirement, people are living longer and Medicare and Medicaid have fewer workers paying into the system. With more baby boomers reaching retirement age, more benefits will have to be paid out. Back in the day when the Social Security system was established, retirees received their checks in the mail, walked into a bank full of tellers, and drove their Chevrolet or Ford to a mom-and-pop store to purchase American-made products from salespeople who made commissions and paid payroll taxes. Today, people drive their foreign cars through the drive-through at the bank to cash their check, then motor on to Walmart to buy items produced overseas by workers who contribute nothing to Social Security. Past reforms have sent American jobs overseas, caused corporations to lay off workers, and hurt small businesses, some closing their doors for good. Your party wants bread-and-butter basics for everyone, no matter who pays for it. The other party wants lesser government and more opportunities for individuals to earn their way without limits. Reforms are giving politicians a quick excuse to accept praise, a quick excuse to blame others, a slow reason to share success, and never a reason to accept failure. Real reform is bipartisan and voted on by the public.

If our politicians want to do something to change health care and make our country better, the first line of business should be making our veterans hospitals world-class establishments staffed by our best doctors and nurses. Care for the military coming back from war unquestionably should be a top priority. Careful consideration of many difficult issues will avoid some unnecessary disputes later. The military has already sacrificed enough.

Insurers are going to have to abide by the same rules in terms of providing comprehensive care, and this could include reproductive care, which would greatly increase the number of abortions paid for by Americans. Our president is elected for the common good of all the people. Going back to the three elements of common good, remember one of them is respect for life. If Congress does not act to explicitly exclude abortion from any government-mandated health care plan paid for by taxpayers, then those who oppose abortion are not being heard. For this reason, the president will find it very difficult to get the support of the 'Right to Life' people in the next presidential election.

Health care isn't free. Why should the people who work to pay for it, pay higher premiums so others can get it at a discount or for free? Just as families need to exercise fiscal discipline, our government can't spend our way to economic recovery and prosperity. More taxpayers' dollars spent for more bureaucrats interfering between you and your doctor raises costs and does nothing to monitor the accountability of anyone.

To the people who are broke and uncomfortable, home does not seem like the luxurious abodes you see on television or in the movies. To the homeless walking the streets who want to work, to the unemployed who want to work, there is nothing particularly exotic or beautiful about life. For these people time passes slowly. Forever, if they don't have jobs or money, this is enough reason for these people not to care about you. Our government and our private sector should be doing everything we can to help businesses create jobs with health care benefits so that people are protected if they become sick, but not spending money on more new handout programs for those strong enough to work. Give a man a fish and he will be back for more free handouts; teach a man to fish and he will become self-sufficient.

Most hospitals are nonprofit organizations, and therefore, they are exempt from sales taxes, income taxes, and property taxes. That means that Americans have even a greater stake in insisting that their hospitals are efficient operations. Patients and their families must pay attention to billing statements and report errors when charges seem wrong or unbalanced.

Workers and senior citizens have watched their incomes decrease during your first term, while your healthcare plan schemes to direct more taxpayers' dollars to government coffers and the insurance executives you cut deals. You might want to direct some straight talk towards our young people. To pay for this massive tax, (yes, the highest court in our land called your "Affordable Healthcare Act" a tax, so you could pass your legislation) businesses will raise prices. You might want to tell the college students to start paying attention to food prices, gas prices, and consumer goods prices. You might tell them to watch to see if the electric company, the sewer company, the water company, and all the other utility companies apply for increases to help pay for your government healthcare plan.

Next time you visit a college campus to tell students how your healthcare plan is magically making everything wonderful in la-la land, you might want to add some truths to your message. Presidents can make lip service for their immediate agenda, while secretly planning more shenanigans with money that more health coverage will generate.

Working against the theme of efficiency is the abhorrent amounts of money already paid to CEOs at health insurance giants. The story is the same at Aetna, Cigna, Coventry Health Systems, Humana, and WellPoint. With all that personal greed, many of the CEOs of these companies have already announced double-digit premium increases for their customers next year. Generous compensation is the rule throughout the health care industry, but flat-out greed by executives has the American people questioning how these CEOs give us value for our dollars. I know the crony friends of your administration visiting Washington love government-directed health care. Costs never go down under government direction, because friends of politicians always share in the proceeds, robbing money from the masses. You don't understand the competitive market. Insurance companies are now protected from competition. Your less-than-angelic administration is fooling the public. Please stop railing against arguments no one is making, policies no one is proposing. When is the media going to start questioning all the straw man analogies distancing citizens from the truth about healthcare and start demanding real discourse about understanding how fairness and creativity works? When is the media going to follow up arguments with intelligent questions offering some degree of insight? The Tea Party wants more than just watching the media pander to you, and watching you appease college students in a lecture hall. College students have little knowledge of the history of politics, and even less experience with healthcare. The Tea Party wants to see an end to all these special arrangements made by Democrats only. They want an end to your partisan constructed health care because your plan only puts more taxpayers' money in the hands of government and highly paid CEOs, and does nothing to help control health care costs. Here is a revelation. A fair health care plan would include more representation from the Republican Senators and input from a panel of Fortune 500 executives, the persons paying for large portions of company-sponsored health care. The main ideas of all the new health care legislation could be lumped into a few more simply proposed bills and put in front of the House and Senate for a vote.

Our health care system is filled with perverse incentives that encourage doctors and hospitals to provide more services, extra tests, and more care, not necessarily better care. Our culture has changed from getting lots of exercise to playing video games and eating more. We are increasing our number of office visits, and doctors are treating more illnesses and more cases of heart disease and diabetes. The health care reform bill seems to be full of pages explaining lots of access for patients, but not much talk about cost containment and prevention.

Your administration has not been transparent with the details of the future costs and hidden taxes written into health care reform policies. You said fines will be levied on taxpayers who don't sign up to obtain a health plan and the government will levy surcharges on employers who don't provide health coverage to full-time employees. I guess another agency will be created to perform this work. The government will add and collect excise taxes on health care plans. The IRS will pay close attention by auditing health care tax credits taken by small businesses and corporations. The government will enforce collecting employer penalties for failure to follow the rules to provide employer-paid health insurance. One big change to health care reform purposely shadowed from the public was the plan making only medical expenses that are at least 10% of income tax deductible. Since this requirement used to be 7.5% of income, raising it will mean the tax deduction vanishes for many, a disguised tax for all those affected by the change. Many of the enforcement and collection duties will fall to the IRS, disguising some of the true costs of administering your health care plan. The IRS may have to add as many as 20,000 employees to enforce the new legislation, another huge expense to taxpayers. Up until this point in time, many businesses have held off hiring new workers because of the uncertainty caused by the many new mandates, taxes, and requirements in your health care legislation.

Some businesses are facing immediate regulatory changes from health care reform. Indoor tanning salons are charging customers an excise tax because of the risks of skin cancer, which must be collected and then remitted to the IRS. Hospitals, Blue Cross/Blue Shield, United Health care, and other insurance organizations are facing significant additional regulatory and tax provisions. Group health plans now must cover preventive services and eliminate lifetime coverage limits. Colleges and lending companies are giving loan forgiveness to certain medical professionals opting to practice in underserved areas and the money is tax free. Your administration, Mr. President, is throwing darts trying to sell your plan to the public.

Future historians will write about how Americans saw their standard of living and their freedoms decline during your first term as president. They will write about all your newly created laws, like the Affordable Healthcare Act, the Wall Street Reform Act, the Consumer Protection Act, Dodd-Frank, and the Consumer Financial Protection Bureau. You told us all your new laws would protect us, but we now see how they stand in the way between businesses and customers and how too much idealist change kills jobs in a real economy. Your continuing expansion of mandates is creating more confusion and uncertainty. What is next? The First Lady wants to penalize food-manufacturing companies, citing them as the cause for the high rate of obese black children in our country. There are plenty of obese children of other races too. The problem is not food companies force-feeding children. The problem stems from parents not educating their children about proper nutrition and spending time with them to shape positive behavior. If we teach proper diet and exercise to our children, the free market will dictate changes in the food industry. It is better to govern for all people, instead of picking sectors of the population as winners and losers of taxpayer dollars. Tea Party Patriots are tired of watching White House policies fund more class-action suits. Your record thus far suggests that your first term was more to do with change (you did warn us about this) than it was about finding solutions. It is time to stop picking winners and losers. I now believe your policies are all about how circumstances can gain you votes, rather than how you can fix problems. Maybe if you and your administrative officials had to pay the start-up costs for all these new laws and attendant agencies, as an entrepreneur has to pay all the costs to start a company, maybe the public would see better models for change.

The health care industry is growing by leaps and bounds, but so are the charges to patients who need medical care or stay at a hospital for any length of time. Health care is such a political hot button, mainly because the government pays such a large part of the bill and people without insurance coverage are behind the eight ball.

One of the great things about the health care industry is that it employs so many people around the country: administrators, doctors, physicians, surgeons, technicians, dentists, anesthesiologists, nurses, orderlies, billing clerks, and all the engineers, groundskeepers, and maintenance staff that help keep the equipment and facilities running. It is the hope of every patient to benefit from a well-run hospital, but it would be nice if everyone could afford it. This is somewhat of a different perspective, but why couldn't there be more caps put on some of the regularly occurring expenses and treatments administrators and doctors are charging at our hospitals? A little goodwill would go a long way in keeping patients and making sure they get the treatment they need. Insurance companies could stand to lower their premiums a couple of percentage points by finding ways to cut waste or cut a point off sales commissions. Patients with insurance coverage could raise their deductible one level, if they haven't already. With a well-thought-out plan of government regulations agreed upon by Republicans and your administration and the top administrators of our hospitals across the country, a less aggressive approach of tweaking the current system will work. Here is a stab in the dark. Why don't you let the people vote on your proposal? If a reworked plan is fair, it will work. Because people have compassion for those who are sick, they realize everyone needs basic affordable health care, using common sense to help the bootless person who cannot lift himself up by his bootstraps and pay for his own care.

Middle-class people have health problems like everybody else, the aristocrats, the lower-income individuals, all people. If the breadwinner of a family pays for the insurance needs of himself, his spouse, his children, and aging parents, should he also be responsible for other families without health insurance? It's not that good people don't want to help the "bootless" out of the goodness of their hearts. They just want those capable to start doing more of their part. If a breadwinner puts in the hours working and makes the sacrifices to be able to afford and pay for health insurance, should he be responsible for health insurance of other people who didn't plan, make the effort in school for a career, make the sacrifices, or provide the sweat equity to buy their own? Excellence is what makes freedom ring. The focus of health care should not be solely about how much it costs, but more importantly about how much it buys. The only way to improve the standard of living in the US is to move people off welfare and into jobs.

During your campaign, Mr. President, you promised that there would be no new net spending of taxpayers' money during your administration. Americans just want their president to keep his word. *Your Patient Protection and Affordable Care Act represents a new height of federal doublespeak for hinterland. It will provide neither. There are at least eighty different programs already where the individual can request help from the government. When did it become fashionable for people to expect the government to solve all their individual financial woes? Medicaid was created in 1965 and it absorbed most welfare dollars. It was set up for children, the elderly, and people with debilitating injuries or illnesses who can't fend for themselves. Children can't cast ballots, so their problems don't always get enough attention, because helping them doesn't garner more votes for elected officials.*

Your Democratic platform now revolves around the idea that individuals can only gain success by government intervention. It is transforming the Declaration of Independence into the Declaration of Dependence. Peddling handouts will only give power to a politician trying to gain votes. Handouts will not help people earn success or help them contribute to society. Please cancel your health care plan and do something to stop the hundreds of thousands of swindlers milking the system who certainly are healthy enough to work and make an honest living. Our country doesn't need any more welfare programs. Your policies mean nothing if your actions reveal an opposite example of your rhetoric. All this expansion of government is making it more difficult to pursue life, liberty, and happiness. I am afraid with your style of fighting poverty, poverty will win in the end. How much longer will taxpayers have to pay for new reforms every time a politician thinks of another way to make a money grab for another handout, more foreign aid, or help for another business sect bailout? Please stop interfering in private business, because it is starting to feel like your administration thinks it is its duty to treat adult businesspersons like children. Legislators want teachers paid according to their effectiveness as evaluated by student test scores. Maybe we should pay legislators according to their effectiveness as evaluated by job growth, economic prosperity, decrease in crime, and reduction in drug abuse. It is time for all people to start showing more ambition and more patriotism. Tea Party Patriots don't have to be told to remove their hats at the playing of the national anthem.
Thank you for your time.
Best Wishes,
Arthur Hobson
Community Organizer

Epilogue

Arthur was eternally curious. When ideas floated away from his brain and onto a computer screen and eventually onto the pages of a speech, there were always assurances that someone in his community would listen to his words. Never really completing his work, he filled the pages of his speeches with everydayness and elements of whimsy, at times experimenting with plot and the element of surprise. He resisted the pressure to write defensively and only spoke to citizens about what he knew: politics and life. He felt it was a waste of time to speak only about the obvious. Sometimes a thought or an opinion wasn't popular. He spoke about things that disturbed him, particularly if it bothered no one else, by shifting away from superficial details and toward an examination with emotional impact. He used the power of the English language to try to influence politics, media, business, and gender roles. He believed any ability to manipulate and shape opinions and cultural attitudes is one of the worthiest goals of communicating, but only if the words were spoken honestly, because of the important issues facing an increasingly complex multicultural America. His mother taught him the English language, with its flexibility and richness and how it is supposed to be used responsibly and effectively in communications. She stressed that words take people inside the boardrooms of America's largest corporations, within the viscera of a Pennsylvania Avenue screening room, behind one-way mirrors in places like Heartland and Rainbow Creek, in the middle of a double-paned window of a mayoral meeting, and they describe the view from the top row of a sports stadium. Politicians use words in the hope that they will magically impress their constituents when they use them. Arthur learned that if a writer or a politician is going to gain support based on merits, he has to play by the rules, but know how to throw a thoughtful punch too.

Down deep, Arthur knew he would never fall into a "happily ever after" trap. There would always be another conflict worth fighting for and needing a solution. The characters in his own family and group of friends will supply some of the twists in his life. He was driven to teach the complex system of American politics to anyone who would listen, but he wished more young people would follow his lead to be part of it, because places like Rainbow Creek need them more than ever.

Rampant alcoholism and drug abuse, dishonest business practices, children raised without any form of parental supervision or guidance, the destruction of traditional morals and respect for law and order, and a refusal to see the dangers of failing to insist upon government policies that protect the Constitution are contributing to the deterioration of our society. Arthur knew if people don't start paying more attention to the things that matter in our culture, this kind of social destruction will soon infect and ultimately destroy everything good about Western society. He selfishly hoped his speeches left his listeners breathless, sleepless, astounded, or joyous. Whatever others thought of his politics, Arthur tried to speak up to people, not down to them. Most importantly, he hoped others would want to figure out another way to contribute to society. If he motivated others to think about viewpoints they hadn't considered before, then he had accomplished his mission.

Life is about searching for the truth. Arthur came to understand how patience is a virtue and that anything worth working for and waiting for, had real value. He wanted everyone to share in his belief that passion is a key ingredient to life. Just as Sandra and Susie Hobson were coming of age about their own political views, the next generation of young people in America are seeking the truth delivered plainly, using clear words and logic, rather than muddled graphs, impenetrable fabricated statistics, fraudulent formulas, and double-talk.

American soldiers, including hundreds of GIs from Rainbow Creek, deserve credit for living up to the ideals of fighting for liberty and fighting off dictators. Margaret Hobson spoke to her three sons about showing great respect for all our men and women who have fought so bravely to protect the nation, so they would know the value of their freedom and work hard to help supply American soldiers with whatever they needed to fight the enemy, build roads, conduct tribal councils, grow security forces, or help build schools for boys and girls around the world. She was sure our soldiers have always encouraged more of us to stand up for our beliefs, honor our right to vote, appreciate our freedoms, and look to a future that is full of promise, goodness, and prosperity.

Though the lines of distinguishing one class from another are quite blurry these days, it would be fair to say that during the early part of the twenty-first century, America needs politics that protect the rights of the individual. Individual liberties, property rights, the laws of our country, and the Constitution are more important than who belongs to the wealthy class of Americans. Tradesmen, shopkeepers, factory workers, deliverymen, and laborers deserve the same considerations of the Constitution as professionals with university degrees, doctors, lawyers, professors, architects, scientists, journalists, engineers, and corporate executives. If in the eyes of some, this characterization of class warfare still exists, it is not just about money. Some trade workers have such high-demand skills that their take-home pay far exceeds that of some professionals. It's all about workers making themselves a more valuable commodity and bettering their earning power when the opportunities arise. And as these opportunities arise, anything can get accomplished with the right people in place. But in businesses and in government, too often the wrong people have too much power.

America is still free, but sometimes it feels like all this change is painfully taking away some of the individual freedoms and opportunities our soldiers fought for. Why should the person unwilling to work be entitled to all of the same benefits of the working person? The worker putting in long hours and sometimes working weekends, the person working two jobs or the worker who puts in all the extra effort earns the right to make more wages and benefits. Too many people are being rewarded for joyriding the gravy train of free welfare handouts, an insult to the brave soldiers who put their lives on the line for all of us.

Everybody knows others who have lost their jobs and most people would want to help them get by, but this is where Washington should be doing everything it can to help successful businesses create jobs. America needs more private-sector jobs. That means real jobs where people produce real goods and services. Burdensome federal corruption, earmarks, illegal immigrants, street drugs, entitlement programs, wasteful spending, borrowing money from China, dishonest tax funneling, and unqualified politicians are strangling small businesses and our agricultural economy. All these wrongful acts are costing billions of dollars and saddling our children and grandchildren with debt. It is extremely important for middle-class Americans to vote out politicians that refuse to protect and don't share our American values. Politicians who aren't committed to our children's financial future turn hope into an empty wish when they smother opportunities for our young people. It is time to lock up the middle-level drug dealers, who without a conscience are killing our young people. Without the middlemen, there is no distribution system for the drug cartels.

Arthur made a point of telling people to realize that we all are human beings, not that much separates the middle class from any other class, not nearly as much as once thought. Everybody has a right to walk on this planet, but everybody has a duty to contribute to it too. Do your best to make yourself indispensable, he believes. Read, learn new things, develop communication skills, network, share, love, excel, create something, innovate, overcome obstacles, help the sick feel better, share, teach what you know, make a difference, give real effort, don't let people take advantage of you, take responsibility, try to keep a positive attitude and live a healthy life. "If someone says, you are not smart enough or good enough to do something, prove that person wrong. If someone tells you that you are not college material, go to graduate school and prove that person wrong too. Turn a bad situation into a good one." Arthur made it a point to tell his two daughters these things often.

Ideally, Arthur would have liked to come up with a theory that explained the origin of the universe from first principles. However, because Arthur understood he was a human being with theoretical limitations and complexity, he did not want to be one of those people who never admitted mistakes or realized any boundaries. Therefore, he assumed a set of initial conditions living on this planet, but he continued reading and listening to the ideas of Tea Party Patriots, analyzing new policies of politicians and paying attention to planned events by his constituents at the community center.

Arthur certainly gave his share of political speeches, and for a change of pace, he was considering writing a book about the combined powers of crystal healing, leaf reading, fortune telling, hypnosis, and magic. He figured this might require some more research about Beckett's waiting for Godot, Sartre's Nausea, Don Quixote, Marcus Aurelius, and Meditations of Saint Augustine. All these people ate and slept just enough, so they were reenergized enough to spend the rest of the time in their days arguing and contemplating everything, only to swap hats later, after having a change in heart from involvement in wrongful deeds. Our current ways of solving problems hasn't been an exact science anyway, and because books cover a varied set of topics, it might be worth mentioning that the most interesting books contain some history and informative facts that reveal the truth. Most important, Arthur Hobson was sure about one thing: now is the time for our political leaders and institutions to govern in noncorrupt ways. It is time to build the bridge to the next century and quit bickering about old ideas that don't work, because America needs to be great and politics needs to be an honorable and respected profession again.

The issues of our country are important. Every citizen who is old enough to vote should try to stay informed about local, state, and national legislation that affects households all across America. People who do not take the time to vote do not exercise their First Amendment rights to encourage fairness. By understanding what is at stake and voting, the middle class can show its mettle and earn respect. Ultimately, injustice and corruption fails because people are meant to live free.

Arthur's mayoral loss certainly was not the big news in the grand scheme of things affecting the world at the time. The military was doing their part trying to make a huge impact in the war on terror. Navy SEALs brought Osama bin Laden down in a daring mission planned for several months and ending in firefight. The bastard was not living in a cave far away from any other civilization, as was reported by many in the press. He was living with women and children in a three-story compound in Pakistan complete with armed guards and carriers to protect the complex and bring food and supplies as needed.

President Obama gave the go-ahead for the helicopter mission in lieu of a fighter jet bomber mission because senators and military generals were hopeful of confiscating bin Laden's body as proof, whether he was brought back dead or alive. It is the best of times when Americans realize that no more suffering will occur directly from the commands of this man, but it is the worst of times when we are so hungry for celebration that we rejoice in a man's death. Two of bin Laden's Pakistani cousins, Arshad Khan and Tareg Khan, were trusted help at the compound, running errands and managing the property. They were killed along with bin Laden.

Now when Arthur drove anywhere in his hometown, he thought about glorious parts of its past and he still envisioned far better plans for the future even though he would not be mayor. He hoped for progress from the Tea Party and he hoped enough smart people would figure out how to replace the decay with good fortune. Arthur's idea of a good politician was one who served humanity, not one who tried to dominate humanity. The closeness in the polls and in the voting at elections tells political leaders that the middle class has its own problems and it is time to stop making them responsible for paying for aristocratic mistakes, giving away their hard-earned money to pay for more entitlement programs that don't work. Too much new local, state and federal legislation continues to layer taxes on the middle class, some of it transparent and some shrouded in charges at a government office, the gas pump, the cash register, or in the fine print.

But life was returning to normal. Karen from across the street still tried to tease Arthur whenever she saw him out at the mailbox. Susie was getting closer to earning her degree in biological sciences. Sandra's focus was now split between her career and on a new man she met. She was already thinking about when to introduce him to her parents. She signed up for two night classes at the community college's school of nursing and accepted a full-time position at the retirement home where she had been working part-time. Studying phlebotomy and medical records analysis helped her learn skills she applied at work, as she earned credits toward her goal of a nursing degree.

In his personal life, every time Arthur tried to hold on to the good parts of what was, there always seemed to be something to change it or make it go away. To the best of his ability, he tried to keep closeness with his two daughters, hoping to overcome the difficult position a divorce imposes on a father. To him, having two parents who love their children was more important than two parents forcing a relationship that did not work anymore. For him and Jane it was the right decision to divorce and live apart so each family member had a chance to live a happy life. He and Jane both knew it was important to stand down and walk away from a situation that poorly articulated and poorly applied opposite parenting styles, playing the children against one parent or the other. While other family members were finally taking responsibility for the energy they brought into each other's space, Arthur and Addison couldn't resist playing one little joke on Stuart just for fun.

Intending no harm, the two filled out an Internet order form to request free samples of Instarise and had them shipped to the Hobson House in Stuart's name. The free samples arrived four weeks later. Every time Arthur and Addison saw Stuart or someone mentioned his name, a smile flashed across both of their faces as each of them imagined his reaction when he received the package. Arthur and Addison were proud to be Americans, proud to live in a country that allows its people to laugh, to cry, and to express their feelings.

Arthur felt good about temporarily helping save the life of heroin-addicted Johnny, knowing he was well intentioned, though AIDS did his brother in at the end. He felt proud about always paying his bills and that he owed no one any money. He felt good knowing that much of the growth at the community center and the improvements the Rainbow Creek School District enjoyed, and focus on mayoral issues, he played a part in ensuring some success. He felt good about having Addison, who thought he was amazing, as a friend. Sandra and Susie were now doing what every young American of the next generation should do: getting an education, staying away from drugs, taking control of their own expenses, and getting involved in their communities to make the world a better place. Sandra and Susie were becoming an indispensable part of the middle class.

Now that the weather was warming and Arthur's semiretired life meant extra free time, Arthur and Addison started planning a vacation together to ride bikes on the flat trails of Central Netherlands in hopes of enjoying the colorful and plentiful tulips marking the beautiful landscapes close to the home of Rembrandt. Addison also tried talking Arthur into a trip to explore the island of St. George's rich colonial history and its pink sand beaches, multicolored storefronts and turquoise waters, which make it one of the world's most breathtaking environments. But Arthur was more interested in considering a trip to discover the many wonders of the Mediterranean, giving himself and Addison a chance to gaze upon Michelangelo's masterpiece at the Sistine Chapel, a chance to brace their toes in the starting blocks that launched a thousand athletes in ancient Greece, and an opportunity to watch the streets come alive at night in Barcelona. If Johnny were still alive, another consideration not for the faint at heart might mean all three of them participating in the racing of a herd of stampeding bulls through the narrow city streets of Pamplona, or dancing with the nearly half a million tango revelers in Buenos Aires at the annual summer event where Johnny once traveled.

Arthur and Addison did not have the money to do everything they wanted to do, but they now had much more time to make big decisions and narrow down their choices. As Mark Twain wrote, "So, throw off the bowlines, sail away from the safe harbor, and catch the trade winds in your sails. Go explore, dream, and discover." Arthur believed Mark Twain was way ahead of his time and he was sure he and Addison had earned time off for a vacation.

Susie, for her part, accepted an offer as one of the students to help with the oceanic studies aboard the shipping vessel with her fellow students and three professors from the biological sciences department at the Columbia. Together they flew to San Francisco Bay to board the shipping vessel that would be their home for most of eight weeks. Their temporary home was a giant recycling machine and the students quickly learned there is no such thing as trash. A manufacturer used thousands of recycled potato chip bags to make the outdoor patio furniture on the deck of the vessel. A sign on the top deck read, "If we keep our waste out of watersheds and landfills, almost all materials can be recycled." The professors hoped that the experience of the next eight weeks might inspire a few of the students to flourish as entrepreneurs later, developing new ideas on how to use recycled materials to make new products. A waste industry expert on the ship estimated that growth is exponential in the recycling business because manufacturers are using only a very small amount of available recyclable materials.

On the trip, Susie also learned more about America's problem with waste, most of it generated by throwaway packaging used by the middle class, the people with enough money to buy more of the paper and plastic products. If all other countries consumed at US rates, the world's population would need four planets. With the growing middle class in China and India, the professors told the students to give serious thought to packaging and throwaway containers, mainly for reuse and recycling, because more biodegradable materials needed to be incorporated into our packaging and shipping products.

Susie was starting to form her own opinion of how companies are chasing the fast dollar, cheapening everything they make. If they just would think a little longer and spend a little more time improving what they knew how to do well, then the economy would grow and the environment would stay protected. To her way of thinking, a double victory takes place when people win with the environment and a company wins on the balance sheet. She was learning much about how the different materials in trash have value and how they are reusable. The waste in trash converts into methane gas, saving billion of dollars on energy bills and helping double revenue for waste-hauling companies with intelligent recycling policies.

Susie's view of recycling, reusing trash, and cleaning up pollution was now different from the cap-and-trade policies the Obama administration was talking about on his circuit. The president's policy is supposed to deliver results with a mandatory cap on emissions, while providing companies and energy sources some flexibility in how to comply. Any new national energy tax bill that increases the cost of gasoline and other utilities, but does not reward innovation, efficiency, early action, and accountability, isn't better if it doesn't help create jobs and isn't ratified by the House and Senate, in Susie's view. Her father taught her that many of the business owners in Rainbow Creek already felt taxed enough and though the issue is important, adding too many green taxes to manufacturing makes it even more difficult to compete with the global economy and the rapid growth of China, India, and Brazil. "If energy legislation cripples businesses with taxes that are too high, it won't work, at a time when my college friends and I will need full-time jobs soon," Susie often told her summer professors. Whether she realized it or not, Susie was learning to voice her opinions.

Arthur Hobson was a good man who refused to compromise his principles to gain a bigger platform, but he hoped of better days for the next generation, and like most hardworking middle-class people who do not accomplish all of the things they hope for, he made small contributions along the way. Because the wrinkles of life slowly accumulate while few of us notice, eventually everyone's time runs out and it is too late to negotiate anymore, and any hope for reprieve must pass along to the next generation. Arthur's daughters were still learning how to sift out the vast and growing mountain of information flung upon young people through computer search engines and cable TV shows, but he was confident they would go forth bravely if they discovered something new and genuinely useful. He hoped for the day his daughters could look into his eyes, and without needing to say a word, they would have a mutual understanding of pain, forgiveness, appreciation, love, and respect. Forever, with Arthur's contributions, combined with the small contributions of all the other men and women like him, there's a good chance the next generation will enter the realm of possibility, learning how to live in a way which makes the world a better place.

Sandra: "Hi, Dad, this is Sandra. I am glad you have your cell phone along with you. Susie and I have been talking and hanging out. Have you noticed the cable TV went dark several hours ago and hasn't come back on yet?"

Arthur: "I know cable providers who are at odds with programming providers were threatening to do that. They must have made good on their threats. Fox, Disney, Cablevision Systems, News Corp, Charter Communications, and several other large entities have a stake in the outcome of negotiations. I heard that a state senator out West wants legislation to regulate how retransmission lines operate and charge fees. The middle class can once again watch more services decline as high-level politicians make sure they share the biggest slice of pie with their high-level executive friends."

Sandra: "This cable dilemma sounds messy, but it's not what I called about. When you and Addison get back from vacation, we all need to sit down and talk. It would be nice if Rainbow Creek had an opera house like the Peabody Opera House in St. Louis. Let us see if we can get enough citizens interested in a smaller-scale version, and maybe we could name the project after Uncle Johnny. 'The Johnny Hobson Opera House of Rainbow Creek' has a nice ring to it. Dad, I'm handing over the phone to Susie."

Susie: "Hey, Dad. We were thinking, the townspeople now know more about your political views, and a project to build an opera house could give you a more practical platform to continue using your voice to do well, help the community, and enjoy yourself at the same time. I am considering another project myself, because as you know, I am still building my platform too. After I graduate, I am considering working for this privately funded study to find parallels between ants and human societies, such as labor, communications, transportation, food, medication, and rituals. If I get the job, one of my responsibilities would be writing the blog for the study."

Arthur: "As always, just make sure you research all the details. Find out what companies are involved and who is paying for the project. Make sure your professors endorse the study. Ultimately it is your decision."

Susie: "I would get to travel and the private fund pays for my expenses. Maybe we already know that many species of ants damage crops and invade too many buildings, but I'm convinced studying their successes in warm climates will help discover new ideas for human beings to reverse global warming and pollution trends. Many of our insights into the origins of disease come from the laboratory benches of researchers. Did you know there are over twelve thousand species of ants?"

Arthur: "No, I did not. It would be great if humans worked together collectively to take care of the globe the way ants work together to support the colony."

Susie: "Maybe we can find out if humans get stepped on at the same rate as ants. Maybe studying ants will give us some clues on how to relay some information about environmental issues to small businesses, before large corporations and big government impose their models upon them. Our government spends large amounts of money dispersing grants to study sleep patterns, dreams, and many other conditions. Maybe my work will help lead to some kind of discovery to help build better roads and bridges or bring more happiness to the lives of animals."

Arthur smiled to himself. He understood it was time to allow his two grown daughters to discover new opportunities on their own. The talented chief listener of the Hobson family just might have a few more big decisions to make himself, concerning his relevant social network and pressure from his two blogging daughters.

Arthur was proud of his friend Frank, who kept working hard to increase revenues at his company four years in a row, pressured by mounting expenses from union negotiations, pension expenses, healthcare costs, and the salary of an extra employee relegated with the difficult task of trying to keep up with regulatory changes and tax code modifications. He was proud of Sandra for stepping up to the plate when big problems faced the family and her Uncle Johnny needed help. He was proud of Susie for studying biological sciences and working on research studies, so that one day she could apply her findings to help people, and dogs like Three-Putt and Mud Hazard. He was proud of his brother Johnny for finally seeing the faults of his ways and trying to change his life. The Hobsons were not the kind of people who only participated or talked a big game when they could gain some sort of benefit. They were the kind of people, Tea Party Patriots in the end, who fought to uphold the principles of their country and strived for excellence and genius over conformity and equality. Margaret should get some of the credit for that.

A Note from the Author

It is my hope that this book sheds more light on the interconnections of big government, big business, professional sports teams, drug cartels, and racketeers all fighting to control the country and acquire a large slice of the financial pie. Embracing wisdom and truth should be the common goal of all people. Even when topics are controversial, it is important for all authors and media to have a voice. When government or large corporations monopolize the media, news departments turn into entertainment programs, because research is defunded and fewer sources get checked for accuracy.

Arthur Hobson, the protagonist in this book, certainly does not have all the answers, but great cutting-edge ideas come from awareness and meaningful, thought-provoking discussions on the most pressing issues of the day. Any voter's personal fairness doctrine should include listening to both sides of an issue, liberal and conservative, left versus right, before forming an opinion or making a decision. Yet, dialogue from citizens groups will continue to form the opinions of many voters.

The mainstream middle class has bigger problems than idolizing athletes and celebrities. To do so is conventional, bland, safe, and predictable, while real life and its needs go unaddressed. We are finding out it is not OK to leave behind a mountain of wreckage. All of us need to be part of the solutions to our problems associated with the economy, jobs, environmental issues, foreign affairs, health care, and technology, while helping to convince our politicians to form a balance of regulations between business and government.

Like many of the characters in The Hobsons of Rainbow Creek, middle-class America is full of many hardworking and good people. The middle class still makes up the day-to-day operations of the best country in the world, and the United States of America is strong because of what is in the hearts of its people. We are proud because we suffer enough pain to appreciate what we have, the smaller things in life, but we want to enjoy more of the finer things that sustain life and give us enough happiness to keep our spirits alive. We reelect our politicians for the good things they try to accomplish, even when we do not agree with all of their other policies. We do this because we love our country. Long live freedom, long live our Republic, and long live the United States of America.

About the Author

Steven Michael Hubele has a bachelor's degree in education from Southeast Missouri State University and a master's degree in computer resources technology from Webster University. His first book, titled *Almost Full Circle: A Tribute to Dad*, was released February 2010. A former teacher, businessperson and newspaper carrier, Hubele enjoys working on computers; playing golf; watching Cardinals baseball games; reading books and newspapers; and of course writing. He lives in St. Louis, Missouri, with his two daughters, Amanda and Allison.

Contact Information:
Steven Michael Hubele
9838 Affton View Court
St. Louis, MO 63123

OFFICE: 314-631-6779 (9:00–5:30 CST)
EMAIL: stevehubele@charter.net

www.ingramcontent.com/pod-product-compliance
Lightning Source LLC
Chambersburg PA
CBHW080742250626
47162CB00010B/2996